Sex and Stravinsky

Brother of the More Famous Jack

Noah's Ark

Temples of Delight

Juggling

The Travelling Hornplayer

Frankie and Stankie

Sex and Stravinsky

BARBARA TRAPIDO

B L O O M S B U R Y
LONDON · BERLIN · NEW YORK

First published in Great Britain 2010

Copyright © 2010 by Barbara Trapido

The moral right of the author has been asserted

Bloomsbury Publishing, London, Berlin and New York

36 Soho Square, London W1D 3QY

A CIP catalogue record for this book is available from the British Library

ISBN 978 1 4088 0232 8
10 9 8 7 6 5 4 3 2 1

Typeset by Hewer Text UK Ltd, Edinburgh

Printed in Great Britain by Clays Ltd, St Ives plc

FSC **Mixed Sources**
Product group from well-managed
forests and other controlled sources
www.fsc.org Cert no. SGS-COC-2061
© 1996 Forest Stewardship Council

www.bloomsbury.com/barbaratrapido

For Megan Vaughan

Chapter One

Josh Meets Caroline

Josh meets Caroline in a shared student house in London. The time is late 1970s so everyone in the house looks hideous. That's everyone except for Caroline, but she doesn't live there. Not yet. All the men have got too much hair, which tends to come lank, matt and flecked with dandruff. The women wear floaty purple cheesecloth things – either cropped floaty purple things, worn over flared jeans, or full-length floaty purple things that go from shoulder to ankle. Josh remembers this as the Purple Time.

The women also have lots of hair, long, lank and drooping from centre partings, but theirs has less dandruff since it's better cared for. Josh, like all the others, has too much hair, but because his is so curly it looks shorter. He wishes it would grow in a Jimi Hendrix fuzz but because his curls are looser the effect is more Harpo Marx, except that it's red. Josh's hair, in his youth – in the Purple Time – is a dark, chestnut red. And, since facial hair for men is more or less obligatory, he discovers that his beard and moustache grow in an interesting speckle of red, black and white, like the chalks in a Watteau drawing. His work on the evolution of the clown has caused him to look at Watteau drawings. Whenever he sees photographs of himself these days, twenty years on, in the 'now' time – that is to say, 1995 – he thinks it is he who looks like a clown, but then everyone looks pretty weird. Except for Caroline.

Josh is quite short because his legs are short. He's been told several times, by Greek persons, that this has to do with the Greek in him. That's if ever he lets drop that the man who fathered him – a small-time crook, an unscrupulous, loutish ne'er-do-well, a man he never met beyond babyhood – was Greek. And his name isn't really Josh, come to that. It's George. Caroline always looks fabulous in old photographs, except that sometimes her head has been cut off. This is because she's taller than everyone else in the picture. Caroline is blonde and six foot tall.

Josh meets her one Sunday morning when he trundles woozily downstairs wearing a long cotton tunic that comes from Tanzania, courtesy of his parents. Adoptive parents. He's feeling the need for instant coffee and hasn't yet surfaced properly, so his focus, behind his lenses, is fairly restricted. First, he takes in that the area of kitchen worktop around the kettle is devoid of its usual clutter and that his housemate Keiran's saucer of squeezed-out reusable tea bags is no longer in evidence. There's a nice corner-bakery smell that has taken over from the odour of dustbin and then when he looks up, widening his range, he sees that there's a blonde Amazon standing at the sink with her back to him and that she's wearing big yellow washing-up gloves.

The blonde, from behind, has what looks like regulation long straight hair, only nicer, because hers has thickness and lift like curly hair that happens to be straight and for the moment she has gathered up half of it to the crown of her head, with a large tortoise-shell clip. The Amazon is wearing loose black drawstring trousers that hang on gaunt, jutting hip bones and on her torso she has the top half of a black bikini. The faint outline of her ribs is visible under the flesh and Josh can see that her spinal cord is indented slightly, like rope under the skin. Her shoulder blades are two beautiful, almost-rectangles, one just slightly higher than the other, that hold him in thrall. Her neck is elegantly long. Everything about her is long. Then she's finished rinsing the crockery and she pulls off the washing-up gloves. Sensing Josh's stare, she turns round. Grace Kelly sort of face, Josh notes. Broad cheek-bones. Squarish jaw. Widely spaced blue eyes.

He takes a step backwards, thinking, Oh my God, just look at yourself, would you? Morning dog-breath. A bloke in a dress. Where is your nightcap, Mr Scrooge? Where is your candlestick, Mr Wee Willie Winkie?

'Hi,' he says. 'Excuse me. I'll just get the kettle on. If that's OK.'

It's a whistling kettle that sits permanently on the gas hob, so it's always encrusted with the grease that splatters from student fry-ups. Except that now it isn't. The kettle is revealing itself as a thing made of gleaming dark-green enamel. Racing green, as it's called these days in ad-man speak.

'Something's happened to this kettle,' he says, staring at it hard, his lazy right eye drifting slightly outwards behind his glasses as he holds it under the tap, so that, for a moment, he sees two slightly overlapping green kettles, before the edges once again cohere.

'I cleaned it,' the Amazon says. 'With washing soda. I'm Caroline, by the way. I'm visiting Tamsin.'

Ozzie, Josh notes. The girl's from Oz. Love the vowels. A bit like home, only different. Diphthongs as monophthongs. It's Josh's drama school training that accounts for this tendency to see phonetic symbols dancing in the air when people speak. Josh is from Durban, but he's been in London for a year. Everyone else in the house is English except for Tamsin, who's Australian. Marty's parents are from Jamaica but he's been raised in Lewisham.

'Hi,' Josh says, 'I'm Josh.' Then he says, 'It smells kind of different in here. It smells nice.'

'Could be that I've emptied the bin,' she says. 'Plus I've got muffins in the oven. Fancy a muffin with that coffee? They're just about ready.'

The muffins are made with bananas and a sprinkle of wheat bran, so they're moist along with having texture. It's quite a while since he's eaten a muffin. The only approximation he's managed to find in London is what he thinks of as a cup cake. Then there are those crumpet-type things called 'English muffins' that taste like ceiling tiles. Well, that's until your housemates tell you they need toasting.

'They're called Seven-day Muffins,' Caroline says, 'because you make up the dough and keep it in the fridge for seven days, you see. Then every morning all you need do is take out enough dough for that day's breakfast and pop it into a muffin tray. Bingo.'

'Bingo'. Who the hell says 'Bingo'? He wonders, Is the woman speaking tongue-in-cheek? Josh, whose mother – adoptive mother, that is – combined her professional life not only with political activism, but with large dollops of Yiddishe Mama, is familiar with basic cooking procedures, only he's wondering, now, how on earth the Amazon has come by the muffin trays, not to mention the washing soda. Does she cart baking tins and household cleaners around in her luggage?

'I reckon these should be called One-day Muffins,' Josh says. 'They'd never last seven days.'

'You can make up the dough in larger batches and freeze it in seven-day portions,' Caroline offers helpfully. 'I could show you guys how to make up a batch for the freezer, only you'd need to get hold of some decent plastic storage boxes.' Then she says, 'Have another. Feel free.'

'Tell me,' Josh says. 'Are you a being from earth? Or what manner of being are you?'

'Come again?' Caroline says. 'I'm from Melbourne.'

'I really like your clothes,' he says.

'Thank you,' she says. 'Actually, I quite like yours.'

Caroline is wearing the bikini, she explains, because she's been sunbathing in the yard.

'Before breakfast is the best time for sunshine in England,' she says. 'Only time, I should say. Most students miss it. They're always asleep.' Then, unexpectedly, the Amazon smiles. 'Still,' she says. 'You're awake, aren't you? Well, sort of.'

Josh doesn't yet know that Caroline has made the bikini from a paper pattern, along with the drawstring trousers, but being patronised by a beautiful, judgemental creature strikes him as quite entertaining. And being smiled on by her is an altogether pleasing sensation. It's a bit like being smiled on by the Blessed Damozel.

Caroline is a graduate student at Oxford, she tells him. History. She's been in the country for eight months on a three-year scholarship. That night she, Josh and Tamsin go to the cinema in Tottenham Court Road. They see Polanski's *Chinatown*, with Jack Nicholson and Faye Dunaway. Then, within the month, Caroline has invited him to be her partner at her college ball. And Josh, who knows that he will never completely get over his passion for Hattie Marais, née Thomas – Hattie, his first love, his dainty five-foot ballet girl back home; Hattie, who turned him down in favour of Herman Marais, that loudmouth architectural student, that brawny rugger-bugger – is nonetheless both beguiled and entertained by Caroline. Beguiled by her grace and beauty; entertained by her remarkable spread of ability, which she combines so relentlessly with motivation. Caroline is quite simply Wonder Woman, and that's in itself diverting, even though she herself is not a person with whom one can giggle and conspire. Caroline is not a 'fun' person and Josh is almost never really funny with her; not in the way he always was with Hattie. Caroline is not comfortable with what she calls his 'clowning'. 'You do it because you're short,' she says.

But then Caroline is such an awesome creature, so gaspingly prodigious, that Josh doesn't really notice at first how much she is given to wrong-footing him. Or, combined as it is with that eager, early-on sexual attraction, it acts as a sort of come-on. Mistress Caroline Killjoy, with her repertoire of fabulous clothes. In her interactions with him, there's almost always an element of put-down.

Caroline, even in her student days, is no mean cook. She knows the uses of coconut milk and cardamom pods. While her contemporaries are stuck with pulses, and tinned pilchards, and mounds of oily grated cheddar, she's already making her own pesto with fresh basil that she grows from seed in flowerpots and her careful student budgeting allows for tiny bags of pine nuts and pecorino cheese. She has bought herself a stone mortar and pestle from a homeopathic pharmacy in Regent's Street and she keeps it sitting next to her copy of *The Crusades through Arab Eyes*. She makes glazed fruit tarts. She makes a fruit mousse, mixing dried apricots, stewed and puréed, with gelatine, whipped cream and frothed egg whites. For Josh, she makes an airy angel whip, contrived from what she's recycled from the college fellows' discarded champagne flutes. Gleanings from the Warden's garden party, for which she'd offered services as waitress.

Though Josh is shorter than Caroline by more than half a ruler, this doesn't stop her from wearing four-inch heels to the ball. Caroline not only dresses beautifully, but she makes all her clothes herself, like a girl from the 1950s.

'You're kidding,' Josh says, when she reveals that she has run up her own ball gown. Furthermore, as is the case with almost all her outfits, she has made it out of something else. Caroline, that night, is a vision of beanpole loveliness in a toffee-coloured Thai-silk dress with a wide V-shaped neckline that falls in papery folds from her naked shoulders, revealing small white breasts that have the gradients of shallow meringues. The dress is close-fitting and ruched like a festoon blind. This is because Caroline has made it out of a festoon blind that she found in the Broad Street Oxfam shop, just a stone's throw from her college. And she's honoured her undertaking to clothe her partner as well. She's assembled the complete black-tie get-up from a retro-heap near the bus station and has, for a mere two pounds fifty, bought Josh a pair of Savile Row black shoes.

'But how did you know they'd fit me?' Josh asks in wonder.

'Because I walked around in them myself,' she says. 'We've got the same-sized feet.'

'But how did you come to know that?' he says.

'There's was a "9" printed in your flip-flops,' she says. 'You kicked them off that day I met you. In the kitchen, when that kettle started to whistle.' Caroline's shoes are toffee-coloured ankle-straps.

'Hey, but you're a great dancer,' she says, looking down into Josh's Harpo curls, since his face is currently level with Caroline's non-cleavage. And it's true about his dancing, thanks to Hattie Thomas, his ballet teacher; his beloved. Not only the two years of lessons with her, but the time spent staging things together at the university back home. A sequence from *The Indian Queen*, inserted into that production of *A Midsummer Night's Dream*; that little *Pulcinella* duet they'd used in their Italian mime. And right now, given his current studies in mime, he's somewhat preoccupied, day by day, with various theories of movement. He's been brooding on the idea that all emotion is movement; all about push and pull. I love: I pull. I hate: I push. The previous night Josh was pleased to find that he had woken from a dream about Jacques le Coq's 'Movement Rose'. The thing was glowing there, no longer a mere diagram, but a great luminous window; a rose window, such as one might see at the altar end of a cathedral, diffusing light behind his sleeping eyelids.

At 4 a.m. he and Caroline retire to her room, where they take off their clothes and wake naked at midday in a warm tumble of bedlinen. This is Josh's first time in Caroline's room and, waking seconds before she does, he takes in that the room is as beautiful as she is. Her cloud-grey trouser suit is hanging from a hook on the back of the door; a thing she's made from old union-cloth loose covers. Caroline has previously told him that she got the loose covers off the back of a truck at the access to the council dump. Having noticed the fabric on a three-piece suite, she'd had time to get off her bike and rap on the truckie's window, which caused him to pull over.

'Help yourself, my love,' he said.

Then there's her black-and-yellow plaid coat, made out of an old travelling rug – from a paper pattern, Vogue Paris Original. It looks like origami and has one flat, plate-like white button that she's picked from a rusted toffee tin on a market stall. Caroline has two pretty upright chairs that she's pulled, minus seats, from a builder's skip in the Turl. Having cut them new seats made from scavenged plywood, she's painted them with oyster satin-finish and made them pillow-ticking box cushions to match her pillow-ticking curtains. Pillow-ticking, Josh reflects, is one of her favourite fabrics. He envisages that, one day soon, he may well be the recipient of a home-made pillow-ticking suit.

By the following October, she has made Josh a camel-coloured winter coat out of two undyed wool blankets she's had sent out from Australia. Josh is lost in admiration, both for his girlfriend's range of skills and that she should so often find her raw materials not only in skips and on market stalls, but in those unspeakably horrible second-hand clothing shops in which he can never find anything except crumpled mounds of dead people's underwear and ugly polyester shirts that come with turd-brown swirly patterns and figure-hugging darts.

In between, Caroline spends long hours in the Bodleian Library, displaying more application than anyone else in the place, as far as he can see. She also spends time in the language laboratory with earphones, teaching herself Farsi. And isn't it just like Caroline, he reflects – brilliant Caroline, who already has better mastery of his own two necessary research languages – that is to say, Italian and French – to go and choose for a subject something that requires her to learn a wholly alien language before she can begin to read the documents?

'But it's *not* an alien language,' Caroline says. 'It's Indo-European. And can we please call it "Persian"? "Farsi" sort of erases the richness of the past.'

She's working, he knows, on something to do with old trade routes through Persia, and watching her at it is making him feel that there's something delightfully soft-option about his own PhD subject, which requires him to visit archives and theatre museums in Paris and Naples, along with making trips to the ballet and the theatre. Sometimes he goes to the circus and to the comic opera as well. The major stress factor for him is having to board that puke-inducing Hovercraft, which is his cheapest way across the Channel to France.

Caroline is suitably put-down about the area of his research.

'It's kind of a girl's subject,' she says. 'Know what I mean?'

When Josh and Caroline decide to get married, it's very much a youthful, spur-of-the-moment affair, sparked by Caroline's discovery that her college will make self-contained accommodation available to graduate couples – that's as soon as an apartment should fall vacant. It's a daring and radical step to be taking, though each, with a little frisson of excitement laced with fear, is secretly thinking that a marriage, what the hell, can always be undone – that's if things do not appear to be working out as they should. So they make a date with the registry office and plan a small party at Caroline's college with twenty-five of their friends. Families are not an option, since Josh's parents are decamped from Durban to Dar es Salaam and their pensions will not stretch to long-haul flights;

9

especially not these past two years, when they've been funding Jack, their old housemaid's son, through school.

They are fairly old for parents, in any case. Having never intended to have children, given the high-risk nature of their political commitments in the apartheid state, old Professor Silver was already over forty when Josh came into their lives and he has, of late, become quite frail. Both banned from pursuing their careers, the Silvers were eventually obliged to cross borders in the dead of night and, thereafter, to sell their property – disadvantageously, from a distance. Josh promises to send photographs when he treats himself to a five-minute long-distance call from a public phone box, during which time Bernie and Ida Silver, jostling eagerly for turns with the receiver, yell down the line at him, as if they were required to make themselves audible across the miles, without the assistance of technology.

Caroline's mother, on the other hand, spry and just turned sixty, has already expressed her family's unwillingness to make the trip. She has done so in one of what Josh does not yet know are her characteristically brief and poisonous letters.

Dear Caroline

About the wedding, what a surprise, it doesn't sound much of a do. Dad will be much too busy to come and I've got my health to consider. Your sister as you will appreciate is much too delicate to travel all that way, especially now what with all her schoolwork it has become so hard for her, because healthwise Janet as you should try to remember has always been less fortunate than you.

Love Mum

Then she's added a postscript.

When you send Janet a birthday card this year I hope you make it a special one, not home-made as usual, do NOT forget because

this time it's her sixteenth!! Quite a milestone, sweet sixteen!!!
Mum

'Oh well,' Caroline says, sounding to Josh, for the very first time, a little less than invincible.

The letter is somewhat puzzling to Josh, because why on earth should one sister's birthday take precedence over another sister's wedding?

'What's the matter with your sister?' he says.

'Oh,' Caroline says. 'She's frail.'

'Frail?' Josh says.

'Yes, frail,' Caroline says, beginning to sound edgy. 'She needs to take care, that's all.'

'Are you saying she's mentally unstable?' Josh says, after a pause.

'Of course not,' Caroline says. 'Of course she's not mentally unstable. She was always sickly as a child, for heaven's sake. Aren't people allowed to be frail?'

'Yes,' Josh says. 'But –'

'Look. Stop interrogating me, all right?' Caroline says.

The episode causes Josh a flash of memory that has to do with Hattie Thomas. The unfavoured sister. Another talented girl of his acquaintance who was possessed of a preferred sibling of whom she almost never spoke. Weird that he should have found his way to both of them. Weird that they should both be so reluctant to open up. Josh finds this impossible to comprehend; he whose adoptive parents spoke of anything and everything and usually over dinner. From circumcision rituals to the theory of surplus value. From Non-conformism in *Adam Bede*, to the trafficking of women. By the time Josh is ten years old, he knows that his own birth mother had herself been effectively trafficked; tricked into a proxy marriage with a sleazy gold-digging stranger.

'I'm sorry, Caroline,' he says. 'But I hate to see you upset.'

11

'I'm not upset,' she says. 'End of story.'

And that afternoon she embarks upon a birthday card for her sister; a labour-intensive and highly skilled affair; a pull-out concertina construction made of thick, antique-white etching paper with intricate cut-out sections giving a filigree effect. Each frame depicts a stage in her sister's growing up. Janet at four with a new puppy. Janet at eight with a bicycle. Janet at twelve in a party dress. Janet, Janet.

Josh has never before been witness to this particular aspect of Caroline's talent.

'Christ,' he says. 'You're not going to give that card away? Caroline, I reckon it should be hanging in the Tate. Anyway, didn't your mother say not to send "home-made"?'

Caroline makes the envelope out of the same thick etching paper. He watches her address the envelope in her large italic hand. 'Miss Janet Abigail McCleod.'

'I thought perhaps if it was especially nice,' she says. 'I mean, the bought ones are usually so crappy, aren't they? That's unless you've got fortunes to spend, which, as you know, I have not.'

Caroline makes her wedding dress from five yards of cream-coloured crêpe de Chine that have been left behind, as an accidental bonus, in a small chest of drawers she's bought in the Animal Sanctuary shop. She's stripped the chest with Nitromors but not before encasing the crêpe de Chine in a linen pillowcase and putting it through a cold wash in the college launderette machine to remove a faint, rust-coloured fold-mark.

The day before the wedding party, Caroline sends Josh to pick strawberries from a farm on the edge of Port Meadow, while she bakes a ham and makes a vat of potato salad. She makes two large, buttery onion tarts and prepares bowls of tzatziki and hummus. She devises a way of poaching a salmon in the absence of a fish kettle. Having first rigorously scrubbed the small steel sink in the student kitchen, she places the fish within it and covers it with boiling water. Then she seals the sink with a sheet of baking foil, which she weighs down at each corner with a large baking potato.

Josh, who stays over with her in Oxford that night, discovers that Caroline has also made these amazing nuptial pyjamas out of a pre-war satin bedspread. Silver Hollywood pyjamas which she puts on the night before the wedding. Josh is knocked out by Caroline in the pyjamas. He finds them incredibly provocative and, with hindsight, remembers them as the high point of his marriage. She is like a lithe and slippery silver fish, and next morning, lying with his face in the crumpled satin folds of her crotch, as she sits, knees apart, hands around a cup of coffee, it comes to him that Caroline is glimmering; glimmering, like that disappearing dream-girl in the Yeats poem about the hazel wood. A girl who, transformed from a silver fish, then vanishes on the air. There's that bit about the golden and the silver apples belonging to the sun and the moon. An old man looking back. His life consumed with yearning; with seeking out the object of desire, through hollow and hilly lands.

Josh, at that moment, does not know quite how quickly the hollow lands will hove into view, or that the hilly lands are just around the corner.

'There was this beautiful quilted medallion in the centre of the bedspread,' Caroline is saying. 'I've kept it because I'll maybe make it into a fire screen. For one day when we've got our very own house.'

'Yes,' Josh says.

'I want us to have one of those little Victorian terraced houses that's got a fireplace with pretty tiles and a garden with climbing roses,' she says. 'Two up, two down. That's all. It would be bliss to decorate a house.'

Josh has had no thoughts, to date, on the subject of interior decoration and probably never will have, so in this respect Caroline faces a future of unimpeded freedom to pursue her own vision of homemaking, though he's noticed that, between the historical tomes, Caroline keeps a stack of glossy magazines with pictures of bedrooms and gardens and bathrooms. These are items she plucks from around the back of a local hairdressing salon, which means they are always just a month out of date.

It has never crossed his mind before that such things could play a part in the life of a woman with a serious brain. The Silvers' furniture, beyond Bernie's remarkable over-large desk and his collection of interesting art works, had the look of having been chosen randomly and for purely functional purposes. And the art works – mainly local – had on the whole been gifts over the years, in repayment for endless small loans and handouts to impecunious black artists. Josh could remember Bernie once laughing in the face of a gallery owner who had paid a visit in hopes of prising a particular painting from him; a painting of three rusted shanties on a windswept Eastern Cape wasteland.

'So it's the fashion these days for the bourgeoisie to have a slum hanging in the house?' he said. At the time he had no intention to sell, but in the end it was the sale of all the paintings that made paying Jack's school fees possible.

'And let's have a dear little baby,' Caroline is saying. 'I mean, just as soon as we can. Actually, can we have four? I've always wanted lots of children.' Then she laughs and says, 'I suppose we'd have to make an extra bedroom in the roof? A "loft conversion" with a little spiral staircase. Kids would love a spiral staircase.'

'Or a fireman's pole,' Josh says, who has not as yet considered having children; hasn't quite got his head around the idea of being a grown-up himself, and he right now assumes that Caroline's speaking of making babies is merely a form of pillow-talk, which is certainly having its effect.

But Caroline is quite serious, though she doesn't question why. She remembers vividly being seven years old and awaiting her sister's birth. She remembers a fistful of drawings made in tribute to the baby and her almost unbearable eagerness to push the baby in its new pram. But after that she has a large blank. Before Janet. After Janet. She has no conscious memory of being pushed out to the periphery; of being that small child who went through a ruthless withdrawal of maternal love; an experience that would have triggered her strategy of trying ever harder and harder – and, given her natural abilities, it materialised as a strategy that always paid off handsomely with schoolteachers and sports coaches and university lecturers. It paid off repeatedly with committees that gave out prizes. Essay prizes; art prizes; scholarships.

Caroline has no memory of when such strategies began. They are simply too much a part of the person she has become. And, along with it, she carries a strong urge to have a baby. Another baby. A baby to love and cherish, and to be loved and cherished in return. She has a need to go back into that blank space and fill it with hope and light, as people do in the case of certain dreams; dreams in which they urge themselves back in, because they are in hopes of changing the outcome.

'A fireman's pole would be good,' she says. 'I suppose I ought to get dressed.'

'Don't,' Josh says. 'Don't get dressed. Caroline, will you marry me in these slippery silver pyjamas?'

'Wait till you see my dress,' she says.

'Is that right?' he says. He's thinking that her hair, especially first thing in the morning, before she's brushed it, is something quite extraordinary. Voluminous, like Mary Magdalene's hair. Hair that grew and grew so that, all through the saint's years of desert exile, as her clothes fell from her in rags, she was protected from exposure.

'Think *The Philadelphia Story*,' Caroline says. 'You are going to love it.'

And then there's the buzz of the doorbell. Someone in the street has pressed the buzzer for Caroline's room.

'It'll be some dosser,' Caroline says, sounding somewhat brisk. 'You get the whole bang shoot around here. Old winos, young druggies, drunk foreign-student kids. It's sort of like those buttons are all yelling, "Please press me." Especially at 4 a.m.' Then she gets up and leans out of the window. He watches her suddenly stiffen. 'Oh my God,' she says. 'I don't believe it. It's Mum. And my sister. Josh, you'll have to make yourself scarce.' She's already begun to gather up his clothes.

'But why?' Josh says. 'I mean, we're getting married today.'

'Quick!' she says. He can see that she is shaking. 'Please, Josh. Go and get dressed, but not in here. Go to the bathroom at the far end, OK? Then come back in twenty minutes. But go downstairs and press the buzzer. That way they'll think you've just arrived. And – oh Christ, Josh – please remember to shave.'

When Josh returns, sluiced, shaved and dressed, Caroline's mother and sister are seated in the two oyster-painted chairs with the pillow-ticking seats; two dumpy, mouse-haired women who have the look of visiting the same hairdresser for a weekly wash and set. Caroline has evidently made the bed in haste, which is now playing host to a large suitcase, alongside which Caroline is perched. She is still in the silver pyjamas. Her mother is evidently in mid-flow, filling the air with down-home small talk, while Janet emits the odd whingeing refrain and looks perpetually down-in-the-mouth.

They pause, momentarily, in this symbiotic double act, to acknowledge Josh's arrival and follow through with a brief shaking of hands. Then the performance continues, just as if he were not there. Mother is the talky partner, daughter the silent back-up. It reminds Josh of those Jehovah's Witnesses who always come to the door in pairs. Caroline, he decides there and then, must take after her absent father because, while mother and younger daughter are remarkably alike, in neither can he see the smallest trace of his beautiful girlfriend. Of the two, Janet has the weedier handshake. Otherwise, she's a clone. To take her hand is like grasping the body of a dead herring.

'Yes, it's a shame about Dad,' Caroline's mother is venturing. 'But we decided on coming at the very last minute, so there wasn't the time to make contact. He was off at work, as usual. Quite an adventure, wasn't it, Janet? Coming to the UK. But, of course, we told Mrs Dodds next door, and she'll have passed on the news to Dad by now.' Then she says, 'Mrs Dodds seemed quite excited, by the way – I mean about you getting married, but then she always did play favourites, didn't she? She's sent you a tea cosy, Caroline. It's one she made herself, so you'll remember to write her a thank-you note, won't you? Just a notelet will do.'

'Yes, Mum,' Caroline says. 'I will.' Caroline, recent maker of scissor-work greeting cards and ruched, Thai-silk ball gowns.

'We'd have got you something in the duty-free,' the matriarch continues, 'but you'll appreciate that Janet was much too tired before the flight. When it comes to stamina she's always been so much less fortunate than you.' Then she turns to Josh. 'I hope you'll call me Mum,' she says. 'I've always been very informal. I'm very easy-going, Josh. I take people as they come. I must say, you're not very tall, now, are you?'

It appears that Caroline's less fortunate younger sister was born with a cleft palate which was successfully treated in infancy, as was her childhood asthma. Other than that, there is nothing at all wrong with Janet, except for her markedly less fortunate personality. Josh can't quite see the point of Janet, other than that she evidently exists to act as sidekick and backup to Caroline's mother, along with offering that lady the means to induce guilt in her beautiful and brilliant elder daughter. In short, he finds his in-laws to be a couple of grotesques.

17

The mother has the daughter on a length of invisible string – both daughters, come to that – and she certainly knows how to sabotage the spontaneity of the wedding feast by constantly diverting poor, conscientious Caroline with what seem to him idiotic and spoilt-brat demands for special treatment. Janet is cold. May she please change seats? Borrow a cardigan? Move out of the draught? And how many eggs are in this quiche? Thanks but no thanks. Only one egg a week. Those are my doctor's orders. And onions have a nasty habit of repeating on me. Not exactly the thing for one's wedding night, if I may say so. Fish? No thank you. I've never been one for fish. As you will appreciate, I've never been a fussy woman, but fish has always been a no-no with me. Caroline, could I possibly have a smaller fork? A sharper knife? A riper tomato? Eton Mess you call this? I must say, it certainly looks rather a mess! No thank you, dear. Not unless it's low-fat cream. And Janet can't eat strawberries, as you surely will remember. Caroline, is this decaff? Sorry, but caffeine is not for me.

By nightfall it has become horribly apparent that the ghoulish pair have made no arrangements regarding accommodation and that Caroline's mother is making it clear that it's her daughter's job to play host.

'Well, you surely didn't expect us to go traipsing about in the cold, looking for a hotel?' she says. 'What with Janet having one of her colds coming on, after sitting in all that draught. You do have a cold coming, don't you, Janet? And mark my words, it'll turn to bronchitis if we don't take care.'

'A-tish-oo,' Janet says.

'And aren't the two of you "going away"?' she says. 'I naturally assumed we'd have the use of your room, what with us having come all this way. Whatever happened to hospitality? Not to mention the honeymoon?'

18

'You see, Mum,' Caroline says, sounding, as she has all day, both submissive and apologetic. 'You see, it's not the vacation yet and I've got my field trip to budget for. I'm going to Iran next term and –'

'Well!' her mother says, cutting her short. 'I must say, it's all been *so* romantic, it makes me want to get married all over again – I don't think! I can't imagine your sister making such a poor fist of things. That's when her "special day" comes along.'

'Josh,' Caroline is saying in whispers as, together with a handful of friends, they are clearing up the party debris. 'Josh, we've got to give them my room. After all, she is my mother.'

'But it's our wedding night,' he says.

'Oh never mind,' Caroline says. 'Look. We've got the rest of our lives together.'

'Yes,' Josh says. 'But . . .'

'Come on,' she says. 'It'll be fine. I'll work something out. You'll see.'

And it is. She does. It all works out, because Caroline is nothing if not a prodigious problem-solver. Two of her friends, Sam and Jen, are an artist couple who live in a decommissioned red double-decker bus that they park in the field of a local farmer, just up the Abingdon Road. And Horst, the physics post-doc from Freiburg, has a two-person tent along with camping equipment. So the newly-weds bike out to pitch camp alongside the artists' vegetable patch and bed down to watch a star-studded night sky through the lean isosceles triangle of the tent's open access.

In the balmy summer morning they make coffee and heat up a tin of baked beans on Horst's little Trangia stove. They watch sheep graze in a field. Caroline is in the slippery silver pyjamas and Josh is wrapped in a flowered kanga. Beachwear from his home town.

'We're having a honeymoon after all,' Josh observes. 'You are a genius, Caroline.'

'Thank you,' she says.

Then they go for a second cup of coffee, with Sam and Jen inside the bus. Both Josh and Caroline are enchanted by the bus, with its shiny metal footplate, which now constitutes the floor of the porch, and its ting-ting conductor's bell, which is still in working order. The lower deck, now minus its passenger seats, makes a long kitchen-living room, while up the narrow winding stairs is an elongated, many-windowed bedroom with a tiny shower room. Sam has made a stepping-stone path from the bus to the farm track. Jen's vegetable patch is bordered with tall sunflowers.

'Isn't this heaven?' Caroline says and Josh has to agree.

Then they bike back to the ghoulish pair, who are up, dressed, and waiting for their breakfast with foot-tapping impatience.

'About time too,' says Caroline's mother. 'Don't mind us, will you, Caroline?'

'I'm so sorry, Mum,' Caroline says and off they go to a café in Holywell Street, where – doctor's orders cast aside – the matriarch tucks into eggs and bacon and toast.

'And now you can show us the sights,' she says, neatly placing her knife and fork at twenty-five past.

'Yes, Mum. Of course, Mum,' Caroline says.

'If Janet feels up to it,' she says.

'A-tish-oo,' Janet says.

'You get a fantastic view of the city from the cupola of the Sheldonian,' Caroline ventures. 'It's just a stone's throw from here.'

'No thank you,' her mother says. 'Not if it's going to mean climbing umpteen stairs. You might be as strong as a bull, Caroline, but I think you might show some consideration for your sister.'

'OK, Mum,' Caroline says. 'Sorry, Mum. What about a walk through Christ Church Meadow? It's just off the High Street and you come out via a cobbled lane just opposite –'

'A meadow?' says her mother. 'And what makes you think we packed our gumboots?'

It transpires that what the pair really have in mind is to dawdle round various retail outlets, acquiring armfuls of clothes.

'This way we get the fashions a season ahead,' says Caroline's mother, doing a girly gaiety voice in the aisles of M & S. 'Janet's always had a really good eye. Haven't you, Janet? And what on earth is that thing you're wearing, Caroline – just by the way?'

Caroline is wearing her immaculate Levi's with a simple white cotton top, delicately pleated at the yoke, like a cropped choirboy smock.

That night, since mother and daughter have plans to spend a second night, Josh and Caroline, once again, bike up the Abingdon Road. Then, next morning, the pair, whom Josh by now has inwardly dubbed the Witch Woman and the Less Fortunate, announce their intention of travelling by train to Aberdeen, in pursuit of a maternal cousin, several times removed; a cousin who has had no hint of her relations' imminent arrival.

'I don't like to stand on ceremony,' the Witch Woman says. 'I like to be informal.'

'A-tish-oo,' says the Less Fortunate.

And then, at last, they are gone. And then; and then.

And then the Iranian revolution is happening. And then, alas for the country's long-suffering progressives, it is taking an unfortunate turn. Bearded mullahs are staging public executions in sports arenas and city squares. Black chadors are transforming the female population into a flock of faceless crows – and Caroline's research trip is, of necessity, placed on hold. Josh, meanwhile, has planned to spend the next five weeks in Paris.

'Not to worry,' Caroline says. 'I've got plenty to be getting on with. I'll make a plan.'

The plan she makes during his absence is somewhat unexpected and it casts a black cloud over his return. It also has the long-term effect of binding them grimly together. Because Caroline, unbeknown to him, has received another of those letters, and this one contains a bombshell.

Dear Caroline

I'm afraid we lost Dad ten days ago. He had a heart attack while driving back from work and just had time to pull over. I would have sent a telegram but as you will appreciate Janet was very upset and she needed me at home so it was difficult for me, you people should get a phone. There's bad news as well because it looks like Dad has bonded everything away to his creditors so Janet and I will have nothing to call our own really. I don't know what's going to happen to us because Uncle Julius says he can't help. He says we should sell the house and move to a small flat and that I've got typing and clerical skills and Janet is sixteen so we should both go out to work. But I've got my health to consider and Janet as you will appreciate is much too frail, she needs to stay on at school and get herself a higher education. After all, you had your chance at uni, didn't you, so it's only fair that Janet should have the same, that's if her health will allow.

Love Mum

Again she's added a postscript.

Dad's health had been going downhill for about six months but I didn't like to mention it on your 'big day'. Do you have any photos, by the way, because Mrs Dodds keeps asking about it even though I've told her that it wasn't much of a wedding. Mum.

So Josh returns to his London student house to find that Caroline is not at her Oxford college. She is billeted in his room. It's his

22

room, but minus any speck of dust and with his books arranged in alphabetical order. She has been there for a month. Having spent the first days of her husband's five-week absence weeping for her father, she has then picked herself up, a little paler and thinner, and she's embarked upon a plan. Caroline's grief, as he observes, has already been converted into her own special brand of try-hard action.

'Oh Caroline,' he says, attempting to embrace her. 'Oh my God, I'm so sorry. Oh Christ, why didn't you tell me? I would've come back.'

But Caroline is from a family not much given to communication and, in his absence, she has taken some bold, unilateral decisions. Decisions that now appal him.

'Jesus,' he says, once he's heard her out. 'Just wait, Caroline. Wait, for heaven's sake. This is all much too hasty.'

Caroline, without consulting him, has put an end to the sweet privilege of her graduate student life. She's given up her scholarship and has got herself a teaching job in history and French. The job is in a small private school just outside Oxford.

'The pay is better,' she says. She has signed herself up to complete, concurrently, a one-year postgraduate Certificate in Education as an external student through London University. 'The head has agreed to up my salary once I've got the certificate,' she says. 'She watched me give a lesson, Josh. She knows that I'm damn good.'

He has no doubt that she is good. She has withdrawn her name from the married-student accommodation list, for which, of course, they are no longer eligible, but she's got some 'good news' on the housing front, she says.

'Sam and Jen have taken jobs in Leeds and they've offered us the bus. We can buy it from them in monthly sums over three whole years and for only four hundred pounds. That's incredibly cheap, Josh. It works out at less than twelve quid a month.

Anyway, it'll be such fun. Much better than some crappy breeze-block student flat with no garden and smelling of fish fingers. I need you to say you're pleased.'

Pleased. Josh has been feeling really high these last five weeks and now his heart is somewhere inside his shoes.

'Why are you doing this?' he says. 'It's stupid, Caro. It's too drastic. You're upset. I can't deal with it. I need you to slow down.'

'It's done,' she corrects him. 'I'm not "doing" it, Josh. It's done.'

'We should've discussed it,' he says. 'You should have told me.'

'It's done, precisely because I know that it's our only option and I know that you would've tried to stop me,' she says. 'This way we can both live on your grant and I can give all my salary to Mum and Janet.'

Josh says nothing. Absolutely nothing. His life experience in the household of his adoptive parents has predisposed him to respect personal sacrifice as an honourable thing, and once again he's amazed by Caroline's ability to cut a swathe through every obstacle and emerge with workable solutions. Nonetheless, he has a queasy feeling that this particular solution is an insult to Caroline herself as an unusually talented person; a case of casting pearls before swine. But Caroline, as he's had the opportunity to observe, is clearly devoted to her unlikeable mother and sister. And maybe unlikeable is an irrelevance? Maybe need is simply need?

'I think it's all a bit drastic,' he says. 'First of all, is it reversible?'

'It's done,' she says. 'Of course it's not reversible. Josh, it makes sense. I've had my chance at uni and why shouldn't Janet have the same?'

'You got funded,' Josh says. 'And aren't you quite a lot brainier than Janet? Caroline, you're brainier than anyone I know.'

'And you think that I should use my brain to abandon my mother and sister?' she says. 'They're my own flesh and blood.'

This is true, he's reflecting ruefully, and not for the first time. By some bizarre, inexplicable twist in that doubly twisting DNA, the Witch Woman and the Less Fortunate are Caroline's flesh and blood. But then his own flesh and blood would be that pair of weirdos he's never known and never much bothered about. The puny Greek fraudster and the catatonic convent girl. God Almighty, why should he care? It's Bernie and Ida Silver who have always been his nearest and dearest – and they don't believe too much in flesh and blood. They believe in the human race. And wasn't little Jack, the housemaid's boy, more brother to him than the wretched Janet could ever be sister to Caroline?

'Look, Josh, I'm all they've got,' Caroline is saying. 'And face it, my DPhil's screwed. I'll never get to Iran. Not now. Both of us know that. This way is good. I'm fine with it. The world needs teachers. Who needs another person with a doctorate in something or other?'

There's a long pause.

'Caroline,' Josh says. He's thinking of the wonderful days just past that he's spent poring over the set designs and the scores for Stravinsky's *Pulcinella*, his hands clothed in archive-issue white cotton gloves. 'I'm not giving up my PhD. I can't. I hope you don't expect it of me.'

'Of course not,' she says. 'Go for it, Josh, please. If we live in the bus, then you can give up this place. Getting to London will be an easy commute for you and you've got your travel allowance.'

This is true. Josh has got his travel allowance, for which, mercifully, he is required to submit receipts. There is no way, thank the Lord, that this money can be spent on Caroline's mother and sister.

And Caroline is right, as usual, at least in respect of the bus. The old bus in the Abingdon Road is a smashing place for two young childless people to live. Every morning early Caroline wheels her tall Dutch bike along the stepping-stone path and proceeds to the Woodstock Road, where she catches a bus to her school. Three times a week, Josh takes the nausea-inducing Oxford-to-London coach from Gloucester Green to Baker Street, in order to use the libraries, or to attend and sometimes give seminars. And Josh is

25

lucky because, just as his research funding is being threatened by the decline of the rand against sterling, he submits his thesis and lands a job in the drama department at Bristol University; a manageable commuter distance from the old red bus. This time he buys a season ticket and commutes by high-speed train.

Four years into their marriage; four years during which she's watched several of her same-age friends have children – Caroline, having kept it nobly to herself, is still harbouring longings to have a baby. She has sustained her family through her sister's last years at high school plus two out of three years of higher education. So maybe the time has come? Janet, having been turned down for law school, will soon have completed a teacher-training course and will then be eligible for work. So Zoe is born, a dainty, easy baby with Josh's chestnut curls, whose existence provides Caroline with yet another outlet for her creative talents, because, for all her parents' pared-down income, Zoe is always beautifully attired.

Her jumble-sale Babygro suits have been dyed dark plum, or bottle green, or chocolate brown. Zoe has a quilted toggle jacket made from scraps of Liberty lawn and another made from the edging strips of a large Madras-check tablecloth. She spends her first months sleeping in an antique wooden cradle, rescued from the council dump – Caroline having first padded the interior with sheep's wool gathered from the farmer's fences, and covered the padding with sky-blue pleated silk.

Josh finds he loves to take care of Zoe on his stay-at-home days and sometimes, during her first twelve months, he takes her with him on the train to Bristol in a sling across his chest, and with a Moses basket in tow so that she can sleep through meetings and lectures, which she always reliably does.

They have even started saving to buy that little terraced house.

'It's all going to work out fine,' Caroline says, on the occasion of Zoe's first birthday, as they munch on celebratory slices of home-made almond cake. 'You realise that Janet graduates next month? Then, as soon as she can get a job, it'll make for one less dependant. And with Mum and Janet living together, they can share the household expenses. Plus my sister and I can start to share the cost of Mum's personal needs.'

Caroline has moved on from the small private school to become head of history in a somewhat challenging city comprehensive. It's a job that makes greater demands on her, but it earns her the extra money to place Zoe in the crèche run by her old college.

'We've done it, Josh!' she says. 'We've very nearly done it! Say, one of these days – like in about a year – I could take a cut in salary and see about working part-time. Then we could have another baby. And, I mean – well – the bus is lovely, but it could be that we should try now for a proper house. I mean go for it right away, before they get even more expensive.'

Caroline, alas, has spoken too soon, since Janet duly graduates, but, after teaching for three days in a leafy suburban school, has seen fit to pack it in. The information is relayed to them via another of the matriarch's letters.

Dear Caroline

This is to let you know that your sister has had to give up teaching. The children of today are so badly behaved there is no respect and Janet can't be expected to cope with all the rudeness and noise. As you will appreciate she is much too frail when it comes to stamina, she has always been less fortunate than you.

Love Mum

This time there is no postscript.

'Caroline,' Josh says darkly. 'We can't let this go on. We have to fly there and sort it out. We have to blow a chunk of our savings. There's nothing else we can do.'

Josh has recently agreed with Caroline that he should splash out and take a plane to Dar es Salaam – spurred on by Ida's most recent letter, from which it has become obvious that Bernie is in serious decline. He suffers attacks of angina and has recently undergone a hospital procedure to improve upon his wobbly heartbeat. They have agreed that Josh will take Zoe with him to meet his parents, and both the prospective travellers have had their necessary jabs. Sadly, now he sees no option but to delay the visit to Tanzania, and to spend the money elsewhere.

To his relief, Caroline does not reject the idea.

'But let's give it a little bit longer,' she says. 'I'll write and suggest that Janet try for some less demanding job. Maybe in a library? Just give me one more try.'

As it turns out, Caroline's mother soon saves them the expense of buying airfares. She pays another of her unannounced visits, and this time she is toting a significantly larger suitcase. Josh is home alone with Zoe when he hears the ting-ting of the bus conductor's bell.

'Surprise-surprise!' she says. 'Well, aren't you going to ask me in?'

'Yes, of course,' Josh says. 'Come in. Take a seat.' But his mother-in-law remains standing, as she stares out of the window. 'Really,' she says. 'Can't the two of you do any better than this?' Then she tries her hand at humour. 'And who would have thought I'd have to come all this way to see a sheep farm,' she says.

This time she has no plans to take off for Aberdeen. She ensconces herself in the upstairs bedroom, while Josh and Caroline sleep downstairs on a camping mattress alongside the bus's pretty pot-bellied stove. Zoe sleeps between them. Josh finds that throughout this time it is Zoe – his precious little Zoe – who keeps him safe from drowning.

On her first night, in a mood of ominous skittishness, Caroline's mother has pulled out bundles of ugly canary-yellow hand-knits

28

along with two polyester toddler frocks in harsh Mrs Thatcher blue.

'Now you won't forget to write thank-you notes?' she says, going into a familiar routine.

Thank-you notes, Josh is reflecting bitterly, to Mesdames Blah, Blah and Blah. Etiquette lessons from the Witch Woman, who, in five years to date, has never once thanked him or Caroline for handing over more than half their income.

'Now for the photographs,' she says, with a wink. 'I've got the video as well, of course, but since you folks don't have TV . . .'

'Photographs?' Caroline says. Surprise-surprise.

Her mother's pièce de résistance is a sheaf of professional wedding photographs that depict Caroline's sister Janet, standing in full-length nuptial regalia beside a dark-haired man in a morning suit. In some, the bride is surrounded by a phalanx of female children in lemon bridesmaids' get-up. There is one adult-size female, also in ankle-length lemon. In some, the couple are in the company of both mothers. One matriarch is in lilac ensemble, complete with lilac bag, shoes, gloves and hat; the other is in tangerine.

'Uncle Julius gave her away,' the matriarch says, before going on to produce what she refers to as the 'informal snaps'; a stash of posed lovebird studies in which the bride has taken her shoes off and is dabbling her feet in a pond.

'Gosh,' Caroline says, visibly gulping down hurt. 'You both look really great, Mum. What a fabulous hat.'

'Well, you know your sister,' replies Mrs McCleod. 'Only the best will do. And, of course, Mark is a very successful accountant. Need I say more?'

The couple met at an evangelical summer school. The Less Fortunate, as it transpires, has been Born Again.

'So how long have you got with us, Mum?' Caroline says, but Josh takes note that his mother-in-law is suddenly very busy organising the photographs back into their respective envelopes.

'Now, Caroline,' she says. 'My blood pressure. You'll have to remind me to take my pills. Every morning and evening. Janet always reminds me to take my pills. And please remember that the doctor says I'm not to be upset.'

On day one of week two, Caroline's mother, after haunting the bus, hour after long hour, wrong-footing Josh in Caroline's absence and bearing down upon poor little Zoe in a manner denoting the unconditional entitlement of grannyhood, finds herself suddenly in need of retail therapy and orders herself a cab to Marks & Spencer. This is when Josh, at last, can seize his chance. He dives upstairs and falls upon the matriarch's hand luggage, in which he finds a one-way ticket to London Heathrow. The Witch Woman, as he's begun to suspect, has no return ticket. He also finds a self-help book entitled *Codependent No More*. On the flyleaf of the book, Janet has written a chilling inscription.

Dear Mum
    I hope that reading this book will help you as much as it has helped me. It will show you why I need to cut my ties with you completly.
    Best of luck and God bless. You will always be in our prayers.
    Love Janet

Josh stuffs the book and the air ticket back inside his mother-in-law's cabin bag. He is shaking so violently as he comes downstairs that he almost twists an ankle. He drinks a glass of water and tries to compose himself.

He checks on Zoe, who is happily engaged with a pile of plastic bricks. He seizes a red marker pen from one of Caroline's jars.

'Hold on there, Zoe babe,' he says and he blows her a jaunty kiss.

He mounts the stairs. He reaches for the self-help book and opens it at the flyleaf. He makes an insertion mark between the 't' and the 'l' in the word 'completly'. Then he adds a bold red 'e'. After that he goes downstairs to wait for Caroline to come home.

'Oh poor Mum!' Caroline says, when Josh tells her about the book and the inscription and the one-way ticket. 'Oh my God, how terrible for her.'

They are speaking in whispers from the lower deck, because Caroline's mother, having tired herself out, is now having a lie-down upstairs.

'But we have to confront her about her plans,' Josh says. 'We have to know where we stand. Caro, even you would have to admit that we're a little bit crowded in here.'

'OK,' Caroline says. 'OK. Let's talk about it after supper.'

And she sets about preparing a porcini risotto and a green salad made with lettuce and endive gathered from her vegetable patch, along with some young dandelion leaves.

As an unpropitious prelude to the imminent confrontation, Caroline's mother, having picked out all the porcini mushrooms from her daughter's risotto and arranged them pointedly in a ring around the outer edge of her dinner plate, then turns her attention to finding fault with the salad.

'I must admit that when I'm offered salad I expect it to be salad,' she says. 'I don't expect to find myself wrestling with a pile of garden weeds. Caroline, if I'm not mistaken, you've got dandelions in here.'

'Yes, Mum, but it's just the new leaves,' Caroline says. 'Try them. They're really good.'

'No thank you,' her mother replies. 'Dad always put dandelions on to the compost heap.'

Josh can suddenly stand it no longer.

'Mrs McCleod,' he says. 'There is something I have to ask you.'

'Call me Mum, you silly boy,' she says.

'Mrs McCleod,' he says. 'We need you to answer a question.'

'Please, Josh,' Caroline says. 'Maybe not now.'

'We need to get something sorted out,' he says, and he clears his throat. 'Have you decided to emigrate?' he says. 'Or do you have plans to go home? Either way, we need to know how long you plan to stay with us.'

In the extended silence that follows, Josh can hear the rise and fall of his sleeping daughter's breathing. And, finally, when his mother-in-law speaks, it is not to him but to her daughter.

'You haven't been reminding me to take my pills,' she says. 'Janet always reminds me to take my pills.'

And then Caroline is reaching for tissues and soothing words as she gently helps her mother up the stairs.

It is an hour before she comes down again, by which time Josh is resolved.

'I'm taking off for Heathrow,' he says. 'I'm flying to Tanzania. I really need to see my father – and I'm taking Zoe with me.'

'What? Right now?' Caroline says.

'Yes. Right now,' he says. 'Tonight. We'll go standby. We'll stay about a month. I'll take good care of Zoe – and you can trust me to bring her back.'

'Yes,' Caroline says. 'Please. I know that.'

'As to this business,' he says, jerking his head irritably towards the ceiling, to indicate a certain person ensconced on the floor above. 'You can sort it out in my absence any which way you like. Only I want her out of our bed and out from under our feet.'

'Yes,' Caroline says.

And Caroline does indeed 'sort it out', so that, once again, when Josh returns, he finds that she has made a plan. It's a plan that he's too worn out to query, given that his Tanzanian journey has concluded with a funeral – albeit a funeral with fabulous singing; African mission-school singing for a benign old unbeliever. His father, post-surgical procedure, had picked up a bug from one of his pupils; one of those activist Soweto kids who had made it across several borders. Then came the news that Jack was gone; vanished as if into thin air. Brilliant Jack, the housemaid's son, who had been doing so well at school. These things made for a sufficient coming together to bring down a frail old man.

Josh and Caroline fall with relief into each other's arms, with Zoe sandwiched between them.

'I'm so sorry, Josh,' she says. 'I'm so truly sorry about your dad. But how wonderful that you could be there for him. He always sounded such a darling man.'

'He was beyond being aware of much,' Josh says in reply. 'He'd completely stopped speaking. He'd even stopped needing to pee. Just a corpse on a bed, but somehow still breathing.' Then he says, 'Shall I tell you the one and only thing he said, all the time I was there? He opened his eyes and looked at Zoe. Then he said, "Beautiful baby." He even tried to raise his hand. It sort of fluttered on the sheet for a moment.'

Both of them promptly start to cry. Their tears fall on to Zoe's chestnut curls.

'Thank you, Caro,' Josh says. 'For letting me take her. What I mean is thank you for trusting me.'

What he doesn't say is how seriously he thought about not coming back; about packing it all in and staying there, on the east coast of Africa; how it had crossed his mind as he sat there on the veranda of his mother's little single-storey house. The three of them sitting at one of those wood-and-raffia tables that African craftsmen sell in the street. A set with matching chairs; the whole roped in a bundle and carried on the head. There was a beaded-mesh cover protecting the milk jug. His mother was wearing the sort of period-piece apron that she always wore in his childhood. God only knew where she'd got it. Rickrack braid on the pocket, he noted, as she fed Zoe blinis with blobs of her home-made cream cheese. She filled his coffee cup and talked to him, as she had always done, about the International Labour Organisation, and the statistics for agricultural production and the need for speeding up the training of local paramedics.

She's got so old, Josh was thinking. And her breathing isn't great. And now she's on her own. But she wasn't really. Not on her own. As of old, streams of comrades came and went, day after day. And the kids from the nearby Lutheran Sunday School would go home via her kitchen, where she taught them how to make rock cakes and got them to do subtraction sums with the raisins. Ten raisins minus three raisins makes three to eat and seven to throw in the rock-cake mix. Then there was Liesl, the maid, who was roughly as old as Ida. The two of them were more like sisters. Intermittently embracing; sharing a little weep over the old man's death. Interesting, Josh thought, how ethnic difference begins to leach from the features with age.

He noted that, while Bernie and Ida had transplanted themselves, what they had recreated around themselves felt much the same as before. He tried in his mind to put Caroline and Ida together; both with that resolute productivity. All that sewing and growing and organising. And yet. And yet.

Ida hugged him when it was time for him to go.

'My boy,' she said. It was all she said.

She gave him a cow-skin album pasted with all the photographs he'd taken during his visit. Most of them were of her and Zoe, or of Zoe with the Sunday School kids. One, taken by Liesl, had the three of them together. A couple were of Zoe with Liesl. Ida had added a few old photographs of Josh in childhood, with Ida and Bernie.

'For the little girl,' she said.

'I was foul to you before I left,' Josh says to Caroline. 'I'm sorry. I was stressed.'

'No,' she says. 'No. It's OK. Look, Mum's in a B & B, by the way, but it's only for a few weeks. She's been there since yesterday evening.'

Caroline's 'plan' has been to put on hold their own intended house purchase and to buy for her mother instead.

'She'll be right on the edge of the city,' she says. 'We did a massive consumer survey and she fell for this brand-new little semi. The good news is that, because it's so new, it needed quite a small deposit and the developer sorts out the mortgage. She'll exchange contracts in about two weeks. It's all going through very quickly. It's using up nearly all of our savings, Josh, but I promise we'll build them up again. And I'll be responsible for the monthly payments and Mum's allowance. You won't need to notice a thing.'

Neither of them has the stomach to bring up Caroline's previously stated intention to work part-time and have another baby, or to move out of the bus. Josh finds that right now he's so wrung out that he's completely beyond caring. He's desperately in need of sleep. He's home again. The Witch Woman is patently no longer in his bed. Besides, it's not he but Caroline who longs to have more children. Josh is wholly focused on Zoe. He's more than happy to have her remain as his precious only child.

'It's fine,' he says. 'It's all fine, Caro. Just so long as we've got each other.'

Then he climbs the stairs of the old red bus and he falls asleep in his clothes.

Chapter Two

Zoe

Zoe is really upset about the French exchange, and all the more so because it hasn't even started. She's feeling extra apprehensive, not only because it's going to be three whole weeks, not two, on account of Mrs Mead, head of French, believing in what she calls 'total immersion', but she's the only girl in the class who's been teamed up with a boy. All the boys in her class have got French boys for partners and all the girls have got French girls – that's except for her. Unfortunately, there's been a not quite correlating boy–girl take-up in each of the two schools. This is what Mrs Mead has explained, so somebody's got to have the extra boy on the other side of the Channel. And – guess what? – that somebody is going to be her. Zoe Silver. *Of course.*

And it's so unfair, because it could have been Gemma, or Gemma's best friend Becca, both boy-mad and both with their proper grown-up lacy bras and their scary mixed-sex birthday parties that they've been having since they were eleven. And now Gemma's been moaning her head off non-stop because her thirteenth birthday is going to happen while the class is away on the French exchange and she's going to have to postpone her party till they get back. Just like other people didn't have much worse things happen to them – e.g., like being teamed up with a boy, when the whole idea of having to go and stay with a bunch of people you don't even know is quite scary enough. Zoe just can't stop worrying about it.

Most of her class have given up birthday parties for the moment because at twelve, and especially thirteen, you can't very well go on having those babyish all-girl parties with treasure hunts and loot bags, and pin-the-tail-on-the-donkey, and with your mum making you a novelty cake of your choice, with candles on it. Well, you can if you're Emily, of course, but then Emily is so kind of floaty that she doesn't even notice. And, on the quiet, all the girls really enjoy her parties, because Emily's mum keeps everyone so busy there's no time to get bitchy or to feel left out, like there is at Gemma and Becca's parties, where you stand there wishing you had different shoes on and that your mum had let you have your ears pierced and that you knew about kissing and stuff.

Zoe's mum, Caroline, used to do those four-star kids' parties for her, except that she always insisted Gran come and only once, two years ago, did she agree to make Zoe a ballerina cake.

The next year she said, 'Not again, Zoe. That's just boring. And aren't you getting a bit too old for all this ballet stuff? What about the belle époque, if you're wanting something a bit girly? Or how about we make you a map of Middle Earth?'

Zoe really doesn't like Tolkien. It seems to her it's a lot of weird boy-stuff that, for some reason, her mother thinks would be better for her than reading ballet books. It's probably because her mum was young in the 1970s, so she thinks that girls should be forever doing plumbing and welding along with cooking and sewing, to show how liberated they are. And she won't let Zoe have ballet lessons, because she says they're much too expensive and that Zoe must absolutely not go leaning on her dad.

'You know what a pushover he is,' she said. 'He'll start going without lunch just to pay for you to have lessons.'

So Zoe hasn't said a word to Josh about it. She's kept it to herself.

But, about the birthday cakes, the only really embarrassing time was once, when her mum and dad had to be away and Gran did her party instead. She just insisted and Zoe didn't know how to tell her not to. Gran made this horrible iced cake like a Christmas cake that looked like a tombstone and inside was that kind of claggy fruitcake, when everyone knows it's a chocolate cake you're supposed to have. Anyway, nobody ate it. They just broke it up into bits and then Gran kept saying cringeworthy stuff out loud in front of Zoe's friends, like, 'Personally, I can't abide the waste!' and, 'It makes you wonder what sort of homes they come from!' that just made everyone giggle – especially as most of them have got quite smart houses and it's Zoe's family who still live in a bus – though not for very much longer because when she gets back they're going to be moving into a house where she'll have a 'proper' bedroom.

Except that, last weekend, when her dad had a sneaky plan that he and she – just the two of them – should go and camp in her new bedroom overnight, they'd got there and Zoe had refused to sleep in the house, because the bedrooms had these really horrible old nylon carpets that stank of wee, with creaky floorboards underneath, and all the door panels were painted orange and lilac with, like, brush hairs stuck in the paint, though her dad said that Caroline was going to 'work miracles' on the house while they were away. But, anyway, her dad said never mind, they'd just practise a few headstands against the walls downstairs for a bit and then they'd go back home to the bus.

Her bedroom in the bus is just about big enough for her bed with drawers under it, plus with about forty centimetres running down the side, so that she has to keep all her 'hanging-up' clothes in her mum and dad's room, but at least the bus is kind of stylish-looking inside and her friends really like it.

Doing the headstands was fun and now Zoe's really sorry that she wouldn't sleep in the house with her dad, because she's not going to see him for ages and ages until they both get back. She's quite good at headstands and so is her dad. She used to be scared of doing gym, but when she was six he'd taught her to do forward and backward rolls on this big trampoline they'd found on a rainy beach in Devon and after that she'd got much braver about it.

Anyway, about Gran and the embarrassing birthday party, she said all Zoe's friends had to eat up the sandwiches first before they were even allowed any cake, so no one had room for it by then. Emily's mum's a widow and she's a doctor who works with people who've had head injuries, so revolting Sadie once passed this note around the class saying that Emily must have had a head injury, which was where her mum had got all the practice. But, instead of passing the note on, Zoe just shoved it into her desk, because it was so mean and horrible. Sadie had only written it because Emily's a bit goofy-looking and her ears are quite sticky-out. And just because she's got this quite big sort of a mole thing on her chest, Sadie's note also said had anybody noticed Emily had got 'three nipples'.

Then, later on, one of the senior girls, who must've been snooping in Zoe's desk during geography, had gone and found the note and given it to the head and Zoe'd got the blame for it, just because she wouldn't tell who'd sent it. Well, you can't tell on people, can you? Even if it's someone gross, like Sadie. Then afterwards Sadie thought it was all dead funny about the head and all, and she started behaving like she and Zoe were kind of 'together' because of it.

But, anyway, about the boy thing and the French exchange, Zoe's already tried getting her mum to go up and have a word with Mrs Mead, but Caroline's refused, because she says Zoe should learn to fight her own battles, and anyway she thinks it's 'a bit silly and bigoted' of Zoe to mind having a boy. And, worse luck, her dad, who's usually better at understanding about when you're scared, was staying over in Bristol all of that week, though he's usually only there over three nights. It's because of some funny little opera thing he's putting on together with the music department, which is all about this lechy old tutor who's in love with his beautiful young orphan pupil, and everyone ends up getting married to the wrong people. Her dad says this is fairly unusual for a comic opera, but that it's maybe a lot more like real life.

Anyway, Zoe's even tried doing something she's never done before – i.e., going up to Mrs Mead on her own and pretending that her mum wants her to try and swap things round, so she can have a girl – but there's nothing Mrs Mead is prepared to do about it. That's except for producing a whole lot of soft soap in a letter that she tells Zoe to pass on to Caroline, which is really embarrassing. I mean as if it wasn't hard enough telling Mrs Mead a lie like that in the first place.

Dear Mrs Silver
    Please be reassured. Zoe is such a sensible girl. She is always so dependable and resourceful that you really need have no fear with regard to the French exchange. I know that she will cope splendidly.

Then she's signed it 'Regan Mead', which is really weird. I mean for teachers to have first names at all, even though her own mother's a teacher of course, but that seems different. Anyway, isn't Regan one of the daughters from hell in that Shakespeare play where the eyes get gouged out onstage? The letter is burning a hole in Zoe's pocket all the way home, so she walks round and round the long way home and finally goes down this little alley that leads to the back of a shop and she tears it up and puts the pieces into the shop's litter bin, but even then she's terrified that she's going to be found out for reading somebody else's letter. For 'dependable', she's thinking, read orthodontic braces; read red hair that's too curly; read freckles and nearly flat-chested; read second-to-shortest girl in the class. In others words, read not blonde and not boy-mad, with not underwired uplift bras. That'll be why she's got the French boy. Mrs Mead thinks there's no chance that he'll want to get smoochy with her. Still, at least if you haven't grown boobs yet you can go on day-dreaming about becoming a dancer, like in *Dream of Sadler's Wells*, or like in her current top favourite, *Lola Comes to London*.

'Do I have to go?' Zoe says to her mother, once she's got home. 'Please can I not go? I'll work extra hard at French, I promise.'

'Of course you're going,' Caroline says, and she's sounding all upbeat about it.

Zoe can tell that her mum is really enjoying the idea of the French exchange. She's making it into one of her eager educational projects. And it's only because, even though she can speak French really well and she backpacked all over before she came to England from Australia as a graduate student, she and Zoe's dad never have proper holidays now, like going to Provence, or Malta, or the Canary Islands, or somewhere else nice, like Maggs and Mattie's families do.

They're on a tight budget because of having to provide for Gran, who lives near them instead of in Australia, because of some 'difficulty' she's had way back with Zoe's Aunt Janet whom Zoe's never met, but it wouldn't be 'kind' to talk about it, Caroline says. So, even though they both go out to work full-time, they can still only ever afford to do stuff like taking tents to St Ives and walking Offa's Dyke.

'If I didn't go to France, would it save enough money for me to start ballet lessons?' Zoe says. 'Because I'll soon be too old.'

'Oh stop it, Zoe,' her mother says. 'For heaven's sake. This is all too silly and babyish. You're far too old already. And I just know that you'll love France once you get there. You'll be half an hour from Paris. Just think how exciting that'll be. You'll go on lovely trips to Versailles and Fontainebleau. You'll go to the Louvre. You'll be walking along the Seine to Notre-Dame and peering into all those little art galleries and boutiques. And the food will be just wonderful. You can buy *crêpes* in the street. And think of the little *brioches* and *pains au chocolat* you'll be having for breakfast. I expect at supper there'll be all those delicious soups and terrines. The French are so much better about sitting down to proper family meals.'

But 'soups and terrines' are what Caroline makes at home from her French cookbooks. And, anyway, Maggs's older sister, who did the French exchange two years ago, says that all her Maman ever gave her to eat was sort of instant chicken-nugget things and bags of cheap cup cakes with lots of vanilla in them, like those ones you can get in a plastic bag at the Co-op on special offer.

'I want you to say I'm a vegetarian,' Zoe says, 'because otherwise I'll have to eat liver.'

'But you're not a vegetarian,' Caroline says. 'I don't mind writing a letter to Maman saying that you'd prefer not to eat intensively farmed meat.'

'Please don't write a letter,' Zoe says in sudden panic. 'Promise me you won't write a letter, or they'll think I'm a freak.' Then she says, 'How do you say "liver" in French?'

'*Foie*,' her mother says. 'But it depends on the animal, of course. So calves' liver would be *foie de veau*, for example, and pigs' liver –'

'And now,' Zoe says, 'how do you say, "I don't like"?'

'I'll make you a list of useful words and phrases,' Caroline says. 'Oh, and I've ordered you some really good maps of your area. Ones like an Ordnance Survey map only bigger – and, don't worry – it's in English. Then there's a really good street map.

42

They're from a special map shop in Covent Garden, and they're very hard to come by in this country.' Meaning that her mother has already done a whole lot of research into the French exchange project. 'So, you see,' Caroline says, 'you can't possibly get lost, even if the famous French boy gives you the slip and goes off with his mates to play football.'

Zoe can't bear it that her mother can think it's funny when the whole thing has been tormenting her for weeks.

'Or maybe he'll teach you how to play?' Caroline adds, with a twinkle.

The maps come in the next day's post. They show that she'll be staying in a newish housing development on the outer edge of the town, between an ancient aqueduct that gets Caroline really excited and a huge area of dense woodland. Meanwhile, Mattie and Maggs will be staying miles away, right in the town centre, near all the shops.

'The French have such amazing forests,' Caroline is saying, as she pores over the maps. 'There's so much more woodland than we have here.'

The only thing Zoe really likes about the maps is that one of them has got a misprint that has turned 'huts' into 'hats'. All the woodland hut-diagrams look like those little houses on the Monopoly board, and next to each one it says 'forest hat'. Then, far up in the woods, it says 'inaccessible forest hat'.

'What's the point of a "hat", if it's inaccessible?' she says.

She knows that the edge-of-town housing development is going to be just like where Gran lives on the outskirts of Oxford, because it's got the same kind of stupid winding roads, just like in *Neighbours* on the telly. Where her gran lives is called Garden Haven, even though all the front gardens have been turned into those crappy concrete spaces for parking a car. Her dad says that he needs a ball of string to find his way to Gran's house without getting lost, because he can't ever remember which winding road to go down next, and that all the houses look the same.

But they don't really, because they've all got different replacement front doors and windows, and some of them have got concrete swans or concrete squirrels and rabbits in the front. Also they have different net curtains, so you can count three houses from the concrete squirrel and four houses from the net curtains that are ruched up in the middle, like when your school skirt's got caught up in your knickers at the back. Then you go past the house with the oval in the front door that's got a stained-glass sailing ship in it, and then, another two from that, is the one that never takes down the Christmas decorations in the front window.

It's just that her dad really dislikes Gran, Zoe can tell, so he doesn't ever want to get there – and Zoe's not that great on Gran either, but just occasionally she has to stay there overnight when her parents are out and if there's some reason why she can't go to Maggs or Mattie's, which is what she usually does. It's always been pretty boring at Gran's house, especially now that she's outgrown the album of Invisible Janet's wedding photographs, and the musical box with the ballerina on top that she used to like so much, but these days Zoe can tell that the way she's got her arms and legs is all wrong. And then Gran has got all these little china figurines on shelves that Zoe used to like, especially the one of a lady wearing a china mob cap and lying in a little china bed, with a man in a china wig and china knickerbockers standing alongside her and holding her hand.

'Since you're so fond of that, I'll give it to you one day, when you're good,' Gran said, but Zoe was always good and Gran never gave it to her, so eventually, one day when she was a lot younger, she stole it. But then she felt so much like a thief that she had to keep it hidden in a box under her bed all the time, and she never had any fun with it.

*   *   *

44

The French boy's name is Gérard. Zoe knows this because on both sides of the Channel the children have had to spend a double language period writing letters to their partners, each in the other's language. They have had to introduce themselves to their partners and say things about themselves and their families and their hobbies. By the look of the letters, they have all been written with heavy dependence on the dictionary. Zoe knows that her own letter was crap, but she's pretty sure it wasn't quite as crap as Gérard's. And at least hers was quite a bit longer.

Dear Zoe

I am a tall merry fellow with brown hairs. The hairs, which are curled, are also short. I have twelve years and my sister has sixteen years. She is Véronique. She likes much the music pop but I like much to make the hunt with my father and with my dog also, which is called Mimi. I like also much the football and also much the football player Zinédine Zidane, which is called Zizou. Indeed to you.

I am your friend, Gérard.

The Tall Merry Fellow has sent Mattie and Maggs into fits.

'He sounds like a stilt walker in a stripy top hat,' Mattie says.

'He sounds like a total nerd,' Zoe says, secretly wondering if Mattie and Maggs's insides are also turning to jelly over the French exchange, or if it's only her. 'And I bet his sister's a cow,' she says.

Caroline, as well as getting the maps, has gone to the trouble of buying Zoe a torch the size of a cigarette and she's soon made that list of 'useful phrases', which she pastes to the inside of Zoe's little backpack. Zoe wishes her mother wouldn't always be so keen to enter into the spirit of school trips and outings, like the way, when they walked the Ridgeway, e.g., her mum went and bought her

45

Puck of Pook's Hill because it had Wayland's Smithy in it. And then, whenever Zoe gets home from anything 'educational', she always wants to know about it. Like when they went to Cirencester on the coach, to look at the Roman ruins, and all Zoe could really remember about it was how she and Maggs and Mattie had got the giggles because there was a used condom in the amphitheatre, as well as lots of old crisp packets. It always ends up leaving Zoe feeling a bit stupid and inadequate, like she was letting Caroline down.

The class goes to France by coach, leaving at 7 a.m. with all the mothers to wave them off. Zoe wishes her dad was there so that at least she could say goodbye to him because she knows he's going off to a conference in three days' time. It's in South Africa, and then he'll be away for nearly a whole month, so there'll be no sense in trying to phone home to ask him to rescue her from the Tall Merry Fellow and his sister Véronique. Anyway, she hasn't got a mobile phone and she won't understand how to use the call boxes, even though Caroline has taped the code for the UK inside her backpack along with all the useful phrases and she's got Zoe some phone cards as well.

But Zoe knows that if she tries to use the cards there'll be a recorded voice talking to her in French that she won't understand, because that's exactly what happened when they went on a school day-trip to Bordeaux to practise 'shopping' in French. In the event, everywhere was self-service, so you never had to ask for anything. You just put your things on the counter and handed over whatever money it said you owed on the screen.

Zoe is always the last to get stuff like a mobile phone and she hasn't even got a personal stereo, because Caroline thinks it's not good for 'the young' to have things that rob them of their resourcefulness. Plus they're much too expensive, and a mobile phone will fry your brain and a personal stereo will give you hearing loss and tinnitus later on, when you're about a hundred and three.

And her clothes aren't usually that OK either, though grown-ups are forever saying, 'Oh Caroline, your Zoe's got such beautiful clothes. She always looks so elegant.' This is because Caroline finds these designer bargains at jumble sales and in charity shops, usually in snot green or chocolate brown, or black, just when Zoe is longing for baby pink and sparkles, but she's never had the nerve actually to refuse to wear Caroline's tasteful finds. 'That green is so wonderful with her hair,' they say.

'But it's Moschino, darling,' Caroline says, about this black bomber jacket thingy. 'Zoe, it couldn't be more stylish.'

And then, just as her peers are beginning to get the black habit, Caroline will suddenly do an ironic take on Barbie gear and she'll come back with a pastel fur-fabric dolly coat, or with little rhinestone shoes. Fortunately, right now, the black Moschino bomber jacket has really come into its own and Zoe can wear it with pride on the French exchange trip. She has to hand that to Caroline, but, even so, she knows she'll never, ever be able to forgive her mum for that one-time floral take on Birkenstocks. Not ever.

All the cases go in the hold, while the backpacks with the packed lunches go with you in the coach. As well as her packed lunch, Zoe has a roll of freezer-bags with sealer clips in case of being sick, because she's always sick on trips, which is another thing to be worried about. Once Zoe said to Josh that being car sick was her 'cultural heritage', because it's true she gets car sickness from her dad, along with being short and having too curly chestnut hair. But her dad said that nausea on coach trips couldn't be a person's cultural heritage; it was more of a genetic heritage. He said that 'culture' has to do with beliefs and customs, so it had to be things like plate-smashing at weddings and wearing corks around your hat, and having to marry your second cousin when you're twelve.

47

Right now, at least Zoe really likes her luggage, because her things are all in a beautiful black hat box with old luggage labels on it that she's persuaded Caroline to give her for keeps. The labels say things like 'Kaiser Hotel, Baden-Baden' and 'Deutsche Europäische Linie', because the hat box once belonged to a piano teacher called Lottie Kirschner who came to England as a refugee in 1933 and started a bookshop. Then, when she was eighty, she put this spidery little notice in the newsagent about selling up her possessions because she was moving into a retirement flat. Caroline went along with Zoe, and they met this dainty, beautiful old lady, who gave them coffee and walnut cake and pressed a little brooch upon Zoe, which made her wish she could've had Lottie Kirschner for her grandmother, instead of Gran, who was a bit of a pain; and her other grandparents – that's her dad's parents – who sound a lot nicer, are both dead.

And she didn't really know them, anyway. She just sort of feels she knew them from what her dad's told her about when he took her to see them in Tanzania when she was just a baby and from a book of photographs she's got that Josh's mum gave her. And also, she used to send these funny little story books sometimes before she died that had been written for African schoolchildren – like her favourite one, *A Little Red Bus Called 'Take Me Home'*, about this old bus driver called Mr Tumbo, who was sad because he'd been made redundant, but then he and this boy called Jonah find a little bus in a scrapyard and they secretly fix it up for weeks and weeks, and it becomes the village bus, so Mr Tumbo's got a job again and so has Jonah, because he's the 'turn boy', which means he puts all the bicycles and sacks of mangos and chickens and stuff on to the roof rack, and everyone in the village is really pleased to have their own bus.

Her dad's mum died quite suddenly, when Zoe was five. She just went to bed one night and then in the morning she was dead. It made her dad go very quiet for a long time and, after he got back from her funeral, he used to go for really long walks all by himself for ages and not talk much.

It's quite hard to pack a case that's round, but Zoe's case is very neat. That's because she gave up and let Caroline do it and her mum's a packing genius. She's even remembered to slip in a flat-pack zipper bag, because she knows that Zoe most probably won't be able to fit her things back in the hat box when she comes home. When Caroline packs, she tessellates, like in maths, leaving no spaces at all, while Zoe and her dad use the 'stuff' method.

Each child's case contains a small gift as instructed by Mrs Mead.

'A small gift for your hostess,' she says. 'Nothing expensive or flashy, please.'

So Caroline has starched and pressed two antique white-linen guest towels with handmade lace trim that she's wrapped in pink tissue paper from Paperchase. Zoe is really worried because she doesn't think that a present should be second-hand and it must be that her concern is showing in her face.

'Maman will love them,' Caroline says firmly. 'The French appreciate good linen.'

She's also made the family a batch of fudge, which she's bagged in Cellophane and tied with a gold ribbon, saved from last year's Easter egg, but Zoe decides to pass the fudge round the bus, once they're beyond the ring road, because presents, as well as not being second-hand, aren't supposed to be home-made either. It's that lovely crumbly fudge like you get in Scotland because Caroline has got the recipe from Gran, who says she's Scottish, even though Josh says that she sounds like Dame Edna and she's only ever been to Scotland once, in the year that Zoe's parents got married. Bonnie Scotland is her heritage, she says – though she sometimes calls Zoe '*ma petite*'. Her name is Mrs McCleod. Mrs Catriona McCleod.

'Your mum's brilliant,' Mattie says. 'Your mum's cool.'

Mattie and Maggs are Zoe's two best friends, and they're sitting together just behind her in the bus. Meanwhile, she's got revolting Sadie sitting beside her, whom nobody else wants. The trouble is, if you're just a little bit sweet and kind like Zoe, then you always have a moment of feeling sorry for people like Sadie, because everyone else is giving them the brush-off. But as soon as you weaken and let her in, then she starts patronising you and order-ing you about, just as if she was doing you a favour by sitting next to you. So Sadie starts being a spoiler almost as soon as they've got under way. The class has begun singing, but when Zoe joins in Sadie shuts her up by putting her hand across Zoe's mouth, which is horrible, because it's kind of clammy and it smells like old dishcloths that have been left to dry in a ball.

'You really shouldn't sing with a voice like that,' she says.

'Like what?' Zoe says, all mumbly, from under Sadie's hand, and she looks at Sadie indignantly but Sadie just laughs and says, 'You should see your face. You look all gawky and stupid like that.' Then she lets her go.

Zoe slumps silently in her seat. She knows what's going to happen over the next four weeks.

Mattie and Maggs are good friends of hers, but it's kind of under-stood that they have a prior claim on each other, because they've been friends since the preschool playgroup and their mums met in the antenatal class and they do Pilates and Book Club together. Sometimes the families even go on holiday together, and now Mrs Mead has gone and partnered them with a pair of French girl twins in that downtown apartment, so they'll be in and out of the shops and cafés together, as a foursome, while she'll be stuck in no-man's-land with the Tall Merry Fellow and his sister Véronique, and most probably having to do all those crappy outdoor boy things like whittling, and cataloguing how many yellow Lego bricks you've got. Thinking about it is just too excruciating.

And any time when she's actually free of the Tall Merry Fellow – like on the class outing to Versailles or somewhere – then Sadie will be there, insinuating herself, which will make all the others run away; Sadie, who is right now chewing her packed lunch with her mouth open, but Zoe knows better than to tell her not to, because she's the kind of person who'd think it's hilarious to stop chewing and open her mouth really wide, so that you can see all the mushed-up food and saliva swishing around on her tongue.

Behind her, she can hear Mattie and Maggs giggling softly together about nothing and everything and, every now and again, either one of them will lean forward and whisper something in her ear, but if ever she turns round, then she right away starts to feel car sick, even though she's wearing her special pressure-point wristbands. Once, a few years ago, for the outward-bound trip to Glasebury, Caroline had got her these amazing little sticking plasters from the doctor that you stuck behind your ears and they worked brilliantly, but now you can't get them any more, because the way they worked was to leak toxins into your ears or something. Anyway, right now Mattie and Maggs are having a giggle about their sandwiches.

'My mum always cuts the crusts off,' Maggs says. 'It's because she thinks she's making canapés.' She pronounces it 'can-*apes*', which makes them giggle some more.

'Mine too,' Mattie says. 'Why do they do it when they know we like the crusts?'

Zoe half turns round.

'I expect your mums like the crusts as well,' she says. 'They're probably sitting in the kitchen dipping your crusts into their morning coffee.'

'Dipping them in blobs of Hellmann's, most likely,' Mattie says. 'Oh yum.'

'Zoe's mum's probably making hers into bread-and-butter pudding,' says Maggs. 'God, but your mum's so brilliant.'

'Stop fidgeting,' Sadie says, and she takes Zoe's chin in her hands and jerks her head back to face the front.

'Leave me alone,' Zoe says.

'Leave her alone,' Mattie says.

' "Leave her alone," ' Sadie squeaks, in would-be mimicry, giving Zoe a poke with her elbow.

But Maggs, who is pulling the lettuce out of her sandwich, has started putting the bits on Sadie's head, which is causing them another bout of giggling. Zoe's mum doesn't use Hellmann's because the eggs aren't free-range, so she always makes her own mayonnaise.

'Control yourself, *child o' mine*,' Sadie says to Zoe, not realising she's got bits of lettuce on her head.

'I'm not your "child",' Zoe says. 'Stop saying that.'

'*Child*,' Sadie says.

Zoe sighs. She takes her new Henrietta Marchmont ballet book out of her backpack, just for the pleasure of holding it in her hand, because she couldn't possibly read it on the coach without wanting to puke. This one is called *Lola Keeps a Secret* and it's the third book in the series, so Lola is now living in London, in 'digs', while she attends the ballet school, and, if she's lucky and works hard, she'll maybe start dancing with 'the Company' in a year or two. Lola has come from a remote farmhouse thousands of miles away in Africa, and now, because she's a scholarship girl and having to watch every penny, she can't ever afford to fly home and see her family, or even go to the cinema, or buy new clothes, so she has to darn her tights and scour the school noticeboard for an outgrown tutu.

But ballet is her passion; ballet is her life, even though everyone else on the farm where she comes from just likes cattle breeding and horse riding and they don't understand where she gets it from

– and also, they're all about thirty centimetres taller than Lola. At the end of the last book, when she was newly arrived in London, Lola had just met this boy called Sergei, who is also at the ballet school, and he was really kind and helpful to her and it turned out they were in the same digs, but he's got a past life in Russia that he never talks about.

Zoe only discovered the Lola books about six months ago and they've made her long to do ballet even more, but Caroline thinks it's just because she wants the pink satin shoes and the pink angora crossover cardigan and the leg warmers. Zoe has read the first two books in the series about five times each and she's also sneaked in another ballet book right at the top of the hat box, because it's very flat and she could do it once Caroline had finished putting in all the clothes and toiletries, et cetera. It's called *Ballet Class* and it teaches you about all the ballet positions and exercises and warm-ups to practise by yourself.

'Do you still read those babyish books?' Sadie is saying, just as if Zoe's new Lola book was *Postman Pat* or something, so she sighs and puts it away and pretends to fall asleep.

School trips are always in a coach, even though ever since last year they could have got to Paris on the Eurostar. But no. It's got to be the sick-making coach that takes all day. Coach, coach, ferry, coach. Then it's all those hours through France on the motorway that mostly looks just like England, except with more crashed cars by the side of the road and the hoardings are in French. Then comes the moment she's been dreading, when they finally end up exhausted in this tarmac playground at the French school, where the exchange kids are waiting for them along with their mums and dads. That's except for Zoe's.

Because the Tall Merry Fellow is nowhere, although his mother and his sister are there and both of them reek of cigarettes. Neither of them smiles at her and they're not very talky – well not to her, anyway. The mum is gaunt and creased-looking

53

and her face is kind of putty-coloured, like cigarette smoke has got into all her wrinkles. She seems really angry and crosspatch, while Véronique is sneery and smug-looking, with spiked-up hair, and she's wearing her navy school cardigan with no shirt under it and with the top three buttons undone to show her Wonderbra cleavage. And she does this stroppy-looking, no-blink eye contact with Zoe, which is really disconcerting, so that you don't know where to look.

'*Viens*!' says Maman. '*Vite, vite*!' And she's striding towards her car like she's got a train to catch.

She gestures that Zoe should put her things in the back. She and Véronique get into the front, so Zoe clambers hurriedly into the back alongside the beautiful hat box, and with her backpack on her lap. She's noticed Véronique staring hard at the hat box with all its German luggage labels, and she gives Zoe this horrible look.

Both of them start lighting up cigarettes in the car, which makes Zoe reach for the second of her freezer-bags and ensure the top is open, at the ready. She's only sicked up once so far, and that was on the ferry. Right now, she's not sure whether Caroline has given her the phrase for 'Please stop the car, I feel sick', but she feels too sick to pause and look sideways in the backpack to check and anyway she's feeling much too shy to speak.

Oh, please God, she's thinking desperately, let me think of something else. Don't let me think about puke. Anything but puke. *Je m'appelle Zoe. Je n'aime pas le, le, le livre.* No, that's not right. *Je n'aime pas* – Oh, please, please don't start thinking about liver. Do not. Think about the Tall Merry Fellow. Like where is he? Maybe he was feeling shy as well? Maybe he's feeling really embarrassed about having a girl for his exchange, just the same as she is about having a boy? Oh God! Oh no! Puke!

Maman is driving sort of angrily, veering sideways and lurching back and forth, as she keeps on trying to overtake other cars on the way home. Zoe's been given no explanation for her exchange partner's absence and, while Maman and Véronique are having these rather staccato exchanges between themselves, they're talking much too fast for Zoe to follow a word and both of them are behaving as though she wasn't there. Zoe's stomach has risen unstoppably to her throat and she's just in time to throw up discreetly into the freezer-bag, which she clamps shut, and she then starts reaching for her backpack, but not before Maman and Véronique have noticed.

'*Merde*!' says Maman, without slowing down or even turning round, but Zoe can see her contemptuous expression in the rear-view mirror, while Véronique looks at Zoe and smirks.

Maman makes a right turn and swerves to a jerky stop.

'*Descends*!' she says. And, when Zoe hesitates, she reaches over and wrenches open the back door. '*Descends et jette le*!' she says, making throwing gestures, i.e., that Zoe should litter the verge with her vomit bag. '*Voilà, et maintenant, remonte*!'

 - When Zoe's back inside the car, she hears Maman say to Véronique, as she roars off like she's on a starting block, '*Cette fille est une idiote*!'

They skirt around the town centre, on and on, and eventually end up in this new suburb, where all the roads look like Scalextrics, but the houses are kind of different-horrible to the ones where Zoe's gran lives. These ones have steeply pitched grey pyramids for roofs with plastic dormer windows and white-plastered outside walls and crazy-paving paths to the front doors that look a bit like the Yellow Brick Road. And, while true to Caroline's map there's lots of woodland just behind the houses, the only trees in the gardens that she can see are these nasty little dwarf conifers. It's like there's a rash of them all over the housing development and there's also quite a lot of dog crap. Plus the Tall Merry Fellow's house has got these clinky-clunky wind chimes that are supposed to sound like the rainforest hanging over the front door.

'*Alors*,' Maman says, throwing her fag-end into one of the two dwarf-conifer pots that stand to the left and right of the front door, just as Zoe is deducing that Maman will probably be driving her and Véronique and the Tall Merry Fellow to school every morning, dodging and weaving and lurching, so that she will be throwing up over and over, until soon there won't be any freezer-bags left. Or will they be allowed to catch a bus?

On the floor, inside the conifer house, are those scratchy Dutch carpet tiles and there's an open staircase to the upstairs rooms. It stinks of dog, though there doesn't seem to be any dog, worse luck. No Mimi is there to come and greet them. Véronique is instructed to show Zoe to her room, which she does in a big huffy sulk from halfway up the staircase. She just waves her arm haphazardly in the direction of a bedroom door to the left.

Zoe opens the door and then shuts it behind her. She plonks the hat box and her backpack on the bed. Then she turns round to look at what is obviously a boy's bedroom. It's got shelves with animal skulls – like maybe from deer and rabbits – and there are several torches on the bookshelves. Quite big ones. After a little snoop, Zoe finds a tobacco tin containing a survival kit with a length of fishing line and waxed matches and a compass and a miniature folding knife and water-sterilising pills. Then she sees that there's a football on the desk and a black T-shirt over the chair that says 'Zizou'. Nobody has even bothered to tidy away a pair of walking boots that are standing in the middle of the floor, with balled-up hiking socks stuffed into the tops.

Zoe puts *Lola Keeps a Secret* and her *Ballet Class* book on the table beside the bed, on top of all these Tintin books in French, and she opens a drawer for her clothes, but inside it's full of boys' boxer shorts and socks and bathers, and there's even one of those embarrassing things that makes you really glad to be a girl. It's a thing that's meant to hold a groin guard in place – Maggs once explained it to her when they went to a sports shop to get gym

56

shirts for PE. It's a kind of white-pouch thing, with dangly straps that are supposed to go up a boy's bum crack and they're fixed to an elastic waistband.

There's no way she can mingle her clothes with boys' boxer shorts and especially not with that groin-guard thing in there, so she decides to leave all her clothes in the hat box, except for her pyjamas, which she puts under the pillow. But – oh gross! – someone else's head has been on the pillows. No one has even bothered to change the pillowcases, so she'll just have to spread a bath towel over them and first thing tomorrow she'll have to ask Mattie and Maggs about buying some sheets and stuff. That's if she's got enough money. And even then she doesn't know how she's going to stop Maman from noticing. Meanwhile she's just going to have to sleep on top of the bedspread.

Then, to help block out the awfulness of everything, she sits on the bed and reads her Lola book until Maman yells up for her to come downstairs and eat.

But when Zoe opens the door to come out, she goes mental.

'*Zut! Pas là! Espèce d'imbécile!*' she says, and she charges up the stairs and jabs her finger towards the next door along. '*Là!*' she says, and she flings it open.

It gives on to a sort of boxroom with a camp bed and no reading lamp, but at least it's got clean pillowcases and a clean duvet cover.

'*Mets les choses là-dedans!*' she says, so Zoe scrambles to move her hat box and her backpack – and she remembers just in time to collect her pyjamas.

It's only the three of them for supper – still no sign of the Tall Merry Fellow – but at least, to Zoe's relief, it isn't home-made 'soups and terrines', or even one of those 'family dishes' with animal innards in them that look like bits of chopped-up worms. It's just potatoes *au gratin* and a bit of salad and then some of that not very nice supermarket ice cream that tastes like baking margarine with strands of red jammy stuff running through it.

'*Bon appétit*,' Maman says, with a face like a shrunken head.

Then, once Zoe's in bed, she remembers she's left her Lola book along with *Ballet Class* on top of the Tintin pile next door. She's too scared to go and retrieve them in case the floorboards creak – and anyway there's no lamp to read by. Plus she's feeling too exhausted and stressed.

And next morning they drive, Maman, she and Véronique – stop-start, stop-start – through all the busy traffic and the petrol fumes and the ciggy smoke, until Zoe is sick into the third of the freezer-bag collection. This time the sick is a mix of undigested Frosties and full-cream milk.

'*Merde*! *Merde*!' Maman says once again. '*L'imbécile*!' and Véronique does one of her smirky looks all over again, but this time the car doesn't pull to a stop, so that when she gets to the tarmac playground, Zoe is still clutching the freezer-bag.

School isn't actually all that bad because Maggs and Mattie's bubbly blonde twins are quite good fun and they right away pull up an extra chair for Zoe at their work table. Then they sportingly shout, 'No room! No room!' when Sadie tries to squeeze in, because their dad has got them an abridged CD of *Alice's Adventures in Wonderland*, in English, to prepare them for their hosting duties, so they know 'The Mad Hatter's Tea Party' off by heart.

It's only at home time, just when the five of them have hatched this plan to go out together, that Véronique barges in and pulls Zoe off and marches her to a bus stop. Then the bus carries them all the way back to the conifer house, where nobody is at home.

After that, Véronique spends about two hours locked in the bathroom, with wafts of stinky bath-oil smells coming from under the door. Then, once she's all dolled and spiked up, with lots of make-up, and this really tight skirt that's making the tops of her thighs squeak together when she walks, and shoes with wobbly high heels, she gets both of them to walk back to the bus stop. All the way, she's having to stop and tug at the skirt, because it keeps on riding up her bum.

In the town centre, they meet up with three of Véronique's horrible scary friends, who all stare at Zoe and roll their eyes as if she was either a complete freak or else somebody's pain-in-the-arse baby sister who's insisted on tagging along.

'*J'ai dû l'amener avec moi,*' Véronique says rudely, without even making any introductions.

They spend the next hour in McDonald's, mainly in the Ladies', where they glam up and spike their hair up some more, before starting on Zoe's appearance, completely ignoring her protestations. They stuff loo paper into her treble-A bra, and stick lots of blusher and eyeliner on her face and then they try to straighten her hair with mousse. Meanwhile, the slimmest of them has helped herself to Zoe's Moschino jacket, though it's a bit tight for her under the arms and it's making a stretchy crease all along the back, below her shoulder blades. The girl just dives out of the way each time Zoe tries to grab it back and all of them have a good laugh.

Then they go to a vodka bar, where they do lots of under-age drinking before going on to this revolting basement club down some broken stone steps, where they smoke like mad and drink some pink alcoholic stuff that comes in cone-shaped glasses. After that they get very pushy and loud, and they start giving grown-up men the come-on.

Some of the men come over and sit down at their table and, suddenly, thank God, they're all gone – but still with Zoe's Moschino jacket. Even so, it's a little while before Zoe realises she's been abandoned for the evening. She's been sitting there alone until this lechy guy comes up and she can't understand what he's saying, so all she can think to do is to flee back to McDonald's

59

and seek shelter under the big yellow M. She heads for the Ladies' and washes her face and drags a comb through her hair. Then she finds the bus stop and heads back to the conifer house – though she hasn't even got a front-door key in the event of no one being at home.

It's really hard to see where the bus is going now that the sun has gone down and the distances between the stops are getting longer and longer. She rings the bell suddenly, but it turns out she's already gone too far. She's only just begun to realise where she is, once the bus is bowling alongside the wood-land at quite a lick. Cold and scared, Zoe remembers the map which is still inside her backpack. She spreads it out on the verge under the light of the bus-stop lamp and, sure enough, there is the housing development, there the street, winding its way more or less against the leftmost edge of the woodland. And here must be exactly where she finds herself standing now. There's a dotted line showing a not very long footpath going through the wood that will take her right into the back end of the housing development.

Zoe sighs with relief. She's thinking Maggs was so right when she said that Caroline was brilliant – especially for getting her the maps. And there's the little torch as well, in case it gets darker along the path. For the moment, the bus-stop lamp is casting quite a bit of reassuring light as she heads off among the trees.

It's not long, of course, before the woods get seriously dark and the light from the little torch doesn't spread very far in the circumstances, though a couple of times it stops her from trip-ping over tree roots and falling down rabbit holes. But the walk is surely taking her much too long – like about an hour, maybe? She begins to realise that she must have got it wrong, because by now she should be seeing the lights from the housing development. In fact she should have managed to walk the distance twice over, whereas all that's happening is it's getting darker and darker and, every now and again, there's a scary sort of night noise that's like somewhere in the woods there's an animal murdering another animal. Well, that's if it's not the hooded axe-man having a go at a human baby. Oh my God.

And she's no sooner begun to think these thoughts than she can hear kind of heavy-breathing noises following her and she's much too scared to turn round and look, so she tries to stop breathing for a bit to see if it's coming from herself. Then there's something brushing against her leg, and she nearly has heart failure, but all of a sudden she can see that it's just a dog.

It's a lovely, waggy-tail, chunky Labrador and it's very pleased to be meeting her, because it's sniffing her like mad, and it jumps up and does sloppy kisses on her face. So they sit down together for a minute while she strokes its ears. It clambers all over her, because it seems quite young and bouncy, and it's soon pestering for them to get up and get going. Or maybe it thinks she's going to start throwing sticks for it in the dark?

Meanwhile Zoe's shone a light onto its collar and, as well as seeing that its coat is chocolate brown, she's noticed that it's got a phone number and its name on a metal strip. 'Mimi'! So no wonder it's being so licky and friendly, because, by now, she must stink of the conifer house, all mixed up with the smell of Maman's Gitanes. Zoe is so relieved that she's practically crying with joy and, on top of everything, she's extra pleased because the dog is a girl.

'You're a girl dog,' she says, and she gives the dog a big hug. Then she follows it, because she's sure that it's going to lead her straight back to the house.

But the dog doesn't take her to the dwarf-conifer house, though they eventually reach a bit of a clearing where she can see a glimmery sort of light. It's not like electric light at all, and it's coming from a small wooden hut, which has surely got to be one of the 'forest hats' that she's noticed on the map. Scuffly noises are coming from inside, along with a kind of slurred, drunk-man speech.

The dog trots right up to the hut and scrapes a paw on the wood, but nobody inside seems to hear it. Zoe hesitates, before she draws close up and peers in cautiously at the window, where the scene that meets her eyes is a bit like Pap Meets the Angel of Death in *Huckleberry Finn*, because a thick-set man is wrestling with a boy, and the man is obviously drunk. He's trying to punch the boy in the face, but all he does is knock over a stool, while a spirit lamp on a small rough table wobbles and rights itself. In the light of the lamp, Zoe can see two empty brandy bottles and a tempting little still life with two apples and a heel of bread, and a clasp knife, and a wedge of cheese.

The man, having lunged at the boy, has lost his balance and fallen to the ground, where he goes very quiet within seconds – in fact, he subsides so fast that she can hardly believe it, but it looks as if he's fallen asleep. Soon she can even hear the rhythm of his loud snores. The boy rolls him gently on to a sleeping bag and takes off his boots. Then he covers the man with a coat.

After that he turns round. Zoe can see that the boy is tall and that he's got short, very curly brown hair. It's slightly chestnut hair, a bit like hers, and he's even got the same kind of freckles. Only, right now, he's looking anything but merry.

Then he steps outside to greet the dog and he looks to the left, and sees her.

'*Je m'appelle Zoe Silver*,' she says quickly. '*Je suis* – um – lost.' Then she says, '*Perdue?*' and the boy holds out his hand.

'*Je m'appelle Gérard*,' he says. 'Good night. You have hunger?'

'*Oui*,' she says, nodding vigorously. 'I'm actually starving.'

So he goes back inside the hut and gets the bread and cheese and the apples. They seat themselves side by side on a log and munch in silence.

Then he says, '*Ne t'inquiète-pas.* I can – *t'accompagner* – *à la* – house? Yes? It is *très facile.*'

'Thank you,' she says.

He doesn't say much on the walk back to the house, except that twice he says his father is '*triste*'.

Then he says, 'My father, he is *ne va pas bien.*' Meanwhile he's got a much more effective torch than Zoe's inadequate effort and he's carrying a stout stick. 'There is sometimes *les sangliers*,' he says, by way of explanation. 'Pig?' he says, so that Zoe doesn't find out until much later that there are wild boar in the woods, because she's envisaging the odd friendly Gloucester Old Spot pursuing his cultural heritage as he roots for those Gallic truffles that Caroline's told her about.

And when they finally get to the house, it's plunged in darkness. And it's locked, because by now it's really late, but Gérard indicates that she should wait alongside the back door with Mimi, while he shins up the drainpipe that gives on to the window of his bedroom. After that, he tiptoes downstairs and opens the door to let her in. The only thing is, she's a bit surprised to see that he's not only clutching the T-shirt that says 'Zizou', but he's got *Ballet Class* under his arm.

'I can read this book?' he says politely. Then he says, 'Since tomorrow? OK?'

'OK,' Zoe says and the Tall Merry Fellow does a gracious little almost-bow.

'Visit with me tomorrow,' he says and he indicates the pathway back towards the forest hat.

Then he's gone and she creeps, mouse-quiet, into her little boxroom, where she falls asleep, except that, next morning, Véronique has obviously told her mother that Zoe gave her the slip the previous night. So Maman is going '*Rant-rant-blah-blah-l'imbécile*' all the way along the stop-start-lurch-puke route to the tarmac playground, from which – once Véronique's back is safely turned, and once she has got Maggs and Mattie on side to tell the teacher she's got '*la grippe*' – Zoe walks straight to the stop where the bus will take her back to Gérard, and the forest hat, and Mimi, and the *très triste* dad, which is where she means to play hookey for the first time in her life.

Chapter Three

Hattie

Hattie Marais has once again fallen asleep with the radio on because Herman is off on one of his business trips. He's absent quite a lot these days so the all-night radio has become a bit of a habit. She's also taken to sprawling her little eight-stone person all over the king-size bed. When Herman is there, Hattie sleeps – has slept, now, for eighteen years – in a contained foetal ball, strictly on her own side of the bed, because Herman is quite a light sleeper. He likes a no-man's-land between himself and his bedfellow, along with one of those fancy mattresses where each side functions independently of the other. My craters are not thy craters.

When he's at home, he always takes care to let down the Roman blinds that make a blackout between the room and the east-facing veranda where the morning light comes in. But now the same light is dappling her eyelids as it dances through the unveiled French windows, via the hibiscus and the clambering bougainvillea. And she can see the feathery leaves of the flame tree dipping and rising on a light breeze, which has come at last to moderate the sweaty, subtropical heat.

'See you probably two weeks-ish, Snoeks,' Herman says – always says – giving Hattie a brief conjugal peck on the cheek before he takes off, carting work stuff, golf stuff, diving stuff; fishing stuff, ski stuff; white-water rafting stuff, riding stuff, biking stuff. Bloke stuff in some form. Business or pleasure? Work hard. Play hard. Herman is very good at both. One of the many pay-offs is that, precisely because Herman is such a bloke, he's also a bit of a techie, which means he likes high-quality equipment. So whereas Hattie, left to herself, would still be making do with her crackly Roberts radio, *circa* 1960, the item now residing in style alongside her marriage bed – Herman's side of the bed, admittedly – is a superior, multichannelled, digital affair that means Hattie can now punctuate her sleep with impeccable transmissions from the BBC's Radio 3: snatches of Tom Stoppard interviews; Bach fugues; extracts from Mozart's letters to his female cousin; reappraisals of Samuel Barber (or was it Samuel Palmer? Lots of it is what she hears in her half-conscious waking moments), even, coming full circle, she listens to the aged Mahotella Queens in conversation with Andy Kershaw. Hattie likes to envisage the Queens in Central London, sitting regally in their Zulu headgear and short grass skirts, in the foyer of that BBC building in Portland Place, with the Eric Gill sculpture over the doorway.

And now, on this particular morning, she stirs around 5 a.m. to hear the minuet from the end of Stravinsky's *Pulcinella* ballet; that slowed-up, seductive version of the Pergolesi music that Stravinsky 'recomposed', as he put it – except that her friend Josh Silver from way back once told her that chunks of it were not, in fact, composed by Pergolesi. They were written by somebody else. Stravinsky wrote that he felt 'a sensory and mental kinship' with Pergolesi and also how lucky he'd been that, when he went on the trip to Naples with Picasso, he had found these precious Pergolesi fragments, which had so far eluded the academics. So, maybe, had they not eluded the academics, the misattributions would have been detected before Stravinsky got to recompose them? But, in the event, so what?

As Josh had gone on to observe, inspired people's mistakes are usually in themselves inspiring. That's why he liked it that, when Jesus said whatever it was that he'd said to Mary Magdalene in Aramaic, he hadn't said, '*Noli me tangere*.' He hadn't meant, 'Touch me not.' It was a mistranslation that had inspired a hundred Old Master paintings. And Moses, Josh said, was probably not even Jewish. That's what he'd read in Freud. He was very likely a prince of Egypt with an adoption fantasy. Or had the Egyptian princess and her maidens been stringing Pharaoh along? Look what we found floating down the Nile in a basket. Yeah. Right. A handy story when you'd got yourself in trouble.

The Pergolesi business merely served to underline that the whole, brilliant ballet was about things being not what they seem; about layers of illusion; masks, disguises and deceptions. If you're performing in a mask, as Hattie knows from her dancing days, then your face can't show any emotion. All emotion is gesture. Emotion equals movement. I love: I pull. I hate: I push. Touch me. Touch me not. *Noli me tangere.*

Josh was so passionate about that *Pulcinella* time in Paris, when all the talent of the modern world seemed to be right in there, throwing itself at the Russian Ballet. Hattie knew that he was there in spirit, on the gad with Picasso and Stravinsky as they set out for Naples to find the perfect Neapolitan comedy on which to base their ballet. He was with them in the hole and corner junk shops and when they were watching the acrobats in the street. 'Who is the third that walks always beside you?' Funny how Josh, with his secular, left-wing parents, could always quote more of the Bible than she ever could, even after a decade of regular attendance at the St Thomas's Anglican Church Sunday School.

Now she's back, drowsing again, as the recomposed Pergolesi is turning from pastoral yearning into those rasping Stravinsky discords and dark dance rhythms. And, through her sleep, she's hearing this one word from the text that sounds a bit like 'screw-gender', but it isn't, of course, because the songs are in Italian. Hattie is no good at foreign languages and her knowledge of Italian is confined to the odd tourist-phrase-book item. '*A che ora arriva il treno?*' That kind of thing. And, until she met Josh, she'd never heard of a ballet with songs.

The second time Hattie wakes, it's after a surprising two-second dream, and just before the six o'clock news. The dream hasn't got any narrative; just a flash of audio-visual clarity. Josh Silver is offering her his glasses; those goggly little glasses that he always used to wear. Maybe still does? He's holding them out to her. 'Take them,' he's saying, right out loud, so that she can hear his voice quite distinctly. 'Go on.' The connection will be Stravinsky. For a couple of weeks in his final year, Josh spent time carrying around an autobiography of Stravinsky. It had a photograph of the composer on the dust jacket. One day he'd come with a story about how, at supper the previous night, his mother had cast her eye over the dust jacket and had seen fit to remark that Stravinsky was 'obviously Jewish'.

'No, he isn't,' Josh said to his mother. 'What you mean is you think he looks Jewish. But it's just because he's Russian.'

Josh suspected his mother – adoptive mother – of wishing to claim various persons of distinction for her own ethnic birth-group, even though she believed religion to be the opium of the people and she'd taught him the words of 'The Internationale'.

In the daytime Josh's mother was a human rights lawyer. She operated in a man's world, taking on all manner of bully-boy white-racist employers, which half the time meant incurring the wrath of the bully-boy white-racist state. But once she was home, she turned into this person who grated raw potatoes for latkes and who liked to make her own sauerkraut. She made her own cream cheese as well, which is why, the one time Hattie went there for supper, there was this oozy little bag of milk curds hanging over one of the taps at the Silvers' kitchen sink. There was also this cute little Afro kid who was going mad for Mrs Silver's cream cheese on rye and he loved the potato latkes. He probably liked chicken soup with barley as well.

'This is Jack,' Josh said to Hattie.

The child belonged to the housemaid, but the family often had him to stay over in the house on Saturdays and Sundays, because his mother had the weekends off. Hattie had never heard of a black child sleeping over in a white person's house, which was surely against the law? The place was quite alarming for Hattie, but it was also, in its way, a breath of fresh air. And she was especially impressed that Mrs Silver, on top of all her professional obligations, found the energy to start arguments at the supper table.

So she was always entertained when Josh regaled her with his family's mealtime talk, because at her own parents' dining table, all through her growing up, the four of them sat in glum silence listening to the shuffling feet of the maid who moved in and out with the dishes, sort of like a serf. And then there was the ticking of the grandfather clock – the same pretty clock that still ticks and bongs in the selfsame hall, even though its time-keeping drives Herman up the wall.

They would be eating that dreary boarding-house food in the room that Herman, since those days, has opened up into a big, bright space, all in one with the kitchen. Then he's added those two glass prisms that run down each side of the house, like Toblerone boxes for giants. Herman's fern-and-orchid houses. Her parents' carpets have all gone, except for one large Baluchi rug, because Herman right away called them 'mould green' and 'disgusting' and he said they stank of old mutton fat and pipe smoke and cabbage. Instead, he exposed and waxed the beautiful wide floorboards – indigenous old hardwood, he said – that had been lurking, all through Hattie's childhood, under two layers of cracked lino, which, in turn, had been lurking under the mould-green carpets.

Meanwhile, back to Josh, who was setting the dinner-table scene for her, in which old Prof Silver was busy providing instruction for his wife. There was no such thing as 'looking Jewish', he said. Italian Jews looked Italian and Iraqi Jews looked Iraqi. And Polish Jews looked Polish. And those Eastern European Ashkenazi settlers in Israel – well, they looked like Eastern Europeans. And those Jews who had always been there from before the biblical diaspora – well, they were indistinguishable from Palestinian Arabs, he said, except for their beard and hats.

'But the Arabs have got nicer hats,' Josh observed in an aside to Hattie. 'Don't you think so?'

Hattie hadn't a clue about the hats, but by the time he had recounted the episode they had covered the distance between the admin block and the student-union café, where, though she wasn't a student there, but a young working ballet teacher, she was his frequent guest.

She remembered him placing the Stravinsky book on the table while he unwound a Chelsea bun. Both of them were nineteen.

'So what do you think?' he said. 'Does Stravinsky look Jewish then, or what?'

'Well,' Hattie said, 'I think his glasses maybe look quite Jewish. Actually, Josh, they're just like your glasses.'

She knew Josh wasn't really Jewish, because he'd told her he was adopted. His parents took him in, aged three, when his mother went round the bend. He had this wild story about being got by a crooked Greek upon a Lebanese convent girl in a mining town called Boksburg. He couldn't remember his time in Boksburg. He was too young. He couldn't remember a thing about his mother, except that she'd been dead since nearly for ever. But he could remember a little bit about Dora the teenage housemaid and a lot more about Dora's mother Pru, who had taken him to her own outdoor church, where they did trance states and sang gospel songs and people got baptised by total immersion. He thought he could maybe remember the rattly long-distance bus, designated for black persons, that had taken him from Boksburg to Durban, where Dora's mother lived, but he knew that, in reality, it was probably because Pru had told him about it. He knew that it was little Dora who had saved his life.

'I don't remember very much from before I became a white person,' Josh said.

Hattie had never been to Boksburg. She only knew it from a joke she'd once heard, about a man who kept on missing the train to it.

Josh seemed quite pleased about Stravinsky's glasses.

'So what do you think?' he said. 'Does he look sexy then, or what?'

Hattie knew that Josh was really keen on her, but even though he was her absolutely best friend – the nicest person she'd ever known; the person with whom she felt 'a sensory and mental kinship' – was she in love with him? She wasn't sure how you could tell. And was it all right to fall for a person of dubious provenance, with dangerous adoptive parents? I mean, what would her own parents have thought? A man who made jokes about being white? Well he *was* white, of course. Lebanese people and Greeks counted as white. Sort of.

That was when Herman had suddenly come up and joined them in the student café. Six foot five and powerfully built; shaking sunlight from his thick blond hair; the hair that didn't last. Final-year star student at the architectural school. Blue eyes. White teeth. Penetrating stare. Very in-your-face.

'Hey, Josh,' he said. 'So are you going to introduce me to your friend?'

Suddenly Hattie is properly awake – wide awake and bolt upright – because the six o'clock news is on the BBC and will

71

be happening at eight o'clock – of course – given that she's in a different hemisphere and she's two hours ahead of GMT. And right now she can hear her sixteen-year-old daughter Cat beginning to bang about in the kitchen the way she does these days.

'Crumbs!' Hattie says to herself. 'The time!' She gets up and pulls on a thin kimono over her nakedness. 'Please God,' she says, somewhat fervently. 'Let me please not fight with Cat today.'

In the passage, on her way to the kitchen, she takes down *The Oxford Companion to Music* and enters the kitchen, where she leans the book on the dresser. Stravinsky. There is the photograph – the very same dust-jacket photograph – reproduced on the page. So does Stravinsky look sexy then, or what? Well, yes, she decides, he does, even though he looks quite a lot like Papa Mouse in *Mouse Tales* by Arnold Lobel. Papa Mouse is 'obviously Jewish'; a mouse patriarch in braces. Hattie once wrote a fan letter to Arnold Lobel, but he died before she'd posted it. *Mouse Tales* is a book that she can still recite by heart because she used to read it ten times a day to Cat, who loved all the stories, but especially the one about the mouse who buys himself new feet. That was a decade ago, when Cat was six; when Cat was sweet. Hattie tries not to brood about Cat too much these days, which is maybe why she's concentrating so hard on Stravinsky's glasses.

'Hey, what you doing, Ma?' Cat says, in that single-volume shout voice she has recourse to these days whenever she talks to her mother.

'Hi, Cat,' Hattie says, hating the sound of her own voice; that slightly fake-cheerful, *Children's Hour* tone.

'So what are you doing?' Cat says again. Her consonants are fuzzy and she's dribbling breakfast cereal from her mouth as she speaks.

Hattie can tell at once that it's the horrible chocolate-flavoured stuff, because brown milk is leaking down her chin. Cat may be sixteen, but she still has an infant's sweet tooth. She'll add extra sugar to Coco Pops and she'll sprinkle sugar on those already cloyingly sweet pink yogurts. Cat sometimes talks with her mouth full these days, which is pretty hard to take. She does it because, while she munches and stuffs, she seldom swallows anything, as far as Hattie can see, so her mouth is always full.

Hattie would rather Cat didn't pretend to be eating, but she clearly likes the taste of food too much not to put it in her mouth. So for the past few weeks she's been pursuing a policy of shovelling spoonloads into her mouth, one after the other, without pausing to swallow. She stores the spoonloads hamsterwise in the pouches of her cheeks. That's until congestion causes bits to start falling out. Then Cat will do one of three things. The first is she'll feign a choking fit and spew the chewed pile on to her plate.

She'll follow this with some bogus accusation that she directs at her mother.

'I nearly choked because of you,' she'll shriek. 'There are bones in this. There are peppercorns in this. What are these disgusting leaf things?'

The second thing is, she'll dash for the bathroom, where Hattie is pretty certain that Cat is disgorging the hamster hoard into the lavatory bowl. This is because she hears the cistern flush, not once, but twice. And thirdly, just occasionally, Cat will actually swallow. When she swallows, most of the hoard goes down in one huge gulp. She'll jerk her head like a turkey, then there'll be a bobbing in her throat and her eyes will start to water. Sometimes a coughing fit ensues. Yet Cat isn't exactly skin and bones – not yet – though she has got slightly thinner. She's still got quite big boobs and that pretty, little-girlish round face. Cat comes off the same production line as Herman's tribe of rosy blonde sisters. Except that, whereas they are always smiling their dimpled smiles, poor old Cat looks a constant crosspatch these days.

And Herman, of course, just keeps on denying that there's anything amiss with Cat. Daddy's best baby girl.

'Just because you're such a titch,' he says. 'Calm down, Snoeks. She's OK. No worries. Her eating's just fine. She doesn't like your cooking, that's all.'

Hattie finds it a bit of a wind-up these days, the way he's never stopped calling her Snoeks.

'I *said*, what are you *doing*, Ma?' Cat says. 'Are you deaf, or something?'

'Oh, it's nothing,' Hattie says. 'I heard this music on the radio.'

'So what?' Cat says. 'Who cares about what music you heard on the radio?'

'It's a ballet with songs and masks,' Hattie says. 'It's a Harlequin story, called *Pulcinella*.'

'So what?' Cat says again.

Then, while her mother still has her eyes on the book, she makes a move for the pedal bin, where she deftly relieves herself of the hamster hoard, before resuming her pose of breakfasting normality, spoon once more in hand.

'Say, Cat?' Hattie says, turning from her book. 'What about masks? That art project of yours. It's just an idea, but what about doing it on African masks?'

Cat makes an irritated noise in her throat.

'Masks, for Chrissakes!' she says. 'Pur-leez! Like what have masks got to do with anything? You don't know what you're talking about, so just butt out, OK?'

Twelve years ago Hattie went to Venice with Cat for a treat, leaving the two older children with Herman and the maid. First they went to England to visit her schoolmaster uncle and her engineer cousin in Norfolk. Then, after that they went, just the two of them, to Venice. A four-day indulgence for herself and her little blonde daughter. Cat was a big hit in Venice, where the waiters kept saying, '*Che bella*!'

'But I'm not Kay and I'm not Bella,' Cat would explain to them repeatedly. 'I'm Cat.'

By coincidence her two best friends back home in the preschool playgroup were called Kay and Bella. Cat, who was four at the time of the visit, now says she can't remember going to Venice.

She stroppily denies having been there, even though she still has the Venetian-glass bonbons she chose, sitting in a bowl on her windowsill. She says that her dad brought them back for her. But Hattie can't forget. She remembers Cat's enchanted little face pressed up against the windows of the tourist shops with carnival masks; beaky plague masks, Harlequin masks, leather masks with knobbly foreheads. *Pulcinella*. And she remembers Cat carefully choosing each little glass bonbon, one by one.

Cat has been incessantly unloading moans about the art project ever since the school term began. And she's in a dilemma, poor girl. Hattie appreciates that. She can't bear to admit any interest in things that her mother might find gratifying and yet she really wants good grades. Cat is immensely able and she wants to get into the architectural school to become an architect like her dad, so she knows that the project will have to be good. And it's got to have an African theme, because that's where she lives, all right? In Africa. No more Eurocentric projects, thank you. This is the New South Africa.

Cat has always been Daddy's Girl. She's always preferred Herman to her mother, and now so much of the time he's not here. It appears to be no longer possible for Hattie to offer Cat anything. All it does is make her abusive – and, when Cat's in a bad mood, she starts to thunder about so formidably, making the floorboards vibrate so that Hattie can hear her great-grandmother's china start to tremble and jingle in the cupboards.

All Hattie's three children are big, like Herman, but right now the older two are carrying it more comfortably than Cat. Then again, they've always had each other. Twins. It runs in the family.

Jonno and Suz are imposing, tall, and efficient. They are strong, confident eighteen-year-olds, sporty and big-boned, delighting in their new undergraduate lives. Hattie, by contrast, has always been small; marked out from infancy as a dainty ballet girl. And, having spent eighteen years of her adult life teaching at the local ballet school, it's eight years since she's packed it in, first to take an arts degree and then to start writing her series of ballet stories for girls.

Unlike most of her women friends, who have broadened around the pelvis, Hattie can still buy her jeans in the children's department at Stuttaford's, but this gives her little satisfaction these days, since, like Cat, she's begun to have doubts about her size. She wonders whether her couplings with Herman were maybe inappropriate all along. Perhaps they were like those of the little shivery whippet she once saw getting it together with a St Bernard in the park? Is this why Herman keeps going off on trips? Could it be that her size has become repellent to him? Has it got anything to do with why Cat hates her? Is it her size that's recently made her daughter start doing all this funny stuff with food? Hattie once saw a photograph of a post-war classroom in Saigon. Six doll-like Vietnamese eight-year-olds were sitting around a table, along with one little eight-year-old giant. The giant was a pale-brown Afro girl whose mother had got it together during the war with a seven-foot black GI.

What's slightly unsettling Hattie right now, apart from Cat, is that she's completely stopped minding about not going along with Herman on some of his trips, where once she would have felt rejected. She likes the way it liberates those parts of herself that she puts on hold when she's playing Mrs Wife. It means that, as well as sprawling across the bed and listening to the all-night radio, she can more easily get on with her writing.

'Snoeks, it's not worth it,' he began saying – that is, when he still felt it incumbent upon him to make excuses. 'Snoeks, it's not much of a trip.' 'Snoeks, I promise it'll bore you stiff.'

He promised her that she would be bored stiff on the trip to Mauritius – that short hop from their home on the east coast of South Africa to the island in the Indian Ocean; white sands and feasts of seafood; indigenous pink pigeons on the terrace; blue-and-white enamelled street signs to make one feel one was in France.

She would get in the way of the golf, Herman said. Golf, as he has repeatedly explained to her, is never simply golf. There is nothing quite like it for clinching a deal. He's assured her, over the years, that she'd be bored rigid by his business trips to Lagos and New Orleans and Tokyo. Too much golf. Once he took his favourite sister instead. Lettie. Five foot nine and bossy to a degree – that's under all the master-race charm and the radiant, dimpled smiles. Scary with a tennis racket in her strong right hand.

'Listen, Snooks, don't knock the golf, all right?' Herman says. 'It's always worked for me. Every move I make translates to the boardroom. And what do you think is paying for the kids to be at uni?'

The 'kids', to be sure, are pretty high-maintenance. Always have been. It's the way Herman's enjoyed bringing them up. Like him, they have always been addicted to those huge American refrigerators with double doors like wardrobes, crammed with iced drinks and top-range snacks. They like tennis coaching and Pony Club and skiing and white-water rafting and deep-sea fishing and holidays in Thailand. They like stuff. High-quality stuff. Electronics and digital stuff and constant, unremitting upgrades. They like clothes with labels. The right labels. They like cars and boats. And now that Jonno and Suz are both at university in the Cape, their dad has seen fit to buy them each their own little brand-new car and their own little brand-new apartment.

'The halls of residence are not what they were in my day,' Herman says. 'You can't expect our kids to live in places like that.'

By which Herman means to say that, now the halls of residence are racially integrated, the room next door may be occupied by a needy black student on state funding, whose three even needier country cousins will be dossing illicitly on the floor. And the country cousins (unemployed) will not necessarily be familiar with the workings of first-world accessories. The flush toilet, for example.

'It's not racist, for heaven's sake, Snoeks,' he says. 'It's about the great unwashed.'

To be sure, in times past, it could have been the Irish, or Romanian Jews, or itinerant Greeks, like Josh Silver's father – or poor white Afrikaners, come to that.

And Hattie, for sure, needs no convincing that it's never been her ballet classes that have funded the children's lifestyle. Nor, more recently, the royalties from her children's books, though these have begun to pick up. Even so, it irks her a little that Herman persists in regarding her writing as a little bit of a hobby, now that she's done with the ballet school. And when, two years ago, she aired the idea of converting the unoccupied servants' rooms into a work space for herself, Herman didn't appear to take the idea on board as a serious proposition. He merely said, 'No worries, Snoeks. One of these days we'll make a plan.'

Then he suddenly went ahead, without consulting her. He drew up the plans and transformed the servants' rooms, not into a work room for his wife; not even into the standard 'garden cottage'. What has emerged within the last few months is a fabulous, opened-up space, a machine for singleton living, which he has arranged to rent out to a young Italian academic. It's become one of Herman's projects and Herman loves a project. Naturally, he has no recall with regard to Hattie's original suggestion. And it's not as though he needs the rent, but Herman likes to utilise his assets. The tenant is due to arrive during his absence. In fact, on this very day. Giacomo Moroni. Somebody new and junior in

78

the drama department who has come from Milan – and Hattie is expecting him at noon.

'Snoeks,' Herman has assured her, just prior to that parting peck on the cheek, 'my hunch is that you'll love him. He sounds right up your street.'

By which, she assumes, he means that the tenant, being a drama type, is probably fond of the ballet. Or he's gay. Or both. A gay boy aesthete would be just the person to take good care of Herman's property.

Someone in Herman's company has done the actual conversion, but Herman has managed to carve out the time to be quite hands-on about it, even though he's on several government committees. He advises the Housing Ministry about this, that and the other. Herman goes fishing with prominent members of the new ANC government. And Hattie can't not admire his energy, along with his amazing genius for always being in the right place. It's weird, she reflects, a little sadly, that people like Josh's adoptive parents – people who spent their whole lives working, at great risk to their personal safety, for the kind of social change that the new government now espouses – have either melted into exile, or invisibility, or they've quietly died. And people like Herman, the well-off sons of white farmers; yesterday's eager upholders of the apartheid state, are now the best of buddies with the new black elite. But of course. One should have predicted it. Because those persons who have the flair to be in there with the in-crowd – those are going to be the same persons who will always be right in there, no matter who's in charge.

'Get real,' Herman says. 'It's the way of the world. Anyway, Sam's a good bloke.' 'Sam' being an ethnic Zulu and Herman's favourite government minister. 'He's a drinking buddy, no more.'

Little point in carping that Herman, along with his parents and the whole tribe of jolly sisters, was yesterday's comfortable advocate of the prohibition laws. That is to say, the prohibition against the sale of alcohol to black persons.

'So why dwell on the past, Hat?' Herman says. 'What for? Move on. Times have changed. We've all changed.'

He likes to talk the jargon of 'transformation' and of course he's got to be right. It's no sin to trade in one's value system for a better one. So why is she being such a witch?

'All this nit-picking,' Herman says. 'It's because you've gone and done your history exams. For Chrissakes, there are times when history is best forgotten.'

It's Hattie's impression that Herman's absences have grown more frequent since she became a graduate. At the time she began her degree course he couldn't seem to see the point. She already had a career, didn't she? And now she can't deny that the experience has made her into a slightly different person. She's sharper and more critical. She's more assertive and more clued-up. More open-eyed.

Years back; sixteen years back, Hattie had decided that her marriage was a mistake. She'd begun to think about leaving Herman, but then she got pregnant with Cat. And then, once Cat was four, she'd taken that trip to Europe.

Hattie loved it. *Loved it!* Loved her time in England; loved it and longed to stay; was surprised how much she felt it to be 'her' place; loved the delicate, shifting light, the shades of grey, the urban terraces, the corner shops; the silver birch trees, the London Underground, the broadsheet newspapers, the chance to wear winter clothes. And little Cat, seated there, in the café at the National Gallery; little Cat in Regent's Park, wrapped up in her red bobble hat, bright tights, fleecy red coat. Ankle boots with novelty laces. Only that Cat was forever chattering to her daddy on the phone. Daddy, Daddy, my daddy. When will I see my daddy?

So Hattie accepted that she hadn't the temperament for rocking anyone's boat. She half suspected herself of having got pregnant in order to hang on in the marriage. Like a limpet, Mrs Wimp. That's you, Henrietta Louisa Marchmont-Thomas Marais. Don't you ever go down to the end of the town. Not ever. So, stay if you must, but don't be pathetic. And she resolved, there and then, that when she got home she would work towards becoming a university student; English and history. She sat the necessary qualifying exams and waited until Cat had started school.

At this time, Hattie put her own stamp on her brother James's one-time bedroom in the turret, since it had hardly been used in years, given the five larger bedrooms of Marchmont House. She made it into her study; her private place in which to write her essays. And then, one day, between the essays, she suddenly found herself doodling into being the first page of her first Lola story. The essays and the lectures had given her back the fun of putting pen to paper that she recalled from primary school. And she had bought herself a PC.

It was strange that on the very same day – the day she began that Lola story – she should have found her father's pen. Oh my God, 'that' pen! The thing had been lurking, concealed, behind one of the miniature top drawers of her brother's old bureau; the desk that had become her own. It was lying on a narrow, half-inch ledge between the drawer end and the bureau back, as if deliberately placed. The pen had been missing since the day the maid had got the sack for it, because   along with his inscribed wristwatch, his cigarette case and snuffbox (snuffbox!), his grandfather's silver baptismal cup – it constituted one of her father's significant dynastic hand-ons; a fetish object by which he defined himself. So when, some twenty-seven years ago, the pen was suddenly nowhere, there was serious trouble. For poor old Gertrude, accused of theft, it had meant the end of her employment. For Hattie, its reappearance served to mark a new beginning.

Throughout her childhood, Hattie was always required to play second fiddle to her twin brother. James Alexander

Marchmont-Thomas was the boy for whom neither expense nor effort was spared. Because James, unlike his sister, was destined to carry the family name and to inherit Marchmont House. James was the one in whom her parents vested their ambition and, in return, he had sucked them dry. Neither Hattie nor her parents have seen James, now, for something like eighteen years. He has gone to ground, God only knows where, or upon which continent. Or could it be that James is dead? And it was thanks entirely to Herman's talent, both with money and with buildings, even from his early twenties, that her parents and the house were saved. Herman bought the house from his in-laws when he and Hattie got married, by which means he was able to save their faces by keeping it in the family and, at the same time, could take it on as the first of his post-student projects; a project guaranteed to make a splash in *The Architectural Review*. Because Marchmont House was a fabulous period piece; a marvellous opportunity. The parents, in their turn, could use the sale money to acquire a nice retirement flat in a location they considered sufficiently salubrious to accord with their social status. And then there was a decent lump sum left over, which, when properly invested for them – by Herman, of course – afforded them an acceptable income. Hattie's parents were, by these means, grudgingly impressed with their son-in-law. He was, regrettably, from Afrikaner stock – 'a Boer', as Hattie's father put it – but Herman was acceptably anglicised and, what with his surname being Marais, he was probably of Cape Huguenot descent; something which would have made his settler lineage somewhat older than that of Mr David Marchmont-Thomas.

Hattie's parents, on both sides, were descended from the 1820 Settlers. Their antecedents were, respectively, a one-time Suffolk seamstress and a basket-weaver from Norfolk, but they had quickly got to see themselves as a settler aristocracy; the Cape's own *Mayflower* descendants; makers of the new Albion. Sailing to the Cape Colony on a British government promise of umpteen hectares of fertile farmland – land recently wrested from indigenous pastoral clansmen – their role, unbeknown to them, was to make themselves into a buffer zone between the Colony's existing settlers and the disgruntled rump of the dispossessed. Hattie's antecedents, like many of their fellow settlers, had not much idea of farming practice, especially on unfamiliar terrain, and at some time early on they had sold the land and moved on to start a clothing shop in town, which, over the course of a hundred years, had grown into a nationwide chain of prominent gentlemen's outfitters.

By the time of Hattie and James's birth, however, in the first half of the 1950s, the business, which had not managed to move successfully with the times, had already closed four of its seven branches and, by the 1960s, there was just the one. And, for all its crowded window displays of dowdy flannel trousers and boring ties and brass-buttoned school blazers, along with those disheartening signs that shrieked 'Back to School!' at the soon-to-be-afflicted, the last branch could do little to stop the populace defecting to the OK Bazaars, or to the cheaper Indian emporiums.

Yet the family still had trappings. It had the aforementioned Marchmont House, a charming, turreted Victorian landmark, a colonial gem within an acre of garden, high on Durban's Berea, where, having taken on a slight whiff of haunted castle, and surrounded by post-war apartment blocks, it was beginning to look a little ominously like a candidate for the eager developer's mallet. The Marchmont-Thomases had the Royal Crown Derby dinner service, complete with its forty place settings, and the portfolio of heirloom drawings by the much-revered colonial artist, Thomas Baines. They had the miscellaneous, framed sepia photographs of the family's founding members, buttoned to the neck and seated, side by side, in cane armchairs, on the verandas of various handsome homesteads, some in the Cape and some in Natal. There was also a reserve of money, but since Hattie's parents made a rigorous distinction between their income and their capital, the day-to-day tone of family life was cheese-paring. Much of the capital had been set aside, even before the twins' birth, for the education of the male heir at an English public school; the selfsame school attended by Hattie's father and his father's father.

Hattie's appearance, fifteen minutes after the arrival of James Alexander Marchmont-Thomas, was, in truth, a relief to her parents, because, had two male twins been born to them, their capital would have been challenged. Compromises made. The boys sent off to a local public school. Something like that. But Hattie, being a girl, would require no more from the education system than a fee-paying girls' day school of the more traditional sort, while the need for higher education would simply not arise.

Hattie's father, in the hospital lounge, was busily cracking open champagne.

'A son and heir!' he said.

Throughout her infancy and childhood Hattie stayed small, which for a while caused health professionals to define her condition as 'failure to thrive'. But Hattie somehow or other managed to thrive in her own understated and low-maintenance way. That's when her sibling would allow it. For James Alexander Marchmont-Thomas was a thumper and a hair-puller; an ingenious tormentor, who never cared to stand still. He liked to stamp on his sister's bare feet and to spread her sandwiches with red ants. But 'Boys will be boys' was the watchword, and he soon moved on to more sadistic forms of domination. He liked to dismember Hattie's dolls and to bring discredit upon her, by shutting her out of the nursery bathroom until she wet her pants. He gave her enemas with the garden hose, which he would bully from the hands of Joseph, the gardener.

Yet, once the children went to school, Hattie found a breathing space in her well-ordered, single-sex establishment, where her gracefulness, neatness and application did not go unacknowledged. Hattie loved all the schoolwork. She loved the reading books in the 'quiet corner', and the nature walks and the sessions when they did writing stories in special 'composition' books. She liked scripture and sums and sitting cross-legged in the hall with her friends during morning assembly. She was the sort of easy, undemanding child for whom all schoolteachers are grateful. And the children were fond of her as well – the more so because, in this all-girl context, being the smallest in the class had the curious effect of conferring status. Of all the lessons, Hattie particularly loved the music-and-movement class, where Miss Cayhill, thumping at the hall piano, invited the children to be moths and fairies; frogs and flowers; trees and bears.

'Very good, Henrietta,' Miss Cayhill said. 'Stop, children. Now I want you all to watch Henrietta.'

James, for all his apparent mental agility, did not get on with school. He could never concentrate for more than a minute and he was one of those children who plays up in class and likes to wind up the teachers. Regrettably, he always did these things in a way which was not so much amusing, as tiresome and inopportune. He interrupted the teachers. He elbowed his desk partners, causing them to smudge their work, so that no one wanted to sit with him. He tripped up classmates as they moved down the aisles. As time passed, he turned out to be always cribbing his homework – would-be verbatim – from others; verbatim, that is, bar the puzzling flurries of misspelling and missed-out words. He did this by filching prep notebooks from his neighbours' desks, or by threatening the smallest of the form's swotty types in the lavatories alongside the swimming pool. This was while he still bothered to hand in work. His reading was always pretty hopeless, his number work all scrambled, and – in the parlance of his deeply traditional and time-warped school – Marchmont-Thomas was, quite simply, a dunderhead. A dunderhead and a nuisance.

'Sir, I think McNolty must have copied my prep, sir,' he would say, but the masters were completely open-eyed about the Marchmont-Thomas son and heir. He told tall tales, he slouched and, as Hattie's mother chose to put it, 'James has always found it hard to study.'

To his father's chagrin, at the age of twelve, James was denied access to the English public school but, thanks entirely to last-minute interventions from influential members of the Rotary Club, the board of governors and possibly the Freemasons as well, he was grudgingly accepted by a high-status public school in his own country.

Meanwhile, having been pressed into it by Miss Cayhill, Hattie's father had reluctantly agreed to fork out the requisite sum for his daughter's weekly ballet lessons in the local church hall. This on condition that she earned it back, by helping her mother with the mending. Mrs Marchmont-Thomas, *circa* 1965, was a little old-fashioned, perhaps, but not altogether aberrant, in keeping a mending basket full of socks with holes alongside her favourite wing armchair. And now each evening she had her little helper while James was away at school. But by the time he was fifteen, James's predicted exam grades were such that they were thought to reflect badly on the school's academic record, and his parents were asked to remove him.

So James, after a summer filled with crammers – from whose grasp he frequently effected his escape – was sent (oh dear!) to a neighbourhood state boys' high school of thoroughly good repute. But even there, his career did not last long, because he was caught taking drugs; a habit that Hattie's parents considered so wholly unmentionable that Hattie was unaware of it until she came upon James's scorched tinfoil, lying alongside a rolled-up banknote, on the old Lloyd Loom table in one of the garden sheds. James, she had taken note of late, had begun spending more and more time lurking near the sheds and the servants' rooms. Then, shortly thereafter, came the business of the stolen fountain pen.

Hattie, aged fifteen and sitting at her desk, had become aware one afternoon of an altercation taking place in the garden, between Gertrude, the housemaid, and her father. It appeared to her as a sort of mime sequence, because she was unable to hear either party's words. Gertrude, divested of her shapeless maid's overalls and standing, hands clasped, beside a cardboard suitcase tied with rope, was making what looked like a last-ditch appeal. She was standing sideways on to Hattie, who was realising, for the first time, that Gertrude was definitely pregnant. Her yellow polka-dot skirt was tight and riding up over her belly. Her blouse buttons were straining across her breasts.

Just a month before, Hattie had been witness to one of those routine maid-and-madam exchanges in the kitchen of Marchmont House, in which her mother, poking a finger into the plump front of Gertrude's overalls, was undertaking a sequence of that would-be Creole-speak that made white madams imagine they were thereby making themselves intelligible.

She was doing so by omitting certain parts of speech and inserting others instead.

'Gertrude, say for madam – no lies – you got piccanin dis-side?'

'No, madam,' said Gertrude.

'You eat too much the *putu* or you got foh piccanin?' said Hattie's mother. 'Madam she say foh piccanin.'

'No, madam,' said Gertrude.

'Madam she say foh piccanin,' said Hattie's mother again, wagging a finger before allowing herself another poke at Gertrude's front. 'Madam she say foh Zulu boy come native *kaia* make foh piccanin. Zulu boy him too much fight make trouble. Zulu boy him no good.'

'No, madam,' said Gertrude.

87

'Master he say no visitor,' Hattie's mother said. 'You got foh Zulu boy visitor him no good? Make master foh too much cross – too much – he say no Zulu boy.'

'No, madam,' Gertrude said.

'Zulu boy him too much drink,' said Mrs Marchmont-Thomas. 'Too much lazy-boy smoke dagga no good foh garden boy. Dis why master he like foh Joseph him make foh good garden boy. Joseph he from far-far-dat-side. Not lazy drunk like foh Zulu boy.'

Joseph, the wizened ancient, hailed, originally, from Mozambique. He lived in the room adjoining Gertrude's and had done so for as long as Hattie could remember.

Gertrude was now on her knees in the grass, attempting to clutch at Hattie's father's hand, but he shook her off, without regard, and moved away towards the house. Then Gertrude clambered to her feet and began to walk away. One yellow polka-dot skirt, one pair of worn-out gym shoes, one card-board suitcase tied with rope, and then Gertrude was gone; dismissed without a character. Pregnant and on the road; the road to nowhere. No job equalled no right of residence within the municipal area.

Hattie, that afternoon, had been regressing in her reading, since the high-summer weather was somewhat enervating. She had put down her school copy of *Silas Marner* in order to reread one of her childhood favourites, *Ballet Shoes*. She had just got to where the new lodger had gained the three girls entry into Mademoiselle's ballet school, where Posy was to prove herself a star. But after witnessing the Gertrude episode, Hattie found herself too trou-bled to read on. She felt impelled to chase after Gertrude and say a proper goodbye. She wanted to give her money, but she didn't really have any to hand. Things, perhaps? Valuable things? There was nothing she could hand to Gertrude that wouldn't make her a suspect. 'Hey, you? Native girl? Where from you get this gold watch?'

At supper that evening, it materialised that Hattie had been mistaken. It was not so much Gertrude's pregnancy that had led to her dismissal. It was theft. Gertrude had evidently helped herself to the heirloom fountain pen from Hattie's father's desk, because it was gone; missing without a trace. It was an item that until this day had always sat in a special green marble tray, alongside that blue-black bottle of Quink that Hattie found so pleasing, for the wide prism of its shape. Gertrude had obviously stolen the pen, even though she could hardly write. Because who else could possibly have done so?

Supper was more than usually glum, and her father spoke abruptly to his daughter.

'Henrietta, will you shift yourself there and help your poor mother in the kitchen?' he said.

And in the kitchen, Hattie found her mother was on a roll with martyred sighs.

'Now I shall have all the work of training up some raw young native girl, straight from the kraal,' she said. 'Just as I had to do with Gertrude. Honestly, Hattie, you get no thanks from these people. I hope you'll remember that when your time comes to keep house.'

'Is Father certain that Gertrude took the pen?' Hattie ventured, but her mother was in full flow.

'They can't help themselves, these people,' she said. 'They'll steal anything that isn't screwed down. Do carry the peas through for me, Hattie, would you?'

So Hattie did as she was told. The peas, as usual, came a virulent green, since Mrs Marchmont-Thomas liked to add a spoon of bicarb to the cooking water; a handy trick that Gertrude would be carrying with her, along the road to nowhere.

By the time Hattie had reached her sixteenth birthday, her father had decided to stop paying for his daughter's ballet lessons. The decision came just as she had managed to win a trio of coveted medals at the annual national eisteddfod. She had had her photograph in all the papers, wearing a tutu that her teacher had given her – 'Only for you, dear Hattie' – a treasured item that had once belonged to her previous star pupil, Margaret Barbieri. A local girl who was, by then, a principal dancer with the Royal Ballet in London.

'And we're planning for you to follow in her footsteps,' the teacher said to Hattie. 'I have my eye on you.'

But right then there was James, who needed his parents' money to buy him into the beginnings of a career, of sorts, in business. Something to keep him on the straight and narrow, but his record was such that the effort was proving both difficult and expensive. It was also requiring the twisting of several influential arms. Hattie's teacher was incensed by Hattie's most recent disheartening intelligence, and, on this occasion, she kept her pupil company all the way home.

There she confronted Mr Marchmont-Thomas and offered to waive Hattie's fees.

'Your daughter, as you must surely know, is really talented,' she said. 'It's a privilege for me to teach her. And we have plans for her future, she and I. Don't we, Hattie dear?'

Mr Marchmont-Thomas was deeply affronted and asked her to leave at once. Then he sent his daughter to her room.

'The cheek of the woman!' he said to his wife. 'As if we were beggars, Kathleen.'

'She meant it for the best,' said Mrs Marchmont-Thomas, on one of her martyred sighs. 'It was kind of her to make the offer.'

'It's completely out of the question,' Mr Marchmont-Thomas replied. 'Hattie must simply start pulling her weight. It's time she left school and found employment. That's until she gets married.'

Mr Marchmont-Thomas had not been employed since the recent closure of the last of the gentlemen's outfitters, though he was wont to don his business suit each morning and bustle off to his club.

'Oh blah!' said Hattie's ballet teacher, when she was informed of this decision. 'Forgive me, Hattie. I know he's your father, but what is the matter with that man? I tell you what, my darling. I'll employ you – full-time and from today. But you must make me two solemn promises. No handouts to that brother of yours and we're going to drop all this "hyphen-Marchmont" business. Lose it, all right, Hattie?'

So Hattie left school and became Hattie Thomas. She gave classes while she prepared herself for a scholarship to London's Central School of Ballet.

'We are going to get you there,' her teacher said with conviction. 'Upward and onward, Hattie! But we've got to toughen you up, my dear. You need to be tough in this profession and you're a bit too much of a pushover.'

'Do you think so?' Hattie said.

And Hattie duly won the scholarship, but her success coincided with an unfortunate event that neither Mr Marchmont-Thomas nor his wife could sweep under one of their mould-green carpets. James, having been wheedled into the offices of one of his father's one-time business associates, had soon been discovered with his fingers in the safe and, furthermore, he was concurrently in the Juvenile Court on a charge of stealing a sports car. Hattie's mother was taking this very badly and had had to get pills from the doctor. She had hardly risen from her bed in fourteen days and she'd been refusing food. Her blood pressure was rising and she had begun to suffer from a constant buzzing in the ears.

'Your mother is not at all well, Henrietta,' Mr Marchmont-Thomas told his daughter. 'We are all of us having to make sacrifices and that must include you. The scholarship is out of the question. You are badly needed at home.'

Then, some years later, when her teacher retired, she'd handed over the school to the pupil for whom she had once had such high hopes.

And Hattie, pliable, pushover Hattie, who has spent her years between sixteen and thirty-four giving ballet classes to children, now writes ballet stories for girls. She keeps Margaret Barbieri's tutu hanging over the desk where she writes. Lola, her heroine, is a strong-minded girl, who leaves her home on the east coast of Africa, against the wishes of her family. She takes up a scholarship at the Central School of Ballet in London, where she toughs it out through hardship and success. The first book Hattie dedicates to her little daughter Cat, who just then is eager to start lessons, but within the year Cat has packed it in.

Once Cat has done with her breakfast Coco Pops, and has so effectively slapped down her mother, she dons her regulation school hat and takes herself off to high school. Hattie makes herself a piece of toast, which she nibbles as she proceeds upstairs to the turret, where she sits down to deal with her correspondence. Then she takes a shower and she puts on her clothes. She sets off on foot for the local shopping mall, but meets the postman at her gate, who hands her a sheaf of envelopes.

'Thank you,' she says. She stuffs the envelopes into her bag and walks on.

Once there, she enters the music shop, where she buys herself the CD of Stravinsky's *Pulcinella*. Then she sits down at a café table with a mug of cappuccino. Hattie loves this little ritual of lingering alone in cafés; loves the anonymity of it; loves getting out of the house. She takes the notes from the sleeve and starts to read the words. It isn't 'screw-gender' that she's heard, of course. What she's heard is '*struggendo*'. '*Struggendo si va. Per voi il core struggendo si va.*' For you my heart languishes. Then she glances through the letters. All of them are for Herman except for one, which she opens and reads. It's from the drama department of the local university and it's asking her, with apologies for the shortness of notice, to take part in their conference on mime.

Hattie blinks. She reads the letter again, feeling a twinge of excitement. Me? she's thinking to herself. Me? Speak at a conference?

Then, as she reads it a third time, she takes note that someone is planting an overlarge tuna sandwich on the table, which is almost making contact with her letter. Blast! How she hates this, especially as the café isn't even particularly full. The sandwich is quartered and it comes on an oval platter festooned with rocket leaves. It is soon followed by a tall fluted glass of what looks to her like guava juice.

'May I?' says a familiar voice; a voice from way back, but one that so recently has happened to gatecrash her sleeping brain. 'It *is* you, isn't it?' says the voice. 'Of course it is.'

When Hattie looks up, she sees that Josh Silver is standing there and he's staring at her hard. Josh Silver, in the flesh; tousled curls, turned half-and-half to grey; the chestnut almost leached out. Same glasses; Stravinsky's glasses. Thick lenses that shrink his eyes. Her hand flies to her mouth as she looks up at him. Then it falls back on to the tabletop, on to the open letter, and she smiles at him with pleasure.

He unhitches a canvas backpack from his left shoulder and eases it to the floor. Then he leans across the table and kisses her cheek.

'Hat,' he says. 'How amazing. This is amazing. I saw you from the counter. Well, I thought I did. I couldn't be sure. But of course I'm sure. You're so –' He stops and glances down at the letter and the sleeve notes.

'*Pulcinella*,' he says, and he laughs.

'I've just been asked to this conference,' she says.

'Great!' he says. 'That's great. Me too. It's why I'm here. Only I've come early. I've got this little room near the beach, but I took one of those combi-taxis up the hill. You know. To prowl old haunts. I just walked past your church hall.'

And then – oh no! – she has to go. *Has to*. Herman's tenant will, at this moment, be arriving at her front door.

Josh is visibly flustered.

'Give me your phone number,' he says. 'Please, Hat.'

She watches with a sinking heart as he writes the number in biro on his hand. Will he maybe forget and wash his hands?

'I'm still in the same house,' she says, as back-up.

'Can we meet up later?' he says. 'Anywhere. Mitchell Park, maybe?'

Mitchell Park, where the mynah birds will be doing their Hitchcock screeching as they home in, en masse, to roost.

'Yes,' she says, and she gathers up her stuff. 'Yes, I'd love that. Call me. I'll be at home all day.' And then she's off, on her little dancer's feet; off at speed to meet Herman's tenant. Giacomo Moroni.

Chapter Four

Josh

The night before Josh leaves for South Africa to attend that conference on mime, he's in the car, returning home with Caroline and
his mother-in-law. Zoe, his darling lookalike daughter, has already
left for her French exchange, and he hates it that he wasn't there
to wave her off. He was tied up in Bristol. Opera production. Joint
production with the music department. And now, on his first free
evening in weeks – his wedding anniversary, no less – the woman
has seen fit to take control of the occasion. Tickets for the opera in
London. Splashy treats courtesy of Caroline's money; *their* money,
of which they have precious little, thanks to the Witch Woman's
monthly allowance and mortgage payments – but Josh has long
since ceased to air this grudge directly. He's never coped well with
confrontation, and what's the point if you can't win?

'It's your bronze, my darlings,' he hears the woman say. (Or
did she say tin? Or copper? Or plastic?) He wasn't listening to her,
because who gives a bugger about this sort of rubbish? Bronze,
lead, zinc, chrome, uranium. Trust the Witch Woman to know
this sort of crap. She who evidently drove her own husband to an
early grave.

And it's been three tickets for the opera, not two, because Mrs
McCleod likes to see '*les jeunes* enjoying themselves', as she says.

And she wouldn't be able to see them, would she? Not if they'd gone off on their own. Caroline, as usual – prodigious Caroline, who can hold almost anyone in the palm of her hand – has not uttered a word to deter her mother from the opera project; Caroline, who, since taking on the headship of a local comprehensive school, can hold in thrall six hundred adolescents as a matter of daily routine.

'Mum's lonely,' Caroline says to Josh.

And there is every good reason why she should be lonely, Josh thinks, because any person of sound mind will be giving her a wide berth. Plus it really gets on his nerves when the old woman calls them '*les jeunes*', because, leaving aside that he has recently turned forty-two, it brings him up against her idiotic assertion that 'spiritually' she's French.

'My heritage is Scottish,' she says. 'But in my soul I'm French.' Josh is never quite sure which he hates more: '*les jeunes*' or 'the bairns', but either way, he's aware that her intent is to disempower. And, to underline his disempowerment, Josh is right now seated in the back of his own car because, thanks to his lousy eyesight, Caroline does all the night driving and his mother-in-law, by long-established tradition, claims rights to the front passenger seat.

'When you bairns get a car with four doors . . .' she says.

Josh hates to travel long distances by car. It always makes him feel sick. Without Caroline's mother they could be travelling home by train, but Mrs McCleod is of the opinion that public transport is exclusively for plebs.

Rigoletto. That's what they've been to see. 'I know how much you like clowns, Josh,' she has explained to him earlier that evening. And, sure as God, she must also know how much he hates these big, boom-boom operatic affairs. He likes early opera, for heaven's sake; chamber opera; tightly plotted comedies in which everyone is in love with somebody else's betrothed and sundry marriage contracts are called into question by a range of incompetent stage lawyers. Foppish drunken halfwits or scheming rogues. He likes it when the entire dramatis personae is cheating, spying, playing dead, and dressing up in other people's clothes. He likes those stagy assignations in moonlit shrubberies and the constant dropping of love letters in regulation privet hedges, where the wrong people are always destined to pick them up. He likes precipitous conclusions in which all is resolved by timely revelation. A telling birthmark. An ancient nun with a very long memory. A mysterious stranger with a significant secret. A twin brother lost and found. Life redeemed through wit and coincidence, heady plot lines and acrobatic dexterity.

Josh has just produced such an opera. Aged Tutor loves Beautiful Orphan. Hideous Crone loves Aged Tutor. Beautiful Orphan loves Twin Brother X. Twin Brother X loves Hideous Crone's Daughter. Twin Brother Y loves Beautiful Orphan. Hideous Crone's Daughter loves Twin Brother Y. A perfect balance of cruelty and choreography. Six people dancing in a box. Dance, dance, for there is only the dance. Josh likes entanglements with rope ladders and chairs. And he's especially irritable right now, because, on this night – *this very night* – and not half a mile from where he has sat squirming through *Rigoletto*, was the last performance of that wild, astonishing Schoenberg, in which Pulcinella, in a frenzied dance, wrestles the moon from his clothes.

So now, after the opera and from the back seat of his car, Josh is exercising the futile rhetoric of the ineffectual. He's indulging in a degree of sarcastic carping after the event.

'Time was,' he says, 'when Italian street actors dressed up in clown masks and threw piss pots at each other all over the piazza. Or they beat each other over the head. That was before the French got hold of the idea and – being French – they turned the clown into this toxic, self-obsessed introvert. So they end up with Pierrot. He of the chalk-white face and the painted teardrop. "Look at me.

97

Feel sorry for me. Me, me and me. I'm so lonely. I'm so sad. And, by the way, I'm a psycho. But it's all because nobody loves me." '

Josh is aware, throughout this wind-up, that he actually adores French theatre; that what he's doing is attacking the Witch Woman's claim to a French 'soul'. He's also aware that Zoe has a white-faced Pierrot doll, given to her by Caroline's mother. It sits on her bookshelf in the old red bus, alongside the plaster Beatrix Potter figures and the collection of little glass Bambis.

And, yes, they are still living in the bus, but not for very much longer, because, for the second time in sixteen years of saving, Caroline's dream of the little Victorian house is just about to come true. Within the month, they have 'completed' on the purchase of a house. Two up, two down and a lean-to kitchen at the back – and no need, after all, for the fireman's pole. Caroline's plan, throughout the period of Josh's absence in South Africa, is to sand the floors, paint the walls and make improvements to the kitchen. She has plans to re-pot her clematis and honeysuckle, and to run up calico Roman blinds for all of the five sash windows. She will move the necessary furniture and effects while her husband and daughter are abroad.

'It'll be easier that way,' she says. Infallible, put-down Caroline. Meanwhile, the bus will stay in the farmer's field, to do service as a communal study. 'And I'll keep up the vegetable garden, of course,' Caroline says. Of course.

'Thank you, Mum, for a lovely evening,' Josh hears her say. 'It's really been a very special treat.'

'Well, I should say so,' says the old woman. 'I won't embarrass you both with the price of the tickets.'

'Then the French sell their psycho-clown back to the Italians,' Josh continues, though he senses that no one is listening to him. 'And that's how we get to *Rigoletto*. Hey presto. The clown has become a serial killer.'

98

Caroline's mother responds by snapping on the radio, just in time for them to hear the tearful father of a runaway twelve-year-old being questioned about his feelings. His daughter has made it from Scunthorpe to Calais in the company of a forty-year-old penpal, before being recovered by the police.

'How do I feel?' the dad is saying. 'I dunno. Joy. Exaltation. All the adjectives.'

'Those aren't adjectives,' Josh says. 'Those are abstract nouns.'

'Think if it was Zoe,' the Witch Woman says. 'I mean these people she's staying with in France. Do you know anything about them?'

Josh lapses into brooding silence. There's a car game he and Zoe like to play, in which they compete to spot entertaining news billboards, or outlets with idiotic names. Recently, because the signs have got too easy, they've given themselves a handicap. All words on the billboards have got to be monosyllabic. So 'Brad Pitt Haircut Boy Banned from School' was one they'd had to forgo, though Zoe had quibbled for a while over 'haircut'. 'It's "hair cut",' she said.

'Lottery Dinner Lady Charged with Theft' was another to bite the dust. 'Man Mugged at Mum's Grave' was one of Zoe's triumphs, as was 'School Run Dad has Mug of Gin'. And, right now, as they finally enter the outer reaches of Oxford's townscape, Josh's eye catches a gem in the brightly lit forecourt of his mother-in-law's local Sainsbury's.

'*Yess!*' he says out loud. 'Yes!! "Cold Flat OAP Found Dead".' He pronounces OAP as 'Ope'.

'You don't say "Ope". You say "Oh-Ay-Pee",' Caroline says. She who has never before deigned to play along. '"Cold Flat Oh-Ay-Pee".'

'Well, I say "Ope",' Josh says.

'No, you don't,' Caroline says. 'You say "Oh-Ay-Pee", just like everyone else.'

'I don't,' Josh says. 'I say "Ope".'

'Please,' says Witch Woman, massaging her temples. 'Bairns. Bairns, both of you. We've had *such* a lovely evening. Give me a break. It's late.'

Given Josh's early life experience, it's no surprise that he avoids confrontation; avoids rejection; prefers emotion contained and stylised, as in those ingenious comedic structures. He prefers life choreographed by acrobats and floating on verbal dexterity. He has long ago shaken off his past, hasn't he? He has moved on. It's Caroline who is in thrall to her family, as the Witch Woman's rapacious and looming presence these eleven years past bears witness. Yet now, what with the trip coming up – his first journey 'home' in almost two decades – Josh finds himself intermittently exhuming elements of his past: Hattie Thomas and little Jack, who so inexplicably vanished. He thinks about Bernie Silver (dead) and Ida (dead) and (long-dead) loving Pru. And then there's the drama department, where now, in the post-apartheid dawn, the conference is to take place. There's the jacaranda tree beyond the Silvers' front veranda and back, beyond that – but only rarely and in dreams – he has been surprised of late to find himself groping blindly in a sulphurous, theatrical mist towards a shadowy figure: a distant woman in layers of clothes – clothes that appear to be made of dust – who is always walking with her back to him; walking further and further away; as if back into her own past.

Josh was born in the early 1950s in what was then the Transvaal, a few miles east of Johannesburg. He was the child of a woman who, within three years, had become a half-mad, shoeless creature; a woman who had stopped speaking; a woman to whom Josh, in infancy, knew better than to try and cling. Instead, he was routinely tied to the back of little Dora, the teenage housemaid. By the time of his birth, Josh's mother was already no longer recognisable as the person she so recently had been; a bourgeois

Lebanese convent orphan with a nice little nest egg and a trousseau filled with the best French linen and handmade family lace. Not that Lilette Habibi had ever seen her own money, or handled statements pertaining to its extent, given the cloistered life she'd lived. Her mother died giving birth to her and her father, expecting a son and thrown into confusion by his pretty young wife's death, gave her over to the care of a nursemaid and then, at six, to the nuns of a teaching order in his native Beirut. Since he travelled a lot on business and had no other children, his daughter spent her holidays at the convent and when he, too, died young – just before her fifteenth birthday – *la petite chère Lilette* simply stayed on at the convent as a cherished and useful, if ambiguous, young spinster; an accomplished young woman with a trousseau and a way with the younger girls.

Lilette, for the time being, was not a novice, for reasons to do with the trousseau, which existed as evidence of her late father's wish that she should one day marry, but such a significant decision was simply, indefinitely deferred. Meanwhile, the girl always rose at five for the convent's ritual devotions and she was never without her rosary. Lilette would probably have entered the order, given a little more time. That is, had she not, all unbeknown to her, been possessed of a certain paternal male cousin, whose parents, twenty years earlier, had made the journey south from Lebanon to Johannesburg.

The cousin was an unmarried chancer, a wide boy, who one evening met his like in the bar of the Royal Hotel in Boksburg. His companion, a hang-loose drifter, born to immigrant Greek corner-shopkeepers, was likewise a disappointment to his parents from whom he was now estranged. Both sets of parents had once cherished hopes of pushing their sons into one of the professions; upward and onward in a strange new country where the streets were paved with gold. Both men did indeed harbour dreams of rising, but without the effort of passing professional exams. They dreamed of making it from small-time fiddle to big-time money bags. They dreamed of ways to generate surplus income without bestirring themselves in any area beyond their common inclination to cheat. In this, the convent orphan's cousin was already a step ahead, since he had moved up from running an eating house for poor black migrant workers, where – by serving up a regular slop of watery stews made from illegally sourced and flyblown meat – he had accumulated the means to run a bed-bug boarding house for the humbler white commercial traveller.

The Greek had not accomplished much, other than to buy and sell knock-off goods acquired from crooked railway employees and then to blow the surplus in a range of brothels and bars. Grown mellow now on cheap Cape brandy, the cousin got a feel-good charge in a moment of inspiration. It came to him that he could play benefactor to his companion by turning marriage broker, and could thereby enrich them both. At fifty-fifty on the convent girl's inheritance, he could be doing both himself and his new friend a good turn – and the convent-girl cousin as well, of course, because what sort of a babe would want to spend her life with a bunch of old maids dressed up like penguins?

'Have I got a cousin for you!' he said, of the relation he had never met, though, via his parents' photograph album, he had seen an old picture of the convent girl's deceased but beautiful mother. 'Rich and beautiful, man!' he said. 'She's a convent girl. You know what I'm saying? Innocent, hey? Pure. Not like some of these dollies nowadays.'

The Greek was nodding sagely. Having some years back tried, without success, to get himself a niche in the girl-running trade, he had found the space already taken by immigrant Romanians and Poles.

'Bleddy Yids,' he said wistfully and half to himself, but he nonetheless had some experience of girls, through his role as paying client. He was partial to dainty blonde prostitutes, though he was fussy about their personal hygiene. Being on the short side, he went for 'petite'. He liked a well-scrubbed, smiley, blue-eyed girl, pink as a newborn piglet. And naked, of course, except for some classy bits and pieces. Tassels, maybe. And a G-string. And pointy high-heeled shoes. He liked the titillating rituals of subservience, especially all the cute doggy stuff.

There was a girl whom he especially liked to visit, who played poodle-doggy for him. She'd wear a little diamanté collar and offer him her lead between her teeth. The Greek appreciated refinements. He liked to pour Babycham into a dog bowl and push doggy choc-drops into her mouth. Good Girl treats, because he knew how much a real lady loved to eat chocolates. The convent girl would be dark-haired, of course, but good-looking like her mother. He could always get her hair bleached, couldn't he? And the money'd got to be good.

'Just so long as she hasn't got a moustache, hey?' he said, and both of them had a laugh.

Negotiations over the convent girl were duly put into motion, though the business took quite a time; a whole lot of stupid foreign palaver before the bar-room friends could get their hands on some of the money. There were documents to be signed; telegrams to fly back and forth – telegrams which were frequently unintelligible. The dowry had to be established and arrangements made for sums to be transferred, in cautious chunks, via the cousin's bank account. Proxy nuptials needed to be simultaneously enacted in the presence of respective Catholic priests.

Then, with the help of the devoted sisterhood, *la petite chère Lilette* finally packed her things into a large wooden trunk – the bedlinen and handmade lace, the crêpe de Chine knickers and nighties – and she departed to meet her Prince Charming. She packed the little boxes containing her family jewels and, though she'd worn it already for the proxy wedding, her mother's veil and somewhat mortifyingly amended full-length dress with all those extra satin panels let into the sides, because Lilette was a very different shape to that of her small-boned mother. She also packed the bridal calfskin gloves, although her hands were much too big for them.

She washed and combed her long black hair and began that night-and-day, day-and-night, interminable sea journey from Beirut to Port Said and then on down, down, all down the Red Sea, between Egypt and Arabia, to Djibouti and the Horn of Africa, past Somalia, to Mombasa. Then on, again, to Dar es Salaam, where she could see the dhows in the harbour and she smelled the cloves of Zanzibar, and on, through the Mozambique Channel, to Beira; landscapes, seascapes, mingling with glimpses of tall, dark people and the sounds of unfamiliar languages floating up from quaysides. Finally, it was into Durban harbour, where she disembarked and was conveyed, by rickshaw, to the northbound train for Johannesburg; on and on, until there, at last, on the station platform, her unknown husband and her unknown cousin were waiting.

But the husband was not best pleased. His wife, he observed, was anything but dainty, since the convent girl was on the solid side, with broad shoulders and heavy breasts. Her hips were wide, she had an hour-glass figure, not right then showing to great advantage in her long, loose travelling clothes, and her shoes were unambiguously flat. The fact that her garments didn't conform to current female fashion trends gave the husband especial and immoderate cause for indignation. No swingy skirt! No stilettos! Evidently no tweezers in her toilet bag, since her eyebrows were unplucked! And, after the sweaty heat of Durban, followed by those stuffy hours on the train, the convent girl was not quite exuding an odour of scented soap and lavender.

'Jeez, but you lied to me,' he said, turning to the cousin with feeling. 'Shit man, but she's ugly like a baboon. And her bum's too big. Just take a look. *Boesman* bum, I'm telling you.'

'*Ach*, it's just from all the travelling, my friend,' said his drinking companion. 'Keep your hair on, OK? Use your imagination. She'll tidy up really nice, all right?'

'Well, I won't take her,' said the husband. 'Not for fifty-fifty. I'll only do seventy-five. Anything less and she's taking her big fat *Boesman* bum straight back to where she's come from. Understand? Jeez man, but she even looks like a *chut*. She could be a half-caste for all I know.'

'You saying my family's got *chuts*?' said the cousin. 'Lebanese is white people, hey? Just like Greeks, if you don't mind.'

All the while the convent girl was standing stock still and uncomprehending on the platform, with her trunk beside her on the ground. Her eyes were modestly cast down, as she stared at the little vanity case she was holding in her hands.

'OK. Sixty-forty,' the cousin said, after a pause. 'It's a deal.'

'Sixty-five,' said the husband.

The cousin shrugged. Then he laughed.

'Spit and shake on it,' he said.

Though the marriage had already taken place, the nuns had pressed for an on-site blessing, in a local Catholic Church. There was nobody present, next morning, at the sorry little ceremony; just the priest, the cousin and the bridal couple. But the bride, once again, wore her mother's wedding dress, with its quantities of tailored satin. She also wore the veil.

'Jeez, but she's a sight for sore eyes,' the husband said, jittery and discontented, in his drainpipe trousers and bootlace tie. 'Even with her face covered up like that. She looks like she's wearing about a million doilies.'

'*Ach*, belt up, you're in church,' hissed the cousin. 'Anyway, you've got her money, haven't you?'

'Ya, but why she's got so much clothes on, hey?' the husband persisted. 'Is she mad or something? She looks like Mother Monkey stole the net curtains. It's like she's wearing all of Ackerman's haberdashery.'

Both men were suddenly trying to smother laughter.

'Slim her down and shut it with all the moaning,' said the cousin. 'You can get her some different clothes. Nice dresses, hey? Sexy colours. Cerise and that. Mauve.'

'And how come she no-speaks?' said the husband.

'She can't speak English,' said the cousin, who, having accommodated his relation overnight in one of the bedrooms of his boarding house, had himself been flummoxed by his own almost total lack of French. 'She speaks foreign, that's all, but she'll soon pick it up,' he said. 'Anyway, no-speaks means there's going to be no nagging, hey? No yackety-yack.'

But the Greek was fond of chit-chat in a girl.

'So what kind of foreign does she speak?' he said. 'Shit, I reckon she's a retard.'

And then the bride and groom were on their own. For all his womanising habits, the husband was not one to be easily aroused, except by daintiness and dog leads, but that night, after he had got himself boozed up, the marriage was sort of consummated in a room in the cousin's hotel, on a creaking bed under a fly-spotted ceiling, with fly papers hanging from the lampshade. After that, the husband, having left the bed, repaired to the nearby men-only bar of the aforementioned Royal Hotel, where, with his new-found wealth, he treated a miscellany of hard-luck victims and exhausted travelling salesmen.

'It's on me,' he said. 'Head in the noose and all that, hey? Let's drink to it.' Which they did.

They drank and played cards until the husband's pockets were empty. But it was nice to know that there would always be more of it. Always. Even if you'd had to go and get yourself married to the Missing Link.

*   *   *

106

With his wife's money, the husband bought a nice suburban house in mock-Tudor style, complete with mock-Tudor double garage, because he really liked cars. He filled the house with new high-street furniture. Lounge suite, dining-room suite, bedroom suite, glass display cabinet with mahogany claw-and-ball feet. ('Clawed balls', as he said, being a wag.) Candlewick bedspread on the marriage bed in swags of pink and green. Dressing table (kidney-shaped) with monster pink powder puff in its own glass bowl. Pink mother-of-pearl vanity set. The lav boasted a crinoline lady to cover the toilet brush, with her dress made all of mauve ribbons, and there were mauve hand towels to match. The garage had got the new MG and the new pink Chevrolet – 'nipple pink', like the dealer called it. Sexy, or what?

Soon he'd had a pool dug in the garden, with a niche at one end that had a naked-lady statue. '*Ach sies*,' he liked to joke to his mates, 'her drapes is just falling off her pussy, hey? But it's all right because it's art.'

The husband, in addition to Dora the maid, had hired a garden 'boy' and a pool 'boy', though he himself couldn't swim and his wife, who had never really looked at her own body, not even in the bath, had a vague idea that the pool was intended for fish. They were fish that never materialised. Meanwhile, the husband's pride in his house did not extend to the mouldy-oldie contents of his wife's heirloom trunk and, since he liked to smoke in bed, he'd soon burnt holes in the French linen sheets and in the hand-worked lace cloths with which the convent girl had presumed to cover the bedside tables and the chests.

Most nights he abandoned the marriage bed in order to visit his dainty blondes and, sometimes, at two in the morning, he brought the women home; diminutive, giggling peroxide creatures in laddered stockings, suspenders showing through their flimsy skirts, their feet in tottering glass slippers. The convent girl could hear him cavorting in the adjoining room. That was until she was banished there herself, so that the husband could take sole possession of the master bedroom.

Sex and the convent girl had not got on – not since her first baffled attempts to understand her husband's particular niche-requirements. And his attempts to demonstrate his canine role-play proclivities had had a counterproductive effect, leaving her resolutely vertical and rigid with panic, flattened up against the wardrobe door. Having fled his clutches, she stood breathing too fast, uttering little cries of terror – a reaction which had a detumescent effect on the husband, though it did arouse his anger. He aimed the odd savage kick at her, and, twice thereafter, blacked her eye. By the fourth week of marriage, he had slammed her jaw into a door frame, which caused her face to lose its symmetry, along with two left-upper teeth. After that, he left her alone. Even so, by the end of the first month of her marriage, the Greek had somehow managed to get the convent girl with child.

Since the husband had never been out with his wife, had never taken her to the cinema, or for a stroll in the park, or even to the greengrocer; and since, in all her past cloistered life, she had never had cause to get the shopping habit, the convent girl, traumatised by brutality and strangeness; silenced by the total absence of French or Arabic speakers, confined within the walls of her baffling mock-Tudor house, had, within the year, become an agoraphobic, non-speaking person, completely dependent on Dora the teenage housemaid – and on the husband, who would appear sporadically, bearing the wherewithal to cook. He arrived occasionally with lumps of brisket and dubious bulk-buy sacks of unrecognisable vegetables, which liquefied in the dark of the larder floor. And, since there were no visits to the doctor, no antenatal consultations, she also found herself dependent on little Dora when she went into labour with Josh.

*   *   *

Meanwhile, the absentee husband was having fun with her money. He began to play the stock market and enjoyed shifting money around, usually at injudicious moments. He liked proposing joint ventures in this and that; all of them ill-fated alliances which he made with the sort of human flotsam to whom he was naturally drawn. He tried a high-interest loan-sharking venture directed at black mine workers; people who were so evidently and abjectly poor that they couldn't not default on future repayments. He bought into a township bus company just before angry boycotters burned twenty per cent of the fleet and stoned to a standstill those vehicles that didn't catch fire.

As the money began to dwindle, his instinct to work on the wrong side of the law came once again to the fore. For a time, the MG and the nipple-pink Chevrolet were sharing the garage with increasing volumes of stolen goods. Then he sold his wife's mother's jewels. After that, once the lounge suite, the dining-room suite, the bedroom suite had all been repossessed; and the MG and the nipple-pink Chevrolet were no longer gracing the garage, the husband – mercifully – stopped coming home. The pyramid-selling scheme had collapsed and the Greek was wanted for fraud. And all this time, the convent girl, who, twelve months earlier, on scavenged scraps of shelving paper, had written a letter, in her neat French cursive, to the Mother Superior of the convent in Beirut, had not been in a position to post it, for want of an envelope or a stamp.

By the time the electricity had been cut off, Josh was three years old; a non-speaking but tactile little boy who was fixed almost permanently to Dora's back. The maid wore him, tied in a blanket, while she went about her work. She cooked bowls of maize-meal porridge on a Primus stove from the servant's room, which she spooned into Josh's mouth along with whatever she could rescue from the bits of brisket and rotting veg. And, while she did not quite spoon-feed the convent girl, she placed food before her.

The convent girl ate rapidly these days, spilling from the side of her mouth where the husband had knocked out her teeth. She no longer brushed her hair or her teeth and she had more or less ceased to wash. Her thick hair, matted and bushy, gave her a somewhat Neanderthal look, her legs and forearms lined with fine black hairs.

On the day when the police came by, it was Dora who acted as interpreter. She drew a picture for her mistress, of prison bars with a stick man stuck behind them, cartoon mouth downturned. She tapped at the stick man on the page and each time she said, 'Madam, it's the master.' The convent girl got the message.

When notice to repossess the house appeared, it was Dora who opened the letter. She hadn't been paid for three months by then and she had come to the end of the line. Way down the south-east coast was Durban, where her mother Prudence lived, not in a poky backyard room, but in a township house of her own. Pru worked for Bernie and Ida Silver, who treated her needs with respect, so she wasn't the regulation on-call skivvy, to be summoned at all hours, like a genie from a bottle; no boyfriends, no drink, no visitors. Not that Pru did boyfriends these days. She got her highs from Jesus, who had proved an altogether more reliable male companion. Pru worked nine to four with two half-days and Sundays off. She had a pension plan, thanks to her employers. And every Sunday, without fail, she was in attendance at the St Moses Holy Apostolic Church, down by the riverside.

Two years earlier, when the Silvers relocated from Johannesburg, they had made special efforts to get their maid permission to move south with them; a thing that took an eternity of form-filling and standing in long apartheid queues. Unfortunately, there were no forms in the land that, at that time, could swing it for little Dora to come with her.

Now, at four in the morning, as Dora planned to cut loose from the convent girl for good, she placed a banknote from her own meagre savings under a jam pot on the kitchen table. Then she slipped out into the darkness and headed for the 'non-white' bus depot. Yet, uncannily, her mute mistress, via a sort of animal radar, had managed to get her sussed. Shoeless and trance-like, her child tied clumsily to her back in a parody version of Dora's blanket, the convent girl had left the house and was following at twenty yards' distance.

Dora clicked her tongue.

'*Hamba*!' she said. 'Go back!'

But her mistress kept on coming. Dora stopped; the convent girl stopped. Stop, go. Stop, go, all the way to the end of the road. Entreat me not to leave thee. Finally Dora gave in. Fearing for Josh's safety in the badly knotted sling, she took the child from the convent girl and tied him to her own back. Then she returned for the banknote, which the convent girl had left untouched, lying under the jam jar.

People may become brown persons as much by context as by physiognomy or pigmentation, and the convent girl already had dark and curly hair. People may become brown persons by dint of poverty, body language and the expectation of exclusion. So nobody questioned the convent girl as she followed Dora on to the bus that was reserved for persons of colour. It was only that she proffered no fare. Dora paid for them both. And then, in a filthy cloud of exhaust fumes, they were off for the south-east coast.

In the yard of Pru's tiny township house, the convent girl gnawed at a heel of bread and drank strong tea from a mug. Then she went to sleep, on a mattress in a lean-to shed-like extension, roofed with corrugated iron. Dora and Pru then sat down at the oilcloth-covered kitchen table while Dora told her story.

'This is a white woman?' Pru said in disbelief. 'This is your madam from Boksburg? Dora girl, you bring trouble. Your madam – she can't stay here.'

But Pru had no way of shifting the convent girl, who, once she woke, sat mute and unresponsive on a plastic chair in the sloping sun of the yard. Meanwhile, Josh was staring at Pru with two enormous, myopic brown eyes and Pru was staring right back at him.

'Hey-hey, hungry boy,' she said.

She took a small tin of condensed milk from a blue-painted shelf and pierced it in two places. Then she mixed its contents in a mug with warm water and dipped in a piece of bread.

'Bread, baby,' she said.

Josh reached out his hand and took the bread from her.

'Bread, baby,' he said.

This was the first thing that Josh had ever said. By the second chunk of bread, he had offered her a smile. She clapped her hands. He clapped his hands. His eyes were fixed on hers.

'You got sleep in your eyes, Mr Baby,' she said. 'Come here to Mama Pru.'

It was Friday night, but by Sunday, though the convent girl had remained impassive as ever, impossible to shift, bedded on the mattress, or making little rushes upon chunks of bread and mugs of tea, Josh was following Pru round the house like an eager, jaunty puppy.

'What's your name, baby?' she said.

'Gorsh,' Josh said.

'Hey-hey, Josh,' Pru said. '*Sawubona*, Josh.'

Then, when it was time for church, while Dora stayed home to mind the convent girl, the child was hoisted in his blanket and tied to Pru's back.

And Josh, whose memory has held no image of his own wretched mother, finds that, all through his life, his earliest recollections are all bound up with Pru. There is Pru and there are the Silvers, with their house – his house – on Durban's south ridge. And there is the St Moses Holy Apostolic Church. He has an idea that his interest in the performing arts must have begun with that introductory Sunday visit to Pru's church. Within the silence and gloom of his early life, it was his first theatrical experience; a transfiguration via joyful noise; clapping hands and swaying hips; trance states and ululations; fabulous harmonies of the human voice; down by the riverside.

By Monday morning, Pru had still got nowhere in her attempted communications with the convent girl, though she had tried in English, Afrikaans and Zulu.

'Where do you come from?'

'What is your name?'

'Where is your home?'

And, having decided upon a day of spring-cleaning in the Silvers' house while the couple were away in Cape Town, Pru tied Josh in his blanket and took him with her on the bus. Upon her arrival at the house, she had the bad luck to run into the next-door neighbour, a person already suspicious of the Silvers' way of life – white people letting the side down, 'spoiling the native girl', letting in callers of African and Asian aspect, who, in defiance of local etiquette, went in and out through the front door.

'Nanny, whose is this child?' he said, looming at Pru over the fence. Above the low growl of his Dobermann, he added, 'This not a native child.'

'No, master,' Pru said, all too aware that, thanks to her nightly baby-bathing efforts, Josh's hair was now less matted and less densely curled. It was revealing itself as distinctly non-Afro and its colour, in the vivid sunlight, was showing up as chestnut brown.

'No, master, this is my daughter's madam's child,' Pru said. 'She is very sick, master.'

'And does the sick madam know you're running round with the *kleinbaas* tied to your back like a piccanin?' he said. 'Where's your daughter?'

'She's looking after her madam, my master,' Pru said.

The interrogator, half satisfied, decided to change tack.

'Your madam and your master's gone away,' he said. 'How you going to get in?'

'I've got the key, master,' Pru said, slightly regretting that Ida Silver had given her the front-door key, where a back-door key would have been a better thing for the purpose of appeasing the neighbour.

And then she was indoors and the episode had passed. Pru sighed with relief that Josh had kept on sleeping throughout the exchange because, these three days past, the child had burst into speech and his talking had become incessant. The problem was that his accent was tellingly like her own. Josh was not as yet speaking in the accent of the master race.

So the Silvers returned from Cape Town to a small, dark-eyed child, who confronted them with a winning smile and with Pru-like hand-clap gestures. He offered them a welcome-home song that he'd picked up at Pru's church. He sang to the tune of 'What A Friend We Have In Jesus' but, naturally, he did so in Zulu. *Namhla Niyabizwa.*

Bernie and Ida Silver, who existed as a sort of two-person Citizens' Advice Bureau, were swiftly alerted to the problem of the mute white woman, whom, they could fully appreciate, had the potential to spell a bundle of trouble for Pru. Ida promptly broke the law to drive back with Pru and the child into the native location, where the two women entered the yard. The convent girl was seated on her plastic chair, staring expressionless at the wall.

And then, a sort of miracle occurred – or at the least a stroke of good fortune. As a one-time Polish refugee, Ida Silver had spent five years of her early adult life in British Mandated Palestine. There she had not only chatted with Arab children in the street and bought falafel from the street vendors. She had also worked as a teaching assistant in a small convent school run by French-speaking nuns.

Now, as she scrutinised the convent girl, she had a lucky hunch.

'*Bonjour, Madame,*' she said. '*Comment vas-tu?*'

The convent girl swallowed hard and kept on staring at the wall. Then she turned slowly, very slowly, and she began to stare at Ida.

'*Je veux rentrer chez moi,*' she said.

'*Je comprends,*' Ida said. '*Madame, où habites-tu?*'

The convent girl turned her gaze back to the wall and stared so fixedly that Ida thought she had lost her.

'Beirut,' said the convent girl at last. Then she added, '*J'étais volée de mon couvent.*'

'*Volée?*' Ida said, though nothing startled her these days, what with the stories people brought to her; people tricked, hijacked, enslaved, abused; people taken far from home; coerced into unspeakable forms of labour.

'*J'étais volée de mon couvent,*' the woman said again. '*Je veux rentrer chez moi.*'

'*Tu es religieuse?*' Ida said.

'*Le couvent,*' said Josh's mother, '*est mon chez-moi.*'

'*Et l'enfant?*' Ida said. '*Ton enfant, Madame?*'

The convent girl glanced, expressionless, indifferent, from Josh to Ida, from Ida to Josh.

'*L'enfant peut rester,*' she said.

The women agreed that the convent girl, along with her child, needed to be transferred at once to the Silvers' white suburban house, where at least her presence would not be illegal while the business was properly thought through. So the convent girl, on the arm of her redeemer, was coaxed into the front passenger seat of Ida's VW Beetle.

The convent girl appeared to have no papers, though, at last, she had her own name. Lilette Habibi. She had no passport, no birth certificate, no nuptial document, but she remembered her address. That is to say, she remembered her address in Beirut, not her address in Boksburg. It was Dora who provided this last.

And Bernie Silver, though he made the tedious train journey north and gained access to the repossessed mock-Tudor house, found that the place had been stripped bare – that was except for some undated pages of cursive French handwriting, neatly executed on the back of what looked like ripped-up drawer-lining paper. He put them in his pocket for Ida.

Scouring the public records, he found evidence of the woman's marriage in the summer of 1952. He was also able to locate the Mother Superior in Beirut, who, after a space of only four years, was unsurprisingly still in place and patently delighted to contemplate the return of *la petite chère Lilette.* So the convent girl, bathed and sluiced – her teeth fixed, her hair trimmed, her feet once more in shoes, her documents replaced – eventually made the long journey home, this time in the company of a Lebanese Catholic priest, though she made it without her heirloom linens and handmade lace. Also, without her child.

Lilette returned into the arms of the order, in which she at last became a novice and then a fully fledged nun. That was until 1967, when, along with one of the other sisters, she was caught up in an Israeli bombing raid on a village south-east of Tyre. Lilette was undertaking her first and only visit to the place of her mother's birth.

Josh's father, initially traceable, thanks to his prison sentence, died by fire, with uncanny symmetry, in 1967. The fire was in the Boksburg boarding house, still owned by the convent girl's cousin. Started one winter's night by a trio of muddle-headed druggies, who had set light to the furniture in an effort to keep themselves warm, the fire soon engulfed the proxy husband who was sleeping in the room directly above.

So Josh, unimpeded by either of his birth parents, grew up in the house of two benign and bookish human rights activists, whose long-ago decision not to have any children, given the high-risk nature of their lives, was pleasantly confounded by the coming of the convent girl's dark-eyed child.

As the product of neglect in infancy, Josh was never bothered that both his adoptive parents spent long hours at work, or that he was required to share them with that mass of needy humanity which passed through their front door. Then, of course, there was Pru. That was until she eventually retired, by which time Josh was fifteen.

And he was fifteen when, though quite able to drive but as yet without a licence, he offered himself in an emergency to undertake an illicit mercy errand for his mother. He drove into what was then rural northern Natal with several boxes of food and clothing for the indigent family of a black political prisoner. And on his way back, in rainy darkness, he almost collided with a woman – a pregnant woman – who was walking in the middle of the road. She was carrying a suitcase on her head and she had lost her job that day. She had also lost her papers, which her employer had withheld. Josh gave her a soft drink and coaxed her into the car.

'Come home with me,' he said. 'My mother can get your papers back. She's a lawyer. It's what she does.'

So the woman spent the night – and many nights thereafter – in the unused servant's room in the backyard of the Silvers' house. And after four months her little son Jack was born.

Though Josh turned out to be an academic sort of boy, this always ran in tandem with his enthusiasm for performance; an inclination which was somewhat alien to his adoptive parents, though they enjoyed the diversion of his home theatricals, his love of toy-cupboard puppet theatres, his flair for backward somersaults and singing and mimicry. From early on, Bernie Silver took note of Josh's impromptu abilities whenever those dreary white church services were relayed over the radio. In the past he would simply have reached out and switched them off but, with Josh's coming, he noticed that, where the congregation sang in unison, the boy – and no doubt he'd learned it from Pru – could ad-lib his own alto line. Bernie bought him a piano and arranged for him to have lessons. Later on, Josh saved his pocket money and bought a red electric guitar. While at junior school he joined the gym club, in which he was the only boy in a group of nineteen little girls; a lone male participant in black shorts and T-shirt, enveloped in a cloud of feminine pastel.

As a high-school student, Josh was small, popular and comfortable with himself; a curly-haired, myopic person measuring five foot three, who involved himself with the school orchestra and acted in all the school plays; an uncircumcised, sort of Jewish-unJewish boy from a secular, agnostic Jewish-unJewish family; a boy with a bent for Zulu harmonies and a repertoire of Apostolic hymns. And, though he was required to tolerate the odd teasing pleasantry with regard to his family's politics – 'Sir, sir, Silver's reading *Pravda*, sir' (that's if he was ever observed reading the *New Statesman* under the desk) – Josh was never seriously picked on, except briefly in his sixteenth year and by one particular pupil: a public-school thicko, as Josh assessed him; a tall, handsome boy, who had entered the school well into the fifth form and stayed for a mere five weeks.

Josh remembered him for not much more than that he stole the red guitar and that he was endowed with an idiotic name; like something out of *Molesworth*. James Alexander Marchmont-Thomas. He was a boy who liked to waylay younger boys in the toilets and shake them down for money. He considered it the soul of wit to use curiously dated insults, such as 'Commie' and 'Yid'. He had a little archaic chant that tended to stale with repetition.

'Crikey Ike-y, King of the Jews, sold his wife for a pair of shoes.' The boy was sent down for reasons undisclosed. Naturally, the whole class knew that it was for dealing drugs in school.

Then at university, where white males were on the whole signed up for engineering and accountancy, Josh opted for French and drama; both areas in which he was once again enfolded by clouds of pastel-clad girls, with whom he happily sketched theatrical costumes from the court of King Louis XIV and staged scenes from Molière and Lully and from Shakespeare's late romantic plays. And, while the predominant mood was for Chekhov and Ibsen, he was more preoccupied with baroque theatre and strolling players and masques. He wanted to connect the drama he was studying with acrobatics and dance. So he was once again a bit of an oddball, but one who was proving extremely useful for playing Ariel and Puck. Then one day, hoping to sign up for lessons, he took himself off to the ballet school, which was where he met Hattie Thomas; Hattie who, on the instant, became the love of his life.

She was sitting straight-backed on the church-hall floor when he approached on a Saturday morning. He could see her through the glass panel in the door. She had placed herself in the centre of a ring of little girls; ten little girls in pink leotards. They all had their hands sticking upwards in the air, palms pressed against their temples, sitting tall and straight, as they mimed putting on their royal crowns. Next, they did wiggling their fingers. They did looking up to the ceiling; looking down to the floor; up and down; up and down. They did lying on the floor making star shapes. They did high-stepping walks; Puss-in-Boots walks, paws bent in front of them. They made frog's legs, knees apart, bending down at the bar.

All this time, Josh, staring through the glass, was transfixed by the dainty young woman in charge. Short schoolgirl hair, sleek, dark and straight. She had large, widely spaced, velvety eyes and a circular patch of natural high colour on the wing of each high cheekbone. To Josh she was nature's Coppélia. She was the girl in a picture sequence he'd perused, of the doll in *The Tales of Hoffmann* who must dance helplessly faster and faster. His own heart had begun to beat faster and faster, until he felt that he might faint.

'Jesus Christ!' he said to himself and he quickly looked away.

Then the class was over and Josh walked into the hall.

Hattie had never taught an adult before, but she agreed to give him some lessons, one-to-one. And Josh, she found, was a most apt pupil; a quick learner who was prepared to work hard. He proved himself to be lots of fun and was soon her inseparable friend. He was always at the church hall. She was forever on the campus. Josh became a feature of her twice-yearly dance shows. She became a part of his student drama productions. *Pas de deux*.

And Josh, who, after completing an MA, was awarded a London postgraduate scholarship, had high hopes of taking Hattie with him; Hattie who had revealed herself to him as a passionate anglophile; a girl for whom the mere idea of Angel tube station induced high excitement for its proximity to Sadler's Wells.

And then things started to go wrong. Hattie appeared to get cold feet. She wavered. She fell for Herman. ('But you'll always be my very best friend, Josh. My best friend in all the world.') The Aged Parents were at this time being hounded into exile; starved out; banned from doing their jobs. Bernie and Ida had clandestine plans for relocating to Dar es Salaam. They quietly began to sell off some of their things. They invited Josh to pick a favourite item, and they did the same with Jack; Jack, the maid's boy, soon to be dispatched to a boarding school in Swaziland at the Silvers' expense.

Prior to their flight, they made arrangements for Jack's mother to be employed as a domestic by kindly, like-minded friends. Then Ida and Bernie crossed the border with one small suitcase each. They had made it to Botswana by the time Josh went, after dark, to the ballet school to say his goodbyes to Hattie, since his own departure was imminent. It was the bleakest night he could remember. Everything was going; going, going, or gone. And even then, in his precious last moments with Hattie, they were interrupted by a demanding male voice that jarred at them from beyond the door.

'Excuse me a moment,' Hattie said and she slipped out into the corridor.

Josh could hear what sounded like some sort of altercation.

'Bitch!' he heard the male voice say – a voice that was unplaceable but somehow familiar to him – and he stepped out into the darkness of the corridor in time to see a tall male figure swinging his way round the corner and out of sight.

Both he and Hattie stood in the silence and the dark. Then, after a minute or so, they heard the clang of the outer doors. There were footfalls on the stone pathway between the gravestones.

Hattie was rubbing her arm.

'Chinese burns,' she said. 'That was my brother.' She had only rarely mentioned her brother, a twin, from whom she was estranged. 'Wanting to scrounge some money off me. But I didn't have any, you see.'

But Josh had had money; quite a lot of it. Bernie had left it with him, in an envelope labelled 'Gertrude'. The money was intended to tide over the maid until her new employers returned from their holiday. And Josh had stupidly left the envelope in the pocket of his jacket, which was hanging on a coat peg in the cloakroom. So on the following day – the day of his own departure – he went to the bank and drew out what constituted a hefty tranche of his UK scholarship money, in order to compensate the maid.

He arrived in London at dawn the next morning, a whole lot poorer than he had meant to be, and he made his way, via the A–Z, into the heart of Bloomsbury. And it was thanks to Marty and Keiran and Tamsin, who offered him cut-price sleeping space on the floor of their shared student house, that he survived his first few weeks; that was the very same student house in which, a year later, he met Caroline.

And now, after the opera; after the performance of *Rigoletto*, as he and his wife and his mother-in-law are on the way home, it's twenty hours before his first flight home in almost twenty years. Caroline is finally driving down the last stretch of winding, sick-making road towards her mother's house. And then they have dropped off his mother-in-law and have seen her safely inside.

'I'm sorry about tonight,' Caroline says into the silence, but Josh doesn't respond. 'Mum had already bought the tickets,' she says. 'There was nothing I could do about it.' Briefly, she takes her left hand from the steering wheel and places it on his knee. 'I'm really and truly sorry, Josh,' she says. 'I'll make it up to you, I promise.'

Josh knows by now that this does not mean Caroline will don the silver Hollywood pyjamas and spend an evening – maybe a whole Sunday – idling in bed with him; takeaway fish-and-chip cartons and an empty bottle of Freixenet rolling about on the floor. Because lovely Caroline – lovely as ever, in that gasp-inducing way – Caroline, who, year in, year out, can make the unworkable work, has unlearned the art of idling.

'I'll work so hard on the house,' she says. 'You and Zoe will stretch your eyes with delight when you get back.' Then she says, 'How was the opera, by the way? I mean *your* opera.'

Josh laughs.

'Oh *my* opera,' he says. 'That was fine. That was good.' And then, in order to exorcise the Witch Woman from his thoughts, he starts to tell her about a little baroque opera house in the Czech Republic that he's angling to visit with his students. That's if he can get the funding.

'It's got all these wooden trapdoors and massive ropes and cog wheels under the floor,' he says. 'And pulleys in the loft space. Maybe you could come with me?'

After that, they go on to the old red bus in the farmer's field off the Abingdon Road. By now Josh is no longer sleepy and, at three in the morning, he gets up and swaps to Zoe's bed, fearing that his wakefulness will be disturbing to Caroline. He snaps on his daughter's little bedside lamp and picks up one of her paperbacks. *Lola Comes to London*, by Henrietta Marchmont. He reads the biographical note on the back. The author is a former ballet teacher who lives in Durban, South Africa. She is married to an architect and has three teenage children. Marchmont, Josh is thinking to himself. As in Marchmont-Thomas? As in James Alexander Marchmont-Thomas? As in the tedious, druggie posh boy who once stole his red guitar? That person was *Hattie's brother*?! Hattie Thomas's twin? Of course! The ne'er-do-well; the bullying sibling; the familiar voice in the corridor. Hattie's brother was none other than the Crikey Ike-y boy.

It takes Josh just over ninety minutes to read the whole of *Lola Comes to London*. He reads parts of it with moist eyes. Then he gets up and goes for a walk along the river from Donnington Bridge to Iffley. When he returns, it is no longer dark and the blackbirds are welcoming the dawn. He faxes the conference organisers, recommending that they issue a last minute invitation to Henrietta Marchmont, local author and long-time dance exponent; also known as Mrs Herman Marais. Then he packs his bag.

Chapter Five

Cat

Cat is so sick of her mother that half the time she wishes the woman would literally drop dead. And she doesn't even have to speak to drive you mad. It's like just everything about her. *Everything.* Like that stupid ballet walk for a start. And like the way she looks in the mirror when she's putting on her eye make-up. Like she was that dumbo Audrey Hepburn from the 1950s or something. D-R-I-P. Sort of Bambified and precious – like she was a nymph in that song 'Where'er You Walk' that Miss Baines got them to sing in choir. Well, that's from when Cat still went to choir, like last term. Anyway, it's the way her mum wears all this 'blusher', so she looks like a doll. Especially because she's such a midget anyway. And the way she sort of tries not to wince when Cat walks past the china cupboard like you were an elephant, or a herd of wildebeest or something. And now that Michelle's gone and stolen all Cat's friends, her mother just knows that something's wrong, so she's forever giving Cat that kind of sideways Oh-God-you-poor-social-cripple look and thinking that you don't notice.

And, as well as that, Cat just hates that boring Englishified crap her mother's got in the house. That stuff she's inherited from her revolting parents, i.e., Grandpa Ghoul and Old

Mother Dribble, though Cat knows her dad's got rid of most of it even before she and the others were born. Like none of her friends' parents have got that kind of snobby stuff – well, that's like when she had any friends to speak of, like before Michelle and them decided to start freezing her out. But anyway, she's got all these old cupboards and desks and things called dopy names like 'tallboy' and 'whatnot' and 'davenport', just like she wanted the whole family to be wearing crinolines and living in la-la land or something.

Like if you take the kitchen – just for example – she's got this like folksy dresser thing that nearly takes up all of one wall and it's got these rows of flowery plates and jugs and blah, like from those kind of places in England where they used to make little kids work in factories, grinding up bones to put in the clay, and then they all got poisoned from the lead and the mercury, or they used to fall into the kilns and burn to death. And it's nearly all stuff they never even actually use. It's just for sitting there and looking Ye Olde.

And then she's got these 'mantel clocks' and this stupid grandfather clock that drives everyone crazy because it's forever making you late for school – but she'll go, 'Oh but the face is so pretty. Don't you think so, Cattie-pie?' Plus there are these wheelback chairs in the kitchen that, like, come to bits when you pull them out and sit on them the wrong way round, and she'll go, 'But the grain on that elm wood is so lovely. That's the thing about elm.'

Then, suddenly, like last week, she goes, 'Oh, Cattie-pie, please don't use that gorgeous jug to wash your bike. For heaven's sake, let me find you a plastic bucket. It's Portmeirion, sweetheart,' when it's just some crappy great thing like probably from before people had washbasins indoors. And it comes like the same size as a bucket, practically. And it's got a crack all down one side. Well, it has now.

And – pur-leez – that's not even to start on this arty sugar-bowl thingy she's like always kept on the kitchen table. Like it's not even meant to be a sugar bowl, it's just like a big silver cup with dents in it that says 'Presented to James Alexander Marchmont-Thomas on the occasion of his confirmation, 23 September 1875', because some ancestor who's got the same name as her mom's unmentionable brother, Uncle James, who's most likely dead for all she knows, and she keeps 'sugar lumps' in it. Note, 'lumps', because she thinks 'lumps' are more posh and Englishified than proper sugar, but most likely she does it to try and stop you adding sugar to your breakfast cereal, or your yogurt. Well, that's just tough, isn't it, because all you have to do is go and get the sugar packet down from the cupboard. Moron.

And then there's even this completely embarrassing thing, like this oar thingy, from some rowing boat that's fixed to the wall, way up on the top-floor landing – OK, so no one's actually going to see it up there, except her, when she's off to her witchy little turret that she calls her 'stud-ee', but it's there because Grandpa Ghoul has made her promise to keep it because of some stupid great-uncle who was a rowing Blue at Oxford and one day it's supposed to go to the unmentionable and probably dead brother, along with the dented sugar bowl etc. Or maybe even the whole house is meant for him as well?

Plus there's this twirly bookcase full of pocky-looking Dickens that no one's ever going to read, especially not her mom, because (a) it's like printed on that old-fashioned scratchy kind of Bronco Bill lav paper that the Ghoul and Old Mother Dribble still have in their bathroom, and (b) she's always too busy writing those dumbo ballet books of hers. Lola. And then if you ever tell her you think the Lola books are crap, she'll go, 'Oh but it keeps me out of mischief, Cat.' Like what mischief, for crying out loud? And she'll like pretend she isn't offended. She just gets this doll-eyed Audrey Hepburn look again, like from her 'favourite' film, *Roman*

Holiday, and she says, 'I mean no harm by it, Cattie-pie. Don't let it bother you.' Cat reckons her mom thinks that anything to do with Italy is 'cultured'.

Cat seriously wants to die these days, whenever her mother calls her Cattie-pie and sweetheart, etc, and her voice can really grate the way it sounds so pathetic and snobby and 'actualleh-actualleh'. But the worst thing – I mean *the* worst – is that, in the very first one of the Lola books she wrote, like when Cat was about eight, she's put in this really freaky dedication and there it is, still in the school library ten years later – well, OK, eight years, but, anyway, it's there and it says 'For dearest Cattie, who danced with me on the Campo Sant'Angelo'. I mean, Jay Christ, how C-R-I-N-G-E is that?

Plus she was always calling her Cattie-pie in front of Michelle, and now, of course, Michelle and them have all pounced on the Lola book and they're being really mean about it, and telling everybody – just because she didn't think fast enough to swipe it off the shelf when they first started being so horrible to her. Anyway, nobody at school has ever called her Cattie, or even Cat – not since last year, when she got all her friends and even all the teachers to start calling her Kate. Except that now, of course, Michelle and the others are forever saying 'Cattie-pie' behind her back and sniggering. Someone's even written 'Cattie-pie ate the pies' in the girls' lav. Ha ha ha. Anyway, she's thinner than Michelle. That's since this week. Michelle's bum is bigger and she's got these really short stubby little legs.

The thing is it was all because Alan liked her and she liked him and she would have said yes to him, except that Michelle went on and on and on about what a slimeball he was. On and on until she had to agree, because Michelle was her best friend, and so she had to tell Alan no, she didn't like him, not as a boyfriend anyway. And then guess who moved in and took him over, just like that? Bloody Michelle. Of course. But not only that, because now Alan's been acting like she was kind of so repulsive, like you could get leprosy or something if you went near her, and between him and Michelle and Eleanor and the others, the whole crowd has just pushed her out.

They've got this special way of going really quiet the moment she comes near, or else they make this kind of growly noise in their throats, as if they were having to warn each other about her coming their way, like they were going to get poisoned if she breathed on them. Then they all start looking at their fingernails like mad, because none of them will look her in the eye. It's been going on now ever since last term began, like about eleven weeks, because Alan and Michelle must have got it together during the holidays before the ones they've just had, and she knows they call her Miss Piggy behind her back, when it isn't Cattie-pie.

And another thing is they make out like she's a big lump by leaving stuff in her desk that they've cut out of magazines about cellulite, etc. It's just like one day she was Kate Marais, with a whole crowd of friends; Kate Marais, who was always best at history and maths and drawing and netball – best at everything, to be honest – Kate Marais, who always got chosen to sing solo in the choir, and then the next day she was the great untouchable. And by now she wouldn't even mind so much if they'd just liter-ally leave her alone, but they don't. They pretend they do, but then they keep finding ways of tormenting her.

And now there's not even anyone to talk to out of school, what with Suz and Jonno gone to uni and her dad away all the time, because he keeps on phoning up and postponing his coming back – and now he's suddenly gone off to Maputo for another week, or it'll be Botswana or London – and with her mom who's got noth-ing better to do than snoop on you, like the way her eyes follow you round the room when you're trying to get your breakfast, or like when you get up from the table to use the lav. It's like you get the feeling she's got those compound eyes like an insect that can see all over the place. Plus it's a really big piss-off, the way she'll try to put these crap cereals like puffed brown rice and Shreddies and stuff at the front of the cupboard, in case you'll just grab one of them by mistake, instead of taking the Coco Pops.

Anyway, about the Coco Pops, etc, Cat's already lost twelve kilos, only no one's going to notice, are they? Not that she wants her mother to notice. She wouldn't give her the satisfaction, which is why she wears Jonno's old trackie bottoms all the time, and his old baggy T-shirts when it isn't school. See, if you've got a sort of podgy round face, then everyone just thinks the rest of you is podgy and round to match. But Cat knows she's got thinner, so fuck her. You just have to pray that she'll soon disappear into her witchy little room – sorry, her 'stud-ee'. That's what she calls it – her 'stud-ee' – where she writes all that Lola crap, and another thing that's disgusting is that her mom has got this like black-and-silver tutu thing that's hanging from the ceiling over her desk, like strung up on some of her dad's fishing line. She says to think of it as 'sculpture' if it bothers you so much.

Well, maybe she hasn't noticed but Cat's stuck her brother's bowie knife through the crotch, so now it's got a slash in it, like in those purply Silk Cut cigarette adverts. That's if she's ever thinking of it as one of the heirlooms, along with all the clocks and 'whatnots' and 'davenports' and crap. Anyway, how can a tutu be sculpture? Because sculpture's got to be made out of stone or bronze or wood or something, hasn't it? Otherwise it's just needlework. I mean, a tutu is like just a kitschy sort of sticky-out party dress that shows your fanny. Plus it's repulsive to think that someone else's been all sweaty in it. And, by the way, her mom's feet are really disgusting as well. It's from all the dancing. It makes your feet go all kind of pervy-looking and weird.

* * *

Her dad would really love to have another massive blitz on the house, she can tell. She reckons maybe that's why he goes away so much, because of the 'davenport' factor. It's started getting on his nerves. Because now he's sent an email saying he's got to go to Accra, for God's sake. I mean, it's thanks to her dad that their house is like really nice – that's apart from the 'what-not' and the crap chairs that come to bits in your hand. Like Michelle and Alan and them – they were always like saying how fab her house was, with the swimming pool and the open space and everything. Well, it is. Like it's got all this glass that makes it look like those photographs of the Pyramide at the Louvre, and the sanded floors and everything. And her dad's got this agreement with her mom about how this Persian rug in the big sitting room is allowed to spend six months on the floor and six months in store. Only now, because he hasn't been around, the rug is still on the floor when it should be in the storeroom and she just pretends she hasn't 'got round to it'. Like if it weren't for her dad they'd probably have those horrible carpets every-where, like in the pictures you see of Buckingham Palace, that looks like a tart's boudoir with all the gold and stuff, and the hideous oil paintings.

And her mother would probably be sending Cat to that snobby girls' school, like with the bonnets and the boring green uniforms, like what she went to herself. But at least her dad believes in co-ed. Cat's decided that, when he gets back, she's going to make him send her to another school. Like a boarding school, where no one knows her, and she's going to make sure that, before she goes, she'll be the thinnest girl in the class as well as the brainiest. Well, she nearly always gets top marks for everything.

Meanwhile, before that happens, she's just got to do her long art project, and her mom keeps nosing in, like dropping oh so casual remarks about it, like you don't already know that you've got to hand it in, like in three weeks' time, and you haven't done anything yet, not even thought of a subject, and you're pissing yourself.

'Oh Cat, by the way, that project of yours. What about masks? Just a thought.'

Like thinking has ever been a big thing with her. Stupid cow.

What's more, Cat knows that her parents would probably be divorced if it weren't for her because Suz and Jonno told her that once, when she wouldn't stop pestering them to let her play when she was little. That's because they were always so 'together' and a bit older, so she was the odd one out. So now you can tell her mom's really sorry she never had an abortion – so much for 'dearest Cattie-pie' and 'sweetheart' and 'the Campo Sant'Angelo', and all that bullshit.

What's really even more of a piss-off is that Michelle and them have started ringing her cell phone and then just cutting out whenever she picks up so she's stopped picking up, only now they ring from a call box so she can't tell from the numbers who it is, which means she can't even answer her own phone any more.

Anyway, it's like a week on from when her dad last emailed about going to Accra and meanwhile something slightly weird has been happening at home because first of all her mother's been twittering on about this 'charming young man' that's come to live in her dad's new annexe, and how she really must have him in to dinner, if only she wasn't so 'busy', because she's got 'a deadline', and how she just knows Cat will find him really interesting, etc – as if you'd give a shit about anyone she thinks is charming or interesting.

'Charming' probably means he's like pretended he's heard about all her Lola books, or something. Plus he's probably about thirty-five. 'Giacomo', she says. That's the tenant's name. 'Giacomo', because he's just come from Milan. But, as well as that, her mom's been banging on about how she's got to do this 'presentation' at 'a conference', if you please, and she's pretending like she wants Cat's advice – well, that's until she's started suddenly staying out all hours, like from about three days ago until yesterday, when she comes home with this weirdo bloke who's about as much of a midget as she is – i.e., he's about twenty centimetres shorter than Cat – and they've got these takeouts from the Italian deli that they spread out all over the kitchen table for supper, like about a million calories per item when she usually eats like a bird, and she's saying, 'Do tuck in, Cattie-pie. Join us, sweetheart, do,' and pretending that they really want her to stay and eat with them, but she's buggered if she's going to sit there and watch her mother being embarrassing with the midget, who, she says, is 'working' with her on a mime sequence about that ballet she was banging on about last week.

'Oh Cat,' she says. 'This is my dear old friend Josh Silver from way back. He's here for the conference, you see. We're planning a mime to illustrate my talk. So now you and I have both got projects with deadlines.' Ha. Ha. Then she says, 'He's got a daughter called Zoe – a bit younger than you.'

Yeah. Right. I mean, so what? Does she want Cat to alert the media about it, or what?

'It would be so nice if you could meet one day,' she says.

Anyway, then she and the midget start munching all this lasagne and stuff and drinking all her dad's red wine and then they disappear upstairs and start moving furniture around and Cat reckons any day now her mother will be prancing round in the sweaty black tutu with the hole in the crotch. Especially as, three days later, the midget has become a bit of a fixture and they're forever talking and laughing about shit all and she's even heard her mom tell him that mean little story she loves, about Cat's favourite aunt, Lettie, her dad's sister, who's been going to a Zulu class to make up for how 'badly' she's always treated black people in the past. Or that's what Lettie's told her.

'Shame,' her mom is saying, and she's trying to mimic Lettie, but she's like seriously crap at doing accents. 'To think we've always expected "them", with their low intelligence, to learn both our languages, and us, with our high intelligence, we haven't bothered to learn theirs.'

Well, it does sound a bit funny maybe, when you don't hear Lettie saying it, but her Aunt Lettie is really nice, like the way she always drives the maid to the doctor for her diabetes check-ups and stuff and she'll bake these amazing chocolate brownies, even though she's got four kids and she works part-time as a bookkeeper for her husband and anyway she's like really pretty.

But the good thing is, about the midget, it means that at least her mom's eyes aren't forever like following you to the lav, or squinting at you sideways if you're eating Coco Pops, because, when they aren't upstairs, then they're like gadding off to the NSA Gallery, or the Stable Theatre, or the BAT Arts Centre, or somewhere else they think is cultured enough for them. So Cat's feeling free to dawdle in the downstairs bathroom that faces over the back garden and she's been in there for absolutely ages, but now she's just brushing her teeth like mad before school, because, let's face it, the getting-thin/chucking-up thing can leave you with like serious dog-breath.

Plus Cat's buggered if she's going to get those horrible rattly black teeth like she knows you can get if you're really stupid about it, because of all the stomach acid. Anyway, she's just having a swish with Corsodyl mouthwash when she looks up and out of the window she can see this person walking up the path from her dad's new annexe and she thinks, Well, he's just got to be the new tenant her mother's been going on about while she's been like trying not to listen. And, actually, more fool her, just this once, because, Jesus H. Christ – and just excuse me a minute while I swoon, OK? – this guy is, like er-MAZ-ing.

The tenant is like about one metre ninety – like, well, taller than her – and he's like dressed all in black. Black long-sleeved T-shirt, black jeans, black lace-up shoes, but – really – so cool. I mean, not like trainers, or like school shoes or anything. Really classy. And he looks about like twenty-something, and he's quite thin, but not all weedy or anything. Just narrow, like maybe about size 32 in trousers? And he's like really muscly as well, and also a bit Afro-looking, with this short-short black Afro hair, so you can see this amazing head, just like so beautiful, the way it's like all curvy at the back when he turns a bit sideways towards the vine with the passion fruit. Like he was an ancient Egyptian pharaoh or something. And like cheekbones and everything. And he's got this fantastic mouth, and the beautiful dark skin – well, sort of halfway dark skin, anyway.

And he's like so gorgeous that Cat wants to die of embarrass- ment because the bathroom window's been open the whole time and – OK, so he's still maybe about twenty metres away – but, oh my God, she thinks, he's just got to have heard the sound of her chucking up, so now she won't be able to face him – ever – because he'll just know it was her. Oh, shit-shit-S-H-I-T! Especially as, from the very moment she sees him, she just knows for certain that Alan is like definitely yesterday's news. Anyway, he looks like a slug and she wouldn't go out with him now if he paid her. It's like he thinks he's so cool but he's practically an albino, like with the ears that go neon pink when the sun shines through them and he's forever having a quick dab with that Tea Tree Spot Stick on his so not gorgeous cleft chin, when he thinks you aren't looking, plus his teeth aren't that great either and the back of his head is too flat.

And, right then, Cat knows that she's going out that same day and she's getting like black hair dye and black eyelash dye and all her clothes are going to be black, black, black. Only by evening she's kind of chickened out for the moment, because of how it would be at school next day, with Michelle and them. And maybe she'll get a bit thinner first?

The tenant keeps regular hours. Cat knows this because over the next four days she's always in the same bathroom at exactly seven-thirty in the morning, looking out. And then it's Saturday and Sunday. On Saturday he gets up and does his laundry before he goes out at about ten o'clock. She knows, because after he's gone she goes down the garden and she checks out the washing line. Then he comes home at midday with three carrier bags from Pick 'n' Pay. They must be from the Musgrave Centre. She reckons he must walk everywhere because she hasn't seen a car.

Cat's wandered down the garden on the pretext of using the pool so she takes her towel and cozzie.

'Oh good,' her mom says. 'You're going for a swim, Cattie dear.'

Of course, the more she says 'Cattie dear', the more you know she hates your guts.

Cat goes out the back door in all her clothes – or, rather, all Jonno's clothes – because if her mom sees her in her cozzie she'll be sizing up Cat's thighs and thinking how come they've got so much thinner when she eats all that chocolate and stuff. But Cat knows that her legs have got a lot thinner because she spends so much time in her bedroom without her clothes on looking at them – especially since she's got her dad to put that bolt on her bedroom door, because otherwise her mom's in there, gathering up all nineteen mouldy coffee mugs (she says) and yakking on about how leaving your pants on the floor when they've got blood on them is an 'insult' to the maid – like you do it on purpose or something.

Cat likes it that her legs are so long, but she can still see too much revolting fat and dimples everywhere. Still, there's quite a lot less of it, she knows, because she's been taking measurements

135

with a tape measure like round her thighs and her boobs and everywhere. And at least she knows she can get as thin as she likes and it's nothing to do with how much Coco Pops she eats.

But what she'd really like is to have proper sticky-out bones. Like real angles everywhere. Bones that would make her eyes look really big and her face not so round. And there's something she knows sounds really pervy, but when they started doing the Second World War in history last week, and Miss Band showed them those pictures of people in the Warsaw Ghetto, Cat thought she'd really like to look like that, with the hollow cheeks and the deep eye sockets and everything. Plus, when she's got some proper money, she's going to have a boob reduction and not tell her mom. Or even Lettie, who thinks big boobs are sexy.

Anyway, it's the weekend again, and, for two Saturdays now, Cat's noticed the tenant has hung up his washing down the bottom of the garden, on his little private line, and all of it is either pure white or pure black. None of his stuff has got patterns or colours on it. All his bedlinen and his towels are white and all his clothes are black, except for his pyjamas, which are white, and he's always got three white shirts on the line.

She reckons he does two washes, one after the other. He must do a hot white-wash and then a cold black-wash. He's got black boxer shorts, black socks, black jeans, black trousers, black T-shirts that have either got long sleeves or no sleeves, and two lightweight black lambswool pullovers that say 'agnès b'.

Cat knows the labels and the sizes and the washing instructions and the countries of origin of all the tenant's clothes – well, the washable ones, anyway – because she's taken a good careful look at all of them on the line and, anyway, she likes touching them. They say 'Jean-Paul Gaultier' and 'Adolfo Dominguez' and 'Giorgio Armani' and 'Yves Saint-Laurent' and 'Ozwald Boateng' and then they say '*Non usare caneggina di cloruro*' and '*Repasser à basse température*' and '*Laver et sécher séparément*' and '*Lavar a mano en agua fria*' and '*Lavage et repassage à l'envers*' and '*Non torcere o strizzare*'.

Then she's noticed that, for the one Sunday so far, he mostly didn't leave the garden, but even when he did it was only for a really short time. Maybe he just went to get a paper? So now, anyway, it's a Saturday when she's watching out for him to go to the Pick 'n' Pay, and then she goes down to the washing line again to touch up the tenant's things and then she thinks she might as well go through the little gate in the bamboo hedge, like on to his little private terrace with the azaleas in pots.

Then she stares through the glass of the French windows, being really careful not to make nose marks on the glass. Inside, she can see that it's all amazingly tidy and there's definitely no one inside, so she tries the door but it's locked. Shit. Anyway, after a while she thinks, So what? She might as well go and have a little poke around, and it's not really a problem because she knows exactly where all the spare keys are. They're in her dad's work room, where he's got them all labelled with little plastic tabs. And she knows, as well, that right now her mother is off doing her pirouettes and crap with the midget, so she'll never even notice what Cat's doing.

So she goes to get the keys and she comes right back, and slips out of her backless shoes and she goes inside. Hey! It's all so fab in there, she can't help just lightly touching everything she passes, like this row of little enamel saucepans and pots and the six white mugs on cup hooks and a little stainless-steel olive-oil can like a baby watering can and a small espresso pot with some coffee next to it in a silver tin that says 'Illy'.

Then she looks in the fridge, which is nearly empty except that it's got six eggs and a packet of mozzarella with a picture of a buffalo on it and some rocket in a bunch like a little bouquet of flowers and there's a jar of pesto from Genoa.

After that she crosses to the far end of the room. She sits down carefully on the edge of the tenant's bed, that's all white, white, white, with just these three huge square white pillows in a fat white row, and then she tries lying down on it, on her back, straight out with her hands at her side, hardly daring to breathe. It all makes her feel a bit scared and excited, like Goldilocks in the three bears' house. So she gets up and smooths it all over very carefully, and then she crosses to this wall of pale-birch-wood cupboards.

She opens all the doors, one by one, and stares inside. Some of it has got hanging things and some of it is like square pigeonholes full of folded stuff. Cat doesn't dare to pick up any of the folded things because the tenant's way of folding his clothes looks quite hard to do, but she takes out this plain white shirt on a hanger and holds it up against her torso, so she can see herself in the mirror on the back of the door. Then she takes out this cute black-linen suit and hooks it over the cupboard door. After that, she takes the jacket off the hanger and tries it on over Jonno's baggy T-shirt. It looks pretty terrible with the shapeless trackie bottoms that are all sort of puffy and lumpy around her hips, so first she looks at her watch and then she quickly takes them off. She tries on the suit trousers as well, but, although she can just about half squeeze herself into them as far as just above her knees, they kind of stick on her thighs and she's scared the zip will break, so she has to yank them off and just hold them up against herself, kind of like tucked under the jacket. Even so, because the jacket is so beautifully cut, Cat reckons she looks quite thin.

And then she's just putting it all back in the cupboard when she sees one of her own long blonde hairs on the lapel. Oh shit. Panic stations. But she manages to pick the hair off and she checks like mad in case there's more. Or maybe dandruff, or something. Oh yuk!

Meanwhile, all this time she's sort of been trying not to look at the tenant's desk, because she's been saving it for best. It's just

that, all along, out of the corner of her eye, there's been this amazing thing, like nothing she's ever seen before, because it's like a
normal pedestal desk with two rows of drawers, except that it's
all kind of silvery and shiny. So finally she goes up to it and she
can see that it's veneered with chrome or silver, or maybe it's tin
that looks like silver? And it's got these amazing glass handles on
the drawers, like they were bits of chandeliers. Sort of pear-drop
shapes. And, God, it must weigh about ten tons, she reckons. On
the surface he's got a fat grey stone jar with all these pens and
pencils in it, so she picks them up, one by one, and puts them
back.

Then her eyes move up towards the pictures that he's put on
the wall above the desk, because they're all so fab. It's just these
three narrow black frames in a row, with drawings in window
mounts of old-fashioned like actors in tall hats – or maybe like
acrobats – wearing those like beaky masks. Then, on the next bit
of wall, along from the desk, he's got another row of four narrow
black frames, just the same, only these have got like drawings of
bits of horse's armour, that look like maybe from the Renaissance,
because there's Italian writing on it, but best of all, on the opposite wall, all on its own, he's got this exhibition poster in a frame,
that's also just black-and-white, and it's a photograph of this fabulous skinny person – well, it's sculpture, not a real person – and it
says 'Giacometti'.

Then her eyes are back on the desk, where there's a pad of
paper that says 'Fabriano', plus there's this huge glossy book
called *Africa Explores* that's got these Benin bronzes of Portuguese
soldiers on the dust jacket, as well as some sort of bird masks
carved out of dark wood. Cat starts to flick through the book,
which is quite fun, because it's got a whole chapter on these kind
of modern paintings that get sold in street markets like in Congo
and Malawi and places, with people getting their shoes shined, or
looking in a grocery shop with lots of tinned food in the window

and Coca-Cola signs, and sexy-looking women wearing sort of batik cloths, and some of them have got speech bubbles above their heads with writing in French. Then there are all these kind of spiky sculpture things from Zimbabwe.

But what's most amazing, Cat thinks, is this whole chapter where the tenant's like put in a bookmark from a shop in Milan, and it's all pictures of these incredible tall, tall, very thin people dancing, like in a kind of procession, all in a line, and some of them are looking even taller – like about four metres high – because they're dancing on stilts. And they've all got these kind of red skirts that it says are made out of special hibiscus flowers, because the red colour is symbolic and everything. And these like mask things – well, like sort of weird tall headdresses and masks all in one that completely cover your face and there are lots of different kinds. They're like birds or animals, or other things like hunters, or trees, or spirits and stuff, and the whole person is called 'the mask', not just the mask.

What it says, like under the photographs and in the text that she reads a bit of, is that it's about special mask festivals that only happen about once every twelve years and it's to do with these people who live up in the hills in Mali called the Dogon, that she's never heard of before, but – worse luck – you have to be a man to be 'a mask' and the women aren't ever allowed to see you like while you're spending weeks in secret making the costumes and you only speak to each other in a special mask language called *Sigi-so* but mostly you don't speak at all the whole time and it's all to do with a story about how like long ago the spirits had these masks but a bird stole them and dropped them, but then this woman found them and put them on to frighten her husband and make him do what she wanted, but then an old woman told him where she'd hidden it all. Bitch! So now the mask-making and the dancing gets kept very secret until the dancers enter the village from the bush, except that mostly in Mali there's getting to be less

140

bush and more and more desert because of climate change, and the Dogon are really poor, but at least the dancing people come from high-up villages where it isn't desert.

But shit, Cat thinks, like this would be just er-MAZ-ing as a subject to do her project on. I mean, wouldn't it? And wouldn't it be like sucks to Michelle, who's started doing this really stupid project on Ndebele houses, that she thinks is so wonderful, but everyone's done it about a million times before. Plus she can't even draw to save her life.

And then Cat looks at her watch, and panics, and flees, pausing only to square up the book and grab her shoes, and, of course, lock the French windows, leaving everything just as it was. But for Cat, everything has changed. For one, she's really excited about the project and she just can't stop thinking about the book and about how she's got to get her hands on it. And also how this weekend, she's definitely – but definitely – going to do the hair dye and eyelash dye and everything. Definitely. Everything about her is going to be black. Even like her nail varnish and her lipstick. And her underwear. And Alan can eat his heart out, because she's going to be so cool. Just like that Giacomo. Just like that Giacometti.

All through the weekend, Cat is making her plans. First of all, on Friday night, she looks on her computer to see if there's stuff about the Dogon, and there's loads of it, as it turns out, but nearly all of it's rubbish. Still, she prints out some of it anyway, but, even when it isn't rubbish, none of it is as good as what's in the tenant's book. Then, on Saturday morning, she goes to the Musgrave Centre, because, just maybe, they've got that same book in the library, but they haven't. There isn't really anything much about the Dogon, just lots about the Zulus, but she takes down some references from African art books and also some anthropology books, so she'll be able write a bibliography, which is where you have to make this list at the end of your project of all the other books you've pretended to have read.

To tell you the truth, Cat's quite relieved they haven't got the book – *the* book – because, for one, it'll mean no one else in her class is going to get hold of it, and another thing is that, although it's like a really scary idea, it's kind of magic, the idea of being in there in the annexe, sitting at the beautiful tenant's silver desk for hours, and with all his beautiful clothes and things around you, and being able to work from his very own book without him even knowing. Or her mom, or anyone. Like just to be bunking off school and sneaking in there day after day for a whole week. So cool.

But first of all she's just got to have the black hair and the black clothes and all. That's for sure, so that's her second reason for being in the Musgrave Centre that Saturday. She's got to go to the pharmacy and check out all the dyes. So she goes and gets this box of eyelash dye that says it'll do eyebrows as well, and then she goes to the shelves with all the hair dyes, only these are more difficult because there are so many, so she reckons she might as well just buy the cheapest. She gets two of these little sachet things with like dotted lines on them where you have to cut open the corners with scissors, and then she goes home.

She does the eyelash dye and the eyebrows in her bedroom that same day, with the door bolted, and it works really well, even though she's terrified all through that she's going to get this stinging stuff in her eyes, so she's really careful. You have to put these pads under your eyes first of all, and then you use two separate lotions from these two tiny tubes, one after the other, and then you have to wait for about fifteen minutes before you sponge it all off. But, hey! When she's finished it all looks so fab. Like even without any eyeliner or mascara or anything, her eyes look about twice as big as normal and her lashes are really long, like about nearly a centimetre, which she's never even noticed before, because they were always so weedy and pale. Anyway, she puts on black mascara, just to make her eyelashes look really thick right to the ends, and she puts black eyeliner on her lids as well.

Then she goes downstairs, where her mom doesn't even seem to notice, except that she gives Cat a kind of smuggy-looking smile, but it's kind of pleased-ish in a vague sort of way, and anyway, at least it's not that Oh-God-you-poor-social-cripple look that she's been doing recently.

She just says, 'You look so nice, Cattie-pie,' but then she starts being chatty, just when you want to look in the fridge. Finally she says, 'But I must go and work, sweetheart. Work-work-work.' And then she's like babbling about her 'deadline'. 'I've got corrections to do on my book,' she says. 'And I'll not get much done all Monday, because Josh and I are planning a hookey day. We're off to one of the lunchtime jazz concerts up at the uni, first of all, because there was no music department – believe it or not – when Josh was a student there, way back. Then, if there's time, we'll head out and do a stretch of the "Midlands Meander", just as an eye-opener for him. Everything is so changed since he was last here. Shall we bring you back anything, Cattie-pie? Are you OK? Please tell me if I'm neglecting you. All right?'

'It's fine,' Cat says. 'I'm fine.'

'Good,' she says. 'There's a really nice baked-aubergine thing in the fridge if you're hungry. How's the art project, by the way? Have you decided on anything?'

'It's fine,' Cat says, gritting her teeth. 'I don't want to talk about it.'

'OK, sweetheart,' her mom says. 'I know you'll do something good.' And, finally – *finally* – like after taking nearly for ever, she goes tripping back upstairs.

And all the time Cat's thinking, So, OK, you're not the only one who's having a hookey day, smart-arse. You and your dear-old-midget-friend-from-way-back. Ha! Cat's going to tell her dad all about the midget one of these days, except maybe they're like already getting divorced? Else why isn't he back from bloody Addis Ababa, or Accra, or wherever? And then she thinks, Hey, if they're splitting up, maybe her dad'll take her to Mali? Just him and her. Then she goes to the fridge and she pulls out this like whole family-size foil tray of tiramisu from the Italian deli that her mom's put right at the back behind the snot-green aubergine thing, and she eats it standing up until she starts to feel really sick. And then she makes a dash for the downstairs lav.

So, anyway. First thing after the weekend, Cat's going to do the hair dye and then she's going to make a start on the tenant's book. So she watches until the tenant goes out and then she goes down the garden, all in her school uniform. That's after she's given her mother this bullshit about how she's decided to start using her bike for school, which is like kept in the garage, down the bottom.

So then she has to wait for her mom and the midget to go out as well, which is quite early, and after that she goes back and collects up the sachets and a pair of scissors and two clean towels from the linen cupboard and she gets into the shower, where, first of all, she washes her hair, ordinarywise, like it says on the instructions. Then she snips the corner of one of the sachets, but it like spills all over her hands and goes under her nails and everything, because it's so much more runny than she expected. Anyway, she quickly squeezes it all on to her hair, which she's forgotten to towel dry, so it starts dripping into her eyes and on to the floor of the shower, even before she's got round to snipping open the second one. Shit. Anyway, she grabs one of the towels and wraps it round her head to stop the drips and then she uses the other one to scrub all the black off the shower, which, thank God, comes off right away, only the towel's pretty buggered, but so what? She can just throw it away – and the other one as well, nobody will notice. Then she quickly does the same routine, only with the other sachet, and she puts the towel back on her head.

But then, when she's trying to comb it all through, she can see she's got these kind of horrible runnels all down her forehead and round her ears and that, so she doesn't even bother to rinse her hair, like it says on the sachet. She just picks up the two revolting towels and she dashes out to lock herself in her bedroom, where she sits down at the dressing table and stares at herself. Shit. Her hair's gone this kind of horrible charcoal matt colour, with her scalp all full of charcoal blotches, and her forehead's got these like hideous charcoal streaks, like dirty rainwater, that won't come off.

So she's just sitting there shivering and staring at herself and it's all so disappointing that she starts to cry. Then she thinks – of course – to phone her Aunt Lettie on her cell phone, because Lettie will be like just about ready to leave her office for home right now, and she won't have picked up her kids yet. So, anyway, all through the phone call she's crying into the phone like mad, but Lettie is just great about the whole thing and she talks to Cat in this like joky, half-Afrikaans lingo, just to cheer her up.

'Ach, cookie, *moenie* worry *nie*,' she says. 'Auntie's going to fix it for her favourite niece, isn't it? I'm coming to get you now-now. Just you put on a *doek* over your head, all right? Just in case I faint. *Liewe Hemel*! Or maybe a paper bag? *Ach sies*, I'm only joking. But don't you know about how gentlemen always prefer blondes? OK. I'm on to my hairdresser for you right now. Right now, cookie.'

So then, about fifteen minutes later, Lettie's there, hooting, in her four-by-four and they drive all the way to Westville, near where Lettie lives, and she drops Cat at this hairdresser's, where all three of them, even Cat, have a bit of a laugh about the ugly charcoal hair, because the hairdresser says it's no worries, she can fix it so that it'll look really nice.

Then Lettie goes off to get some novels for her book club from Exclusive Books at the Pavilion, and after that she goes to collect her kids from school, while the hairdresser is taking about two hours to do this amazing hair-dye job on Cat's head, with special brushes and rubber spatulas and lots of different little plastic bowls. Because as well as the dyeing she first gives Cat this fantastic haircut, like all sort of feathery, so when it's all finished, it's like a bit like Meg Ryan, only black, of course – really black-black and shiny – and she's even managed to get off most of the charcoal runnels, but she also calls over the in-house beautician, who shows Cat how to use this like concealer-stick thing and she does a manicure and she paints Cat's fingernails kind of pearly purple-black while she chats to her about conditioners and moisturisers and about how Cat should drink three litres of spring water a day, instead of all the Diet Coke, and about not eating sugary food. She tells Cat she's really lucky to have such beautiful skin at her age, with no enlarged pores or spots or anything, and she says to keep it that way Cat should make smoothies for breakfast with Cape raspberries and a banana and some grape juice, and just to get her ma to buy her a stick blender if she hasn't already got one.

'Go well, now,' she says, and she gives Cat this little bag of like sample lotions and gels to play with at home.

So then, when Lettie comes back with all the cousins, who are much younger than Cat, because Lettie's the baby of her family, just like Cat is, and she was the last to get married, they all jump up and down and shriek with excitement while Lettie goes and pays this massive bill.

Then she says, 'So now we better go and get madam here some sexy new clothes to go with the new hair, OK?'

Lettie's really fun to shop with, because she's like a seriously big spender and she just tells the store's 'personal shopper' to gather up mounds of stuff for them. Then she gets both of them these plunging black lacy bras and special Lycra magic pants that make them look really skinny and the underwear all says 'Le Bourget' on the labels. Plus they buy Cat these black Armani jeans and really nice black T-shirts.

And in the changing room Lettie pats her bum cheeks and she says, 'You always had a bum like me, Cat, and now it's like you've got someone else's bum. A nice little film star's bum, maybe? Cookie, you look like straight from Bollywood, no kidding.'

And on the way back to Cat's house, Lettie tells all her kids, when they ask about why everything's got to be black, that Cat's going to a funeral, that's why.

'She's going to a witch's funeral tomorrow,' Lettie says.

'Is it Meg's funeral from *Meg and Mog*?' says the youngest one anxiously.

'*Ach* no, Snoekie,' Lettie says. '*Ach sies*. As if Meg could ever die, my baby.'

She even comes into the house when she drops Cat back, and Cat's mom is there, worse luck, having a cup of tea with the midget.

'Hi there, Hattie,' she says. 'Now look, I don't know where your Cat's gone, but I found this one on my way home. She's like maybe one of those cute Muslim girls from Mayville?'

And because her mom's in such a good mood from having the midget with her, she just laughs and says, 'Hey, Cattie-pie, you look really great! Gosh! Wow!' And that's it. She doesn't even ask about school.

School. Cat's not been anywhere near her school all week and now it's Friday. She's been getting into her school uniform and sneaking down to the annexe every morning with the new jeans and one of the T-shirts in her schoolbag. Then she changes in the shed before she goes to sit at the tenant's desk. Giacomo's desk. Because having the black hair and the new black gear and all is making her feel much more poised about what she's doing and she's been working really hard. Much more than she'd ever have done at school.

So far she's done six really nice drawings on lovely thick cartridge paper, because she's always been good at drawing. She's done the stork mask and the stilt mask and the tree mask as well as the healer mask with the four figurines on the headdress and the hunter mask and the antelope. And she's made lots of notes as well. But, even so, she's kind of known all along that, come Friday afternoon, she's going to have to sneak out the book and photocopy some of the colour pictures, and also some of the text, because she's running out of time.

So, anyway, she's got it all worked out, because Friday is when the tenant stays out about an hour later than usual, and the plan is, she'll sneak in early afternoon at about five past two, after she's seen him go. That's because he usually comes back between 1 p.m. and 2 p.m. for some lunch. So she's tipped everything out of her A3 art portfolio and taken it with her to the shed to put the book in because, that way, if her mum sees her coming back with it, she won't start smelling a rat. Anyway, it'll be quite easy to stick the book in the portfolio, although it is quite big and heavy. Well, it kind of weighs like a ton of bricks, to tell you the truth.

So she takes the bus one stop to the photocopy place in the Musgrave Centre, which is a bit of a piss-off, because if her dad was there she would be able to get him to scan it for her, but as it is she doesn't yet know how to do it. And like last time she wanted to scan something that slimy Alan insisted on doing it for her. Anyway, when she gets there to the photocopy shop, they tell her she'll have to come back in an hour – and that's after this guy gives her a whole lot of shit about copyright and stuff, like what's she going to use it for etc, but eventually this manager girl comes up and says for God's sake, it's only for a school project, so they agree to do it.

Then for a whole hour Cat is like nearly dead with nerves, because she's so scared they might lose it or damage it or something, so she can't stand still and she just keeps on riding up and down on the escalators. Up and down. And she goes all round the different avenues inside the centre. In the basement she buys this packet of Rolos and rips it open and sticks three in her mouth all at once, but then she spits them all out into the litter bin and chucks out the rest of the packet as well. But then she goes back after about a minute and picks out the packet. After that, she empties all the sweets one by one into the bin, and pokes them right down to the bottom, underneath this kind of revolting old smeary carton of takeout chicken tikka that somebody's dumped, just to make sure she won't be able to go back for them.

After that she just keeps on buying more and more bottles of fizzy spring water and pouring it down her throat, like Lettie's beautician said to do. She even looks at all the boring old ladies' 'needlecraft' stuff and the shop with household goods like posh tin openers and juicers, because she's starting to get scared that Michelle and them might get out of school a bit early and be hanging around the clothes shops or the cafés on the floors higher up.

And when she finally goes back, after what feels like about five hours, they tell her sorry, but it'll be another half-hour. Shit! Anyway, she says that's OK, though she's practically pissing herself that maybe they've lost it or something, and they're not saying, but she's got no choice. So finally, she's just got to sneak into Truworth's, so she can check herself out in the full-length mirrors, with the new hair and the black jeans and all, and then she tries on these crap jeans that aren't nearly as good as the ones Lettie bought her and they make her stomach stick out. Oh yuk.

And then, finally – *finally* – at bloody last, and after another bottle of spring water – she goes back and, phew, they haven't lost the book or anything, and all the photocopies look seriously

149

fantastic. They look exactly like the real ones. So then they put everything in a plastic bag, even the book, and she sticks it all in her portfolio and she pays them, like millions of rand, and then she's zooming up the escalator, worried as hell, because she's been cutting it all a bit fine, and she's got maybe half an hour before the tenant gets back and it'll be getting dark already, even though it's like all sparkle-sparkle inside the shopping centre.

Anyway, she suddenly looks up and there are these two people just passing her on the going-down escalator and they're staring at her like really hard with their mouths wide open like goldfish and it's Michelle and Alan. And there she is, looking right through them, with her new black eyelashes and her feathery black hair and the uplift bra and the Armani jeans and all, and carrying a black portfolio, like she was an art student or something, and they're just looking like dumbo schoolkids in their crappy uniforms, and Michelle's like got her skirt all hitched up at the waist, which is supposed to make her look sexy, but all it means is you can like see these two fat knees and how short her legs are and Alan's hair is looking all kind of yellow under the bright lights, that are like making his skin look really terrible as well.

So Cat's feeling pretty OK once she's finally made it back to the annexe, and she's got the key in the lock, though she can't see a thing, of course, and she's feeling her way, like doing baby steps, carefully-carefully, across to the other side of the room where the desk is. Then she gets out the book, and puts it like exactly squared up on the corner just like it always is, with the bookmark and all, and then she's just about to go when suddenly she needs to pee so badly, what with all the spring water and the hours of hanging around in the centre, she realises she's been practically holding it in all day and that she's about to wet her pants any second, so she does what she's absolutely never done before. She goes for a wee in the tenant's bathroom. I mean she's been in the bathroom before where it's got all this lovely pale-green glass, like a green-glass washbasin and stuff, and with his wash lotions that say '*per uomo*', but she's never ever actually dreamed of using his lav, like right now, when she's got her jeans and her pants around her ankles and she's thinking, Oh my God and hurry up, hurry up, HURR-EE UP, because this pee is going on and on and on for ever. And then she's just about to flush and hoick up her pants, when she hears this weird noise.

But seriously weird noise. Like tap-tap, tap-tap-tap. And it's coming from right behind her, like from up on the wall near the lavatory cistern, because it's one of those high-up ones. So now she can't even flush, of course, because she's too scared to make a sound. Oh shit! And now he'll know it's her, because boys don't need to use loo paper when they pee and who else could it be except for her? The dumbo girl that like stares at him out of the bathroom window, because the other day she could swear he looked up and saw her watching him. Or maybe not? Anyway, right now, she's literally shaking as she's trying to pull up the Lycra magic pants that have gone into a kind of tight, scrambled-up ring, like they do when you're in a hurry – of course – and she's trying to yank up her jeans as well, but like just at the same time she's turned to face the wall behind her, where the sound's coming from. And then she's holding her breath and – Oh my God, she's thinking – I'm out of here, right now, but then some-thing really weird starts to happen.

There's just a bit more light there in the bathroom than in the rest of the place, because there's like this long, high-up window that faces on to the side street and so there's this slightly orangey street light glow in there and, in the beam of light, Cat can see that little bits of plaster are fluttering down from the wall and they're falling on to the lid of the loo seat, that she's just closed really quietly, and some of it is even falling on her.

And then there's like a little shiny tip of metal coming through the wall, like a chisel or the point of a knife or something. It's a bit like in that story about the knives in the walls that close in on you. And suddenly Cat can't help it but she just starts to scream. She's standing sort of stuck to the spot in her snaggled-up magic pants, and she's screaming so loud that she doesn't even hear the crash on the other side of the wall, or the groan that follows.

She's standing, rigid, in the dark and screaming.

'Mom-*meee*! Mom-*meee*!'

And Cat just can't stop screaming.

Chapter Six

Jack

'You'll be Giacomo Moroni,' Hattie says. 'I'm Hattie. Please come in. I'll take you to the garden cottage.'

Jack hasn't quite got used to being called Giacomo Moroni. It's a recent nom de plume; a name of convenience. For so long now, he's been Jacques: Jacques Moreau. Admittedly Eduardo, when in fatherly mood, had occasionally called him Giacomo, but then the name had come out sounding a whole lot more like Jack. '*Jack*-omo'. Now there is something that startles him about the extra syllable in the mouth of a native English speaker. He is not much accustomed to native English speakers. 'You'll be *Gee-acc-omo*,' his landlady said. For the first time in his life, he has been travelling on a passport that calls him by his real name. Sipho Jack Maseko.

But his rented studio is a dream. It's even nicer than it looked in the pictures.

'It's perfect,' Jack says. 'You've made it all so perfect.'

His eyes are taking in the black-brick floor tiles, diagonally scored; the narrow oblongs of roof window through which he can see a heavenly Magritte-blue sky. An African sky after the notorious grey skies of Milan. He takes in the slate worktop that runs the length of his shining new kitchen. And here, at the far end – the 'sleeping' end – are these lovely pale-wooden wall cupboards whose doors come uninterrupted by handles; doors that open at the touch with a satisfying push-click.

'There's just one thing,' he says. 'I have a desk. I would really love to have my own desk.' Then he says, 'Not that this one isn't beautiful.'

He and Hattie are staring at Herman's purpose-built desk table with its solid legs and chunky mortise joints. She knows that Herman will not be best pleased. The studio is a machine for living and Herman is god of the machine.

'My desk is very special to me,' Jack says. 'It was left to me by a friend.'

'Ah,' Hattie says.

'A friend who died,' Jack says. 'A benefactor.'

Hattie glances quickly at the tenant. Giacomo Moroni. He is young, tall, slim, light brown and very good-looking. He has close-cropped Afro hair and a beautifully shaped skull. He has those alluring eyes that come as one of the benefits of mixed-race parentage; eyes that look as if permanently enhanced with eyeliner. His lashes are long and black. He has the slightest hint of peachy glow across the cheekbones. Giacomo has the sort of pale Afro looks that modelling agencies go mad for. In addition, there is a lovely fluidity in his gesture and movement – something that Hattie appreciates. Inwardly she's speculating that the 'friend', the 'benefactor', could have been a partner who died of Aids. In which case, how dreadful for the poor young man, especially at his age, because Giacomo looks too young to be a member of staff in the drama department, even in the humblest junior capacity; more like an undergraduate. He certainly looks younger than his twenty-seven years. Could it be that the friend was an older woman who loved him in a motherly way? She can tell that older women will fall for Giacomo; will long to nurture him; to put themselves out for him. Right now she's doing it

154

herself. Yet his body language is unambiguous. It says to her, 'Touch me not.'

'But of course,' she says. 'Of course you must have your own desk. It's no problem.'

And she thinks, What the hell, Herman's table can go in the garage – especially since he's incorporated almost all of the one-time shed space into 'the studio'. Or better still, she'll have the beautiful desk table for herself. She'll get it hauled up to her study in the turret – that's if the legs will manage the last bend in the stairs. Then, by the time Herman returns, he will be confronted with a fait accompli. The desk will replace her brother's old bureau, which allows her little space to spread. The latter can go in the drawing room. Or maybe she'll flog it? Dispatch it to an antiques auction? It's time she got some practice in discarding elements of her past life.

'Thank you,' Jack says. 'You're very kind.'

The desk, his beautiful silver desk, is one of the few material possessions that have become important to him, though in general he carries little baggage. There is Josh's old copy of *Treasure Island* along with a small box of books. There are the three engravings given him by Eduardo, along with his framed Giacometti poster. There is his Moka espresso pot and a bag of clothes. There is his pistachio-green Vespa, which is currently in transit on the high seas. He hasn't seen the desk since he was nine years old but Bernie Silver's desk still gleams there on the edges of his mind; a thing to focus on in this oddly familiar yet altogether different place. He can almost not wait to go and claim it. And it's so amazing that, after all these years, after the deaths and disappearances and God knows what, his desk should still be there waiting for him – as confirmed by a recent phone call from Milan. It's exactly where Bernie left it; at the university, in social studies.

Bernie's old room is currently occupied by a Professor Nathan Lewis and it is he who was able to make Jack aware that both

Ida and Bernie were dead. The academic staff will doubtless have changed several times; persons moved on as part of the global diaspora; the anti-apartheid brain drain. Some retired to one-bedroom flats in Marylebone or Montmartre. Some working for human rights on the West Bank, or in Sierra Leone. Some in Perth or Auckland or Winnipeg. Some heading Cambridge colleges, or chairing committees of the British Medical Association. Yet the desk is still there, its large adhesive label apparently intact within the top right-hand drawer. 'This desk is a present from Bernard Silver to Sipho Jack Maseko. To await collection. He may be quite some time.'

'Thank you,' Jack says again to Hattie. 'It is quite big, you see.' And he smiles his rare but enchanting smile.

'You're very welcome,' Hattie says, making as if to withdraw. 'I'll leave you to get settled.'

With his elegant manners, his fluent but somehow unplaceable English, Hattie takes Herman's tenant for a Euro child, a child of sweet first-world privilege; father a diplomat, mother an art dealer, international schools in Geneva and Prague – something like that. Well, you've only got to look at his shoes.

'Let me know if there is anything you need,' she says.

Each morning over those first few days, as Jack surfaces to a hundred bird calls and to that slice of bright subtropical sky, his first half-awake thoughts are all of Dakar. Then he remembers where he is and he thanks God for the studio. It's really quite weird to be back here, but he has always loved a few beautiful spaces. He recalls, to his puzzlement, that his landlady had referred to the studio as 'the garden cottage'. A 'garden cottage', as he has already discovered, is a term much in local use for an upgraded one-time servants' billet. For Jack a cottage is a literary concept, having to do with northern Europe; a picturesque, timber-beamed minihouse, as depicted in those illustrated fairy

156

stories that he long ago read with Josh; a low rustic dwelling, dwarfed by a charming topknot of thatch; wild eglantine and beanstalks clawing at tiny leaded windows. And a witch lurking within, bent double over a cauldron.

Witches in hovels he does know about from his own too personal experience and it's thanks to his hag-like grandmother, who had dominion over him in 'the native reserve'; the horror time that carved three years out of what, until then, he had assumed was his rightful childhood at the Silvers' suburban house. They were years that changed him for ever; years that taught him the ugliness of want and the indignity of ever disclosing emotional need. The hag is probably long dead. Ditto his mother, who abandoned him there at the age of six. He does not know for sure, of course, and frankly he cares less. Good riddance to them both. Gertrude, who dumped him, and the witch, who shook her broom at him; a broom with which she would rearrange the dust of the hovel's wretched mud floor. Do not think of it, Jack Maseko aka Jacques Moreau. Do not go there.

Jack loathes the imperfections that poverty brings; its power to bend the spine, roughen the hands, blacken and loosen the teeth, make for rheumy eyes and pinched, lopsided cheeks. He loathes its power to compel co-existence with cockroaches and bugs; with mosquito bites and stomach cramps and intestinal worms; its power to bring on birth defects: club feet, untreated squints, blindness and withered legs. But here and now, his studio – this lovely space – is no cottage. The studio is a haven of artful, filtered light. The studio is both perfect and perfectly monochrome. Well, that's except for the cool greenish tinge to the bathroom's translucent glass fittings.

Standing, as it does, at the end of a fabulous garden, hidden from the main house by a hedge of tall bamboo, the studio has bougainvillea and a passion fruit vine clambering up a plastered wall that borders his terrace. Azaleas grow on his terrace in large clay tubs and those flowers that he remembers as red-hot pokers. Jack appreciates the privacy and the dimensions of the studio, because in the past he has either lived in cramped back rooms or he has shared. First there was the bunk bed, where he slept above his mother in the Silvers' backyard room. Then there was his grandmother's hovel where five of them slept on the floor. After that there was boarding school; then his five square metres in a storeroom at the back of a baker's shop in Dakar. Living with Eduardo was always rather deluxe – whether the holiday house in Senegal that overlooked the sea, or the apartment in Milan – but his bedroom in either place was always next door to the two little boys. Bastiano and Vincenzo, his pupils. So the studio, for all his complex misgivings, is a sort of paradise. A place all his own and undefiled.

On his first afternoon there, Jack, having walked the distance to the local shopping mall and back, bakes biscuits in his small new oven – four almond cookies on a baking sheet twenty centimetres square – and he eats them, two and two, sitting out at his garden table on the terrace. The first two, he eats at 4 p.m., with a wide white cup of mint tea. Then, as the light goes, he eats the second two, dipping them into a glass of chilled Vin Santo; or a delicious local version of Vin Santo that he's bought in the 'bottle store'. That's what people used to call those places; those shops in which black persons were forbidden to buy alcohol. The Vin Santo is from a Cape wine estate called Klein Constantia and it tastes of flowers and apricots. It tastes of honey and marmalade. It tastes the way he remembers the contents of Ida Silver's fridge.

An avocado and a pawpaw tree are visible to him, heavy with fruit, over the vista of low neighbourhood roofs. He's taken aback by the unremembered lushness of this place, his once-upon-a-time home town; by the depth of its shiny greens. Jack is aware that his studio would once have been a shed-like row of basic rooms to house domestic servants. And where his green-glass bathroom is, there would have been a concrete appendage with utility cold shower and hole-in-the-floor flush toilet. His sloping slate roof with its oblong inlets of glass would once have been sheets of corrugated tin with gaps that let in mosquitoes and spiders, along with that fierce, slanting rain. The interior walls would all have been black with paraffin smoke from rickety Primus stoves. He knows – albeit sketchily, because his mother, being taciturn, never furnished him with detail – that it was from a servant's room in a grand sort of house like this one that, long ago, she was evicted and sent packing. He knows that this happened shortly before he was born. He knows that, afterwards, she went to work at the house of Bernie and Ida Silver, where he'd spent his early childhood. That was before his horror time in the witch's hovel, of course. And, after that – after his rescue – the Silvers packed him off to boarding school, and he never saw any of them again. Bernie, on that last day, drove him as far as the Swaziland border, where one of the school staff members was waiting to pick him up.

And Gertrude? She never turned up at the house where the Silvers had so carefully arranged for her to be employed; the place for which Bernie had given him the address and the telephone number. Not that he had ever tried to phone his mother, but he had got letters from her would-be employers. They had made efforts to discover his mother's whereabouts, but all without success. So Jack never heard from his mother, who was in any case near illiterate, for all Ida's determined efforts at adult education. She simply dropped out of his world. This never really bothered him; not after she'd delivered him up to the mercies of the witch's hovel. Both Josh and Ida wrote regularly, though his need for them had passed. He'd been schooled by then in emotional self-sufficiency. He was Jack Maseko, Swaziland schoolboy. That was until the day he decided to cross another border and walk out of his schoolboy life. At that point, Jack became Jacques. He moved on. He wore a different mask. It was thanks to Josh, admittedly, that he'd always been so interested in masks.

Jack is not much of a 'people' person. And, given how much the turn of his life has been dependent upon a handful of wind-fall benefactors, it would have been burdensome were he to have embraced all those to whom he was beholden. He would have had to experience the complicated ambivalence that can come with too much dependence; an endless see-saw of resentment and gratitude. So Jack is not grateful and he likes to stand alone. He is himself. He is whichever version of himself he chooses to present. And if he never felt much for his mother, it can't be denied that the woman had never appeared to feel very much for him. The circumstances of his conception were hardly the most felicitous – not that she had ever properly filled him in on these – and, though she took over Pru's job as the Silvers' domestic servant, Gertrude was never a spontaneous and warm-hearted woman like Pru. She entered the household by accident, clammed-up and emotionally opaque; a person who had early on bought into the idea of her own racially inferior and servile status. Gertrude was always a firm upholder of caste barriers and, as such, for all the convenience of her unconventional billet, she resisted the Silvers' aberrant and colour-blind style. There was nothing for it, since, however unwillingly, she herself had crossed those barriers of caste – and the shaming evidence of this transgression was her offspring's paler skin.

Gertrude's taking up residence in the Silvers' backyard was something that nobody had planned. It was not a relationship that quite dovetailed – which was why, on that first evening, a muted and somewhat suspicious Gertrude watched in puzzlement as the Silvers scurried about finding sheets, pillows and candles for the unused, cobwebby maid's room at the far end of their small yard. Ida gave Gertrude a Thermos of milky tea and a box of Ouma Rusks. She gave her two bananas and a bath towel and a slice of her home-made chocolate-and-almond cake. There was a mattress in the room on a small iron bed frame, which Josh made up with clean linen, and a rickety kitchen chair. Both were items that pre-dated the Silvers' purchase of the house.

And early next morning, Ida went and did the thing she was best at. She haggled on behalf of the dispossessed, confronting a besuited Mr Marchmont-Thomas on the doorstep of Marchmont House. He was on his way to go marking time at his club. Ida first presented him with her card. She told him she had come to collect the illegally withheld papers of one Mrs Gertrude Maseko.

'*Mrs?*' said Hattie's father, knee-jerk sarcastic. 'Well, bless my soul!' But he capitulated almost at once. 'A silly misunderstanding,' he said. 'Good Lord, the stupid woman. She only had to ask.'

Ida waited, as grudgingly invited, in the gloomy mould-green drawing room of the amazing colonial villa she had driven past almost every day on her way to work from her own more modest three-bedroom house. As a serious cook, she was disappointed that the interior should smell so much of boarding house; of boiled cauliflower and beef shin; all evidence of a depressing cuisine that comes devoid of tomatoes, or olive oil, or herbs. But this was precisely the kind of time-warped diet that the Marchmont family clung to as 'plain English food'; admirably non-devious food; food of a kind that would always ensure against what Hattie's father called 'gyppo guts'.

Then Mr Marchmont-Thomas, his teeth bared unpleasantly in place of a smile, wanting to be shot of the woman, appeared with Gertrude's papers.

'Here we are then, Mrs . . . urm.' He glanced at Ida's card. Bloody trouble-maker. 'Mrs Silver,' he said. Jewess, of course. Nice little earner. Funny how these people were so often called Silver or Gold. 'She steals, you know – your Mrs Gertrude Thing,' he said. 'Light fingers, I'm afraid.'

Gertrude stayed for the next ten years. It solved the problem of the absent character reference and she was dependable and hard-working. The Silvers doubled her wages and Jack was born three months after her appearance, by which time the still somewhat basic servant's room had been fitted with electric light, a pair of gingham curtains and a carpet. Ida was not an 'interiors' person, but the room boasted a decent new single bed and a small folding cot for the baby, while the adjoining servant's washroom now had a lavatory bowl and a shower that ran hot and cold. And Gertrude had access to the Silvers' washing machine so that Jack's little vests and nappies hung on the line in the yard. Yet Gertrude never loosened up; never accommodated to the family style; never became quite comfortable with her own son Jack, who, in all sorts of ways, was a different kettle of fish.

Since, unlike the garden of Marchmont House, the Silvers' backyard was small, the servant's room was not much more than twelve metres from the constantly open kitchen door, which granted Jack ease of entry. Josh loved to play with Jack; welcomed him into the enticing den of his own bedroom where they read stories together, clapped hands and stomped, dressed up in funny hats, drew pictures and did cutting-out. They also did headstands against the wall. For Jack, Josh's bedroom was an Aladdin's Cave of puppet theatres, art materials, tape recorders and walls of books, which still included, between the more adult tomes, a feast of childhood favourites that Jack quickly took to heart. *Scuffy the Tugboat*; *The Wind in the Willows*; *The Little Prince*; *The Box of Delights*. Jack loved *Little Bear* and the big flat Orlando books. He especially loved *Treasure Island*. He adored Josh's electric keyboard. And, across the hall, was Bernie's study, where before very long the marvellous silver desk with its pear-drop, cut-glass handles yielded up quantities of scrap paper and Sellotape and paperclips, along with scissors, glue and rubber bands.

Jack knew that one day, when he became a white person, he would own a desk like this. He knew that he would be a white person, because the evidence was before him. He was already a whole lot lighter than his mother, so it was clear to him that, while everyone was born dark brown, some people would then start to fade, after which they would go on to own all these beautiful things. People like himself. Special people. Meanwhile Jack's determinedly barefoot mother cooked pots of maize porridge for his breakfast, but Jack liked toast and marmalade with lots of oozy butter. He liked dates and sugared almonds. He liked the cartons of peach and apricot juice that lived inside the Silvers' fridge.

For Jack, though it had been better fitted out since its days as an untenanted concrete hutch, his mother's room couldn't compete with what he thought of as the 'big' house, with its separate kitchen and living room and its special rooms for sleeping. And while his mother maintained the barriers, refusing herself ever to sit on the comfy living-room chairs; yanking little Jack off them with a click of her disapproving tongue, he, on her weekend visits away, curled up there on Josh's knee, or joined the family in the dining room, where he enjoyed second helpings of Ida's lemony chicken.

Jack, who spoke to his mother in Zulu, nonetheless spoke English with the Silvers in the accents of a white person – something that always made his visits to the corner shop a problem. And the problematical nature of Jack's marginal status in a society so rigidly stratified by race had not bypassed the notice of Bernie and Ida Silver. But, being always busy and much preoccupied with more dramatic human problems among the dispossessed, they were not particularly hands-on with Gertrude's child, whose dilemmas, for the moment, were fairly low down in the hierarchy of human suffering, examples of which they witnessed day by day.

'Try not to steal that child from his mother,' Bernie said warningly to his adopted teenage son. 'Just take care, all right?'

Meanwhile, Ida's solution was to raise up Gertrude with one-to-one classes in adult literacy, though Gertrude proved an obdurate pupil and faded out as soon as she could. Jack, on the other hand, thanks to natural talent and to Josh's copious read-aloud time, could read *Little Bear* and *Cat in the Hat* and several of the Blue Pirate books before the age of four. He also loved the epistolary art, as he and Josh wrote letters to each other in an ongoing game in which they posted their efforts into a home-made, red-painted cardboard post box with a slot cut into the top. The box sat on the back veranda, alongside an old stone sink.

> Dear Jack
>> Please will you come and play with me today?
>> From your loving friend,
>> Josh

Josh always used an envelope on which he wrote the Silvers' address, followed by 'Southern Hemisphere, the World, the Universe'. He made tiny pretend stamps cut out from magazine pictures and faked the graphics of the Post Office franking machines, including the bilingual exhortations to drive safely home. 'DRIVE SAFELY/*KOM VEILIG TUIS.*'

Jack, though his mother regarded these items with suspicion, kept a shoebox of paper and fibre pens on a shelf above his pillow on the top bunk bed that had come to replace the cot in which he once slept.

> Dear Josh
>> I will come.
>> From Jack

Then he decorated his letters with marvellous pictures of tractors and busily crashing cars. He drew Hannibal crossing the Alps with great numbers of elephants. He drew King Arthur and his knights in armour. He drew castles with moats and drawbridges. Jack drew tightrope walkers and clowns. He never drew Zulu warriors with assegais and shields.

Because the Silvers were oddballs, they never demanded of their maidservant that the boy be dispatched, as most black infants were, from the time that they were weaned; sent away as toddlers, back to the 'native reserve' – the reserve that, in Jack's case, had now been redefined as the Bantu homeland of KwaZulu – because a native child was, by law, an unproductive unit who had no automatic rights of residence in town by virtue of parental employment there.

So Jack, devoid of peer-group playmates, lingered content-edly in the Silvers' backyard through the period of his preschool life – until Gertrude one day without prior consultation simply, unilaterally, removed her son to his maternal grandmother and left him there, her precocious, urban, pale-skinned child, and she beat a hasty retreat. The removal took place towards the end of Josh's 3rd year at university and in the very week of Jack's own guest appearance in the drama school's production of *A Midsummer Night's Dream*; Jack, 'the little changeling boy', Titania's ward, the stolen child. Gertrude took Jack, still dreaming of greasepaint, in the bus along that same bumpy road upon which she had once met Josh; Jack, who had no previous knowledge of rural life, had never met his grandmother, knew nothing of this eroded scrap of washed-up land on which those too old and too young were eking out a half-life at somewhere below subsistence. Gertrude had, thus far, always made her visits there without her son – and Josh's invariable, eager offers of sleepover had made this easy for her. But now the time had come.

These years of rural exile have etched themselves upon Jack's brain. They have made their way into the bone and marrow of his being. The grim, joyless grandmother, the ragged, teasing children – several of them, apparently his own nieces and nephews – offspring of a feckless adult half-sister he never knew he had; the hovel that smelled of grass and mud and unwashed bodies and rags stiffened with ancient sweat, where he was required to sleep on the floor along with all the others; all under a low grass roof from which bugs and crawlies dropped on to his face and limbs in the night. Angry red itchy bumps made their appearance on his arms and legs, where they remained as a semi-permanent fixture. He was soon dressed in rags himself, because Grandmother had seized her chance to sell all his good town clothes.

School was a barefoot three-mile walk to a windowless garage-type construction, laid out with rows of backless benches, where the children sat jammed up in rows before a teacher who had, himself, not gone to school beyond the age of fourteen and often reeked of drink. Sometimes the teacher would fall asleep with his head down on the table, allowing the bolder students to creep away before their time. Jack discovered himself devoid of techniques for bonding with other children and it did not help that his reading and writing were glaringly proficient, while those years older than himself were spelling out monosyllabic words in time to the teacher's dreary tap-tap at the blackboard. All classroom learning was by rote and most of it – for want of paper – was chanted out loud. The teacher kept a big stick and frequently lashed out. Grandmother also kept a stick and she lashed out as well.

Some days he had to skip school and take a turn minding Grandmother's goats. He didn't care too much for the goats but he preferred them to the schoolroom. He disliked the smelly intimacy of drawing the goats' milk, and then the hazardous prospect of carrying it back – what with the terror of spillage, or the other children grabbing the pail to slurp at it before he had made it home. Grandmother would always notice if there was less milk than there should have been and she'd have cause to reach for her stick.

Grandmother, like all the malevolent hags in storybooks, appeared to have only one tooth. Her cheeks were shrivelled. Her eyes had a yellowy film. She went in for mean-minded pinches that left purple bruises on his skin. She grabbed his ears and cackled. Everyone was in threadbare clothes, including Grandmother herself and the teacher. Some of the smaller boys wore grown-up men's jackets for want of more appropriate clothing; jackets that hung below their knees and were vastly too wide on the shoulders; snot-encrusted cuffs covering their hands.

Food was maize porridge that sometimes came with sharp soured milk curds, or with a smear of sludgy greenish veg. Just occasionally, the porridge came with little bits of animal: chicken's feet; a boiled head; washed-out innards like those big rubber bands on Bernie Silver's desk. Oh do not think of Bernie's desk. Not now; not any more. Everywhere had flies because no one had a fridge and there was no electric light. The lav was a box over a reeking hole in the ground into which small children had been known to fall and drown. His shrunken homeland was a hell of dust and turds and flies, and of the sort of green-eyed watchfulness that can accompany extremes of deprivation. Jack hated the smell of the fermenting grains when Grandmother made her vats of beer. He hated all things to do with local rituals; with skins and feathers and gall bladders tied in a person's hair, or the skeletons of snakes. There were bent-up old men with bleary eyes and head rings and feathers, who would babble around smoky fires about ancient and glorious times before the white man came and took the land. For toys, the children played in the dirt, skimming dusty stones with dustier hands into dusty hollows in the earth.

Then one day it was three years on and Jack spotted his chance. Kept behind as a punishment for he cannot remember what, Jack observed that the teacher was once again asleep, with his head upon the table. But on this occasion something else was lying there as well. There was a letter, addressed to the teacher, and the envelope, he could see, bore an unfranked stamp. Jack approached and reached out with care, because the teacher would always beat his pupils more readily after he had been drinking. Letters had not been a feature of Jack's life, not since Josh and the red-painted post box, but in a moment the item was in his pocket and he had tiptoed from the schoolroom.

The relentless absence of privacy in the village, along with the paucity of resources, meant that it was several days before Jack had managed to reseal the back of the envelope and fix a scrap of paper over its existing address with a smear of stolen schoolroom glue. He still knew the Silvers' address by heart, though he left off 'Southern Hemisphere, the World, the Universe'. He fed the teacher's letter to one of the goats and his own letter was written on the yellowing, torn-out title page of the only book that he had snatched up from Josh's bedroom three years earlier: a small paperback copy of *Treasure Island*; the version he'd made off with in preference to the more enticing but less portable illustrated hardback.

> Dear Josh
>   I ask you please to come for me. *Please.* I ask you to come *soon.* I ask you to come *now.* I ask you, *please, soon, NOW.*
>   From your old friend, Jack

He entrusted the letter in a last daring minute to a young adult migrant worker, who was returning that day to his packing job in a Durban warehouse. Then he could do nothing but wait, and wait, and hope.

When Josh got Jack's letter, he had just recently had good news about his application for a graduate scholarship in London. Josh had got himself a little car – his very own third-hand 2CV – along with a driving licence, and Hattie Thomas, his dance teacher, had become his constant companion. At this time, he still had hopes of persuading Hattie to leave the country with him and the two of them occasionally indulged in pleasant fantasies about flat-sharing in Pimlico – or maybe near Hampstead Heath?

'Hey, remember little Jack?' he said to Hattie, who had met Jack during the play rehearsals three years earlier and also, just once, on that weekend visit to the Silvers' house when Gertrude was out of town.

Then Josh pulled the letter from his pocket.

'Come,' he said. 'He needs us. He's written me a letter at long bloody last. It's written from this nowhere-land, but I've *finally* screwed out of Gertrude exactly where it is. The bloody woman, she's such a lump, and getting anything out of her is like drawing blood from a stone. God only knows, I've given her umpteen letters for him – letters and books and all sorts of stuff – that's whenever she's gone up there on a visit, and I've never heard a single word back. Not until now. Anyway, let's go. We're going to drive there right now and get him.'

'Does Gertrude know?' Hattie said. 'I mean –'

Josh fixed her with a look.

'Of course she doesn't know,' he said. 'I mean. *As if.*'

After a few false turnings and a quick stopover at a filling station where the shop afforded Josh the opportunity to buy a range of appeasement gifts for Jack's grandmother – twelve tins of pilchards in tomato sauce, eight tins of evaporated milk, three spit-roasted chickens sweating in foil-lined bags and a tray containing eighteen nearly ripe peaches – the 2CV bumped into the settlement towards the end of the afternoon, raising clouds of dust. Everyone stopped and stared: ragged children with a plastic football; adults lingering in doorways; scrawny dogs. And, at a distance, the furthest distance, leaning on one mosquito-bitten leg against a red mud wall, was Jack, who was not staring. Beautiful Jack, taller, skinnier, wearing frayed khaki shorts and reading *Treasure Island*.

In his head, as he'd been doing for years, he was choreographing the story. Blind Pugh, coming up the hill. Tap-tap-tap. He waited for Josh to get out and approach him, with the cardboard box in his hands. Jack moved hardly at all. With his right hand, he gestured towards his grandmother's hut. His face was like a mask. Then Josh, while Hattie waited in the car, proceeded to the doorway and made over the gifts, the pilchards and tinned milk; the sweating chickens; the peaches.

'I come from Gertrude,' he said and he hinted at a little bow. He spoke to the old woman in Zulu, which he'd once learned at dear Pru's knee. 'I've come to fetch the boy,' he said.

Grandmother took possession of the tribute. She put it down in the hovel. Jack waited, leaning against the wall, as Josh took his leave. He fetched nothing, spoke to nobody, looked neither to left nor right. He waited until the courtesies were done. Then he followed Josh to the car and climbed into the back. Josh undertook a three-point turn, raising a further cloud of dust. He gave a swift parp-parp and waved his hand in the air through the open window. Jack stared, expressionless, into the back of Josh's head. His hands were in his lap, holding the book.

Oh dear. Irresponsible Josh. Gertrude was certainly not best pleased and the Silvers were facing another domestic headache. This could be considered the third time that Josh had made a problem for his kindly adoptive parents. The first, admittedly not of his making, was when he'd turned up in infancy, as the child of the catatonic novice. The second was when he'd appeared with pregnant Gertrude. The third occasion was now. Because what were the Silvers to do with the boy, in a place where there wasn't a school that was eligible by law to take him? Decamped, without legal status, in the backyard of a dissident family under the increasing scrutiny of the state was not a viable option, especially as Ida had recently been declared a banned person. She couldn't work. She couldn't be quoted. She couldn't attend gatherings. She'd had her passport impounded and Bernie had a reasonable hunch that his turn would come before long.

For some weeks Ida used her enforced idleness to tutor Jack at home. She and Bernie tried telling each other that Jack was merely on a 'visit' from the rural homeland. They attempted a family meeting with Gertrude but, as ever, it was hard enough to get Gertrude to sit at the dining table; harder still to solicit her participation in the matter of her hijacked child, to whom she'd always seemed so curiously muted. Clearly the boy could not stay where he was and he was adamant that he wouldn't go back. The only option, as the Silvers saw it, expensive as it would prove – and at a time when their own future was looking somewhat shaky – would be to place the boy in the junior department of a progressive, private boarding school across the country's border.

Gertrude appeared neutral. She made no objection. Josh was happy. Jack was on board. The Silvers, in the circumstances, were admirably sanguine. Having done well by one bright, creative nowhere boy who, twenty years earlier, had landed in their lap, they now accepted that life had landed them another. This time it was talented little Jack, who, through no deliberate intent on their part, had become a marginal child, a stolen child, a child who, thanks to Josh's warm embrace and his own mother's curious indifference, had long ago been lured by the charms and resources of an unusual white bourgeois household, with its open door to a treasure trove of books and puppet theatres and scissors and glue. And a big silver desk with cut-glass, pear-drop handles.

It was the Silvers' plan to ship out of the country, passports or no, which meant that they could not return. With this in mind, they began discreetly to make their plans. Josh would be leaving for London and Jack for Swaziland. Things were drawing to a close. Bernie called in both the boys and suggested they might each like to choose something special from among his possessions to have as their own. Josh, with the logistics of packing in mind, chose four Leon Bakst lithographs that Bernie had once been given by his one-time academic mentor, an émigré anthropologist who had come out of pre-war Vienna. Jack, somewhat less practically, chose the big silver desk.

'OK, Jack!' Bernie said, and he laughed. 'OK. The desk will be yours.'

And then they made plans for its storage. The desk would be waiting for Jack, he said. It would be up at the university. He'd have it moved into his office in the social studies department. That was room number twenty-seven, on the first floor. It was the second door on the right. Bernie made a large notice and pasted it into the top right-hand drawer. 'This desk is a present from Bernard Silver to Sipho Jack Maseko. To await collection. He may be quite some time.'

And then Jack was at boarding school, year after pleasant year; transplanted into a royalist mountain kingdom, too small, too landlocked, too powerless to be anything but acquiescent with its looming, well-armed neighbour to the south, but sort of independent, for all that. School offered a gentle and privileged existence, and a nice ethnic mix, among whom the offspring of South Africa's exiled or imprisoned 'struggle royalty' was adequately represented. Then there were those whose parents were bankers, farmers, tribal heirs apparent, regional bishops, and the heads of independent African states. School made a context in which Jack, the illiterate housemaid's child; cool, self-contained, brainy Jack, soon prospered and became a schoolboy star. The resources of the art room, the library, the music room, the theatre were all versions of Josh Silver's bedroom, writ larger and more wonderful.

Jack shone in everything at school, but it was literature and theatre studies with its related arts that held particular appeal for him, not only because of Josh's early influence, but because these things offered him opportunities to take on alternative identities. And Jack, who had long ago come to understand that he would never become a white person, was confident by now that he was nonetheless able to become whosoever he wished. Self-sufficient, touch-me-not Jack, who had no holiday journeys home and no person from his earlier life who was able to come and visit, considered these things to be a matter of little consequence. He found favour with the teaching staff and, in the vacations, was quite content to be billeted, as arranged, with a local doctor's family whose own slightly younger boy was a pupil at the school.

Gifted and bookish, Jack took as his birthright what the Silvers were doing for him; had no sort of yardstick, had never had any own-age friends and was, by now, quite open-eyed in the matter of what he considered to be the Silvers' respective personal shortcomings. Josh, at the time of their parting, appeared to him morose, self-indulgent and preoccupied with the business of losing his girlfriend. Bernie, as always, was somewhat boringly pedagogical, and had offered him edifying lectures on the heretical Bishop Colenso and on the Industrial and Commercial Workers' Union, as they had made that final drive together towards the Swaziland border. Ida, for all her flair with food, he remembered as forever banging on about health care and crèches and human rights violations and workers' education. God only knew, she'd even had a shot at teaching his own dead-end mother. Jack was glad to have all that behind him because, right here, at school, he belonged to no one but himself.

And then he began to learn French. Jack discovered a profound and romantic passion for French. He loved its sounds; loved what it did to his gestures and to the shapes it made with his mouth; loved it for being so different from the language of those white corner-shopkeepers who'd distrusted him for his accent; an uppity little brown boy who had presumed towards white-boy speech. And thanks to the accident of an art-theory essay, Jack one day encountered a thing that caused him to imagine for himself a vision of francophone Africa. It was something about which, until then, he had known nothing, though he chose from now on to construct it in opposition to all that he associated with that lingering British-settler imperialism of his birthplace; that pathetic small-minded mix of racism and royalism, which – thanks largely to the Silvers – he had early on learnt to despise. The Union Jacks in white suburban flowerbeds, the portraits of Queen Elizabeth II and her incessantly smiling mother, always in those appalling feathery hats. Lemon and lilac; matching accessories; hat, gloves, two-piece, handbag, shoes; colour photographs that his own abject mother would cut from glossy magazines and stick obsequiously to walls of the maid's room.

He had imbibed enough of the Silvers' anti-monarchism to find it a little stifling that, even here, in the agreeable mountain kingdom, the Swazi royals, tinpot as they may have been, should loom so large in people's minds; should command such loyalty and respect. So Jack chose to despise the local rain-dance rituals; for all that he knew the pretty, grass-skirted maidens who appeared before the king were often enough studying higher maths or history of art – some of them at his own school. He was especially repelled by the prospect of that annual display, in which a young, public-school-educated Swazi male royal could be observed, naked, and straddling a large black bull.

In the French class; in French language and culture, he saw only the beauty of otherness, a disposition that was helped along by the persuasiveness of his pleasant young teacher, who was very good at her job. In quick time she had her classes up and running; singing French songs, performing simple one-act plays, filling out vocabulary sheets, marking diagrammatic maps that transfigured for Jack all those ordinary things that he was required to label

– *hôtel de ville, église, boulangerie, musée, bicyclette, chien.* Then there were the real-life maps; maps of Toulouse, maps of Montpellier, maps of Paris itself. Notre-Dame, the Île St Louis, Montmartre, the Louvre.

Miss Lundy fleshed out her lessons with meanderings through the history of French culture. There were the republican Romantics – Jacques Louis David; Delacroix and Ingres. And before that, the courtly Romantics – Watteau and Fragonard. She played her pupils tapes of French music: Lully, Fauré, Messiaen, Edith Piaf. She had videos of French films – sometimes even films about French royals who were so distant, so strange, so unlike the British Family Windsor, that Jack found himself enchanted. Beautiful, long-dead and deadly royals; a ballet-dancing Sun King, twirling in golden shoes.

And then, coming up sixteen and working in the library on an essay he had entitled 'Picasso and the Theatre', Jack came upon Léopold Sédar Senghor, poet, intellectual, cultural icon; first black member of the French National Assembly; President of Senegal; patron of the arts. And here, on the page, was the man himself, writing about Picasso. The greatness of Picasso's art, Jack read, was that it came from a combination of 'assimilation and rooted-ness'; that Picasso, by use of symbols, assimilated a wide range of cultural forms that welded together modernism and ancient traditions. And, in this, the art of Africa had played a hugely significant part. Likewise, the great new national force of Senegalese art, Senghor wrote, would be forged in pan-ethnic assimilation; a cultural inheritance that would incorporate 'Berber Arab, Black African, Mediterranean and Indo-European'. And this particular inheritance would be played out in a constant 'dialectic with modernity'.

This is all about me, Jack found himself thinking, because the whole enriching drift of what he was reading had nothing to do with Grandmother and gall bladders and feathers. It had to do with the forging of a new urban identity in an independent French-African state which, from that moment, became the focus of Jack's intense and romantic imaginings.

He read about the Senegalese National Ballet and the Senegalese Film School. He pored over such photographs as he could find of pavement cafés in Dakar; of agitprop artists' workshops, of busy little blue-painted buses run by brilliantly robed Mourides. He began to envisage his own inheritance, no longer in terms of Grandmother's hut or the maid's room in the backyard, or that hey-boy-no-change style of white corner-shopkeeper, but as 'Berber Arab, Black African, Mediterranean and Indo-European'.

He left the library wrapped in a cloak of his newly made plural identity. And each element was splashed on it like a bright star on a fabric of inky midnight blue. Way Up. Way Out. Way to go.

His Picasso essay was excellent. And Jack would duly have proceeded in predictable fashion towards a string of A grades in the International Bacc, had it not been for his French teacher, who, by chance, had returned from a vacation in Paris, laughing gaily, tossing back her head as she slammed the passenger door of a hired car, which had been driven by a young Parisian Senegalese whom she had befriended at an arts event in the 16th arrondissement. The young man was a poet who was on his way to visit family members in northern Senegal, but only after a term which he would spend as writer in residence in Dar es Salaam. As a French citizen he could travel easily – oh, easy for some! And Miss Lundy, who had a bit of a thing for clever, creative young Afro chaps, had quickly fallen for his impulsive, somewhat madcap plan to make a brief detour via her school in Swaziland, where he'd offered himself for a couple of poetry readings and a workshop or two. They would fly together from Paris to Johannesburg, yes? Then the poet – protected, of course, by his Euro status from the absurd local race laws – would hire a car at the airport and they would drive to the school in Mbabane. Once done, he would bid her farewell and drive the hired car to the Mozambique border, where he would hand it in. Then he would cross the border and linger to eat gigantic spicy prawns on the white beaches of Maputo. After that, he would travel pillion, by motorbike, northwards towards Beira and beyond, until he reached the Tanzanian border.

'You do know that South Africa has begun to stoke a civil war in Mozambique?' the French teacher said. 'A nasty little secret war. I believe they've been planting landmines. And as to all those giant prawns – well – food is beginning to run short. And if petrol should also be in short supply, that just might put paid to the motorbike.'

'Pah,' said the poet. He had 'connections'. He had a friend called Thierry, who had a friend called Claude, who had a friend called Pedro, who had a motorbike. And Pedro was friends with everyone, including the border authorities. Pedro was friends with the government. He was also friends with the rebels. And Pedro was friends with the South Africans as well, who were officially 'not there'. But Pedro fetched and carried for them. Pedro would always have petrol. Pedro would always have access to food. Pedro would collect him at the border and they would ride into Maputo. Then on and up. An adventure, *n'est-ce pas?*

The poet made Miss Lundy laugh – and Jack as well, to whom she had, at once, introduced him; Jack, her rising star; Jack, who had read Léopold Sédar Senghor.

Like Jack, the poet was tall and slim. Like Jack, his skin was pale. He looked young for his age, though he was seven years Jack's senior. He had cute round tortoiseshell glasses and longer hair.

'*Je m'appelle Jacques,*' he said and they shook hands.
'*Moi aussi,*' Jack said.

As they sat, a threesome over Miss Lundy's buns and tea, the poet talked about himself. He had a white French father, an anthropologist from Nantes, who taught in Paris, but now he was dead.

'My mother also,' he said. 'She is *descendue* from *l'aristocratie des Wolof* Kingdoms of Jolof.'

He drank his tea without milk. He did a lot of charming eye contact.

Jack, finding himself suddenly in want of a similarly interesting context, borrowed one from an old friend.

'Mine are also dead,' he said. 'I was taken in by eccentric white Communists. My mother was from Beirut. She abandoned me as a baby and returned there to take the veil. Then the Israelis dropped a big bomb.' With his hands he made graceful lotus gestures. '*Pouf!*' he said. '*Boum!*'

The poet laughed. He did more charming eye contact. He gestured a big explosion.

'*Boum-BOUM!*' he said.

At the reading in the hall that afternoon, the poet intoned a sequence of his somewhat lengthy lyrics, which were based on Homer's *Odyssey*; a West African odyssey to do with meanderings among Berber Arabs, Black Africans, Mediterraneans and Indo-Europeans. Some of the time he sang his lyrics – a thing he did without embarrassment, throwing his voice far into the hall. Since the poet's English was not very good and the school's French somewhat rudimentary, Miss Lundy had put Jack on the platform as translator, though she was there as back-up. So Jack and Jacques sat, heads together, sharing a microphone, sometimes bumping hands.

Once the event was over, the trio repaired to Miss Lundy's rooms for dinner – a private dinner for which her lamb was cooked almost to rags on account of Jacques's poetical offerings having been so very extended. It was clear by now to the French teacher that she had lost the poet to her pupil but, in truth, she no longer cared. His verses were, after all, not particularly good and his egomania had begun to disenchant. Its waning charm decreased with the man's excessive loquaciousness, which was being exacerbated by drink, because the poet's contribution to the evening meal had been a large bottle of duty-free whisky, which he drank unassisted by either one of his companions.

By halfway through the bottle, the poet was pushing aside the lamb shank on his plate. He was giving his audience an extended lesson in the care of his exquisite hair. He washed his hair like this, like that, he explained; never like that, like this. He combed it always exactly so. Never, ever, like so. And the only comb he had always to use – please to note – was this one. Observe. This was the only one he had always about his person. The comb was made of ivory. The teeth were of exactly such a depth; of such a width; spaced precisely so; the handle never too short; never too long. Always exactly so. To be used – observe – like this. The poet's hair made an attractive halo around his head. He would have no truck with braids; even less with extensions. Never! His hair was all his own.

Miss Lundy had begun to yawn.

'Jack,' she said finally. 'Jack.' She spoke in whispers as they coincided in her kitchen. 'I'm really sorry to ask this of you, but do you think you could get our guest to his room before he collapses here on me?'

So Jack, with his arm around the poet's waist, the poet's arm across his shoulders, proceeded with caution, step by step, along the path to the guest room across the garden and he wrestled Jacques in through the door. But the poet, suddenly upright, looked about him with interest. He resumed his state of animated wakefulness. He became coercively affable.

'Please,' he said. 'Jack, please to sit.'

But Jack kept on standing. He saw that, on the bedside table, the poet had a second whisky bottle, which he soon began to uncap. He gathered a tumbler and a plastic mug from the bath-room, filled both, and took a hefty swig. He scrabbled within a cabin bag, from which he pulled out more poetry.

'*Écoute-moi*,' he said.

The poems were long and boring and Jack was very tired.

'Come,' the poet said, looking up in time to see him yawn. He was patting the bed beside him. 'Pretty boy,' he said.

'*What?!*' Jack said; touch-me-not Jack.

He took a step backwards towards the door, but the poet was quick to intercept him.

He was on his feet and breathing into Jack's right ear.

'I know why you are here,' he said, and his breath, with its stale, grainy odour, was not unlike the smell of Jack's grandmother's home-made beer – albeit that the grains had been twelve years in the barrel.

Jack gave the poet a forceful shove, which had him tottering backwards, but he landed, quite softly, on the bed. For some-thing like five seconds, he looked nonplussed. Then his expression changed to anger. He rose and grabbed at both his travel bags. He threw in his few scattered items and closed the zips. He pulled on his leather jacket and tried, without success, to stuff the whisky bottle into one of its pockets. Then he snatched up the car keys.

After that he turned to Jack.

'I go,' he said.

'No,' Jack said. 'You can't.'

'I do not stay,' said the poet. 'I go where I am – *admire*.'

'Please –' Jack said.

'I,' said the poet, somewhat pompously, thumping his own breast, 'I am more better than Rimbaud. And Rimbaud, he is more better than Apollinaire. You will regret, *mon ami*. You will regret.'

'Please,' Jack said. 'Stay. It's dark.' He hesitated to observe that the poet was too drunk to drive the car. 'Where will you go?' he said.

'Mozambique,' said the poet. '*Bien sûr.*'

'Look,' Jack said. 'The roads aren't great. There are mountains and wild animals. You know. Game reserves. Big animals.'

The poet laughed. He darted forward and kissed Jack teasingly on the mouth; a brief assault of tongue and saliva that left Jack in shock.

'*Au revoir,*' he said and he was gone.

Jack wiped his mouth on his sleeve. He bolted the door. Then he sat down, stunned, on the poet's bed. He heard the car's engine start up in the car park. He waited, hardly daring to breathe. No lights flicked on in the body of the school. Nobody appeared to wake. He saw a brief arc of light cross the wall of the gym as the car reversed out of the parking bay. Then he stretched out on the poet's bed with his hands under his head; numb, corpse-like, appalled.

'Shit!' he mumbled. 'Oh shit, what now?'

He became aware that he was shivering and he wrapped himself in the poet's duvet against the thin mountain air. Then he couldn't stop yawning. His eyelids began to droop.

And when he woke, his bed seemed strangely aligned and the room was full of daylight. Jack saw that he was still in his clothes and that his shoes were on his feet. He sat bolt upright and looked at his watch. Thanks be to God, it was actually not that late. He hadn't even missed breakfast. If he was quick about it, he could slip out of the poet's room and fall unobserved into the slipstream of school life. And then, in the bathroom where he went for a first morning pee, he had yet another surprise. Oh my God. The poet's leather travel purse – a small, A5-sized item – was lying on the cistern. Alongside it, were the poet's ivory comb and his tortoiseshell glasses. Inside the purse were his passport, his return air ticket between Dar es Salaam and Dakar, his Visa Card and seven hundred US dollars. There was also a small notebook containing addresses and telephone numbers. Jack swished water through his teeth. He stuffed all the items into the wallet. Then he strode out of the guest room and closed the door behind him. His first port of call would be the staff room, where he was in hopes of catching Miss Lundy.

But something unscheduled was clearly going on. The school was not conforming to its usual morning routine. The teachers were not in the staff room. They were huddling in the foyer. There were two policemen in their midst and the talk was all of the poet. The car had been found, burnt out and turned over in a ditch. Material relating to the school – Miss Lundy's material – scorched but not entirely illegible, had been found in the glove compartment. The poet was dead. Tickets, documents, personal effects were all irrelevant now. Jack moved off, not wanting to intrude. He stashed the travel purse in his locker and went to get himself some breakfast. Within the hour, the school had resumed its normal workaday schedule.

Days went by and then weeks. Nobody asked about the poet's documents; nobody raised a question. After a month, as Jack approached his sixteenth birthday, the passport and the ticket had become his precious, secret things. Had it not been for the poet's effects, Jack's next two years would have been running their predictable schoolboy course, but now December had become his deadline. The air tickets had been issued by Kenya Airways. The flight was from Dar es Salaam on 15 December. He knew that by then he would be in Tanzania and that his hair would be quite a bit longer. He knew that he would be in Dar es Salaam. He would have got there by crossing the border into Mozambique with the help of one Pedro, who was friends with everybody; Pedro, whose telephone number was contained within the poet's small notebook.

Before he inherited the documents, there was little chance that Jack, as a black South African, could have crossed and recrossed borders. But now he had an EU passport; one belonging to Jacques Moreau, a comparably pale-brown person; an Afro-French person of similar height, similar build. And Pedro, who owned a motorbike, would always have enough petrol. Over the next three months, as he brooded on his secret treasures, Jack made himself ready to become that other person. *'Je m'appelle Jacques,'* he said. The utterance gave him much pleasure. It was, after all, what he had learned to say in Miss Lundy's very first French class. It was an identity with which he was comfortable; a version of himself that he preferred. His preparations were meticulous. He worked even harder at French. He read Camus. He read Aimé Césaire. He worked his way through all Miss Lundy's audio tapes from French radio. He watched French films. Then one day he made a trip into town and consulted with an optician. He had the poet's glasses in his bag. The glasses were needed for a play, he said. He wanted plain glass in the frames.

It was just at this time that Josh wrote suggesting that Jack might like to apply for a student visa for the UK; that, with Josh's guidance and recommendation, he could submit the relevant application and put in for sources of funding. Naturally, this might involve making a journey with no return, but Jack might nonetheless like to consider it. Jack didn't reply. France would have been another matter, but for the moment he had no interest in the Anglo-Saxon world. His focus was elsewhere. He was about to embark on another sort of journey with no possibility of return. He had read what he could about Chad and Mauritania and about the Côte d'Ivoire. He had read about Mali and Burkina Faso. Mostly he had read about Dakar. He could draw street plans of that city, from the avenue Pasteur to the Route de N'Gor; from the Stade Léopold Sédar Sénghor to the Pointe des Almadies. Though the poet's air tickets were in his possession, he daydreamed, occasionally and just for fun, in a *Boy's Own* sort of way, about taking the Bamako–Dakar railroad into the city all the way from Mali, or about making the journey by river in a dugout canoe. He knew all about the Île de Gorée and the art studios off the avenue Pompidou.

Jack waited until the Christmas holidays, when he announced to his host family that he was off to spend a day in the library. Then he headed out on a tourist bus for the Lebombo Mountains that made the border with Mozambique; a young French traveller in tortoiseshell glasses, who travelled on an EU passport. At the border crossing he heard, with a small shiver of excitement, that people were speaking Portuguese; that strange sound, a bit like Spanish crossed with Russian. And Pedro was there to ease his transit. Jack rode pillion the short distance to the white beaches of Maputo, where, flashing down avenues of flame trees, they paused to eat giant prawns in the beautiful, crumbling shell of an old colonial hotel.

Jack and his courier encountered little trouble as they hugged the coast, heading north. It was early days yet in the dirty-tricks war and they travelled almost unimpeded. They stopped at a series of enchanting small towns, each one edged with a sparkling turquoise sea. They proceeded, via pretty archipelagos, where they paused among reed houses and time-warped pastel villas for plates of peanut-and-cassava stew and bowls of boiled crabs. They made river crossings and skirted the national parks. They came upon a Makonde mask dance on the Ilha de Moçambique. And then they arrived at the Rovuma River, where Pedro came to a stop. Jack made the crossing without him, in – yes – a dugout canoe. And then he was on the Tanzanian border, where his visa was perfectly in order.

'Welcome to our country,' said the border guards, who spoke both English and Swahili. A bus took him into Dar es Salaam, where for three days Jack slept on the beach, living off bread and root-vegetable crisps that small boys sold him in paper cones made from used school jotters. The same small boys sold him cups of Arab coffee, brewed up on little camping burners. There was no way, even if he'd wanted to, that he could have visited Bernie and Ida Silver. He would have given himself away and, besides, he adored his isolation.

Then he headed out on the airport bus for the Kenya Airways flight. Jack had never flown before and he didn't know the procedure, but he knew that the plane would touch down in Nairobi, where certain passengers would alight. The airport, mercifully, was not very large and he was well on time. Once in the departure lounge, it was obvious to him which passengers were flying to Dakar. Everything about them was different. Their clothes were markedly different and they were speaking French or Wolof. Jack's forearms goose-pimpled with excitement as he opted to get in line behind a man who was carrying a kora. And then he was in the air.

Chapter Seven

Caroline

Having seen off her daughter on a three-week French exchange and her husband on a month-long trip to his one-time home town on the east coast of South Africa – a trip that will culminate in a conference on mime – Caroline, infallible, industrious Caroline; prodigious Caroline, has been making progress with her renovations to the family's recently acquired Victorian terraced house; a house that is the realisation of her modest, graduate-student dreams, all those years ago. Two up, two down and a lean-to kitchen at the back.

Within the week she has paint-stripped the window frames and the banisters, blow lamp in hand, and wearing a mask and goggles. Then she has waxed the exposed wooden surfaces. In the kitchen, where the furnishings are of sufficient an age to charm her rather than repel, she begins by sugar-soaping all the walls and the ceiling. Then she cleans up the old Belfast sink, with its nice wooden draining board, and she undertakes an invisible mend to a small chip in the glaze. Caroline removes several decades of grease from a pretty antique cooking stove, an electric item shaped like a Queen Anne cupboard on cabriole legs, but veneered in mottled enamel. There is something about old mottled enamel that always lifts her spirits, so she's delighted to discover that all the stove's parts still work.

Making liberal use of the Spar shop's Own Brand washing-soda crystals, she cleans up a 1950s blue-and-cream plywood dresser, its name fixed to the front in raised chrome cursive: 'The Pantrix'. It has a pull-down, enamel-work surface with integral wooden bread board and several door panels made of dimpled glass. Prior to Caroline's ministrations, it also has forty years of toast crumbs set in sausage grease, which coat all its outer surfaces. The kitchen's open wooden shelves all exhibit a disgusting, glued-on compound: a sort of caramel substance in which several small insects have met their end. But Caroline, who enjoys a challenge, has a strong and splendid right arm.

Next, she rips off the textured, swirly orange vinyl that covers the kitchen floor and is rewarded by the sight of old red quarry tiles beneath. All the same, it puzzles her that the red quarry tiles should themselves have been coated with red floor-paint. She removes the blistering paint without much trouble, before scrubbing, sealing and polishing the quarry tiles to a lovely, matt-brick richness. Then, covering the floor with two large groundsheets, she paints the kitchen ceiling white and the walls pale blue and cream, to match The Pantrix. Finally, she fixes a repro laundry rack on pulleys to the ceiling; a thing she has acquired from Scotts of Stow by mail order, and on it she hangs a miscellany of pots and pans, along with her ladles, whisks and colanders. The laundry rack is one of the very few items that Caroline has bought new – and it is with a touch of Ozzie feminist irritation that she takes note of its name. It's called 'The Sheila Maid'.

Immediately outside the kitchen door is a small flagstone yard, which, with Pathclear and a sturdy garden broom, she transforms from its drain-and-dandelion dankness to a shady scented patio, with the help of her clematis and honeysuckle, and her several old fish kettles of kitchen herbs. Mint and parsley; marjoram and sage; fennel, rosemary and chives.

Having previously employed a builder to knock through the two tiny ground-floor living rooms, the house, once dark and poky, is now filled with light, and the walls here and there are coated in new sepia plaster which reminds her of old walls in Rome. What a time it is since she has travelled anywhere – but upward and onward, Caroline! In the bathroom she removes the tacky hardboard bath panels to discover that her tub has pretty feet. She spends a morning treating patches of rust on its iron underside and, next day, paints the treated surfaces a soothing pastel grey. Meanwhile, having applied mould repellent to the walls and regrouted the white ceramic tiles, Caroline sets herself to papering the bathroom with three rolls of pale-grey Jane Churchill polka dots, which – being Caroline – she has found for thirty pence each in a basket of bin ends in the Red Cross charity shop.

In the bedrooms she rips away the cladding from both the cast-iron fireplaces and sweeps up two dead starlings from one of the grates. She throws the pocky nylon carpets out of the front sash window, before gathering them up from the pavement and carting them off to the dump. Then she washes and undercoats the upstairs floorboards, before painting them pale grey. Meanwhile, she's collected the floor sander she's hired, complete with edging attachment, and, having checked the downstairs floors for loose nails, Caroline switches on the great roaring kidney-shaking machine and proceeds to sand the living-room floorboards.

Oh dear! It is precisely because of the great roaring machine that she doesn't hear the three calls from her mother to her mobile phone. Caroline's mother has been phoning her daughter to complain of chest pains. Her 'heartburn', as she calls it, is getting worse. In between making attempts to reach her daughter, Caroline's mother has been swallowing over-the-counter antacids in a peppy mix with blood-pressure tablets and her daily dose of Warfarin. Then, for good measure, she has taken all of it twice.

And it's because of the great roaring machine that Mrs McCleod, who has suffered a cerebral haemorrhage, lies for twenty-four hours, unobserved and unattended, in a heap alongside her bed in the house at Garden Haven. Because Caroline, after a day spent operating the sander, has driven back home to the bus up the Abingdon Road and has then, uncharacteristically, fallen asleep, exhausted, without checking her messages; without so much as washing her feet, or brushing her perfect white teeth.

Caroline spends the following day finishing off her downstairs floors with the edging attachment and vacuuming up the quantities of sawdust created by the big roaring machine. Then, at evening, she finally goes home to spruce up. She takes an indulgently long hot shower, washes and dries her beautiful thick hair, anoints her skin with thrifty E45 cream and drives off to her mother's house in freshly laundered clothes. She has with her a wholesome supper for two – a home-made cucumber soup; pork medallions on a bed of creamed spinach, along with some braised fennel; a salad of plums tossed lightly in a dressing of yogurt, mint and honey. Having rung the bell and knocked at the front-room window, Caroline finally lets herself in with her key. On a first round she doesn't see the old woman, slumped unconscious and hypothermic, on the far side of the bed and she goes back downstairs. It is only a delayed mental image of the half-made bed that causes her to take a second look. Then it's all stations go.

The ambulance arrives with laudable speed and it's hands-on emergency care by a skilled paramedic, before Caroline's mother is carefully stretchered out of her house. And it's 4 a.m. before the old woman, tagged, assessed and processed, is carted off for a brain scan. Finally Caroline goes home to the bus and catches two hours' sleep. At 9 a.m. she is telephoned by a neurosurgeon from the hospital. There is evidence of her mother's having had several previous small strokes, he says, probably over the past year and all of them undiagnosed. Right now she has a significant subdural haematoma, a blood clot the size of a bath sponge, pressing down on her brain.

The neurosurgeon plans to operate within the hour, he says, and he assures her that the prognosis for recovery is reasonably good – though age could be a negative factor. The surgery he describes sounds to Caroline like prehistoric trepanning. The surgeon will drill a hole in the side of her mother's skull and draw out what Caroline envisages as a Petri dish full of half-set red jelly. Unfortunately, he tells her, there is a possibility that the cavity will refill with blood, in which case, after a second scan, he will need to operate again.

By now Caroline is in no frame of mind to focus on sanded floorboards. The home-improvement project is put on hold as she spends anxious days at the hospital, alternating between the League of Friends canteen on the ground floor and the neuro-science ward upstairs, where the old woman, her eyes firmly closed in sleep, lies motionless, with what look like several Frankenstein bolts jutting from the side of her shaven head. In between, Caroline pays brief visits to Garden Haven, gathering up basic toiletries, dealing with perishable foodstuffs, searching hurriedly through her mother's drawers for address books and letters, in the hope of finding some way to make contact with her sister. Since she has no luck here or, being agitated, gives up too soon, she decides instead to contact the Australian Embassy and place the matter in their hands.

She then makes equally unsuccessful attempts to contact Josh at the beachfront hotel where he is booked in for the three weeks prior to the conference. Josh never seems to be in and he doesn't respond to her messages. I will not worry about him, Caroline tells herself, though she's feeling unusually vulnerable and just a little bit needy. I will not think of gun crime. Josh will be busy, she tells herself. He'll be out of town. Visiting old friends? Old family servants? Something like that. Then there is Zoe. Caroline, with her first two calls to the household of her daughter's French exchange, is unlucky enough to get Véronique, who is monosyllabic, ungracious and unhelpful to a degree, even when speaking her own language. On a third attempt she gets Maman, who tells her, somewhat abruptly, that her daughter Zoe is 'out'.

'*Vueillez la dire que sa grandmère est très très malade,*' Caroline says. 'Please, Madame, will you ask her to call me?'

'*D'accord,*' says Maman. '*Certainement.*' But Zoe does not phone back.

Next day, Caroline calls again.

Zoe, Maman says, '*est sortie*'.

'A school trip?' Caroline asks.

'*Oui,*' says Maman. '*Le school-trip. Exactement.*'

By this time Caroline's mother has begun somewhat feebly to open her eyes and has sipped a few teaspoons of Lucozade. Caroline, who has eagerly followed up this development by bringing in a jar of thin, carefully strained chicken broth and a small home-made pear smoothie, finds that her mother simply spits these out the moment tiny particles of either are deposited on her tongue.

'Jam,' she says. This appears to be her only available word. 'Jam,' she says again.

Caroline is convinced that her mother is asking for Janet; the estranged but favourite daughter.

'Don't worry, Mum,' she says. 'I'll find Janet for you, I promise. The Australian Embassy has got it all in hand.'

'Jam,' the old woman says.

'Is there anything you'd like me to bring in for you?' Caroline says. 'Anything at all, Mum?'

'Jam,' is all her mother says. 'Jam. Jam.' Her speech is barely above a whisper.

191

By the next day, she is relieved to find that the Australian Embassy has left her a message. They have a contact number for a person they believe to be her sister. Janet has not been difficult to find, since she holds the position of editor at a national family magazine based on 'Christian values'.

Back home in the bus that evening, Caroline calculates the time difference and psychs herself up to phone her sister. As a preliminary, she checks out Janet's magazine on the Web. It materialises as a cringeworthy publication of such unbearable homespun smugness that it embarrasses Caroline as a form of emotional bad faith in conjunction with intellectual death. Cosy advice, interspersed with judgemental harangues, advertisements for virginity merchandise and novelty reach-out projects for the promotion of community goodwill.

'Do you experience negative feelings about a colleague, friend or neighbour?' trills the editorial, under a small, homely photograph of Janet, sixteen years on from Caroline's last sighting of her. 'Try making a batch of our scrumptious Grudge Fudge and take it round with a smile (*see p.52*).'

On the telephone, Janet is distancing and cold.

'It's better you deal with Mum,' she says. 'My place is here at Mark's side. His work is very important.'

'Janet,' Caroline says pleadingly, 'Mum's just had brain surgery. She can't speak. She's not eating. She can barely open her eyes. All she can say is your name. Just the one word, that's all. Over and over. How important can Mark's work be?'

'Pardon me?' Janet says, with that upward inflection Caroline has never before noticed she finds extremely irritating. She wonders, for a moment, whether she has it herself. 'Mark is working for Jesus,' Janet says. End of story.

'Mum said he was an accountant,' Caroline says. It's a remark that Janet chooses to ignore. 'Look. Please, Janet. Take my number,' she says. 'Think about it, won't you? Try and find a flight. It would be so great if you could come over. It might make all the difference.'

'Not possible,' Janet says. 'Unfortunately. Tell Mum we always remember her in our prayers.'

Then the line goes dead.

Caroline is shaking all over. She can hardly believe what she's just heard; nor that her sister has simply terminated the exchange. Can this really be Janet; her whiny little invalid sister? Can she have morphed over the years into this judgemental, smug middle age? Why is she being so cruel? What for? No wonder she was so heartless with their poor mother all those years ago.

In some agitation, Caroline tries again to contact Josh. No response. She judges herself too upset to unload on Zoe, who is, after all, just a child, but she's feeling distinctly inadequate, not to say frightened. Caroline concentrates on sleep, but tosses and turns in bed. She sucks her fingers. She tries reading detective fiction. Finally, she manages three hours' sleep until, at 5 a.m., she leaps from bed, remembering the sanding machine. Oh God! She has left the wretched roaring machine in the living room of the little new house, during which time it will have clocked up four days of unscheduled hire charge. Oh shit and double shit! This is not the sort of oversight that Caroline expects of herself. She makes herself a cafetière of coffee and goes outside to calm down, cup in hand. She watches the sun rise over her vegetable garden. She plucks off the odd busy snail. Then she gets herself ready to collect the sander and drive it back to the hire firm, hoping that by putting in an extra-early appearance she'll persuade the firm to waive a day of the fee.

In the hospital her mother is imbibing nothing but coaxed teaspoons of Lucozade and she's barely opening her eyes.

'Jam,' she says impassively, when Caroline kisses her.

This time, Caroline tells herself firmly that her mother, who has a sweet tooth, is simply asking for jam.

'I'm sorry, Mum,' she says. 'I'll bring in some jam for you today.'

'Jam,' the old woman says.

The neurosurgeon is concerned that Caroline's mother is excessively lethargic and arranges for another brain scan. Then, two days later and with no prior warning, Caroline arrives to find that the old woman has been moved out of the gleaming neuroscience ward, with its generous supply of committed and highly skilled nurses. She has gone far down the food chain, into a slovenly and understaffed geriatric ward, where hollow-eyed and hopeless oldies are groaning feebly, calling out in vain for commodes, or shuffling on Zimmer frames in fluffy dressing gowns to a lavatory that's doing its damnedest to scream a warning to all potential users. 'Attention! Superbug! Please Do Not Enter!' The whole ward reeks of diarrhoea. Beds are unmade, there are balls of stained cotton wool and discarded adhesive dressings dotted about the cracked linoleum floor and – try indefatigably as Caroline does, day after day, from now on – no senior doctor is ever available to discuss her mother's case. No one appears conversant with her mother's medical history, nor with the neurosurgeon's previously stated intentions. The neurosurgeon himself is as if teleported to Planet Zorg.

Caroline's mother, who is kept permanently attached to a somewhat grubby-looking catheter, is very soon found to have a urinary infection for which she is given antibiotics. For a day she appears to pick up a bit and even begins to eat; two sultanas and one quarter of a small sawdust biscuit, but she promptly vomits everything she eats. At this point, although she is still on holiday, Caroline arranges six weeks' compassionate leave from her job and, after another week, lobbies to take her mother home as soon as possible. She is confident that her own twenty-four-hour, hands-on nursing care, away from the soiled dressings and the constant threat of infection, could provide the old woman with a better chance of recovery.

In anticipation of her new role, Caroline moves her mother's bed downstairs and researches less dehumanising alternatives to the patient's clumpy, in-dwelling catheter. She goes to Boots, where, for a gasp-inducing eighty-five pounds the box, she acquires two dozen single-use catheters that look like narrow drinking straws, and she teaches herself to use them. She has also researched various rehab techniques for stroke victims, in response to which she's spent hours making picture cards – house, tree, apple, flower, dog, cat, et cetera – and has stuck white name cards on several household items in clear, bold lower case: fridge, door, table, chair, window, lamp, kettle, bed, mug. In between her visits to the hospital, she barely goes home to the bus. Nor does she visit the new house for further home improvements. She beds down, exhausted, night after night, in her mother's house at Garden Haven, begging a God, in whom she no longer believes, to make the old woman well.

Over the days, she continues her attempts to contact her husband and her daughter, asking them please to ring her, or please to leave her a message, but she's getting no response. Neither, of course, has a mobile phone. In between, she calms her nerves by embarking on a Garden Haven spring-clean. She sorts out her mother's fridge. She squares up the clutter of old magazines. She removes the collection of china ornaments to soak in washing-up liquid – the hideous miscellany of shire horses and shepherdesses; the coy Hummel figurines, with their unpleasing crusty matt glaze. Only one little pair escapes Caroline's clean-up: the dainty china lady on her china bed, with her devoted china gentleman standing alongside her, his little china hand in hers. She wonders idly where it can have gone. Caroline dusts her mother's shelves. She neatens the bookcase with the large-print Catherine Cooksons and the copy of *Codependent No More*. Then, having previously rifled the desk drawers, jammed as they are, with old diaries, household clutter, junk leaflets and bank statements, in a frantic search for some sign of Janet's contact details, she now turns her attention to sorting the desk.

There are no half-measures with Caroline and her efforts are nothing if not rigorous, so it is not all that long before a wallet file has fallen from her hands and spewed its contents to the floor. The file contains Catriona McCleod's 'Last Will and Testament', dated 19 August of the previous year – 1994. Curiosity overcomes Caroline. First, the document contains her mother's instructions for burial. No cremation, thank you. She desires that her body be conveyed to Australia and laid in a plot she has evidently purchased, near the domicile of her younger daughter Janet. In the will, Caroline notes that her mother has left all her property to Janet. That is to say, all her 'capital', as contained in an unexpected medley of ISAs and savings accounts, all duly enumerated, including an instant-access higher-rate account worth sixty thousand pounds. It's with the same bank that holds her mother's current account.

Caroline's mother has bequeathed the Garden Haven house exclusively to Janet; the house bought and paid for by Caroline, who has done so by the sacrifice of all her own and her husband's first savings. Pretty well all of it went to providing the Garden Haven deposit, while a twenty-year mortgage made up the rest, taken out in Caroline's name and payable by monthly direct debit from Caroline's bank account. Thus, though the ownership of the property is in Mrs McCleod's name – a thing that her mother had been adamant about – Caroline has been footing the bill for the previous eleven years. She has nine years still to go. Yet the house, as she now takes note, will belong to Janet. If her mother were to die and the house be rented out, any rental income would presumably be Janet's. Mark would doubtless find those fat monthly rental cheques a useful bolster to his 'important work'. The cheques will all be for Jesus, while Caroline will be stuck paying off the mortgage. And were she to renege on paying it? Well then, she presumes that the mortgage provider would be within his rights to repossess her property. That is to say, not the one in Garden Haven, but the darling little terraced house with its newly sanded floorboards and its prettily renovated kitchen. The Last Will and Testament has started to swim before her eyes as Wonder Girl, can-do Caroline begins to feel ever smaller and more hurt. In fact it is easily ten minutes before she is able to read on. That is when she discovers she is not to be left entirely empty-handed.

'To my adopted daughter, Caroline,' says the will, 'I leave all the contents of my house.' The said 'contents' doubtless to include the large-print Catherine Cooksons and *Codependent No More*, the Hummel figurines currently soaking in Fairy Liquid, the mustard Dralon 'suite' and the two busily-patterned, Indian-sweatshop rugs. But worldly goods are, for the moment, not the primary focus of Caroline's attention. 'My adopted daughter,' she reads. Then she reads it again. 'My adopted daughter.' 'My adopted' –

She stares and stares at the document. Her eyes brim with tears. Caroline, who has never allowed herself even a moment's self-pity; Caroline, who never cries, now finds that the floodgates open. She weeps until she's soaked through her sleeves. Then she gets up and fetches a roll of kitchen towel.

Caroline throws herself on the sofa, where the crying becomes a sort of howl. In between the wails and howls, she emits pitiful hiccups and sobs. The sky has gone dark around her. Shivering with cold, she hugs herself in a foetal ball and starts to rock back and forth. She has always so terribly – perhaps excessively – wanted her mother to love her; to admire and value her. And now, for eleven of her adult years – no, fifteen counting the four years before little Zoe's appearance – she has bitten down her longing to have children; has obliged her family to do without holidays; to do without stuff; to live in a bus; has obliged them all, in spite of hard work, talent and two professional salaries, to do nothing but make do and mend. All for the sake of her mother. Caroline has been incessantly, relentlessly ingenious, with scraps of home-grown cabbage and handfuls of dried beans; with old linen sheets and recycled union cloth; with items found in jumble sales and dumped on skips. She has given up her Oxford DPhil along with her beckoning career in academe. Worst of all – oh, unforgivable! – she has consistently, confidently denied her own daughter, her sweet, good and only child, all those things that her girlfriends have; the things that little girls want and need; Barbie dolls, ballet lessons, riding lessons, gym club and mobile phones, Topshop clothes and music players. She has brooked no opposition; has always been firmly, know-it-all put-down – that's if ever Josh has ventured to query the austerity of her regime. Let us, as always, count our blessings. Caroline Clever-Clogs. Problem-Solver Extraordinaire, who has never stopped laying down the law.

Caroline has been cutting her own hair for the last sixteen years. She cuts Josh and Zoe's hair as well. And hasn't she done an excellent job? Oh my, yes! She has never bought herself new clothes, not beyond her M & S basic-range knickers. Even her bras have come from charity shops. And now her cleverness, her triumphs of thrift, have all turned to ash in her mouth. How could her mother have done this to her? And why? Because she was 'adopted'? Did her mother simply fall out of love with her when a biological daughter came along? More than that, does her mother actively dislike her? Resent her existence? Her brains? Her markedly better looks? Has she, all along, been wishing her older daughter ill?

'I bought you this *fucking* house, you bitch, you witch!' she says suddenly, right out loud, raising her voice to full volume, pitching it against the farthest wall. 'This ugly, revolting house! And the monthly allowance – what a con!' She bangs her fist hard on the wooden arm of the sofa and lets out a wail of pain.

Two hours have passed before Caroline has stopped crying. She has moved from misery to rage. She gets up and goes through to the kitchen, where, one by one, she removes the Hummel figurines from their washing-up water and throws them against the wall. Since the wretched things will not oblige and shatter, she smashes them to pieces with a meat mallet, grinding them into the floor. Finally, she is once more in control as rage gives way to calculation.

She has tried Josh yet again, this time not bothering to use the cheap-rate Teledial number, because – what the hell – any debts incurred will be for Janet to pick up. And, on her visit to the hospital next evening, she is gratified to see that her mother is, once again, looking worse – or is it her imagination? It seems to Caroline that her mother's abdomen is swollen, but this time she makes no attempt to seek out the duty doctor for information.

She leans over and whispers into the old woman's ear.

'I've read your will,' she says. 'And shall I tell you something? You are a poisonous bitch and I really hope you die.'

The old woman's eyelids flutter feebly.

'Jam,' she says, in a tiny whisper.

'Oh no!' Caroline says. 'No jam for you. Why don't we rather start thinking about fudge? Janet's "scrumptious Grudge Fudge". Now there's a thing. Or perhaps we should call it tablet, since Bonnie Scotland is your heritage? Make a batch of toxic Scottish tablet and give it to someone you hate. That's dear Janet's personal advice and she's got Jesus on the board.'

The old woman appears to have tears in her eyes, or is it just a rheumy ooze?

'Jam,' she says pathetically, clawing the sheet with her one still-functioning hand. 'Jam.'

Caroline, before she leaves the ward, takes note that her mother's catheter bag is now so full that it's in danger of backing up. This time she makes no effort to buttonhole a nurse. Neither does she undertake the task of emptying it into the bowl of the Superbug lav. She takes herself straight home – home to the bus – and falls into a deep sleep. Before the dawn she is up and doing, filled with vigour and resolution. She knows exactly what she's going to do.

Caroline returns by first light to Garden Haven, where, once again at her mother's desk, she arranges all the old woman's bank statements, policies and chequebooks in a line across the floor. She observes from checking the current-account statements that her mother, contrary to her constant claims of indigence, has evidently been in receipt of a monthly private pension which goes back sixteen years.

These same monthly amounts have been regularly transferred, by direct debit, into her higher-rate savings account; a nicely accumulating nest egg which has clearly been no problem for her since, all the while, she has had Caroline's monthly allowance to provide for her day-to-day expenditure. Caroline fetches her mother's handbag and tips out all its contents. She lines up the debit and credit cards along with the statements and the policies. In her mother's pocket diary she observes that her mother has written what Caroline takes to be her pin code. It's the year of the old woman's birth, but written backwards. And, in the address book – yes! – under 'B' for 'Bank', she finds the TeleBank call number alongside what is very likely a five-digit security code – this last, somewhat inadequately disguised as a local telephone number. The Witch Woman has prefixed the five secret digits with her local telephone code, but the local numbers, as Caroline knows, should total six, not five.

Before she visits the hospital that day, Caroline spends an hour on the phone. She deals with the matter of the monthly allowance, cancelling the standing order from her own bank to her mother's for an amount that, until yesterday, she had always wished could have been larger. Then she taps in the number of her mother's TeleBank. She follows this with the security code and the sixteen-digit number on the front of her mother's debit card. Bingo! Open Sesame! Alongside her, by the phone, Caroline has the number of her mother's higher-rate account. She transfers ten thousand pounds from the higher-rate account to her mother's current account. Then, using the pin number, she goes out to avail herself of the nearest cash point, where she withdraws the maximum-permitted daily amount, which appears to be two hundred pounds.

Caroline does this every morning before she visits the hospital. Her tally is one thousand four hundred per week. This she stashes under the newly sanded floorboards in the living room of the Victorian terraced house.

In between, she embarks on a policy of running up the maximum debt on her mother's credit card. She goes for a facial, a massage and a haircut, to include the sort of blonde highlights that, way back in her Australian youth, the sun always granted her for free. Over the ensuing days, she browses in designer-clothing boutiques and buys herself Armani jeans, Betty Jackson trousers, two Joseph cardigans, a buttercup-yellow short-sleeved sundress by Marc Jacobs and an amazing Vivienne Westwood item with off-the-shoulder, whalebone-corset top and Flower Fairy skirt of gauzy pale-blue georgette. Then she buys a capacious Mulberry handbag, before she starts on shoes. That done, Caroline buys three tickets apiece for the entire Glyndebourne Touring Opera season and a trio of tickets for Zoe and her best friends, Mattie and Maggs, to see the Ellen Kent *Swan Lake*, to be performed by a much-lauded touring ballet company from Kiev.

Caroline is not surprised when her mother's bank phones the house in Garden Haven. She is more than ready for the nice young man who has 'some security concerns', since the pattern of withdrawals from Mrs McCleod's current account appears to be a little unusual.

'Am I speaking to Mrs Catriona McCleod?' he says.

'Speaking,' Caroline says.

She has no problem answering his range of easy security questions, regarding her mother's date of birth and maiden name, or what the amount was of the last withdrawal she remembers making.

'The truth is, I don't have much time,' Caroline tells him. 'I'm sorry if I embarrass you, young man. Forgive me, but to put it bluntly, I'm "terminal", you see. I've decided to treat myself.'

'I'm so sorry,' says the young man. 'Yes, of course.'

'I'm also treating my daughter,' Caroline goes on. 'It's a better thing, wouldn't you agree, to give with a warm hand rather than a cold one?'

'Absolutely,' says the young man. 'You take care now, Mrs McCleod. You look after yourself.'

'Thank you,' Caroline says. 'I will.'

Her next call is to order a new top-of-the-range central-heating system for the Victorian terraced house, which she pays for, over the telephone, with her mother's credit card.

That evening, from her mother's phone, Caroline calls her sister, who, given the time difference, will just have arrived at the office of her Grudge Fudge Jesus Mag.

'Janet,' she says, faking good cheer and finding, much to her own surprise, that she's quite good at it. 'First of all, Mum is a little bit better. I thought you'd like to know.'

'Thank you,' Janet says. 'I could tell you were overreacting.'

Good God, Caroline is thinking. Is this a crazy person? I mean, is it possible one could be 'overreacting' to a vast blood clot pressing down on an oldie's brain? But biting her tongue she goes on.

'Mum has been talking quite a bit,' she says. 'But I think she's a little confused.'

'Is this relevant?' Janet says, attempting to cut her short. 'If it's not, I'm a bit busy –'

'She told me that I was adopted,' Caroline says. 'I mean, does that ring any bells with you? Or what is she thinking of?'

'Of course you're adopted,' Janet says. 'Mum and Dad thought they couldn't have children. That's until I came along.'

'Any idea where they got me?' Caroline says. 'I mean it's the first I've –' Her hand is shaking so badly she can hardly hold the phone.

'Sure,' Janet says. 'Mum told me. From some blonde tart on a bus.'

'How do you mean tart?' Caroline says.

'As in tart,' Janet says. 'As in the sort of slut who gets pregnant out of wedlock and gives away her baby on a bus.'

'Where?' Caroline says. 'A bus from where to where?' She has suddenly found herself overwhelmed with relief to have it confirmed that she once had another sort of mother, whether tart or no.

'Somewhere in the boondocks,' Janet says. 'Could've been somewhere like between Chillingollah and Pinnaroo. Or maybe between Tintinara and Dimboola? Or what about Wangaratta? How about Gol Gol? Take your pick, Caroline, because, frankly, I haven't got a clue. Things could be quite informal back then. And I happen to know that there was no exchange of names and addresses. Mum, understandably, made it "strictly no contact". Why don't you ask her if you must?'

'I will,' Caroline says. 'Thank you, Janet, I will.'

'I reckon you owe Mum a lot,' Janet says. 'Think about it, Caroline.'

'I will,' says Caroline. 'I am thinking about it.'

'Well, if there's nothing else,' Janet says. 'We go to press this afternoon.'

'Yes,' Caroline says. 'Thank you, Janet. Thanks a lot.' But once again, she's talking into the air, because Janet, the Witch Woman's heiress, the whining, one-time Less Fortunate, has already hung up on her sister.

The call concluded, Caroline sets out from Garden Haven to visit her mother, who is looking markedly worse. The old woman is groaning feebly and appears to be in pain. She's developed a sudden fever and she's back on a glucose drip. Somewhat to Caroline's astonishment, a senior consultant actually seeks her out to acquaint her of new developments. The old woman has not only developed a lower-bowel infection – doubtless thanks to the Superbug factor, whose existence is discreetly not mentioned – but, in addition, she has managed to rip out a catheter with the result that bits of its rubber bulb have come adrift within her urethra, which are likely to cause blood poisoning. The only option on both counts, the doctor tells the patient's daughter, is urgent surgery. They will need to cut away some of her bowel, in addition to removing the bits of rubber. He desists from making the obvious point that the patient, given the current state of her, is not likely to survive further surgery.

Caroline is given some papers to sign, after which she returns to Garden Haven, where she tries once more to phone her husband. His resolute inaccessibility over these last two weeks has suddenly begun to make her frantic and she bangs down the phone in a fret. Why is Josh always so bloody ineffectual? Why is he never there when things get tough? Why does he never take command? And why – bloody why – did he not ever put his foot down over his blood-sucking mother-in-law? Wouldn't a real man have stopped her?

'Or me?' she yells. 'Why did you let me do it? Why? You stood by and let me debase myself before that malignant old leech. I mean, for years and years. And she isn't even my mother! Josh, why the fuck didn't you STOP ME? Why did you let it go on? And on? And ON?'

She's so angry with him that she suddenly knows that she's got to have it out – and soon. If he can't or won't respond to her telephone calls, she'll bloody well confront him face to face. She'll book two return flights to South Africa on the old cow's credit card and then she'll go off on the Eurostar to collect her daughter from France. Why not? By the sound of Zoe's uncharming exchange family, the poor girl will be only too pleased to have the experience cut short, and the two of them can then spend a glorious day in Paris – a day full of shopping and little-girl treats – all courtesy of Gran's bank accounts.

There's nothing that lifts Caroline's spirits like a project and she's on to the airline right away. Seven days' time? Why not? Two return tickets from Heathrow to Johannesburg, plus two internal return flights from Johannesburg to Durban. Two days in France, then back to England in time to deal with her mother, be she alive or dead. Then, to pack for that lovely trip south, which has begun to seem quite an adventure. Caroline has not been on a plane since 1978. Using her mother's TeleBank facility, Caroline shifts twenty thousand pounds from the Witch Woman's higher-rate savings account to the current account. Then she pays off the minimum amount to accord with that quoted on her mother's monthly Visa Card statement; this to ensure that her ensuing purchases will not be blocked through overspend. Both transactions are a simple matter of pushing buttons on the telephone keypad and it's making her feel pretty good. As usual, she goes out to draw her daily limit of two hundred pounds, which she stashes under the newly sanded floorboards. The cash sum now tallies one thousand six hundred pounds.

Caroline's mother survives the surgery, but survives it by a mere thirty-six hours, during which time she can breathe only with an oxygen mask and with a pronounced rattle in the larynx. She never again opens her eyes. Once it's over, Caroline briskly checks the *Yellow Pages*. She arranges to have her mother's body transported to the offices of the nearest burial service for cremation, where she arranges a speedy appointment. There, where all is tasteful carpeting and soothing birch veneer, a young female attendant is suitably sober and respectful. Caroline fills in the proffered form and answers several questions with regard to burial options. These include the offer of a horse-drawn hearse and a flunky in top hat and tails. The young woman has several full-colour plastic-coated albums of casket choices, from mahogany with buttoned satin linings to wicker eco-baskets.

'I don't need a casket,' Caroline says. 'There's to be no funeral service. When can I collect the ashes?'

She pays the charges, on the spot, with her mother's credit card, and collects the ashes after forty-eight hours, by which time the stash under the sanded floorboards totals two thousand two hundred pounds.

In the interim she has visited Argos, where she buys herself a shredder, and she returns with it to Garden Haven with the intention of shredding the will. It pleases her to reflect that it's her mother's card that has paid for the shredder, though she's certain that all she's doing is buying herself a little extra time. The woman will have a copy lodged with her solicitor. Come to think of it, which solicitor is that? She has no memory, from her desk-tidy episode, of coming upon a letter either to or from any such person.

Caroline goes to the cardboard folder and draws out the will once more. She scrutinises the thing from end to end. No evidence

of a solicitor. No headed writing paper, nor sturdy legal envelope. It crosses her mind that this is the first time she has actually
read the will all the way to the end. Last time she simply called
a halt upon discovering herself the adopted heir to the Hummel
figurines and the contents of her mother's bookcase. Now, on
the final page, she observes the signature. Catriona McCleod. It
stands alone. Then there is the date: 19 August 1994. That is all.
The will has not been witnessed and no solicitor has overseen
it. With sixty thousand in her higher-rate savings account, the
woman has nonetheless done her own will the cut-price, self-help
way. She has bought the form from a high-street stationer and
filled it in herself. God knows, as it stands, the thing is surely not
valid – though could it be that Janet is in possession of a properly witnessed copy? And yet? And yet? All the evidence suggests
that her sister's severance from the old woman has been total.
Caroline has unearthed no draft letter, no telephone calls to
Australia, as recorded on her mother's umpteen statements from
BT, no fondly hoarded Christmas or birthday card from yester-
year. Nothing. Only those cloying wedding photos from eleven
years back and the copy of *Codependent No More*, with its poisonous
little message. Yet she can't afford to pick up the phone and sound
out her sister. Well, not yet.

When she goes to collect the ashes, Caroline notes that they are
contained within a transparent plastic bag which is inside a cardboard box. The box is of subdued pastel hue, a bit like a cuboid
tissue box, but with a small adhesive label bearing the name of
the deceased. Once outside the offices of the burial service, she
removes the transparent plastic bag and places it in a Sainsbury's
bag that she has about her person. The pastel cuboid box she
drops into the nearest roadside litter bin, having first picked off
the small adhesive label and put it in her pocket. Then she begins
her journey home.

The sun is shining and Caroline decides to return on foot to the bus off the Abingdon Road, taking a pleasant, long way round, walking through small suburban streets until she gets to those that run alongside the river. She notes that it's evidently refuse-collection day, because the bins are all on the street. One of them has a sturdy rubber lid that says 'Not suitable for hot ashes', which gives her an idea. Caroline lifts the bin lid. She drops in the Sainsbury's carrier bag containing the bag of ashes, which are most certainly no longer hot. Then she puts the bin lid back. She walks on, unencumbered. By the end of the day, she speculates with satisfaction, the Witch Woman will be landfill.

Before she leaves for the Eurostar next day, Caroline does some money stuff, knowing that her spending time will soon run out. She will have to acquire a death certificate and close all her mother's accounts within five days of her demise. So she pays her annual Council Tax along with the tax on her car. She makes sure all her own quarterly household bills are paid. For these expenses she considers it expedient to use her mother's chequebook, predating the cheques to three days before the old woman's death.

Only then does she phone her sister.

'Oh Janet,' she says, 'I'm so sorry. Look. It's Mum. I've got bad news.'

'Spit it out,' Janet says into the pause.

'Janet, Mum died,' she says. 'I'm sorry. It was so sudden. She got this horrible infection in hospital and she went downhill really fast. They had to do high-risk surgery, you see, even though she was so weak. She survived the operation, but only by a few hours . . .'

Janet appears remarkably composed in the face of her sister's news.

'She's gone to a better place,' she says.

Caroline knows that the wretched woman is either still in a refuse bin, or she's on the rubbish dump, but she doesn't contradict.

And then Janet asks a question that lifts a burden from Caroline's shoulders. She does so, Caroline notes, with impressive and uninhibited haste.

'Did Mum leave a will, d'you know?' she says.

'There's no sign of one at the house,' Caroline says. 'Nor any mention of a solicitor. I've been at her house this afternoon.'

All this is perfectly true, because Caroline has used the Argos shredding machine and has carried the shreds back to the bus, where she's fed them to the pot-bellied stove. There is no longer any sign of a will at her mother's house. The will, worthless as it may have been, has gone up in a curl of smoke.

'Well, I guess it'll be fifty-fifty,' Janet says, and she mentions the word 'probate'. 'I'd really like to have those little Hummel figurines,' she says. 'They make such a lovely display.'

Caroline adores the Eurostar. She hasn't been abroad in ages. She loves alighting at the Gare du Nord, where, on the concourse, she enjoys a *café au lait* and a fat *croque-monsieur*. She's wearing the Betty Jackson trousers and one of the Joseph cardigans with a soft cashmere scarf and high-heeled ankle boots. Her face is enhanced and nurtured by a new range of French treatment creams that were sold to her, two weeks earlier, by the beautician who gave her a facial. In the large Mulberry handbag she has a change of underwear and a small travel pack of toiletries and cosmetics. Caroline is fully aware that she is turning heads as she makes her way to the Gare de Lyon, where she boards a second train. After that, she takes a cab to Zoe's exchange house on the edge of the wood, where, standing at Maman's rippled glass door, her six foot frame is towering over the twin dwarf conifers placed to left and right, while her hair makes contact with the overhead wind chimes, causing them a little burst of rainforest resonance. Then she presses the door bell. Ding-dong.

As luck will have it, Maman is on half-day so Caroline is soon confronted by the Brillo-haired Fury in backless mules, who reeks of cigarette smoke.

'*Bonjour, Madame,*' Caroline says. '*Je suis la mère de Zoe,*' and she extends her hand. '*Je m'appelle Caroline,*' she says.

Then she tells her daughter's host that Zoe's grandmother is dead and that, sadly, she must fetch her daughter home. The Fury has granted her visitor admittance and has parked her on a kitchen chair. She lights a cigarette before heading for the phone, where she calls the school. But Zoe, of course, is not at school and neither is the Tall Merry Fellow. Zoe has *la grippe, n'est-ce pas?* She hasn't been in school for over two weeks. As for the Tall Merry Fellow . . . well, where to begin? Caroline is not party to the school's intelligence but she sees Maman bang down the phone and work herself into a frenzy.

'*Merde!*' she says and she knocks her hand harshly against her temple. It's the hand that's holding the cigarette, so it causes a shower of ash. 'Zee girl,' she says. 'Your girl. She eez sheet!'

Next minute she has grabbed a large black bin bag from a drawer and she has made her way up the open stairs. Caroline hears thirty seconds of clanking and banging above, before Maman reappears with the bin bag in her hand; the bag that is now bulging and hat-box shaped, but with assorted extra items thrown in carelessly on top.

'*Allons,*' she says. 'We get zee children. *Ils pensent que je ne sais pas où ils vont!*'

Maman, having hurled the bin bag into the back of her car, where it spills out its top layer of knickers and T-shirts, orders Caroline into the front passenger seat and reverses, hell-for-leather, like a teenage joy rider, and then they're off – stop, start, stop, start – for the pathway into the woods. Maman ignores the concept of 'footpath' and drives, bump, thump and crash, over fallen branches and tree roots. Boughs make a sound like chalk on blackboard as they scrape against the passenger's window.

Then Maman jerks to a stop, just short of a clearing. And there Caroline is suddenly witness to a split-second sylvan idyll that makes her soul sing. Because there before her, like two babes in the wood, are Zoe and her French exchange partner. Their arms and hands arch gracefully over their heads in sweet balletic attitude as they stand, face to face, as mirror images of each other. Both are in black T-shirts, their feet shoeless, but clad in socks. And then the moment crumbles. The children turn suddenly and stare, wide-eyed and frozen with fear, like young rabbits trapped in headlights. Her little ballet-mad daughter and the Tall Merry Fellow *Pas de deux*.

Zoe's *Ballet Class* book lies open on the ground at Lesson Four, because, day by day, Zoe has been instructing her French exchange, as she simultaneously instructs herself. And Gérard has been a quick learner, especially with regard to terminology, which Zoe finds quite a struggle. It's not too difficult for him to take on board terms like '*grand plié*' and '*jeté*' and '*port de bras*' and '*pas de chat*' and '*rond de jambe*' and his assistance with pronouncing them is giving Zoe's confidence quite a boost.

Over the past couple of weeks, having survived the regular early-morning sick-bag experience between the dwarf-conifer house and the tarmac playground, she has made her way back to the small woodland hut by bus, where Gérard, having burgled his mother's kitchen in her absence, is usually to be found proffering basic foodstuffs to his bleary-eyed, unshaven male parent, who will be washing it all down with his second bottle of beer. Gérard's dad, thanks to his drinking habits, has lost his job as forest ranger some two months back and, no longer able to stand the ensuing wrath of the Brillo-haired Fury, is now decamped in the woodland hut; a highly impractical expedient, of course, except in the eyes of a maudlin alcoholic and a protective twelve-year-old – or two protective twelve-year-olds, since Zoe has become very fond of Gérard's dad, who has a kindly, tolerant smile, albeit somewhat toothless.

And, since he spends most of his days asleep, he has never intruded on their balletic efforts to master the arm and feet positions, one through five. And, while on their agreeable nature walks, where Gérard is a mine of information on all things animal and vegetable, Zoe has told him stories of *The Sleeping Beauty* and *Giselle* and *Coppélia* and *The Nutcracker* and *Swan Lake*. So he knows all about wicked Carabosse, the thirteenth fairy, with her chariot pulled by rats, and the Blue Bird, and the Lilac Fairy. He knows about poor Albrecht and the nightly dances of dead brides, summoned from their cold graves, and the lifelike, wind-up clockwork dolls in the Magician Coppelius's house, and little Clara's Christmas dream of the handsome soldier who is really just a nutcracker, and the huge scary Mouse King and the Arabian dancer in the Coffee Dance and the luscious Land of Sweets.

And now, suddenly, Maman is right here, in the clearing – their clearing – in that horrible car, just like the wicked Carabosse. Nobody drives into the clearing and why on earth has she come? And – oh my God! – in the passenger seat. That other person. It's her mother. Her mother with different hair.

Before Caroline has managed to unclick her safety belt, Maman is already out of the car and hurling herself upon her son. She has clouted him twice across the face. Then she grabs both children by the scruff and frogmarches them to the car.

'*Entrez!*' she screams and throws them into the back, alongside the spewing bin bag.

At the door of the hut her husband has managed to appear, blearily scratching his head and just in time to observe Maman as she reverses at speed, zoom, screech and bump. The bump is quickly followed by a more significant bump, which in turn is followed by an agonising yowl.

'*Merde!*' she says, because Gérard, quick as lightning, has flung open his door and has hurled himself out on to the path. Before Zoe can follow him, Maman has clicked the central locking system, so that both Caroline and her daughter are imprisoned.

'It's Mimi!' Zoe is screaming. 'Mum! Make her stop! It's Mimi! She's hurt! Mum! She might be DYING!!'

But the Brillo-haired Fury drives on. And on. Zoe pukes into the top of the bin bag and wipes her mouth on a T-shirt. Maman dumps them at the access to the railway station.

'*Prend le sac!*' she says. '*C'est fini!*' And, screech, zoom, she's gone.

'We have to go back!' Zoe is screaming. 'Mu-u-um! We have to go back!'

Caroline discards the puked-on T-shirt in a litter bin, before mother and daughter jump into a taxi and return at once to the footpath, where Caroline, liberated by a wallet full of the Witch Woman's petty cash, now implores the driver to wait. Then, pausing only to strip off the high-heeled ankle boots, Caroline sprints impressively after Zoe; Atalanta in Calydon, but with a bin bag, along with the Mulberry bag, bouncing at her shoulder. In the clearing, it's a relief to find that Mimi is not dead. She is whimpering softly in Gérard's lap as he sits, cross-legged, on the ground, stroking her chocolate-brown head.

'Her leg, it is – *cassée*,' he says.

'Take her to the car,' Caroline says. 'She needs a vet.'

'It's a taxi,' Zoe says. 'My mum's got us a taxi. It's all right, Gérard. It's not your mum.'

The cab driver is not best pleased to accommodate a canine passenger, but Caroline promptly offers him double rates out of the dead woman's stockpile. At the surgery, they wait on little hard chairs. Then Mimi is checked out for internal injuries and she's taken off for some X-rays. After that, they all watch anxiously as she has her leg set in plaster. Caroline dips into her stash to pay a significant bill. Then she arranges for another cab and, while they're waiting, she avails herself of the vet's handy chairs to undertake a swift repacking job on the black bin bag, so that all Zoe's items are, once again, neatly accommodated within the pretty antique hat box, once the property of Lottie Kirschner, who, before the war, in happier times, had taken it with her to the Kaiser Hotel in Baden-Baden.

And all the way in the back of the car, buoyed up by the Labrador's improved condition, Zoe is chattering to her mother about ballet and Mimi and Gérard, and how his dad got sacked and is sleeping rough in the forest, and how Gérard is taking care of him, which is why they couldn't possibly be at school, and about revolting Véronique and the dwarf-conifer house and how she's even run out of sick bags by now, because of the horrible car, and how Véronique and her even more revolting friends stole her black Moschino jacket and then they dumped her in this repulsive sort of nightclub, but she made her way back, all on her own, on the bus, in the dark, and got lost, until – oh bliss; oh joy – she found Gérard and Mimi in the forest, alongside one of the 'forest hats', just like it said on Caroline's map, except that this one was not an 'inaccessible forest hat', which was just as well in the circumstances, when you came to think about it.

'Gérard is my new best friend,' she says. 'And when he comes to stay next year, please can Mimi come as well?'

'You've got your jacket back, I see,' Caroline says, stalling. 'Well done, my darling.'

Caroline doesn't usually say 'darling', but she seems in a very good mood and there's something a bit weird and glossy about her, like she's holding back on a secret.

'Mattie found it for me,' Zoe says. 'She was fab. She saw it on a coat peg at school and she just went up and stole it back.' Then she says, 'But, Mum, what are you doing here? I mean, haven't you come two days early? And wasn't I going to come back on the coach?' She's not actually all that pleased to have her mother invade her territory – even if Caroline's been so brilliant about getting Mimi to the vet – but she's trying hard not to let her disappointment show.

'Your grandmother died,' Caroline says. 'Zoe, I'm afraid we have to go back.'

'I don't really want to go back,' Zoe says, after a pause to take this in. 'I mean do I really have to? Gosh. Mum, I'm sorry. I mean I'm sorry that she's dead. I mean, that's horrible. Like, when, Mum? Like, how?'

Caroline explains how, day after day, she's been trying to get Zoe on the phone and Zoe's dad as well.

'I decided that the only thing for us to do is to fly to South Africa and tell him, face to face. And, gosh, we do need a holiday, don't we? We'll be leaving almost as soon as we get back. For a fortnight – which means you'll miss a week of school, but I dare say that won't bother you?'

Meanwhile Zoe's thinking, Is this really my mum, who has never let me skive off school? Never, ever. Not once. And what's she done to her hair? Then suddenly she takes note that the taxi is turning into the tarmac playground, where Mrs Caroline Headmistress is right in her natural element.

'Come along, children,' she calls out, as they do their best to scurry after her, still in their stockinged feet; Zoe with the hat box and Gérard cradling the dog. Caroline, as if by radar, is striding towards the head's office.

'Mum,' Zoe is saying. 'But I don't think we ought to be here. And I really don't want to go home. Please, Mum, I don't want to go anywhere. I want to stay with Gérard. We're learning how to do ballet together and it's all so fun and Gérard knows all about trees as well, and, anyway, his dad really needs us and . . .'

And then they are ushered into the office. Caroline does lots of teacher talk and, mostly, it's all in French. She's head to head with the head. She's apologising for the children's truanting. And then she switches to English so that Gérard won't understand. She's doing a bit of *sotto voce* with regard to Gérard's situation. A very decent boy, she says, who is struggling to do his best within a patently dysfunctional family; a drunken, unemployable father for whom the boy feels responsible; a mother at the end of her tether with a bit of a penchant for violence; a troubled older sister. The situation is in need of urgent attention.

'*Ah oui*,' says the French head. '*La soeur*. Thank you very much, Madame. We will look into it at once.'

Finally, Caroline explains that Zoe needs to return home right away. Her grandmother has just died. Then they take their leave.

'I don't need to go home yet, do I?' Zoe says in the car park.

But Caroline isn't listening to her. They all get back in the cab. Caroline tells the driver to take Gérard home. Not home to the forest hat, but home to the dwarf-conifer house, with horrible, smug Véronique and the Brillo-haired nicotine addict.

'*Mu-um*!' Zoe says. 'It's a mistake! The driver's made a mistake. Tell him not here. Gérard doesn't want to be back here.'

'Don't be idiotic,' Caroline says. 'Zoe, the boy is twelve years old. He can't camp out in the woods all his life, taking care of a drunk. He needs to eat properly. He needs to go to school. The head now has the matter in hand. They'll get the appropriate help. I'll follow it up myself.'

Zoe has started to cry. Even Gérard is crying a bit now – just the merest moist eye – but their mothers have all the power. For a while, the children cling to each other in the back of the cab as Zoe's tears fall on to Mimi's soft brown head. Gérard pulls out a Bic and hands it to Zoe. He indicates that she should sign her name on Mimi's plaster cast. Zoe writes 'Gérard, Mimi, Zoe. For ever Friends' and she gives him back the pen.

Gérard gets out of the cab and shakes Caroline by the hand.

'*Merci beaucoup, Madame,*' he says politely, 'for the dog.' Then he reaches in and takes Mimi. '*Au revoir,*' he says.

They watch him carry her carefully along the path to his own house, until he's standing in the doorway. He turns and manages a wave and a smile, burdened as he is by the dog. Then he goes inside.

Caroline and Zoe travel on to the station with Zoe weeping all the way. She's trying not to make a sound in case her mum gets cross. Neither says a word. Not until they are through the gate and standing on the platform.

'Darling,' Caroline says. 'I know this is very difficult for you, but it's all for the best, I promise. In half an hour we'll be in Paris. Won't that be super? I've booked us into a dear little hotel. And tomorrow we'll have a really lovely day. Just you and me. We can do whatever you most want to do. I'll take you to the ballet, if you like.'

So they're not even going straight back to England! They're going to dawdle around Paris when she could've been with Gérard and Mimi in the wood. Zoe has always tried to be a good child, but right now her mother is being so weird. She knows that she's making an exhibition of herself, just standing there crying and crying – right there on the station platform, with other people watching – but she can't seem to make herself stop. For a moment she thinks she might stamp her foot and scream; scream at Caroline that she's *horrible, horrible,* because it's true. She's being really horrible and Zoe can't understand why. And then she simply feels worse than ever, because how can you think like that about your own mother? And especially when Gran has just died? Maybe it's me who's being horrible, Zoe thinks, but I *really, really* don't want to go to Paris. I *really, really don't.* Not now. Not any more. Because everything's gone and got spoilt. For me and for Gérard. Just *everything* – and I don't see how either of us can ever be happy again.

After a while she looks up furtively at her mother. Then she quickly looks away. Because why is Caroline wearing all those modelly-looking clothes? And why does she look so different? Like her face and her hair and everything? And why is she talking about treats and shopping and holidays, when she's never been like this before? And isn't it especially weird when her very own mother has just gone and actually died?

Chapter Eight

Caroline Meets Herman

Zoe can't get to sleep on the long-haul flight to Johannesburg, though Caroline, beside her, is sleeping like a baby. She squirms all night and tries intermittently to reread her latest Lola book in the dark. That's because there's this really fat man to her left who has made her switch off her light. He is spilling over into her space like bread dough rising in a bowl, his huge legs spread wide, his right arm flopping all over her armrest so she has to have her elbows tucked in all night. Zoe could swear that there's ever more and more of him as the hours crawl by, like in that story of the magic porridge pot that keeps on cooking more porridge until it covers the whole town. She can't even get to the loo, because his body has blocked her access to the aisle and the only time she tried to climb over him she got stuck, straddled across his great thighs, which was so embarrassing, because he grunted and woke up.

And the person directly in front of her is this male giant, so that when he puts his seat back into 'reclining' position, it just keeps on coming until it's practically touching her fore-head. The whole thing is a bit like being on that school coach to France, only ten times worse because it's taking about a million years longer, plus it's at night when you're longing to be asleep. Then, just when she's nearly asleep – like about 5 a.m. – there's this little kid behind her, who wakes up and starts kicking the back of her chair.

Zoe has been in what Caroline calls 'a sulk' ever since they parted from Gérard and got on that train for Paris. She's been silent all through that 'treat' day in Paris, when her mum has come over all splashy and smarmy, and they're staying in this 'dear little hotel' near this big kind of plant-nursery place and her mum's like, 'Paris-Paris-ooh-aah' the whole time and she's forever trying to buy Zoe new clothes and coaxing her to eat out in cafés and restaurants, but Zoe's just shaken her head and stared at her feet. She's refused to change out of her same jeans and jumper that she's been wearing with Gérard's T-shirt that says 'Zizou', along with the black Moschino jacket. The only concession she's made is to allow her mother to buy her a pair of cheap black baseball boots. And there's no way she's in the mood to go stuffing her face in restaurants – or to eat anything at all, except for those baguettes with ham and cheese, when she's too hungry not to. Plus she keeps on chewing this fruit-flavoured gum called Hollywood, that Gérard has introduced her to.

She's really wanted to go on the Eurostar – and on a plane the way Matti and Maggs do every summer – but not now. Because of what's happened. Because she and Gérard were having such a fun secret time together, day after day. They were going to be ballet dancers and travel the world together and even Gérard's dad was quite sweet to her – not like that revolting mother and sister – except he was nearly always asleep, or drunk, or being '*triste*'. And now Caroline's gone and told on them all to Gérard's headmistress, just like she was their social worker or something. Zoe thinks her mother has been a traitor.

Anyway, everything has got messed up. Zoe is in quite a troubled state of mind because she knows that she's never going to forgive her mother. Not as long as she lives. And thinking about all of these things just keeps on making her snivel, which is embarrassing, because it's so pathetic and babyish. She knows that. And then the aeroplane lights click on and they all get this box of soggy-looking breakfast plonked in front of them, after which Zoe reaches for the sick bag, because they've started their descent.

Then they finally get off the plane in Johannesburg, where she's hit by this wall of heat and blazing sunlight, which doesn't help since she's been feeling puke ever since the plane began its descent and they've got about two hours to wait for their connecting flight to Durban. But her mum, like from nowhere, has suddenly got these posh designer sunglasses she's put on and then she tells Zoe to stand by the 'carousel' while she goes straight to the Ladies' and changes into these summery clothes that she's obviously had stashed in her hand luggage, because when she comes out she's wearing this amazing little yellow sundress that comes to about twenty centimetres above her knees and she's got these ropy yellow espadrille things on her feet. And she's obviously been putting stuff on her face because her skin and her eyes look all gee-whiz.

Then Caroline is trying to get Zoe to change as well, but Zoe won't even take off the Moschino jacket, though she's feeling really sweaty and she's probably smelly as well, because she hasn't even cleaned her teeth, never mind all her little creases.

After that, because they've got all this time to kill, they go and sit in a juice bar, where Caroline is trying to phone Josh and getting nowhere, plus then the juice bar won't take Caroline's French or English money because she hasn't yet changed it into rands. But just as she's standing there looking a bit thrown, with the two long mango drinks on the counter, this guy butts in, who's really tall and quite hunky-looking, except that he's about mid-forties-ish and he's one of those bald guys with a shaven head, and he goes,

'Please. Allow me,' and he pays for their drinks, which is really quite embarrassing.

Then he buys himself a cup of coffee and he looks round for somewhere to sit because the café is quite crowded and Caroline goes, 'Won't you join us?' so he does.

And then they introduce themselves, and Caroline says, 'This is my daughter Zoe.'

By this time he's said his own name, which is Herman Somebody. It's something that sounds a bit like 'Murray', only it's not. But right away, because of him being so big and tall and muscly, a bit like someone's made him out of one of those giant old-fashioned Meccano sets that middle-aged nerds collect, Zoe thinks, Herman Munster. She doesn't really want to shake hands with him and she's kind of sinking into the collar of the black Moschino jacket wanting to be invisible, especially because her mum is being so smiley and talky, and she's even started explaining all about how she hasn't been able to get hold of her husband because, even though she's got the right SIM card, she can't seem to get through, et cetera.

Then Mr H. Munster says to try his 'cell' and he hands her this fancy-looking, top-of-the-range thing that's making Caroline's phone look like it belongs to Mrs Flintstone. But even then she still can't seem to get hold of Zoe's dad, though at least she gets the phone to ring. It just rings and rings. Zoe has suddenly started getting worried about her dad. Like where *is* he?

It turns out that H. Munster is on the same flight as them to Durban, which is where he lives, so he says not to worry, because he's arranged to have his car waiting for him at the airport so he can easily run them to the hotel where Caroline's 'other half' is supposed to be staying and she can go check things out.

'No problem,' he says.

'Oh, gosh, thank you,' Caroline says. 'That is *so-*o kind,' and she's looking sort of shiny, only it's not because she's sweaty like Zoe. It's more as if she's glowing, which is really weird.

It makes Zoe start thinking again about Gran and how she's just died, so she says, 'Hey, Mum? When is Gran's funeral?'

She only says it because she's anxious to know, but it turns out she's said it right in the middle of when Mr H. Munster is telling Caroline about how he's just come from Accra, where he's been liaising with the Housing Ministry and how he's been doing this and doing that, and her mum is saying, 'How fascinating,' so Caroline looks at her sharply and says, '*Zoe!* Don't interrupt! It's really not like you to be so rude!'

Zoe sort of shrinks, hugging her bruises, because she can't help thinking it's like seriously not fair that Caroline's allowed to come barging in and interrupt her and Gérard any time she likes, and just go and wreck everything, while she, Zoe, isn't even allowed to ask about her own grandmother's funeral. Then, when they finally get on the plane, it's quite small and it's two-thirds empty so Mr H. Munster comes and sits next to Caroline, while Zoe spends the whole time staring out of the window, and hoping that she's soon going to see her dad, but she can still hear Caroline, more or less giving him her whole life history, like about how she was born in Australia and about how even five minutes on the airport tarmac in Johannesburg is such a turn-on for her, what with all that 'marvellous' heat and the 'brilliant' sunlight, which has made her realise what she's been missing all these years.

'To think that for seventeen years I've been living in a country where the natural light is like having a ten-watt bulb screwed into the sky,' she says to H. Munster. 'Oh how the grey of it gets right into your brain!'

Zoe thinks her mum is being quite disloyal, because it's like she's belittling their lives in England. And, anyway, isn't everybody's brain grey? But it makes Mr H. M. laugh and he says, 'Is it?' which is something he says quite a lot. *Eezit?*

And then, once they've landed and they've crossed to the car park through an even worse wall of heat, they get in this air-conditioned BMW that's practically as long as a hearse, and they sort of waft along to this beachfront area to find her dad's hotel and Caroline's all 'Oh-what-fun-this-is' about the seafront, even though H. Munster has explained that this is actually the crappy downmarket bit of the beach, and it's got all these big chain-eating places along the front, called stuff like Heifer and Steer and OK Corral with like gigantic shiny pictures on billboards of what you can eat, like a T-bone steak, or a triple cheeseburger as big as your head that Zoe knows Caroline would really rather be dead than eat. Like she'd be really disapproving if you actually went in and wanted to order a burger and fries and she'd probably make you have the salad option, even if it had anchovies in it.

But when they get to her dad's quite crap-looking little hotel, it's in a narrow back street away from the beach, wedged between this hole-in-the-wall Greek taverna and a tiny sandwich bar. It takes for ever for anyone to come to reception when Caroline rings the bell and then the person who shuffles in just shrugs and says that yes, 'Dr Silver' is booked in and, yes, Caroline can leave a message for him, but Caroline insists that they must actually enter Josh's room, where it's pretty obvious, to Zoe's relief, that her dad has just recently gone out, because his toothbrush and his flannel are still wet and the shower is kind of steamy.

'This is really driving me crazy,' Caroline says, once she and Zoe are back at H. Munster's car, but he says, 'No worries.' Please to hop in and he's sure they can track down the missing husband by contacting him via his place of work.

'You say he's here for a conference,' he says. 'So what's his line of business?'

Caroline tells him it's theatre history and that Josh has come for a conference up at the university.

'Is it?' H. M. says again. 'As a matter of fact, the wife's into all that, only with her it's dance. You know. Ballet.'

Somehow Zoe finds it hard to believe that Mrs Munster's got anything to do with 'ballet', because if she's anything like the size of her husband then she probably looks a bit like Babar the Elephant's wife Celeste, clomping around with pink leg warmers on thick elephant ankles and wearing a pink tutu with a huge stretch waistband. Not that Mr Munster is fat, she's got to admit. He's just a bit like embarrassingly big, sort of like being in the same room as Arnie Schwarzenegger, but she has to admit that he is really trying to help.

'Look,' says H. M. 'Come back to mine and make yourselves at home. Take a shower. Check out the uni in the phone book. Sort this thing out. Meanwhile I'll get some fish on the *braai*, what do you say? Maybe some prawns as well. No problem. I warn you, I make a mean chilli sauce. I learnt it in Mozambique. And the wife would be really interested to meet you guys. No kidding.'

So then they're back in the BMW and, by the time they've floated up the hill to this airy ridge and through these wide electronic gates onto H. M's sweep of drive, Zoe's into one of those hopeless, non-stop yawning phases, where each yawn triggers the next, so H. Munster says, '*Ach* shame, *kleintjie*. You really tired, hey? You know, I've got three kids myself and I'd say you definitely need to go crash.'

But, all the time, between the yawning, Zoe's just slightly wondering like what does her mother think she's doing, letting a strange man whisk them off like this? Because usually she'd be the one who'd be having ten fits if it was Zoe taking lifts from strange men, never mind entering their houses. And especially men built like they could qualify for the Springbok rugby team? I mean, just check out the size of H. Munster's feet.

Zoe can see their host's feet because by now he's parked the car and they've all got out. They're going crunch, crunch up this gravel path between the palm trees that he says the weaver birds like for making their nests; up through this incredible green and flowery space, like it was the local botanical gardens or something. Caroline's done karate, and she's got size 9 feet and, as far as Zoe can tell, her mum just never gets scared. Zoe thinks her feet look silly next to Mr Munster's and her mum's, because hers have stopped growing at size 4.

But God, this house is amazing, because, for a start, it's huge and it's like all on its own on the top of this hill with a turret that's got pointy windows, and with verandas upstairs and downstairs, which have got pretty wooden balustrades running all round. It's got stained glass with birds in the front door that's really wide and just inside it's got this black-and-white stone floor and then just miles of wide wooden floorboards and huge white sofas, just like in a glossy magazine. And, through all the windows, you can see other bits of the garden with lots of trees and huge clambering flowers, sort of almost exploding like fireworks, and there's this twinkly blue swimming pool, like Mr Herman Munster must be a 'media mogul' or something.

Anyway, then right away he brings them these hefty plum-juice drinks with lots of clinky ice and he gives Caroline a phone book and a phone and says to call the uni while he gets some food going, but Zoe's mum is too busy going 'Ooh-aah' about H. Munster's abstract art et cetera. And Zoe's just about to fall asleep all over this massive snow-white sofa, but Caroline shakes her and makes her sit up, because their 'host' has offered them lunch, she says.

'*Ach*, no worries, you just go find a bed – any bed – and sleep on it,' H. Munster says, and then, because he and Caroline have started getting all intense over this massive painting of wavy lines that Zoe, on the quiet, thinks looks like a baby chimp could've done it in about five minutes, she goes wandering off upstairs to find a bed, preferably one inside that lovely turret thingy like a fat, six-sided pepper pot that she's seen from the outside. So she keeps going up and up until she gets to this top landing, where there's a boat oar stuck to the wall with names and dates painted on it. And, after that, there's this funny little extra staircase which is really narrow, and with a low, narrow door that H. Munster would have to bend himself in half to get through.

And it opens on to this room with windows all round, like being inside a lighthouse, but, most of all, Zoe can't believe her eyes, and she draws in one big, gasping breath, because it's just like she's tapped her heels three times and said some magic words, and she's been teleported into what looks like Ballet Dreamland. First of all, there's this beautiful desk table with a computer on it and, hanging directly over the computer, there's this real-life ballerina's tutu that's just got to be for Odile in *Swan Lake* because it's black with an embroidered silver swan-feather design edging all the bodice and going down the front. The tutu is looped on to a quilted silk coat hanger that's been suspended, kind of invisibly, from the ceiling.

Zoe reaches out carefully and touches the tutu, just as though it might crumble to dust on contact. It sways slightly, causing sunlight to flicker across it in narrow shafts from all the pointed windows and a faint sprinkle of fairy dust descends from it on to the computer. Then, when she finally turns from the tutu; turns slowly, right round in a full circle, she sees that there are four framed and mounted watercolours on the walls – and the watercolours are none other than the cover illustrations from all four Lola books! There's a small stack of books on the desk table that are a bit like some of her dad's books at home in the bus – like about the Ballets Russes and stuff – and, on top of the books, there are some A4 printed-out pages with a snowstorm paperweight on top, so she gives the paperweight a little shake and then she peeks at the printout and it's so incredible, because it's just got to be the beginning of a new Lola book – one she hasn't yet read – and it starts out with 'the Company' on tour in the Czech Republic, and Lola's best dancer friend, Sergei, has just had a fall on some steps at the train station in Prague, and he's hurt his knee really badly, which could mean the end of his dancing career. Oh no! But Zoe doesn't dare to turn over the page, so she puts back the paperweight and then – oh my God! – before she's thought about what she's doing, she's left-clicked on the computer mouse and this letter has jumped up.

Dear Henrietta
We are all thrilled to be publishing *Lola in Wenceslas Square* . . .

Zoe doesn't dare to read on. She backs away in some alarm and sits down on this lovely old-fashioned sort of twirly iron day bed, praying that the screen will soon go blank, which it does, thank God. The bed has got a stripy knitted blanket on it in lots of colours, and a rolled-up patchwork quilt at the foot end. From the bed she can see, in a big cheval mirror, that there are some black ballet shoes under the day bed, so she leans down and gropes about until she's got them in her hands. Then she takes off her baseball boots and her jeans, and she puts on the ballet shoes, which are exactly the right size! So what is going on? It's like she's inside a fairy tale. And then, as befits a girl in a fairy tale, all the yawning catches up with her. She draws her legs up on to the day bed, pulls up the patchwork quilt, curls up small and falls into a deep, deep sleep. She sleeps uninterrupted and for hours, until she's suddenly jolted awake by this incredible non-stop scream-ing. Sort of high and shrill, like a girl who is screaming her head off.

The room is really dark and, for a moment, she's too scared to move. Then, still in the ballet shoes, she tiptoes to one of the six little windows and peers out. She sees that lights, like tiny bright stars, are clicking on in the grass, as Mr Herman Munster and her tall, Amazon mother are running together towards the furthest end of the garden. And her mother is wearing different clothes. She's sort of dressed like a fairy. Then the little stars click off and they are swallowed up in the foliage. After that, and just moments later, as she's still staring out transfixed into the darkness, she hears the slam of car doors and a second, daintier pair of people is running in the same direction – click, click go the little bright stars – and one of the people is her dad! Then it's obvious to Zoe that she's still asleep and dreaming, because, though she tries calling out to him, no voice will come. And then it's all gone quiet, and the stars in the grass have gone dark and she's back asleep on the old iron day bed, with the quilt drawn up to her chin.

Hattie has been with Josh all day. That's once she's seen Cat off to school. She watches her daughter make her way down the garden to where she keeps her bike, school hat perched on her newly bobbed, newly black hair. Something has happened to Cat in these last days since her hair changed colour. She seems more purposeful, if as put-down as ever. And biking to school has got to be a plus, at least. Then Hattie takes up her keys and drives to Josh's hotel. She conveys him to a café along a more salubrious stretch of beach, where they idle over coffee and almond croissants. After that, they drive to the drama department; that place where they spent so many of their youthful hours, and they collect their 'conference packs'. From there they go on to a lunchtime jazz concert, snatching a panini and some fruit juice in the student canteen along the way; the canteen which is full of cute skinny Indian girls with their ears clamped to mobile phones.

'It beats all those bull-necked white males with rugger legs who used to swamp this place,' Josh says. Neither of them mentions Herman Marais. Then they're off on the 'Midlands Meander'.

'Are you sure about this?' Josh says. 'It sounds a bit too alliterative for comfort.'

'Go on, it's fun,' Hattie says. 'It's beautiful, as you'll remember. Ignore the Tourist Board Speak. You'll love it.'

Josh knows that he will love anything designed to prolong his time with Hattie. To have found Hattie again has been heaven, though, all through these days, he's become increasingly aware that time has begun to gallop. He struggles to blot out the awful fact of his impending real life, which intrudes, occasionally, on the edges of his mind. He ought to be calling Caroline; has done so only once, and that on the morning of his arrival. He ought to be buying a phone card; making the effort. But then, by the same token, Caroline ought to be calling him. She could always leave a message for him at that pocky little hotel. Not that the somewhat clueless and intermittent 'receptionist' would be one to inspire confidence in the relay of accurate messages. Josh has recently begun to doubt whether the woman can write.

'I sometimes get sick in cars,' he says. 'I can't vouch for myself if we "meander".' Hattie laughs and promises to stop off and buy him a pack of Sea-Legs. 'It doesn't meander that much,' she says. 'And I'm a very careful driver.'

He's enchanted to observe that Hattie – grown-up Hattie – is wearing driving gloves. He hasn't seen such things in years. And isn't it oh, so like her, he reflects, that, given the amazing drama of the local ecology – the wildness of the wetlands, the elating scenery, the fern-capped forests, the Drakensberg Mountains with their massive peaks, the rampant hibiscus beauty of the place – that she should suggest the Midlands; that region of picture-postcard farmland terrain, now apparently dotted about with little tourist tea shops, craft boutiques and alfresco farmhouse lunches in rose gardens; a sweet, verdant landscape that dances to the tune of Hattie's transplanted English soul.

They dawdle together in a leather craft shop, where Josh buys a pair of sandals for Zoe, emulating Hattie, who has chosen the identical pair for Cat – sizes 4 and 8, side by side on the counter.

'I suppose our daughters would hate each other,' Hattie says. 'Were they ever likely to meet.'

The sun shines down on them as they make their way through Dargle and Nottingham Road, Hillcrest and Howick. They stop off among the gentle hills to enjoy a pot of Earl Grey and scones with home-made jam in the stable yard of a pretty farmhouse, turned B & B. Then, by the time they have lingered too long in a basket shop   no ordinary baskets these; exquisite artworks, each and every one – the daylight is threatening to vanish.

'We really ought to make tracks,' Hattie says, glancing at her watch. 'I can't leave Cat on her own for ever, much as one's teen-age daughter might relish such a prospect.'

Josh has been dithering over whether to buy a basket for Caroline, but he's never been much of a shopper and she'd prob-ably reproach him over the expense, especially as the baskets don't come cheap. Good thing too, he decides. The makers are skilled craftspersons, after all, and not the ill-used hawkers they once were; their wares haggled down from nothing to less than nothing on beachfront pavements and street corners. He desists from making a purchase, since Hattie is clearly anxious to be off. Something about the daughter. And, yes, he thinks, as they settle back in the car; yes, there is something edgy going on between Hattie and the daughter, but maybe that's just teens? He's not escaped the girl's noxious glances, but more disconcerting for him by far is Cat's astonishing likeness to Herman Marais, though she has, of late, transformed her hair from blonde to raven black.

By contrast, as Josh marvels, Hattie is ever and always the same, day after blissful day. Her hair, her eyes, her adorable ears, her dainty hands on the steering wheel in those gloves with the crochet uppers, her size, her body weight – all is as ever it was. He can scarcely credit that sweet girlish Hattie can have given birth to the trio of hearty blond giants whom he's noticed, in several framed photographs, dotted about that eye-poppingly affluent and stylish house; a house that Hattie appears to float through with every sign of detachment and indifference.

And then, as darkness falls, he turns to wondering how many murders there might have been in these parts, along this very stretch of winding road, for all the gentle rise and fall of its Constable appearance. How many victims of Inkatha vigilantes; how many farmers currently living behind security fences with guns beside the pillow?

And then, 'Good God!' he says out loud. 'Hey, Hat. This is the place where I met Gertrude.'

'What?' Hattie says.

'Gertrude,' he says. 'Right here is where I nearly ran her over. You know that boring Gertrude who used to work for my parents?'

'I never met her,' Hattie says. 'But she had that cute little boy. I came to supper one weekend when he was about four. He was eating rye bread with cream cheese.'

'It was pretty well around this time of day,' Josh says. 'It had suddenly gone pitch dark. I'd been running a mercy errand for my mother. All very urgent and clandestine. Taking food and stuff to this starving family. The dad was in jail. Black political prisoner. They'd got nothing. No money, clothes. Nothing. I'd had these boxes I'd delivered to them and then, on my way back, there was suddenly this woman right in front of me, just walking in the middle of the road. Absolute pitch darkness. Plus my eyesight's especially crap at night. I never drive after dark. God, I didn't even have a licence. Not in those days. I wasn't yet sixteen. I might have killed her if she hadn't been wearing this bright-yellow polka-dot skirt. Jesus, it scared me rigid. This bright-yellow apparition looming up in the headlights. She was pregnant, I could tell – with this white blouse kind of popping its buttons over her boobs. Cardboard suitcase on her head, tied with rope. You know how people do that? Walk right in the middle of the road, with a suitcase on their head? Fuck me, it must be two decades since I've seen anyone do that – walk along with a suitcase on their head. She was avoiding the snakes, she said.' And then he's suddenly off on one of those little trademark esoteric asides that, in normal circumstances, always gave Hattie so much pleasure. 'You know in *The Pilgrim's Progress*?' he says, but right now something quite other is invading Hattie's mind.

'Yellow polka dots?' she says.

'You know how Christian is forever carrying this "burden" on his back? Well, in Africa he carries his burden on his head. That's in all the local illustrations. The book was a total smash hit in these parts. I heard someone give a seminar about it. *The Pilgrim's Progress* in Africa. It was the Victorian evangelical missionaries' best-ever tract. On a par with the Bible. Isn't that fun? New converts would tell the stories of Christian's journeys when they were on their own journeys, and then they'd tell the same stories backwards on their way home. You know. Oral tradition.'

'You were fifteen?' Hattie says, staring intently into the darkness. 'We're about the same age, Josh, aren't we?' She's thinking back to her mother's kitchen. Marchmont House in the days of the mould-green carpets. Her mother poking at Gertrude. 'Madam she say foh piccanin.' 'Madam she say foh Zulu boy come native *kaia* make foh piccanin.' 'Master he say no visitor.' And then, that follow-up scene she'd witnessed from her window, as she'd sat there reading Noel Streatfeild. Gertrude taking leave of her father. Gertrude, clearly bulging out front. Yellow polka-dot skirt. Suitcase tied with rope. Some sort of altercation. The pale Afro child at the Silvers' dinner table. Gertrude's child. So who, exactly, had been the 'visitor'? *Oh my God!*

'Where was she going, do you know?' Hattie says cautiously, her voice coming out rather small.

'Oh,' Josh says. 'She was walking back into bundu-land. She'd got the sack that day and her shitty white employer hadn't paid her wages, so she'd got the bus for as far as she'd had the fare and then she'd started to walk. I found out that he'd also taken the trouble to withhold her papers, so she couldn't look for other work. She was shipping out to this rural dump where her mother lived. Remember you once came with me to that place? We went there to kidnap little Jack. Oh boy.' And Josh heaves a heavy sigh. Then he says, 'I persuaded her to get in the car and I gave her this can of disgusting sun-warmed Fanta. It was all I had. Then I told her my mother could get her papers back. So that's what happened. She came back with me and after that she somehow just stayed. Then she gave birth to Jack. I remember my dad rushing her off to the McCord Zulu Hospital. No doubt it's had a name-change in recent years.'

Hattie makes no reply. Gertrude. Pregnant. Dismissed without a character. By Mr Marchmont-Thomas. Grandpa Ghoul.

'We used to have this fabulous woman who'd just retired,' Josh is saying. 'Pru. God, I loved that woman. And then, thanks to me, we got poor old stolid Gertrude.'

'And you got little Jack,' Hattie says, deciding against disclosure. She, like Josh, is all too aware that their time together is limited and to what purpose spoil it?

'True,' Josh says, and he sighs again. 'I adored that little boy. And then, at some point – God knows – he just went to ground. At sixteen he stopped writing to me. Left his boarding school. Vanished.'

'Vanished?' Hattie says.

'The school never heard from him again,' Josh says. 'Possibly he hooked up with Gertrude, but she'd disappeared as well. Maybe they went to ground together. By then I'd been in England seven years. Caroline and I were finding life quite complicated, but both I and my mother did whatever we could think of. No show. Not long ago it occurred to me that he just might have applied for a passport. That's assuming he's still alive; a big "if" in a bad world. I mean, given that, with the regime change, a number of black South Africans have begun to use their right to travel. I began to check it out, but so far not a word. And the bureaucracy in these parts is something else. The wheels grind slow. The thing that doesn't quite add up for me is that, at school, Jack was brilliant. Really thriving. Whereas he and Gertrude – well, she was not only a bit of a dumbo, but she was always distinctly unfeeling towards him. I don't think she even liked him. Maybe to do with his conception? I mean, he *was* markedly pale, wasn't he? You must have noticed that?'

'Yes,' Hattie says.

'Do you think some white bastard raped her?' Josh says. Then he says, 'A sad thing for me is that I was so distracted around that time when Jack got sent off to boarding school. The parents were committing a significant chunk of money to it. They were about to hop the country. I was leaving for London. It was such a shitty, awful time. Police spies everywhere, tracking people down. The good guys thrown in jail. Dying in jail. The parents taking such risks. They took off in the middle of the night. They nearly got grabbed. I remember feeling terrible because all I could think about was you; that I was leaving the country and you weren't coming with me.'

Hattie tells herself she must concentrate. The roads can be tricky. People driving without licences; driving on forged and stolen licences; people out to hijack your car. Herman will insist on buying high-status cars. Expensive cars. Even for the wife. She'd feel much safer in a little old banger. Her mind is darting about. Josh. Gertrude. Her father. The pale child eating cream cheese on rye. Vanished. Back again to Josh, who had left the country without her. What a fool she'd been. She's right now grateful for the driving gloves, which are a help against sweating palms. She gives up and pulls over on to the side of the road. She leans her head on the steering wheel and sighs.

'I shouldn't be stopping here,' she says. 'I'm sorry. Give me a moment.'

'Are you all right?' he says. 'Gosh, I didn't plan to be so glum.' Hattie says nothing. He thinks she's not going to reply.

When she does, though it's too dark to see her clearly, he can hear the tears in her voice.

'Josh,' she says. 'About you, I'm sorry. I was stupid and I was wrong. I thought I didn't "love" you. I didn't know what love was. I think it's true to say that there wasn't much of it about in my family. I had some idea about the sort of person that one was supposed to fall in love with and that person wasn't you.'

'Hat –' Josh says.

She's casting her mind over her family; her immediate here-and-now family. Herman, who is admittedly splendid, but in a way that has never had much to do with her and now has less and less. The twins, Suz and Jonno; stridently coping young adults, who are ever more strangers to her. And then there's Cat. Daddy's Girl, who longs for her daddy's return. And the house, the heirloom house – brother James's one-time heirloom – the repository of all her unhappy childhood memories; the house from which, thanks to Herman, she has never managed to escape. She's been bound to it all these years, just as she was in the days of that ballet scholarship; the scholarship she'd been instructed to turn down, because she was 'needed at home'. Home? The house now belongs to Herman, and she thanks God for that. She finds it something of a comfort that it was never hers at all.

'My ballet teacher loved me, I believe,' she says. 'Though my lack of fight left her feeling let down.'

'Hat –' Josh says, but she goes on.

He longs to cup her face in his hands; her lovely pointed face with those enormous, wide-spaced eyes. He wants to hold her hands; her dainty hands. And, of all things, wouldn't she just be wearing those funny, old-fashioned little gloves?

'The parents couldn't help themselves,' she says. 'That stuffiness. The snobbery. It was all they had. They were so crippled and hidebound. Still are. Their sense of being a cut above. They'd focused all their ambition on my brother, who would carry the family name. For God's sake, a shopkeeper's name. Basket-weavers from Norfolk who'd got lucky. Anyway, by the time I met you, James'd already sucked them dry.'

'Hat –' Josh says.

'And then along came Herman and saved me. Boom, boom, boom. *King Cophetua and the Beggar Maid.* He's incredibly decisive, you see. And he's a brilliant entrepreneur. He always was, even then. He picked me up, told me I was going to marry him, bailed out my parents and saved their faces; bought the house off them, which kept it in "the family". Then he transformed it. Herman absolutely loves that house. At the time, he was also quite genuinely drawn to me. I was his "English Rose". Payback for the Boer War. Herman's great-grandfather once led a Boer commando, though he'd migrated rather late in the day from the Cape. He'd been head-hunted by the Transvaal Republic as a legal adviser. His first wife and daughter died in the camps. Their property was razed.' She pauses and looks up at him in the darkness. 'But enough. Really and truly, what is the matter with us, Josh? I mean *us*. Just what exactly is happening to us here? Are we simply regressing, and is it because there's no moon? Is this a joint mid-life crisis? You're the brainy one, Josh Silver. I need you to tell me.'

'Hat,' Josh says. 'All I can say is that I love you. I've never stopped loving you and right now I'm hoping that you love me.' Once again, he thinks she's not going to speak.

237

'But what are we going to do about it?' she says.

'I don't know,' Josh says. 'I'm sorry to say that I'm not like Herman Marais. All today I've been wondering if, just this once, we can both of us clap our hands and change the world. If I dance, will you follow me, Hattie? And, likewise, will I follow you? Can we face this thing down? Are we brave enough?' Then he kisses her on the forehead, on the palms of both her little gloved hands, on each of those bright Coppélia patches on her cheeks, which, right now, he can barely see.

'We'd better go,' she says. 'Statistically, we are quite likely to get ourselves carjacked in this place.' And she switches on the engine. She says, 'I do love you, Josh. I do. And I also really love England, by the way. Do you?'

'I don't know if I'd call it love,' he says, after a pause. 'But being back here has confirmed for me that England is "home". It's become my place. It's where I live. The first week I got here, I did all those predictable things. Stared at the outside of the house in Boksburg. Felt nothing. Went to Pru's old house and to where she took me to church. Wept like mad. Even got to see the inside of Bernie and Ida's house. My house. Awfully smart these days. Backyard's got a pool.' Then he says, 'I went to see my parents once, in Tanzania. Way back. I remember wavering at the time; thinking, Maybe this is my place? Here on the east coast of Africa. But not any more.'

'I went to England last Christmas,' Hattie says. 'For the first time in years. Ironically, it's Herman who goes there all the time, when it's me who's the pathetic settler loyalist. I really love the tone of English life. It's always felt more like "home" to me than home.' Then she says, 'Crumbs! Do I sound like my parents? Come to think of it, you never met my parents.'

'No,' Josh says. 'But I did actually coincide with your brother for a few weeks in high school. He nicked my electric guitar.' Then he says, 'Hat, tell me something. That night before I left the country? In the church hall. That person who came by – that was your brother?'

'He wanted money,' she says. 'Sorry about that. You didn't deserve the intrusion. As it happens, I didn't have any money.'

'I had money,' Josh says. 'I had all of Gertrude's money. It had been left with me by my parents. It was in the pocket of my jacket; an envelope with Gertrude's name on it. Then, when I got home it was gone.'

'Oh no,' Hattie says. 'Oh no. And your guitar as well.'

Josh merely laughs.

'Water under the bridge,' he says. 'Oh Hat! So much water under the bridge.'

And then they drive back in silence, until they reach Hattie's remote-control gates, which open for them, and Hattie drives through. She pulls up in front of the house. Neither makes a move.

'About us,' Josh says, and he sighs. 'Let's take a look at us. We've done OK, the two of us, haven't we? Especially you, dearest girl. We've got by. We've put one foot in front of the other. We've "achieved" things. We've got things done.'

'Yes,' Hattie says.

'But, frankly, that's not good enough,' he says. 'Wouldn't you agree? It's all been a bit of a screw-up. What we need to ask ourselves is, are our real lives ever going to happen?'

'Yes,' Hattie says. And that's when they hear the scream. Both of them pause for one split second. Then they leap out of the car. Doors slam and then they are running; running towards the bottom of the garden; towards the studio. And little, earthbound stars of light are clicking on where they tread.

Caroline's day has been interesting from the moment she stepped off the plane. Putting behind her that frustrating experience at Josh's mismanaged hotel, she persuades herself not to fret about it; to relish the unaccustomed comfort of Herman's air-conditioned BMW, as the car rises from the shoreline to the ridge. Then there are the gates and the elegant sweep of drive between the palm trees; the stone terraces of Herman's garden, the green lawns, the bright splashes of subtropical flowers, the spreading, shady trees. A pool flashes past to her left; set deep within an artful hollow, so that it resides in a green ravine. A gardener in a straw hat looks up and puts down his hose before approaching the car to take charge of the luggage. There's a wooden veranda, heavy with hibiscus and bougainvillea. Then the wide, chequered hallway and that vast white living space, all filled with air and light.

'Oh my goodness!' Caroline says, standing enchanted in the middle of Herman's floor. 'Oh! What can I say?' And she throws her arms out wide. 'Air and space!' she says.

'Who's Aaron Space?' Zoe says, on a half-stifled yawn from just behind her, and she throws herself gratefully on to one of Herman's sofas.

'Get up, Zoe!' Caroline says sharply. 'Our host has offered you lunch.'

'But I'm sleepy,' Zoe says, in desperation. 'And you *know* I don't like fish.'

'This really isn't like you, Zoe,' Caroline says, but she's feeling rather unlike herself.

Then Herman dispatches her daughter and offers her the phone. She makes a call to the drama department where – yes; yes, indeed – Josh has called by that very day, but only for a moment. He'd mentioned his intention to attend a lunchtime jazz concert on campus before going off on a day trip. He'd picked up his 'conference pack' and collected a key for his room – the room, booked from the following day, in a university hall of residence. Caroline is promptly given the name, address and telephone number.

'Thank you,' she says. She doesn't leave a message. Sod you, Josh, she's thinking, but her mood is mellowing by the minute.

Everything about this place, this house, this terrain, this climate, this abundant vegetation, this wonderful, throw-back experience of outgoing southern hospitality, is causing Caroline to confront the person she once was; once might have been; might possibly still become. She casts her mind back to that tall, beautiful, brainy girl from Oz who, nearly two decades earlier, endowed with an overlarge colonial cringe, courtesy of her mother's incessant and obsequious propaganda, was drawn inexorably to the idea of 'the Motherland'. And what better way to fulfil that aspiration than to take up a DPhil studentship at an ancient and prestigious British university, in a place that she has, ever since, determinedly espoused?

But have her seventeen years of northern-hemisphere existence been all the time running counter to her nature; counter to the things she truly loves? Years of struggling towards the ownership of a tiny Victorian mouse house; a terraced workman's cottage of total area eighty square yards, upon which she has so recently expended such immoderate effort? A house in which she will exercise her gardening skills in window boxes and old fish kettles? Can do; will do. What has all that been about? Make do and mend. Make do while living in a bus; make do while walking in the rain. Feed the family on forty-five pounds a week. Think good thoughts about thrifty camping holidays in grey English drizzle. Then there's been the constant, day-to-day striding forth into the graffitied forecourts of a down-at-heel British state school. Schoolmarm Caroline. Oh, for God's sake, what for?

And then, of course, there is Josh. Was he simply another departure from her natural inclination? Small, arty, sweet-natured Josh, so unlike the tall blond athletes who'd competed to date her back home in her undergraduate life. Self-deprecating, eccentric Josh, who doesn't dare drive at night. Josh who can't play tennis because of his wonky eyes; who can't do DIY. Josh with his girly, balletic PhD; his constant Pergolesi and *Pulcinella*; his so-what Stravinsky jokes, his Arcadian counter-tenor CDs. Josh, with his little weirdo chamber operas and his Neapolitan street plays. His back-seat word games to do with shop names and news billboards. 'School Cook Saves Dog.' 'Sex Pest Gets Wed.' What does all or any of that have to do with her? Except perhaps that, as it turns out, both of them were adopted. Good God! Did they not so much fall for each other as cling together through some unconscious neediness? And was it all yesterday?

So now she stands, breathing deeply, in the middle of Herman's floor; stands there in the yellow Marc Jacobs sundress, her eyes fixed on a painting of horizontal undulating lines. Under, over, under, over; tangerine and cyclamen; sea green, yellow and blue.

'Kids, hey?' Herman says from behind her, once Zoe has made her way upstairs. 'My youngest – she's my special girl, I admit. She's Daddy's Girl, for sure – but she drives her mother up the wall.'

'I'm sorry about Zoe,' Caroline says. 'I had to pull her away early from her French exchange and I fear she is not best pleased. That was when my mother died, you see. She died just a week ago.'

Herman's living space has two enormous white sofas that face each other across an expanse of floor. Hanging over each white sofa is an equally enormous, unpainted white canvas, encased in a perspex box. On the wall facing her is the painting of the undulating lines that is making her mind lift and dance. There's a strange, pale, bentwood chair, whose tangle of fluid lines takes the eye on an intricate and winding journey, its bleached wood like ribbons of tagliatelle. A second chair is made of solid iron. The seat and back are two heavy plates like outsize slotted spatulas, hammered in a giant's forge. The arms and legs are two continuous iron curves to the right and left of the spatulas; upside-down U-shapes that remind Caroline of gymnasts doing back bends. She, herself, was once a prodigious doer of back bends.

'That chair,' she says. 'Tell me, was it wrested from the Ancient Kingdom of Benin?'

'Not quite,' Herman says. His eyes are intensely blue. He finds that he can't stop himself from fixing them on this fabulous tall woman in the perfect yellow dress. Short skirt. Long legs. And he loves the ropy shoes.

'I bought it from an art-school degree show,' he says, standing alongside her and rather close. 'It's the student's take on a chair he saw in Burkina Faso. On a field trip.' Then, briefly, he touches her arm. 'Excuse me,' he says. 'I'll go and see to the fish.'

Caroline returns her focus to those horizontal undulating lines. Under, over; under, over; tangerine and cyclamen; sea green, yellow and blue. She feels her heart, like a paper boat, lift and bob with their rise and fall.

Then Herman is back.

'Drinks,' he says. 'Food. This way.'

And they cross the hall into his expanse of kitchen in which, somewhat unexpectedly, there is a large, countrified dresser, dense with dainty old English bone china of the more flowery sort. The kitchen table is twelve foot long and has a curious brass measuring stick, marked out in feet and inches, running the length of its near side. Surrounding it are a dozen elm-wood wheelback chairs.

'The wife's family were in the clothing business,' Herman says, observing that Caroline is running her index finger along the brass of the table edge. He parks a bottle of cold Sauvignon Blanc on the table along with two glasses and he proceeds to pour. 'Gentlemen's outfitter's,' he says. 'It came out of one of their shops.' Then he adds, somewhat indifferently, 'All history now. The shops became obsolete. Suffice it to say they were not the sort of outlets where a lady such as yourself would have gone for her retail experience.'

He places a dish of baby tomatoes and basil leaves on the table, which he anoints with quick sloshes of balsamic vinegar and olive oil. Then he serves up the fish.

'Yellowtail,' he says. 'I go sea fishing some weekends. This fish, I'm sorry to say, is what I had frozen from last time – but thank God for refrigeration, hey?'

Caroline watches beads of water condense on her wine glass.

'When I first got to England,' she says, aware that she is colluding, 'there were places where, if you asked for a "cold" beer, or even a "cold" Coke, it didn't come out of a fridge. "Cold" meant that the publican had been keeping it out the back in a place where there wasn't any heating.' After that, she raises her glass and says, 'Cheers.'

Once they have eaten, Herman suggests that she might like to take a shower.

'Or take a kip. Whatever. Feel free,' he says.

He shepherds her from the kitchen, through a door towards the back of the house, into a thrilling double-volume work room that is evidently his private space. Light is coming in, not only from the windows, but also through a shallow glass dome in the ceiling. The room, she assesses, must be almost twenty foot high, and has a wall of floor-to-ceiling steel shelves with a steel fire-escape ladder running up to a halfway platform, to make the higher shelves accessible. The room is unexpected and it excites her laughter.

'Oh may I?' she says, turning to the ladder.

She climbs up to the halfway platform, which is gridded with little hexagons, so that Herman, standing below her in a shaft of sunlight, is patterned all over in small stars. From her vantage point she can look down, not only on Herman, but on to the heads of two large old Nigerian wooden figures that are standing below her, exhibiting a solidity that is something like Herman himself.

244

Near by, in a heavy old wooden mortar, is a bamboo plant twelve foot high.

Once she is back at ground-level, Herman opens a second door for her, which gives on to a cave-like and dimly lit shower room, in which the floor and walls are lined with slate. The foreground, comprising a sort of anteroom, contains a raised slate slab, topped with a plain white linen mattress, and beyond the slab is a 'wet' area, where Caroline, once alone, strips and sluices herself, intrigued that the water should flow over her person in angled, waterfall sheets. Afterwards she wraps herself in a white waffle-cloth towel and emerges, barefoot, into the bright light of the study, where Herman, now with his back to her, is standing alongside his desk at the far end of the room. He is ripping open envelopes from a pile of accumulated mail.

For a while Caroline remains transfixed. Then she projects her voice to reach him across the room.

'I'm actually not sleepy,' she says. 'So I won't make use of the bed. Your beautiful tombstone bed.'

Herman turns from the desk and smiles at her. Fabulous teeth. For just a second she finds herself wondering about a time when Herman would have had hair. Blond hair, like her own, going by the nap on his tanned, sinewy forearms. And then he has put down the envelopes and has crossed the room to where she's standing. He has taken her naked shoulders in both his hands.

'Your shower is quite an experience,' she says, with a little catch in her voice. And then he is manoeuvring her backwards; back through the door into the slate-grey wet room, where he deposits her on the raised slab. The texture of the linen feels curiously papery. It's the feel of well-pressed starch. She watches him intently, her hands under her head, as he peels off his clothes. She sees the garments drop on to the slate in the gloom. The place, given the outside temperature, is wonderfully cool.

'Herman –' she says. 'Ought we to –?'

245

'I don't have the virus,' he says. 'And how's about you yourself?' But he's merely teasing her because, as in most things, Herman is a serious grown-up. He is not a person ever to be inadequately equipped.

'Me?' she says, with feeling. 'Christ, Herman –'

But then she feels no need to tell him about what a relentless goody-goody she is. Has always been. Teacher's pet. Mrs Goody Two Shoes. Uniformly monogamous, self-denying, stiff-necked; a professional thou-shalt-not. She desists because she knows right away that a phase of her life is over. She knows that, whatever should happen to her from this moment on, wherever she should find herself, a version of her own self is sloughed off and gone.

Afterwards, Herman shows her his orchids. Then they sit on a veranda at the back where they finish the Sauvignon Blanc. Herman follows up on the wine by mixing a couple of Martinis. They eat macadamia nuts and watch the sun go down; that incredible, high-speed African sun that drops, almost as fast as she can blink, below the line of Herman's green garden and switches off its light. Then, as if on cue, she hears the shrill of crickets. Caroline, dressy Caroline, has, just for the fun of it, shed the yellow sundress and put on the gauzy blue Vivienne Westwood. There is still no sign of Herman's wife, nor his daughter; nor of Zoe, come to that, who must still be catching up on sleep.

'I've got a story I'll tell you,' Caroline says eventually. 'It may be I shouldn't, but I will.'

And she tells him all about the Witch Woman and her sister Janet, the Less Fortunate, and about her wedding party in the Oxford college, after which she and Josh had camped out in a field, because the ghoulish pair had swooped down and claimed her bed for two nights running. And then she tells about the sixteen ensuing years of scrimping and saving, and the mortgage she took out for her mother who either couldn't or wouldn't go home. And the monthly direct debits to her mother's bank account and the clothes she was forever making for herself out of other people's curtains and about how she and her family have been living, all these years, in a decommissioned double-decker bus.

She tells him about how she recently discovered her mother's will, and about how she found out she'd been given away by her real mother on a bus – yet again, a bus – somewhere between nowhere and nowhere. And how the woman, all the while, had not been poor at all. She'd been putting away the money for Janet, along with bequeathing her the house. And how she, Caroline, had been so furious about it all, she'd smashed up her mother's Hummel figurines with a meat mallet on the kitchen floor.

And – oh dear me – she tells him about the daily withdrawals of two hundred pounds that she's stashed underneath the newly sanded floorboards of the mouse house and how the airfares for herself and her little crosspatch Zoe, along with a pair of Eurostar tickets and a nice hotel in Paris, were bought, over the telephone, on her mother's Visa Card. Then she tells him that she shredded the will, even though she'd realised by then that the thing had not been witnessed and probably wouldn't count for peanuts in any court of law.

'I bought the shredder with my mother's credit card,' she says. 'I did it merely because it gave me so much pleasure.' She doesn't tell him about the ashes in the refuse bin. To that extent she censors. She thinks it's just possibly in poor taste. She thinks it might be too shocking for him. She finds it pretty shocking herself.

And, having concluded her narration, she realises that Herman is shaking with laughter; that this, the story of her thwarted life, has become a virtuoso party piece.

'My God,' he says. '*You!* I could listen to you for ever. *Ach*, I shouldn't be laughing, Caroline, but you are the funniest person. You're a star. Do you know that? You totally knock me out.' Then he reaches out and places his left hand on hers as it lies, palm downwards, on the table. 'The funniest and the most beautiful,' he says. 'And, my God, sexy as hell!'

Caroline knows that she is beautiful. This comes as no surprise to her. And 'sexy'? Well, it's not a thing she has felt herself to be for quite a long time; not until this afternoon, though the new clothes, the hair, the money have all acted as a sort of prelude. But *funny*? Never! 'Funny' is a wholly new experience. 'Funny' is simply not 'her'. Being the funny person, the entertainer, the wit – she has left all that to Josh and she knows exactly why. Because to be funny is to expose oneself; to lay oneself open; to reveal oneself as vulnerable. It's not the grown-up thing to do. To be the jester is to place oneself in the power of another and that's exactly what she's up to right now. She is finding it a most blissful thing to place herself in someone else's power. Caroline is so tired of being always in charge and Herman has such large and capable hands.

'I suppose I thought it was payback time,' she says, laughing lightly at herself. 'I went a bit overboard. I felt so betrayed and I went bonkers. It wouldn't have happened had I not been left so entirely on my own.' And then they sit in silence for a while, holding hands across the table.

'Last week the toxic sister uttered the word "probate",' Caroline says. 'She threw it out over the phone. Ought I to be worried, I wonder? Ought I to be shaking in my shoes?'

'*Ach*,' Herman says. 'Please. It's nonsense. You can talk to my solicitor. That's my company solicitor. We've got these guys in London. They're the best. It's all no problem.' Then he says, 'It's a great place, London. I always love to visit there.' Oh, Perfidious Albion, but then isn't history sometimes 'best forgotten'? His company, he says, keeps a flat there, in Canary Wharf. 'I'd love for you to make use of it,' he says.

This is not an offer he has ever made to Hattie, who doesn't know of the flat's existence, but as he says it he realises that, Christ Almighty, there is no way that this woman is ever going there without him. No way is she going to be walking back into her old life. It's just not on. He's not going to let it happen. Not this great-fuck, class-act Ozzie blonde. She with the longest legs and the spot-on fabulous clothes. And brainy. And sparky. Shit! Like nobody's business. Not like poor old Hattie, his china-shepherdess wife.

Herman has not been feeling too great about himself with regard to the china shepherdess, who, over recent years, has become to him more and more of a turn-off. He doesn't like what her presence is doing to him; has even noticed himself, on occasion, becoming a shade sadistic, but then it's as if she's inviting it. Like the way he effected that takeover of the one-time servants' quarters. Project Studio. But he couldn't stomach that way she kept on calling it 'the cottage'. Just the thought of her messing up that promising, austere space; filling it full of all her old-lady clutter and chintz. It's enough already that, of all the rooms in this fabulous house that he's so admirably remodelled, she chooses to work in the turret, just as if she was Rapunzel, or as if she was yearning to spend her life inside one of those little Beatrix Potter books that she's got in first editions. And where, just by the way, has the woman got to right now; now that time is so strangely standing still; blessing him with this benign and lovely vacuum, into which the fabulous Ozzie Wonder Woman has walked?

'You hungry?' Herman says suddenly, because he's always had a healthy appetite and it's come round to that time of day when he'd normally be throwing the china shepherdess out of the kitchen for fear of having her embark on something to do with mince. Christ, is it any wonder that Cat goes off her food? 'Pasta?' he says. 'Linguini?'

And that's when they hear the scream; a loud, non-stop screaming that rises above the shrill hum of the crickets; a sound that Herman recognises as the voice of his younger daughter. He vaults the veranda in one bound and Caroline is not slow to follow. One behind the other, they run like the wind across the grass, the tiny pinprick lawn lights clicking on as they go. They streak down the length of the garden towards the studio, from whence the sound comes. And little silver flowers of light are blooming where they tread.

Chapter Nine

Eight People

Jack hears the scream as he returns from another long day in the drama department; a day on which, as with all his days here, he feels himself to be uncomfortably alien; a feeling which is all the more intense for the fact that he is back in the place where he was born. 'One day at a time,' he says to himself each morning, in the lovely private haven of the studio, where he lingers as long as he can over a second espresso and a small slice of panettone; a thing that he finds to buy – thank God – in the local shopping centre.

Jack doesn't 'do' emotion and yet to his annoyance he continues to find himself unsettled. Being back is difficult, even, at times, painful. It conjures occasional thoughts of his mother and his grandmother, both of whom cause him poisoning rushes of loathing where he strives to feel indifference. And the predominant local accent – that white-person accent – brings goosebumps to his skin, the more so because it is the very same accent in which he himself, many years earlier, had addressed the local shopkeepers. They were always needled by it; he, the uppity brown boy who talked like a white boy. So let us wind him up; take him down. Let us refuse to give him his change when he buys a bar of chocolate. Let us claim not to have in stock those much-favoured honeycomb sweets that Jack could very well see for himself, winking at him from behind the counter. Let us claim that we cannot sell him the aspirins that his mother has dispatched him to buy.

Right now, largely thanks to his grandmother's village, he is made equally uncomfortable by the local Zulu predominance. Unlike Ida and Bernie Silver, Jack was never in his youth disturbed by the existence of the disadvantaged; merely by the occasions on which he'd been made to feel he was one of them by the accident of his pigmentation. So he feels himself strange here; always strange.

He casts his mind back over his own sixteen-year-old self; that person who had walked so easily out of his familiar life and stepped into another. He runs his mind over that exhilarating experience; the pillion ride through Mozambique; then crossing the Rovuma River into Tanzania. 'Welcome to our country.' The three nights and days he'd spent on a beach in Dar es Salaam; the frisson of elation as he'd fallen in line at the airport behind that man who was carrying a kora. Then the square, plastic in-flight plates and the bright little blue-painted bus that had conveyed him, via the university campus and the Plateau, from the Airport Léopold Sédar Sénghor to the Palais de Justice in the centre of Dakar. He remembers how his spirit danced in the air around his head as he walked the streets on that first day; as he took in the colour and the sound, the smell, the fabulous urban Frenchness of it. Then it was all about a richness and strangeness of which he so easily became a part. Now it has all to do with an alienating and somewhat unpleasant familiarity.

Jack remembers those years in Dakar as half a decade of heaven; years that had to do with adventure and fulfilment, where the present has to do with capitulation and compromise. Then he had only to billet himself over the first three nights in the cheapest brothel-type hotel and step out, his backpack worn lightly over his shoulder, to slake his thirst on hibiscus juice and to choose between the seductive plates of available roadside food. Lebanese or North African? Dainty meat-and-onion pies or perfumy fish and rice? Spicy tomato-and-okra stew lying on a bed of rice? Everyone around him was drinking a beer called Flag.

And into that intoxicating moment of remaking himself, teenage Jack had come to a decision. He would never again consume the flesh of animals; only fish and eggs. And, thanks again to that rural sojourn with his grandmother, he had long ago resolved not to touch the products of fermented milk or millet. So Jack walked past the little meat-and-onion pies. He subsisted, cheaply and well, on suppers of fish and rice and on breakfasts of French bread and butter. He alternated hibiscus juice with a knock-out strong sweet tea.

'Here am I,' he said to himself, on that first day. 'A born-again vegetarian Zulu with a fake French passport and a pocket full of dollars.' The idea made him high. In jubilation he walked the gracious radiating avenues, the looping giddy loveliness of the city's cliff-top streets; walked tall, past the pink stucco houses of the affluent – and Jack, at sixteen, was by any standards tall, even among the statuesque local Wolofs.

' "My mother," ' he murmured, doing a little skip, patting that open-sesame passport which he carried in his inside pocket. ' "My mother, she is *descendue* from *l'aristocratie des* Wolof Kingdoms of Jolof." '

Within the week Jack had found himself a tiny room at the back of a baker's shop and, while keeping himself well away from the British Senegalese Institute, he had managed to find himself employment by perusing news sheets and notices in the more salubrious retail outlets and hotel foyers. He arranged to give one-to-one English lessons in a couple of those very same stucco houses that he had so enjoyed strolling past. In addition, for two full days a week, he had found himself a job selling designer shirts in a clothing outlet for men. By the end of his fourth week Jack was spending his evenings working on French-to-English translations. He translated programmes for a local dance company and for an information sheet aimed at English-speaking tourists. He also did the odd current-affairs piece for a local journalist.

Having no problem with stepping over homeless beggars, Jack was not bothered by the city's inequalities. He was indifferent to local and national politics, to riots or rigged elections, to whomsoever might, or might not, have been currently languishing in jail. He read the Paris-based weeklies over his lovely breakfasts of *pain au beurre* and *café au lait*. He played the occasional game of chess in a favourite café. From time to time, he treated himself to newly published paperbacks, which he bought in the good French bookshop. He began to take lessons in Senegalese dance and was drawn at weekends to the music clubs that sometimes went on all night; venues in which even Jack – aloof, urbane and self-contained Jack – found that he had to pinch himself in order to avoid disbelief that, every Saturday night, Youssou N'Dour was performing live. On the whole, he avoided all popular pursuits of the sweaty-multitude kind; anything that had to do with wrestling, canoe racing, pilgrimages and *fêtes*. Yet he was enchanted by the indigenous cinema and theatre; also by the ballet and the streets of rickety art workshops – because Jack had no problem with popular culture once it had been transfigured via the lens of the intellect.

It was only after he had met Eduardo that he went to his first football match and visited the one-time slave island of Gorée to watch the lantern processions. Together, they attended the celebration of an African High Mass. They visited an island full of birds. They spent a day in a nature reserve, along with the two small boys. Most frequently, Jack's engagements with Eduardo had to do with visiting restaurants; beautiful expensive restaurants in which Eduardo always paid. Eduardo, after all, had become his patron.

The men met one Sunday as Jack sat alone beside a pink lake on a beach made of bleached white shells. He was, once again, reading Josh's paperback *Treasure Island*. Eduardo, a widower with two small sons, was a Milanese art dealer with an interest in West African art and a house on the Corniche d'Est in which he liked to spend three months a year. This way he could avoid the North Italian winters while keeping his eye out for local talent. The trio were a merry party who had seated themselves close by. The time was almost two o'clock and Jack was beginning to feel hungry, yet he lingered because he was enjoying the sound of the Italian language, bouncing between man and boys as they unpacked their picnic lunch.

In spite of himself, Jack was quite unable to stop his own curious sidelong glances.

'We disturb your peace?' Eduardo said.

'No,' Jack said.

'You are English?' Eduardo said and he smiled. Then he said, 'Your book.'

'Ah,' Jack said. 'No. *Mais j'étais mis en pension anglaise.*'

The older boy was looking sideways at Jack's book.

'*Tree-ah-soor-ay Iss-lund,*' he read out.

'Bastiano's favourite,' Eduardo said.

Jack smiled.

'Mine too,' he said. He put down the book and began to pull on his T-shirt, making as if to leave.

'Please,' Eduardo said. 'One stays because the water – it goes to change from rose to purple.' Then he said, 'You have eaten?' He proffered food and wine, which had emerged from a pretty old Bakelite picnic hamper on to a red-and-white checked cloth.

Eduardo was urbane, cultivated and rich. He was everything Jack found alluring, especially in his courteous restraint. Eduardo enjoyed music and the arts, and he quickly discovered that this aesthetically pleasing and courteous young man was charming and well-read, spoke fluent French and English, knew maths and history, could draw and paint, was conversant with the current state of theatre and the arts, and furthermore – thanks to Jack's early playtime experience in the Aladdin's Cave of Josh Silver's bedroom – he had, for all his unusual rectitude, an unexpected facility with young children. Yet the young man lived hand to mouth, in a low-life part of town. He rented sleeping space in a storeroom behind a baker's shop and he sold shirts two days a week. The boy was an orphan; father a French intellectual, long deceased; mother likewise, a high-born local Wolof. He had clearly fallen on hard times; a not unfamiliar African story.

Eduardo's sons, aged five and six, would soon be in need of a private tutor – that was if their father was to continue his habit of spending three months abroad. And so it was that, by the end of the afternoon, once the lake had indeed turned to purple, Jack had agreed to give the family English lessons and, that same evening, once Eduardo had put his sons to bed and left them in the care of his housekeeper, he treated Jack to the first of many fine dinners in a local fish restaurant.

It sat on a wooden pier and was entirely surrounded by water. Jack drank champagne for the first time in his life and he savoured a fillet of sea bass with a plate of miniature vegetables. He followed this with a heavenly *tarte tatin*, made with caramelised pears. By the time he was sipping a small glass of Barsac, Jack had surprised himself by agreeing to a three-month spell as part-time, live-in tutor to Bastiano and Vincenzo.

The inside of Eduardo's house was beautiful beyond imagining and, though Jack had never been comfortable with yielding up any part of his careful separateness, he understood that Eduardo was sensitive to this, being himself both fastidious and private; all the more so for having been quite recently bereaved.

Jack duly brought to his new job some of the magic of that equivalent time in his own early life – his life before the fall – a time that had had to do with Josh's *Scuffy the Tugboat* and *Orlando the Marmalade Cat*; with scissors and glue and the clapping of hands to the sound of an electric keyboard; with a painted cardboard post box on the back veranda of the Silvers' house and with all those reams of scrap paper and Sellotape; that abundance of rubber bands and paper-clips that emerged from the drawers of a big silver desk with cut-glass, pear-drop handles; a desk that was his own, if he should ever find himself in a position to claim it. 'This desk is a present from Bernard Silver to Sipho Jack Maseko. To await collection. He may be quite some time.'

For his part, Eduardo was not only grateful to Jack but also enjoyed his company, given that his young employee was naturally sensitive in keeping his distance; was never invasive; never pried. Jack – wonderful, thoughtful young Jack – was soon more like a favourite nephew, or an obliging, older stepson; a patently gifted and well-read young man, who, through poverty, through his orphan status, had been cruelly denied opportunity. Eduardo was astonished to learn that Jack had had no formal education beyond the age of sixteen, had not so much as completed the Bacc and, as the three months drew to a close, he made Jack a proposition.

'Giacomo,' he said, using a form of the young man's name that both of them occasionally enjoyed. They conversed quite often in Italian these days, which Jack had been picking up apace.

'*Permesso* –'

He suggested that Jack return with the family to Milan, where, within one year, he could accomplish the Baccalaureate along with perfecting his Italian via intensive private lessons. Then he might wish to enter the university – perhaps a literature course at IULM? In the winter months he would accompany the family to Senegal and resume his part-time tutoring duties. While in Italy, the boys would be in school. Naturally, Eduardo said, he would house and fund his protégé.

'You are family now,' he said.

The two small boys were content with the arrangement and Jack, still relishing the idea of his isolation, was equally inclined to relish the idea of a great first-world city, for what he knew it would have to offer. And so it was that, just in time for his twenty-first birthday – for which occasion Eduardo bought him the pistachio-green Vespa – Jack was right on track to become exactly what Hattie, on first meeting, took him to be: a bourgeois first-world Euro child; a person of sweet privilege; a Milanese intellectual who had come to embrace the de Chirico paintings of the CIMAC as his familiar friends; who never tired of the Scala Theatre Museum; a talented graduate whose excellent long essay on the early works of Dario Fo was included for publication in a collection of papers to be edited by his tutor.

Then, suddenly, on two counts, Jack saw that he could hit the buffers. Trouble never comes by halves. It had, over the years, been a relief to him that Jacques Moreau, Miss Lundy's dead French poet, had, for all his youthful arrogance, turned out to be unheard of outside that small Parisian poetry-reading circle from which the French teacher had plucked him. But actually to publish under a dead man's name? Jack's solution, after giving the matter much thought, was to approach his kindly benefactor and suggest that, in recognition of Eduardo's generosity, he would very much like to use the family surname when it came to publication. For his professional life – if he should succeed in having such, Jack said with a modest smile – he would take it as an honour if he could call himself Moroni. Giacomo Moroni.

Kindly Eduardo was touched. He opened a bottle of chilled Prosecco.

'To your first publication,' he said.

In addition, he made his young friend a present of the three equestrian etchings that, by the next year, were hanging over the silver desk in Hattie's garden studio.

Jack's second problem had also to do with the dead French poet, whose passport was about to expire. Yet here again luck was with him; modified luck as Jack perceived it, but luck of a useful sort. The year was propitious. It was 1994 – the year of that first free and fair election in the land of his birth; an election that had brought to an end the laws of the apartheid state. On television, Jack, along with Eduardo and the boys, had previously witnessed the emergence of Nelson Mandela from twenty-seven years in prison; the global saint, blinking into the flashbulbs of several hundred news cameras. It was the year in which Jack, as a person of colour, could walk into the South African Embassy clutching his real-life birth certificate and declare himself to be Sipho Jack Maseko, son of Gertrude Thembisa Maseko, father unknown; born McCord Zulu Hospital, Overport, Durban, South Africa; a person eligible, under the new dispensation, to receive a passport as a citizen of that country; a passport which, given the visa regulations, would, regrettably, soon necessitate his departure from Italy.

It was clear to him that what he needed to do was use a temporary return to his homeland as a way to help forge a career. And, given that in the new post-apartheid state, all institutions of higher education were evidently making strenuous efforts to increase their quotas of black academics, Jack was confident that he would have a good chance of finding himself recruited in some suitably junior capacity. Jack, who, in truth, had every wish to avoid a confrontation with his own past, was nonetheless resolved that this was the option he needed to pursue.

His taking off was oddly precipitous and somewhat puzzling to his benefactor.

'*Sudafrica?*' Eduardo said. 'But my dear Giacomo, why?'

'Believe me,' Jack said steadily in reply, 'this is something that I must do.' Then he said, as if merely to say it could make such a thing come about, 'But I surely will come back.'

*   *   *

And now, on the evening of the day on which he has collected his Vespa from the Durban dockside, Jack is approaching the studio – that soothing private haven from all the complexities of his homecoming. Yet even the studio in these few last days has seemed to him a little less private. Jack can't quite put a finger on it, but his things have the look of things that have been looked at; maybe of having been touched? Something about the splay of his pencils in their jar on the silver desk. And then there are his clothes; a faint, unfamiliar, slightly almond odour – of shampoo, possibly? Or could it be perfume? Or body lotion? Then, yesterday, a single black hair between the pages of one of his books; a distinctly straight, non-Afro hair, quite definitely not one of his own. Could it be something to do with that rather weird girl, the blonde, who forever follows him with her eyes from what he takes to be a bathroom window? Is it his imagination, or has her hair changed colour?

And then he hears the screaming. He sees that the studio lights are all on and that his door is standing open. In addition, as he hastily parks the Vespa on his illuminated terrace, he detects another sound below that of the screaming; a low, groaning sound, which is coming from close behind him. He turns to see that, in the narrow, shadowy gap between the end of the studio and the boundary wall, a derelict male person is lying on the ground; a shabby and malodorous person who looks to have taken a fall. Good God, what is happening around here? But first things first, Jack decides, and he strides in through his open door.

Inside his violated green-glass bathroom, Jack sees that a tall bald man is cradling the weird girl, who falls silent the moment he enters. She is staring at him now, as if transfixed, her mouth standing half open. Her black jeans, he notes with distaste, are pulled down halfway to her knees. Alongside the tall bald man – and almost equally tall – is a beautiful, statuesque blonde woman in a marvellous gauzy dress. Tight-boned bodice. Theatrical. And, hanging back just a little, as if they were newcomers to the scene, is his landlady, who has her back to him, as does her companion, whom Jack nonetheless recognises as Josh Silver; Josh Silver, with fading, greyish hair. This is less of a surprise to him than it might have been, had he not previously noted Josh's name among the conference delegates. All of them have their eyes fixed on the weird girl.

'Excuse me,' Jack says into the sudden silence, 'but there's a man groaning outside. I think he's taken a fall.' He gestures towards the wall, just above the weird girl's head.

Then he retreats to his living space. He pours himself a small glass of whisky, which he drinks, perched on the writing surface of his lovely silver desk. He begins to glance through the conference papers, just as Josh and the landlady pass right through his room and exit on to the terrace, towards the groaning man.

Once outside, Hattie and Josh peer apprehensively at the stranger, who is now craning towards them and making efforts to speak. In the partial darkness of the narrow space in which he lies, they can make out that he is one of those homeless white losers to whom harsh sunlight has not been kind. His face is a mess of shiny red lumps and rough sandpaper patches. He is blue-black around the eyes. His hair and eyebrows are the texture of straw. His unkempt facial hair is yellow, though darkened with food stains around the mouth. He is missing quite a few teeth.

'*I huthuthmee*,' he says, through the wheeze-box in his chest, his speech slurred, thanks as much to alcohol as to his absent front teeth. The man has evidently pissed himself and he reeks of old sweat and booze. 'Thuth-*uthmee*,' he says again.

'What?' Hattie says. 'What is he saying, Josh? I can't hear what he's saying.'

'Excuse me,' says Caroline, pushing between Josh and Hattie. 'Let me take a look at him. I know a bit about first aid.' Then, having edged herself into position, she adds, 'Josh, I won't ask what you are doing here, but can both of you please get out of the light?'

'*Thuth*,' says the pissed-on tramp. '*Uth-mee.*'

'Who are you?' Hattie says sharply, fear rising in her voice, because it seems to her that the man's bloodshot eyes keep locking on to hers. 'What are you doing here?' she demands. 'And why was my daughter screaming?'

'Quiet!' Caroline says as, heedless of stink and Vivienne Westwood, she eases the injured party into the recovery position. The tramp, it appears, has had some sort of entanglement with an adjacent wooden packing crate. She guesses he'd been standing on it when it splintered and gave way. Caroline, having turned his head gently sideways, checks him for broken bones.

'Try not to talk,' she says to him, but he's still twisting his head round and making efforts to speak.

'*Thuth-uth-mee,*' he says.

'Who *are* you?' Hattie says again, sounding louder and more shrill. 'What are you saying to me?'

'Get me a pillow,' Caroline says to Josh, who is paying her no attention. 'Just pass me one of those patio cushions. And can you tell your little friend to get the fuck out of my light.'

Both Hattie and Josh are frozen to the spot as Hattie stares fixedly at the tramp and Josh stares fixedly at Hattie.

'*Thuth*,' says the pissed-on tramp. '*Ith-MEE*. Dthame-th. *Ith mah-munnay.*'

'He's saying "money"!' Hattie says suddenly. 'Josh, is he saying "money"?' And then she has begun to claw at his sleeve. 'Oh my God!' she says and she's suddenly shaking violently. 'Oh my God! Oh no! It's James. It's my br-bro –'

'Try not to move, OK?' Caroline is saying to the tramp. 'You're going to be all right.' She turns again briefly to Josh. 'Get Herman, for Chrissakes,' she says. 'Get him to call an ambulance.'

The tramp has begun to snivel. '*Ah-cum-fuh-ma-munnay,*' he says. '*Thath-all.*' He raises an arm briefly towards the space alongside the cistern outflow where one of the bricks is chipped loose. Then the arm falls feebly to his side.

By now Hattie has completely lost it. She's yelling at the stinking tramp with a volume so loud that Jack, inside the studio, has no difficulty in hearing her every word.

'What "money", you swine?' she screams. 'And why is my daughter upset? What have you done to her?'

'*Ah-puth-ith-un-vuh-wawl,*' the tramp is mumbling. '*Un-vuh-wawl. Long-go. Un-a-om-valope,*' he says. '*Uth-mine.*' Then he says, '*Ah-NEED-vuh-munnay-thuth an' now-uth-gonn.*' Then the tramp starts to cough. It's a cough that can't seem to stop.

'Easy now,' Caroline says. 'Relax.'

'How "long ago", you bastard?!' Hattie is screaming at him. Pennies are dropping thick and fast in her brain. 'And did that "envelope" say "Gertrude"? Well, did it? DID IT?! WILL YOU ANSWER ME!'

'Easy now,' Caroline says again, as the coughing fit subsides.

'*Uth-mah-munnay,*' the man whimpers. '*I-dunno-why-ith-thed-Gertroob –*'

'Because you stole it,' Hattie is yelling. 'You came by the ballet school and you stole it from Josh's pocket. You miserable bastard! You absolute shit! How could you have done that to her? How could you, after what you'd already done to her? Because it was you, wasn't it? It was you who got Gertrude pregnant, you slimeball, you sleaze. And because of it, you made sure she got sacked! You hid Father's fountain pen, just as later on you hid her money. All afternoon I've been trying to work it out. I've been thinking it was Father who'd got her pregnant. But it was you, you evil bastard! Yes, you! You were always skulking around the servants' rooms. And there was I assuming that was merely to do with your drugs. And here you are again – Christ

263

Almighty – more than twenty-five years on! Exactly where you should be. Lying in a drain. You're a waste of space, brother of mine. You always were and you always will be. Not content with screwing up your own life, and leeching off mine and beggaring our parents – you then excel yourself and get the maid pregnant. You get her sacked. You steal from her. Well, *fuck you*, James! *Fuck you! FUCK YOU!*'

Hattie has never screamed at anyone like this. Not in all her life. She has never, as far as she can remember, uttered the 'fuck' word out loud. Josh is staring at her in wonder. Even Caroline, for the moment, appears transfixed. And, inside the studio, Jack, listening intently above the beating of his heart, is gleaning something astonishing; something that bears significantly on his own life. The groaning tramp is the landlady's brother. The landlady's brother has, at some point in the past, got a certain Gertrude with child; Gertrude, the long-ago resident housemaid, who used to inhabit this place. This very place. The landlady goes way back with Josh, who once had an envelope intended for Gertrude; an envelope stuffed with money. And the landlady? Yes, of course! Why had he not taken note of it until now? She had to be the self-same girl who'd come along with Josh on that rescue mission to his grandmother's village all those years ago; the girl who had, on and off, been around on the set of that production of *A Midsummer Night's Dream* in which, in defiance of the race laws, he had played the little changeling boy.

'And get this, brother James!' he hears his landlady saying, and she's still screeching like a fishwife. 'Herman has been all over this wall; all over this whole building. So there isn't an envelope anywhere in sight – with or without "your" money. You came by the ballet school and stole it. And then, for some stupid, muddle-brained reason best known to yourself, you decided to hide it in the wall. Well, clearly someone else has stolen it off you. So why don't you just drop dead!'

264

And then, suddenly, Herman is there, his voice booming into the night. He's got Cat close beside him, her jeans by now hitched up and zipped.

'Henrietta!' he booms, standing there huge as Africa. He bawls her out in a volley of Afrikaans that all present can fully understand. That's except for Caroline, though she doesn't fail to get his drift. '*Hou jou bek, jou lastige vroumens!*' he bawls. '*Is jy mal? Jy maak 'n verskriklike geraas! Bly stil!*' Then, in the silence, he addresses Hattie and Josh together, ordering them both indoors like two bad children. '*Binne!*' he says. '*Albei julle! Onmiddelik!*'

The pair retreat gratefully into the quiet and order of the studio. Once again, they pass right by Jack, who is still perched on the silver desk. They seat themselves side by side on the bed at the far end of the room.

'My hero,' Caroline says, into the merciful silence. 'Well done, Herman.' She's aware that the invalid's pulse is a little erratic. 'Now that you've banished the children,' she says, 'would you call an ambulance, please? And ask if they can make it quick.'

'Dad's done it already,' Cat says, smiling a little self-consciously at the beautiful lady in the fabulous dress; taking care not to focus her eyes on the smelly old dosser who is on the ground; the cause of all her distress.

'Hey!' Caroline says, and she smiles back at the girl. 'Then it's three cheers for your brilliant dad. Now, would you be one of the grown-ups, my dear? Would you please go back inside and get me some sort of a blanket?'

'But that's the ambulance,' Cat says with relief, her sharp ears picking up the peculiar hum of the engine beyond the gate, because there's no way she's going back in there. Never. Not ever, as long as she lives.

Inside the studio, Josh is wholly focused on Hattie.

'Dearest girl,' he says. 'You're so distressed. And I'm really not at all clear. What exactly was all that about?'

265

'Don't you see, Josh?' she says. 'The envelope that said "Gertrude". It was her money. Gertrude's money. The money from your jacket pocket. Your Gertrude was our Gertrude. I realised that this afternoon – just as soon as you said all that about the yellow polka-dot skirt. Pregnant Gertrude in the polka-dot skirt and the suitcase tied with rope. The woman you met on the road.'

'God Almighty,' Josh says. 'Are you sure?'

'She'd worked for us for years,' Hattie says. 'But that would've been the very day my father gave her the sack. All that time James had been acting really weird. He was always coming from round the back of the sheds and the servants' quarters. Gertrude was living there. Right here, as it happens. There was also an old gardener – Joseph – from Mozambique. It was two basic rooms with a washroom and some sheds. James used to do drugs in the sheds. I'd known that for a while. And of course I knew that he was mean and cruel. But all that summer, Gertrude – well – she was sort of shrinking from him. There was something different about it. I don't know. Call it a hunch. And then one day I saw him make this gesture. He'd caught her eye when she was serving dinner. It was kind of horrible and explicit. And that little Jack of yours –'

'Excuse me,' Jack says, clearing his throat; not rising from the silver desk. Both of them look up and stare at him as though they see him there for the first time; the tenant in the Prada shoes.

'Say,' Josh says. 'Isn't that my father's desk?'

'Excuse me,' Jack says again.

'I'm so sorry,' Hattie says, remembering herself. 'I'm really so sorry about all this. I hope you can forgive us. We've all invaded your space. Josh, this is our tenant, Giacomo Moroni. Giacomo, meet –'

But neither Jack nor Josh is listening to her.

Josh is suddenly on his feet and he's approaching the tenant in strides.

'*Jack?!*' he says. 'Jack *Maseko*?! You're Giacomo Moroni? The Dario Fo thing? Oh my God, Jack, it's really you!' He is laughing as he crosses the room and he has his arms outstretched. He envelops the tenant in a hug. 'You disappeared from the planet,' he says. 'Jesus, can it be you?'

'Long story,' Jack says, and he leaves it at that. He considers it expedient to allow himself to be hugged. He does not stiffen, as he usually does, in the event of physical contact. And, given that he's a whole foot taller, he is able to look over the top of Josh's head towards the landlady, who, as Josh releases him, appears to be preparing herself for speech.

'Let me look at you,' Josh is saying. 'You look so different. Well, maybe you don't. Maybe you look just the same?' It is as Josh says this that he notices the ears. Jack has Hattie's own dear little ears; those ears with almost no lobes. And could it be that these same darling ears are to be seen attached to the head of the odious James? James Alexander Marchmont-Thomas, who stole his guitar once, at school? 'But how the hell did you get to be so tall?' he says. 'Good God, how did that happen?'

'DNA,' Hattie interjects. 'My father and my brother are both very tall. My mother's family as well. I'm the blip; the aberration. Foetal disadvantage. We're twins, you see. James and I are twins. And once we were born my mother reinforced the disadvantage by always feeding James first. She did it without thinking.' Then she pauses and she smiles at the tenant. 'Giacomo,' she says, 'forgive me. I've actually met you before, but it was so long ago that you wouldn't remember. This has been the weirdest day, but – please don't think me too objectionable – I have reason to believe that I'm your aunt.' Her words are met with general silence. 'My brother's son,' she says.

'Yes,' Jack says.

'*What?!*' Josh says. 'You mean Jack is –? Christ Almighty, how weird!' Then, after quite a while, he says, 'Since we are talking weirdness right now – can anyone explain to me how Caroline comes to be here?'

'Who's Caroline?' Hattie says.

And then the paramedics are at the wide French windows, with Hattie's brother on a plastic stretcher. They move briefly indoors, into the light, in order to examine him before conveying him to the ambulance. Hattie, as the next of kin, agrees to travel with her brother. Josh and Jack, on the pistachio-green Vespa, follow the ambulance close behind. Each has his own separate reason for making the journey to the hospital. Josh cannot bear to leave Hattie to cope with the ghastly business on her own. Jack, dreaming of an EU passport, is in hopes that his moment may have come. His landlady, without a doubt, has 'settler English' written all over her. He is confident that there will a paternal grandparent born within the British Isles. And the stinking drunkard – God willing, his own male parent – is just as surely on his last legs, so Jack doesn't wish to waste time. He is reassured because, given that the drunkard and the landlady are twins, her DNA will probably serve his purpose, should the drunkard breathe his last. He knows that he needs to choose his moment with care, but he's determined to approach her within the hour.

In the peaceful aftermath of the hospital party's departure, Herman, Cat and Caroline have made their way back to the main house, where the two women sit down at the kitchen table.

'Well,' Caroline says with a smile. 'That was a bit of excitement. So the wino turns out to be family?'

Herman hisses quietly through his teeth as he sorts out glasses and drinks.

'Don't ask,' he says. 'The wife's relations. You'd know all about relations.'

'Yes, indeed,' Caroline says.

'Grandpa Ghoul and Old Mother Dribble,' Cat says confidingly to Caroline. Having recovered her confidence, she senses a felicitous bond. 'That's my mom's parents,' she says, and she giggles. 'They're real pains, aren't they, Dad? Hey, Dad? Was that stinky old *bergie* really Mom's brother? I mean seriously. Was that Unmentionable James?'

' "Was" should be about right, my *skattjie*,' Herman says, with a somewhat harsh laugh. 'Brother James won't trouble us for long. I'd say that he was heading smartly for the great cardboard city in the sky.'

But Cat has just remembered something.

'Hey, Dad,' she says, in agitation. 'I've left my portfolio in there. I need it. Please, Dad, I really need it. I've got to have it now.'

'I'll go,' Herman says. 'But, baby, what were you doing in there, all alone in the dark? Not trespassing, I hope?'

'I was returning a book,' Cat says. 'And that's the honest truth. It was for my art project. And then I needed to wee. And then I saw this, this – Dad! Don't look at me like that! I'm telling you the truth.'

'I'll go,' Caroline says quickly. 'You two stay right here.'

'You're a doll,' Herman says, without thinking, but Cat appears not to mind.

'Great!' she says. 'It's not very big. It's A3-size. It's kind of shiny black plastic with a red handle. I left it by that silver desk.'

'I know exactly,' Caroline says and she steps out once more into that magical garden, where the little earthbound stars of light click on wherever she treads. Then, having retrieved the item and returned with it to the house, she places the portfolio on the kitchen table and looks invitingly at the girl.

'Now then, Catherine,' she says. 'May I take a look? You are "Catherine", I take it?'

'I'm Kate,' Cat says.

'Kate?' says Herman, planting a kiss on the crown of his daughter's head. 'Since when did Cat become Kate, may I ask? And what's with the short black hair? What happened to my beautiful blonde bombshell?'

Cat prances a bit and giggles.

'Lettie helped me,' she says. 'Isn't it great? And she bought me these jeans. Do you think I look thin? Say you think I look thin. It's magic pants. Lettie's got some too. Only it's quite hard to hitch them up.'

Herman laughs. He watches with pleasure as his daughter brings up a chair alongside the lovely Caroline. Both are women who are right now tugging at his heart.

'Takeout pizza?' he suggests.

He is met with unanimous approval. Cat asks for bananas on hers; a local peculiarity that causes Caroline to blink. They order extra for Zoe, though the girl is still sound asleep.

Cat's drawings are fabulous. Caroline is dead impressed. The girl has always been able to draw and these are the best she's ever done. Plus the photocopies and the sections of calligraphy look great.

'It's for my art project,' Cat says to her admirer. 'It's all about Dogon mask dances in Mali. It has to be African, you see. This one's the tree mask and this is the antelope. And this fancy one here with the four figures is the healer. It says all about it in the text that I've done. I'm doing it all in handwriting, which is maybe a bit showy-off, do you think?'

'Kate,' Caroline says. 'Shall I tell you something? I'm a headmistress, so I've seen a lot of projects in my time and this one is the absolute tops. It's the best.' And then she starts doing that 'entering-into-the-spirit' thing; that eagerness routine in the face of a project that has always driven Zoe up the wall. 'I'll tell you what,' she says. 'If I were you, I'd take one or two of these amazing drawings and I'd make them three-dimensional. Scanning them into your dad's computer could be a good way to start. Have you ever done any 3D art work with folding and crumpling paper? And, do you know what? This project deserves really five-star presentation. Good paper, for a start. You want large sheets of handmade paper that you can bind into a book.' She gestures something the size of the A3 portfolio. 'Japanese bookbinding will give you a great look,' she says. 'And it's terribly easy, you know. Have you ever had the chance to try it?'

Cat is staring at her in wonder. She's thinking that being with Caroline is like having Lettie all to yourself, only combined with that brilliant guy on the TV who shows you how to do your own animation.

'No,' she says. 'But will you show me?'

'Sure,' Caroline says. 'How about we leave it until morning? Let's put it all away for now and make sure none of it gets damaged. But, gosh, Kate, you could get some brilliant textures in here, and the quality of your drawings is just superb. You could always make a matching box file as a sort of companion piece, you know. That's to accommodate any 3D construction. Oh, Kate, this is so exciting. Herman, I'm just mad about this girl.'

'Me too,' Herman says. He's uncorking a bottle of sparkling Pinot Grigio that emanates from his brother-in-law's estate.

That is to say, from the estate of one of his sister's husbands. Not from that of the brother-in-law, who has, meanwhile, been conveyed to a nearby private hospital where Hattie has proffered her Visa Card at reception. He has been stripped of his stinking, peed-on clothes, tagged, bathed and diagnosed as having suffered no more than a minor fracture to his left forearm. The examining doctor is far more concerned about the mass of ominous lesions on the patient's hands and face. The man's breathing is terrible, he notes, and, furthermore, on the out-breath he can hear a whistle which is definitely emanating from the back of James's chest. This is something the doctor has encountered before and he's confident he knows the cause. James will have advanced lung cancer. And the cancer will have spread, beyond the lungs, into the flesh and bone of the upper spinal region. The whistle is quite literally coming from a hole in the back of the patient's chest. This is an informed speculation, which, for the moment, he keeps from the patient's sister. James, in the mean time, has proffered the DNA swab, which Hattie has requested in response to Jack's request.

'No problem,' she tells him. 'I'll say it's for me.' To the doctor, by way of explanation, she says, 'I haven't seen my brother in nearly twenty years and, frankly, I'd like to be sure.'

The doctor is understanding and elicits James's consent. She then reports back her success to Jack, who arranges for his own test.

Josh and Jack have been sitting for an hour, side by side in a corridor on matching plastic chairs, during which time the former has been striving to fill in some gaps.

But Jack is economical when it comes to autobiography.

'Senegal,' he says. 'Via Mozambique and Dar es Salaam.' Then, reluctantly, he adds, 'Look. I couldn't write. It would have blown my cover.'

'Cover?' Josh says, trying not to think of how Bernie and Ida died not knowing what had become of him.

Jack sighs as a prelude to having to state a thing so obvious.

'I was travelling on a false passport,' he says. 'It was the passport of a dead French national. Jacques Moreau.'

'Giacomo Moroni?' Josh says. 'So where does Milan fit in?'

Jack has little taste for personal disclosure. He feels no need to give account of his felicitous meeting with a kindly Italian art dealer and his two small sons, on a white beach made all of shells, beside a pink lake that, at sunset, turns to purple.

'Dario Fo,' he says. 'And, no, I never heard from Gertrude. Well, you were about to ask me, weren't you?'

272

Once Hattie returns from James's bedside, she telephones Herman to say that she may well be at the hospital all night, causing Jack, on cue, to rise from his chair.

'I ought to be getting back,' he says. 'Can I –?'

'You go,' Hattie says. 'Really. Josh and I will arrange a cab.'

On his way out Jack takes a brief look at James Alexander Marchmont-Thomas, who, sluiced and shaven, in laundered clothes, helped on his way by painkilling drugs, is deeply asleep between stiff clean sheets, having previously partaken of a little toast and tea.

A nurse comments, in a whisper, that the patient has clearly been managing quite impossible levels of pain.

'Probably for years, poor soul,' she says.

'Marijuana,' Jack says. 'Lots of it, and often.' He smiles his sweetest smile at her before making his way towards the lifts.

Marijuana would be the reason why his unlovely and addle-brained parent had come staggering into his private space for a way-back wad of stolen money he'd once secreted in the wall. Jack experiences a surge of pleasure as he reflects upon how far he has moved from either one of his dead-end parents. He sees that the pistachio-green Vespa is waiting for him in the moonlight. Way up; way out. Jack feels that his life is on the move.

Once Jack has gone, Hattie and Josh arrange for a cab.

'Where to?' says the driver. Neither is particularly keen to head back to Marchmont House.

'South Beach,' Josh says, aware that he still has rights to his hotel room for what remains of this one night. 'Just off Gillespie Street,' he says.

And then, next morning, as they're about to enter the kitchen, what Hattie sees from just beyond the doorway is Caroline and Cat, who are sitting side by side at the far end of that long kitchen table with the brass measure running down one side.

They are wrapped, after an early-morning swim, in two identical kangas got from the swimming-pool changing room, each fixed, halter-style, at the nape of the wearer's neck. Before them, on the table, is the spread of Cat's beautiful drawings, alongside which are scissors and paper clippings from Caroline's demonstrations of three-dimensional effects. She has achieved these via damping, crumpling and folding, and Herman, who has been busy at the worktop, has approached to watch them at it.

'Christ, babe,' Hattie hears him say. 'Where did you learn to do that?'

'Paper engineering,' Caroline says. 'I learnt it from a book. There's this guy at the art school in Tel Aviv. Paper artist. He runs origami workshops for Israeli and Palestinian children. His graduates make these amazing paper clothes for their degree shows. Ball gowns to die for. Beautiful puckered shirts.'

Herman has yet to appreciate that Caroline can teach herself anything from a book: upholstery and binomial equations; organic-vegetable growing; the Farsi language and pattern cutting; the preparation of gravadlax and the making of Roman blinds; drystone walling and how to espalier trees; advanced computer technology and how to make a boat; Japanese bookbinding and a range of electrical repairs.

'Hi there,' Hattie says, stepping into the room. 'Gosh. I'm sorry we took so long. And I'm truly sorry about last night. All the yelling and carry-on. Say, Cat! Lovely drawings.'

But her daughter makes haste to scuffle her pages together before pointedly turning them upside down.

'Coffee,' Herman says. 'So what's the story with James?'

'Well,' Hattie says, 'for a start, as you may have gathered, we're pretty certain that your drama-department tenant is no other than my brother's son – my parents' first male grandchild. Do you suppose the shock might finish them off?'

Everyone at the table is staring at her, and none more so than Cat.

'Giacomo Moroni is Jack Maseko,' she says. 'Got by James upon the housemaid. James has a minor fracture, by the way, but in general his health is pretty dire. They're planning a lot of tests.'

'Giacomo Moroni is –?' Herman begins.

'Jack Maseko,' Hattie says. 'My nephew. Cat's first cousin.'

Cat leaps up in fury, pushing drawings and paper work before her. She's glaring daggers at her mother, as red blotches spring up all over her throat.

'Shut UP, you stupid thicko!' she screams. 'Why don't you just SHUT UP! You mean bitch, I HATE YOU!! It's all LIES and RUBBISH!' Then she bursts into a flood of tears.

The heirloom china jingles in the dresser as she storms out of the room. They hear her footsteps resounding on the stairs. Then the slamming of her bedroom door.

Once inside, she flings herself on the bed, overcome by howls and snot. Her horrible mother is making a fool of her. It's what she best likes to do. Her lovely, secret liaison with the beautiful dark boy. His classy black clothes. Just like hers. His black etchings; his Giacometti poster; the dream boy for whom she's dyed her hair and her eyelashes. First all the awfulness of last night and now this. Her mother has sussed her secret. It's what she always does. She's like a horrible creepy spy. And it's all a lot of rubbish. There's no way that the beautiful boy could be that revolting James's son. It's all a lie. It's that stupid cow and the stupid midget. And everything this morning was just so fab until they had to come back. Cat wishes that both of them would stay away for ever. She wishes that both of them were dead.

In the kitchen, Herman, biting down irritation, makes ready to go after his daughter. And just what, exactly, is the matter with Hattie that she should behave like this? Ten seconds in contact with Cat and there's another bloody screw-up. And as for that pansified, two-foot Commie – Herman remembers him from their student days. Josh Silver. What the hell is he doing here? Hasn't he been gone for decades?

'Christ, Snoeks!' he says, through gritted teeth. Then he says, 'Excuse me,' and he's gone.

'I'm afraid I've invaded your house,' Caroline says. She is carefully returning Cat's art work to the portfolio. 'I ought to be . . .' She sweeps up the scraps of paper clippings with her hands. 'I'm Caroline,' she says. 'I'm Josh's wife.'

'Please,' Hattie says. 'No need to –'

'Your daughter is very talented,' Caroline says. 'This project of hers –'

'Yes,' Hattie says. She sits down and rests her chin in her cupped hands. 'Forgive me for last night,' she says. She pauses and sighs. 'Herman may have explained about my brother. He was always very handsome, you know. Always twice my size. Golden-spoon James who'd seemed so bright and yet he was always in trouble; always on the wrong side of everything. Useless and disruptive when he was at school. Drugs, cheating, stolen cars.'

'Stolen guitars,' Josh throws in.

'Something came to me only last night,' Hattie says. 'In the hospital, sitting beside his bed. God knows why, as a family, we were always so obtuse – or was it just a sign of the times? If poor old James had been thirty years younger he would have been diagnosed dyslexic. He's severely dyslexic, isn't he? ADHD and dyslexic. It's all so glaringly obvious. These days a child like that would be labelled "special needs". He would have got help. I mean, aren't half the people in prison actually dyslexic?'

'Sixty-two per cent,' Caroline says, who always knows these things. 'That's according to recent research.'

'Gertrude as well, come to think of it,' Josh says. 'She could never get her head around the likes of *Ladybird Book 1A*; not for all my mother's efforts. It was just that life expected nothing of her. That's one advantage of low status.'

'And then there's Giacomo,' Hattie says. 'Life can be really amazing.' She reaches for the coffee pot that Herman has placed on the table, along with a clutch of little white mugs. For a moment they all fall silent.

Then Josh looks cautiously at his wife.

'Caroline,' he says, almost as if in fear. 'Please tell me about Zoe. Like where is she? Is she still in France?'

'I'm here,' Zoe says and the three of them look up to see that the child is standing in the doorway. Minus the Moschino jacket and jeans, she stands bare-legged, a slip of a thing, in ballet shoes and voluminous T-shirt; the T-shirt given to her by Gérard that says 'Zizou' across the front.

What Hattie sees is a sweet, dainty child with short chestnut curls and a small scatter of cinnamon freckles across the bridge of her nose. She notes the turn of the girl's head, the line of her shoulders, the set of her back and her legs. She observes the poise of her out-turned palms and the insteps of her little size 4 feet.

'Dad,' she says, 'I'm here.' She crosses to place herself on Josh's knee. 'Where were you?' she says. 'And where are we? I fell asleep. You should come upstairs with me. Please, Dad. You've got to come upstairs. There's this sort of magic place, with pointy windows all round. It's got like ballet things and there's this tutu. It's all black and silver. It's like being inside a dream. I dreamed I saw you in the garden last night and now you're here. Dad, can I *please, please* do ballet. *Please* say yes. *Pleeez.* I know we've never had the money for lessons, but now that Gran's died . . .' She pauses. 'I know that sounds terrible,' she says. 'I'm sorry.'

'Your gran's died?' Josh says.

'Yes,' Zoe says. 'I'm sorry. It's sort of why we're here, I think. So we could tell you. Anyway, about doing ballet, Mum said not to say anything – and I know I'm most probably too old –'

'Oh my darling,' Hattie bursts out impulsively, before Josh can begin to speak. 'You are most definitely not too old, not you. I can promise you that.'

Zoe turns and looks at her. She stares at a person who looks just like the Coppélia doll in one of the many ballet books Zoe's taken out of the library. For a moment she's caught up in the magic of it, but then everything that's happened in the last few days comes surging to the surface and her eyes are filled with tears. She's turned away from the Coppélia lady and she's staring accusingly at Caroline.

'*She* says I am,' Zoe says, jutting her head towards her mother, and then she hears herself open the floodgates; hears herself spill out grievance, just as if she were somehow hovering above her own head and watching, as if some other force is switching on her voice. '*And* she deliberately stopped Gérard and me – just because we were dancing. *And* she's most probably ruined Gérard's life. Because what if he's not allowed to come and stay? Like next year when it's his turn to come to us?' Then she's turned her face to Josh. 'You've *got* to phone him for me, Dad,' she says. 'Please, Dad. You've got to. You have to phone his mother's house, because I don't even know the code from here and anyway, she'd only scream at me. "*Merde, merde!*" like she always does. And there's that horrible Véronique as well, who always treats me like dirt. I mean, I don't even know for sure if he's still there, after what she's gone and done. I mean, what if he's been taken into care? Then I'll never know where he is, will I?' And then she's crying into Josh's shoulder.

Caroline heaves a sigh.

'Give it a break, will you, Zoe?' she says. 'Really! I'm not sure that I can take much more of this. Nobody wants to hear about it and, frankly, Josh hasn't a single clue what you're on about. So if you would please stop crying and screeching, we can discuss all this a bit later.'

'He *has* got a clue!' Zoe says, jerking her head up. 'He *has*! It's just *you*! You always think you know everything and all you've done is mess up Gérard's life. Anyway, I am not the only one who's "screeching". I don't know what's going on around here, but there's always someone screaming their head off. I heard this person screaming last night. I was nearly too scared to breathe. And just now there was someone else yelling and stamping and banging. That's what woke me up.'

Hattie gets up and goes to her. She puts both her hands on Zoe's shoulders.

'About that black-and-silver tutu,' she says. 'Would you like to try it on?'

Caroline and Josh sit alone in the ensuing silence. They drink their coffee to the dregs.

Eventually Josh begins to speak.

'This is all very strange,' he says. 'Gosh.'

'Yes,' Caroline says. 'Sorry about the *Sturm und Drang*. Maybe it's adolescence? But, as Zoe rightly pointed out earlier, it's a bit like being inside a dream. It's true that we came to find you, Josh. But now I've got something to tell you.'

'Your mother,' he says. 'I'm so sorry, Caro. What happened?'

'Not that,' Caroline says. 'No, not that. Look, that's actually wonderful, to tell you the honest truth. I'm only sorry I allowed the old bat to poison our lives for all that time.'

'No –' Josh says, but Caroline carries on.

'It's given me the chance to start over,' she says. 'And that's what I mean to do. This really isn't easy, no matter which way I say it. Not after all that you and I have been through. Josh, I'm not coming back with you. I really didn't mean for this to happen. It's not what I ever expected. I've fallen in love and I'm not coming back. I'm sorry. That's my story.'

'Who have you fallen in love with?' Josh says, somewhat cautiously, after a pause.

'With Herman,' Caroline says. 'With your little friend's husband. Look. None of this is going to be easy. I do understand that much.'

Josh is quiet for such a long time that she thinks that he's not going to speak.

'Well, Cat evidently likes you,' he says. 'That's quite an achievement.' His response is so unexpected that it provokes, in each of them, a small, cautious smile.

'Me too,' Josh says eventually, staring into the dregs of his cup.

'Pardon?' Caroline says.

'I said me too,' Josh says. 'Hattie and me. I didn't know how to tell you.' He's thinking how brave and splendid Caroline is; how infinitely in keeping with herself. To risk pitching in like this and thereby saving him from himself. 'She wants to come to England with me,' he says. 'It's what she should have done first time round. Listen, Caro – I'm not wishing to diminish what we had. What I mean is that being with you has been incredible. You do know that, don't you? I mean that you're amazing. You do know that?'

Caroline manages a smile.

'I suppose I do,' she says. 'Yes, I think I do.'

But clouds are passing across Josh's brain.

'I want Zoe,' he blurts out in panic. He notes that his hands are shaking. 'Please, Caroline. I want Zoe. I want her to come back with me.' Then he adds, more with hope than conviction, 'What if you had her for the school holidays? Something like that?'

Caroline has placed her face in her hands. Behind her fingers, he can tell that her mouth is contorting with pain. Then she looks up.

'We'll have to put it to her,' she says. It's as if she's completely recovered herself. 'We'll ask her,' she says. 'Zoe's not a baby. It's the only thing we can do.' Then she says, 'I have to concede that I know which way she'll jump.' He watches her examine the beautiful U-shaped arcs of her fingernails, as she struggles to change the subject. 'You can have that little mouse house, if you like,' she says. 'I was working on it when my mum died. You'll find it's in good shape. The kitchen and bathroom are pretty nice and I've sanded all the downstairs floors.'

'Caroline –' Josh says.

'There's a new central-heating system on its way,' she says. 'Courtesy of my mother. You'll find it's top-of-the-range. Oh, and there's a couple of thousand pounds that I've left stashed under the living-room floor.'

'Caroline –' Josh says.

'It's just to the left of the fireplace,' she says. 'What?'

'Nothing,' Josh says. 'Caroline, please. Don't . . .' He's thinking that maybe he and Hattie could relocate to Bristol. That's if Zoe's OK with the idea. That's if – oh please, dear God – Zoe chooses to be part of the picture. But then there's Mattie and Maggs to be considered and – of course – there's the dancing boy; the Tall Merry Fellow, whose life may be in ruins. Better, after all, to stay put.

'Why is she so cross with you?' he says. 'Is this to do with Herman?'

'Oh,' Caroline says. 'No, I don't think so.' Then she says, 'Could be. But only a bit. Mainly it's because I went to fetch her in France, after my mother died. She was living rough with a runaway boy and his boozed-up father in a wood. Her exchange partner. Nice kid, as it happens. They were hiding out in a shed. They'd been bunking off school for days. The mother was like a wound-up spring; like a ball of crazed aggression.'

'Was she in the hut as well?' Josh says.

'No,' Caroline says. 'She was in a house near by. There's an older sister. The family is patently dysfunctional, though the boy was doing his best. I had a word with the head, who has promised to follow it up.'

'Christ Almighty,' Josh says. 'Our little girl. It sounds like *Cold Comfort Farm.*'

'Zoe and the boy were teaching themselves to dance,' she says. 'She's got this ballet obsession; just like a hundred and one little girls, as I've always persuaded myself. I've always insisted she was not to bother you with it. I'm really sorry, Josh. I should have been more indulgent with her. I know that now. I should have respected all our needs before those of my wretched mother. Isn't hindsight a wonderful thing?' He sees her wiping her hand across her eyes. Then she says briskly, 'None of us ever has to enter that house of hers again. The Garden Haven horror house. I've smashed up all the Hummel figurines, by the way.'

'Come again?' Josh says.

'Not now,' she says. 'I don't want to talk about it. It's over. I'm going for a swim.' She pecks him briefly on the cheek. 'Be happy,' she says. 'Oh God, I can't begin to tell you how much I love it here! I really, really do!' And then she's gone.

In her bedroom, Cat is being comforted by her dad, who listens to her staccato, hiccuping phrases as he gently strokes her back.

'I hate her!' Cat is saying.

'Relax, my baby,' he says.

'And that stupid midget!' she says. 'All they do is prance around acting smug and clever.'

'Shsh,' Herman says, and he starts to massage her neck.

'They do!' Cat says, sitting up suddenly. Her face red and swollen, she nonetheless has a spirited shot at mimicry. ' "Oh, Cattie-pie, Josh and I are off to the NSA Gallery, because we're so-o arty-farty, don't-you-know?" ' Then, when Herman laughs, she adds, 'It's true, Dad. They've been hanging out together nearly the whole time you've been away.'

Herman is making circular movements with his thumbs at the points where his daughter's shoulders meet her neck. He observes a small, lingering stain from Cat's recent contact with black hair dye. What she says is offering him the convenient possibility that, instead of appearing the supplicant with Hattie, he can have a plausible shot at accusing his wife of playing away. Hattie the marriage-wrecker. Then, what the hell, he'll take out the rest of the week; billet himself with his sister Lettie for a night or two, along with Cat and Caroline; get his two favourite women out of the fray; give Cat a chance to be a child again with her exuberant younger cousins; then on to the Cape for a couple of days; decamp with Esther, his older sister – the one who, with her husband, owns a wine estate on the edge of Stellenbosch. Look in on his student twins while he is about it. Cat will enjoy a visit to her siblings and get a foretaste of that seductive campus life among the orchards and the avenues of oak trees. And all of them – Jonno and Suz included – will be crazy for Caroline, he's quite sure.

'I wish Caroline was my mother,' Cat says viciously, and right on cue.

'Shsh, baby,' Herman says, still massaging the back of her neck. 'How's about we pay Lettie a visit? We'll invite ourselves over for lunch.'

Cat is as a person instantly recovered.

'Yea-ah!' she says, and she throws off his massaging thumbs. 'And Dad? Can Caroline come?'

Herman encounters Hattie, barefoot, on the staircase as he exits his daughter's room. She has just left Zoe in the turret, still wearing the black-and-silver tutu and with the completed type-script of *Lola in Wenceslas Square* planted in her lap.

'I'd love you to be my critical reader,' Hattie has told her. 'Please tell me what you think.'

Unfortunately for Herman, because she is now two treads above the landing, his wife has added height. Nonetheless, he fixes her, eye to eye, with a cold, stern look.

'I think you've got something to tell me,' he says.

But Hattie has seen him with Caroline that morning; has read his body language as she stood in her kitchen doorway; has heard him call Caroline 'babe'. She has observed the looks that pass between them, their eyes shining with love. Something more than love. Love infused with sexual excitement. It's had the effect of making her remember how once, in her salad days, Herman had had that effect on her; those days when, being green in reason, she had not gone to England with Josh. It has the effect now of making her forgive herself. So she faces him down, making steady eye contact, smiling at him sweetly as she does so, thinking objectively that, yes, he's really quite a catch. She wishes Caroline well with him; thinks what an alpha couple they will make and how delighted Lettie will be at the prospect of a new tennis partner.

'You want to tell me that you've fallen in love,' she says. 'You've found somebody else. Herman, I know. It's all right. I know. It's been waiting to happen for a while. Go for it, is what I say. As if I could ever stop you. I hope she'll make you very happy.' Then she continues her descent, still sleepless and a bit rumpled, in yesterday's clothes, her linen shirt curling up at the hem. After a moment, she turns back and looks up at him. 'I won't be in your way for long,' she says, 'though I need to sort something out for James. Perhaps your company has a "property" for me somewhere? A little condo on the Berea, maybe? Just for a few weeks? I think Cat might welcome having me "offstage". She's been missing you like crazy.'

Herman, possibly for the first time in his life, is feeling himself wrong-footed.

'This house is mine,' he says unnecessarily. 'I hope that's understood.'

She needles him by blowing him a kiss as she moves on down the stairs. He notes with displeasure those abused and undersized feet; dancer's feet that, for quite a while now, he has found a little bit repellent.

*　　*　　*

So both girls get what they imagine they want; that's to be the child of the other one's mother. For Zoe, it's all too thrillingly like what happens in *Masquerade at the Wells*, though she knows that she cannot put this analogy to Cat, whom she's been quite careful to avoid. It's clear to her that Cat despises her as a drippy, flat-chested little crawler. Anyway, they don't get too much of a chance, given that Cat disappears with Herman Munster, before Caroline and Josh have taken her aside to explain to her what's happening. Then Caroline goes off, following the others to Lettie's house. It's Lettie who comes to collect her.

Caroline's goodbyes are like those of a person who is taking a weekend break.

'I'll see you soon-soon, my darling,' she says. 'You be good now, sweetheart.' And she gives her daughter a hug.

It's a public sort of hug, undertaken in front of Cat's waiting aunt, which is necessarily inhibiting – though, inside, Zoe is suddenly thinking that it's all got to be her fault, because ever since France she's been so horrible. And that it's going to be really embarrassing to have to tell Mattie and Maggs, because they're always going on and on about how fab her mother is. There was never any chance that she would choose to stay in this place with Caroline and Herman Munster, but what if Hattie gets tired of her? Because what if she's not brainy enough to say anything that isn't stupid and obvious about the typescript of *Lola in Wenceslas Square*? She's wishing that she could be reading the story in a proper book with a cover, and not having to think of clever things to say about it.

'Your dad is going to sort things for you with Gérard,' Caroline is saying, and then she and her wheelie bag are gone; stowed in Lettie's four-by-four. *Voom. Varoom.* Gone.

Afterword

It goes without saying that Herman and Caroline, Hattie and Josh are better off with their swap. It's wonderful for Herman and Caroline – most especially for Caroline, given all those years of thou-shalt-not – that they can now indulge the shiny newness of their strong mutual attraction. Because from the moment Herman paid for those long, chilled mango drinks and handed her that cell phone in the airport café, the two of them have been inhaling enchantment from the pheromones that began at once to dance in the air between them. Thought-bubbles were forming over their heads, plumped out with cartoon love-hearts and smoochy scarlet lips.

Caroline, as everyone knows, is good at making bold and radical decisions when situations require them and she's brilliant at making them work. She's done this before, when she gave up her DPhil and, using an old red bus as her austerity nerve centre, committed herself to a life of make do and mend. On that occasion she didn't look back and she doesn't mean to do so now. Whatever the faults or virtues of that phase of her life, she's not going to beat herself up about it; certainly not from the vantage point of Herman's fabulous house. Because those days are over and – thanks to her mother's recently exposed treachery – she's finished and done with guilt. Naturally, she understands that things might be difficult for Zoe, but people must learn to make their own way. They must toughen up and deal with stuff; whatever stuff life chooses to throw at them. Isn't that what she's always had to do?

Watching Herman with his daughter – with all of his three children, come to that – has made Caroline concede that she hasn't, after all, been one of this life's greatest mothers, and this is a little bit irksome to her, because she's accustomed to always being the best. She sees now that being a five-star domestic researcher, school-project manager and personal shopper; finder of specialist map shops and black Moschino jackets; world's best home pattern-cutter and baker of birthday cakes – alas, only once a ballerina cake – does not quite add up to the same thing. But what the hell, she's done her best and how was she to know different? For God's sake, would you take a look at the role model *she's* had to grow up with.

She knows from all her years of teaching that it's often a lot easier to deal with children who aren't your own – especially if those children happen to be like Kate Marais. She and Cat have hit it off big time, right from the very start. Cat is an absolute dreamboat. And so are Herman's sisters, who, in their warm and ready acceptance of her, their ebullience and their easy sense of entitlement, their splashy parties and barbecues, make a context in which she feels herself appreciated and loved. All of the sisters dote on their brother, who is their only male sibling, and they rejoice to see him hooked up with a woman who, unlike Hattie, doesn't make them feel uncomfortable. All of them find Caroline to be the soul of wit, which comes as quite a surprise. They fall about laughing at almost everything she says and beg to have her tell them all her stories.

The Grudge Fudge has become a family favourite. Make up a batch of Grudge Fudge and give it to someone you hate.

'So have you made any fudge for us today?' Lettie will say to her. 'We'll soon know when we're not welcome.'

Caroline loves to throw parties for them herself. And she loves it, the way that Lettie's sparkly blue eyes will so readily fill with tears of laughter.

Caroline, being the woman she is, doesn't bring out the bully in Herman, who is now most solicitous in the matter of her new career. Does she want to go back to the language lab and to those old trade routes through Persia? Hell, no. She most certainly does not. She signs up instead at the local art school and becomes a student of fashion. Herman makes over the studio for her use, which is to be her study-workshop. She has plans to start a business in there, designing party dresses and ball gowns. Wedding dresses as well. Flashy frocks, and why not? She travels with Herman quite a lot and has taken to playing golf. London, Tokyo, the Seychelles. They have a plan to follow the bus routes, from Chillingollah to Pinnaroo; from Tintinara to Dimboola, because – who knows? – they might turn up a tall ageing blonde, who once gave away a baby on a bus. To do so would be seriously exciting, and if they don't? No worries.

Hattie finds things more difficult at first, but in the main this has to do with all the immediate, complicated stuff that serves to impede any hopes of serenity in the matter of making a getaway. Unlike Caroline, who has all her current effects contained within two travel bags, Hattie has other sorts of baggage and quite a lot of it. There are her twins in the Cape. And there is James; poor old terminal James, who, in the unlikely event of his surviving his time in hospital, will need some form of sheltered care. She and Josh, with Zoe in tow, undertake a three-day high-speed consumer survey of all available establishments for which James might just be eligible. And Hattie also has the task of speaking to her parents. She tells them first that she has found their son, who

288

is alive but gravely ill. After a while, she tells them that, within the week, she herself is taking off to go and live in England.

Predictably, the former intelligence becomes the focus of all their interest. Mrs Marchmont-Thomas, weeping tears of joy and sorrow, becomes increasingly exercised about the possible inadequacy of Hattie's proposals for James's care.

'But why an institution for him?' she says. 'Why on earth can't James have his nice old room back? His little room in the turret?'

'Not possible,' Hattie says firmly. 'That's simply not an option. For a start, he couldn't make the stairs. Mother, James is incredibly frail. And besides, as I've just told you, I'm going to live in England.'

This is Mr Marchmont-Thomas's cue to come into his own.

'You surely can't think of going abroad,' he says. 'When it's clear that you are needed here at home?'

'Oh but I can,' Hattie says. 'You'll find that I most certainly can.'

She feels herself suddenly to have grown a foot taller as she hears herself say these words – or is it that her father has begun to shrink with age? Having succumbed to this form of blackmail in years gone by, it delights her to know that she will never be doing so again.

'You may remember,' she says now, addressing both her parents, 'that Marchmont House belongs to Herman, who has no responsibility for James.'

She desists from pointing out that her royalties will be covering the cost of James's care; also that their own top-notch retirement flat comes courtesy of Herman, to whose chagrin the place is so perennially crammed with heavy items of dark-brown heirloom furniture that there is barely space to breathe. Yet her father, as always, is looking dapper, in his dark suit with watch chain.

She gives her parents the telephone number for her brother's hospital ward.

'About going to visit him,' she says. 'I'd advise you to make it soon.'

She kisses her mother on the cheek. Her father, who doesn't do kissing, offers his hand instead.

'Back to the Old Country, eh?' he says. 'You'll find that it's not what it was.'

And then – thank God – there is the conference to take her mind off these things. On the platform she talks briefly and personally about what dance has meant to her, how, for all its physical battering, it drew her out from an oppressive childhood, into a world of weightlessness and lift. She talks about how she has chosen, now, to focus on Stravinsky's *Pulcinella* – a thing to which Josh Silver introduced her many years ago; a ballet with songs and masks; a ballet that, for all its unlikely balance of piss-pot slapstick and delicate romance, is revealing itself as capable of having relevance to real life. Because Person A, who was lost – presumed dead – has turned out to be alive. And Person B, who for many years has walked in the shoes of another, is now most wonderfully unmasked. And then, of course, there is Person C. Well, frankly, he has all to do with the business of pairing off; with picking out one's life's dancing partner from the profusion of characters crowding the stage, all leaping and swirling before one's eyes in the same tall conical hats. She says, in conclusion, that her next Lola story will be set in Pulcinella's home town. Lola will be on her way to Naples.

After that, she and Josh take off their shoes and nod to Jack, who is standing in the wings, with his finger on the Pause button of a portable CD player. In response, he releases the sound of that slowed-up, stretched-out 'recomposition', full of rasping discords and pastoral yearnings. Hattie and Josh then mime the last scene in which – via grief, betrayal and bereavement, via ecstasy and muddle – they finally come together. *Per voi il core struggendo si va.*

At Marchmont House, in the five-day space that Herman has

tactfully afforded them, Hattie begins to flap and dither about what to keep and what to ditch.

'That clock,' she says. 'It's so beautiful. And I know that Cat and Herman hate it. Will there be room for it in your house, or am I getting to be like my parents?'

Then she's at the kitchen dresser, pulling out her great-grand-mother's china plates.

'What do you think?' she says to Josh. 'Shall I get massive rolls of bubble wrap and make a start on these? Or shall I get in the packers to do it after we've gone?'

'Leave it,' Josh says. 'For heaven's sake, Hat. Just walk away from it.'

Having been adamant that the three of them travel together to London, he has been obliged to buy new tickets, since the last ones couldn't be exchanged. Their initial flight will be to Cape Town, so that Hattie can go and see her twins. Then, from there, it's on to Heathrow. He's made the booking on his credit card in the hope of being able to pay it off from the Witch Woman's bundle that Caroline has left under the floor.

'Just leave all that, I beg you,' he says. 'Caroline will pack it for you. And she'll arrange to have it shipped. There's nothing she likes better and she's very good at it. Caroline is a packing genius. Zoe will back me up here. Isn't that right, Zoe?'

But Zoe has gone very quiet. She has her nose in a copy of *What Katy Did*, and she doesn't appear to be listening.

'Everything in the turret will be left just so for you, my darling,' Hattie says to Josh's child. 'It will be your very own bedroom – your special place, for when you come to visit your mother.'

Zoe wishes that Hattie wouldn't keep on calling her darling and she especially doesn't like to think about coming back here to stay – what with Mister H. Munster in residence, as well as that tall shouty girl. The thought of it is giving her the horrors. She wishes that they could just go; go quickly; just get on that plane and go home. But Hattie, who is coming with them, has got about a million plates that she's pulled out all over the floor. Zoe has never seen so many plates. It's like she was planning to have a banquet or something.

Hattie and Josh make a quieter pair of lovers than Herman and Caroline. They are smaller and less glamorous and a lot more understated. They are northern-hemisphere lovers. But they are intensely in love, for all that. They relish every minute in each other's company. Their greatest pleasures are simple walks in woods and meadows and on towpaths. They have taken to making weekend visits to old Cotswold churches and they often walk holding hands. Such spare cash as they have, they spend on theatre visits and the ballet. They care so little about their clothes that Zoe thinks they'll end up like those embarrassing oldies who always wear sandals with socks. Hattie loves the gentle drizzle and the slanting silvery light.

The three of them take up residence in the pretty little terraced house that Caroline has so tastefully made ready, and for which they now – rather quickly and indifferently – acquire some additional bits of furniture. Hattie ships out the grandfather clock, but soon commits it to auction, where it fetches a very good price. She has four of the elm-wood chairs in the house, but the plates are permanently in store. Zoe inhabits the small back bedroom while Josh and Hattie share the slightly larger one that overlooks the street. Sometimes one or other of the pair will go off for a couple of hours to do some paperwork in the old bus, but mostly they are together, each bent over their writing at either end of the living-room table.

They sign up Zoe for a ballet class that takes place in north Oxford and Hattie supervises her practice. In the evenings, they usually eat carton soup, or scrambled eggs, or cheese on toast, especially on the days when Josh stays over in Bristol. Sometimes, at weekends, Hattie will rouse herself to roast a chicken, but she never leaves it in the oven long enough, so it's always sort of sloppy and anaemic; not crisp and golden as it should be. Plus Caroline used to make stuffing for a chicken, with things like pine nuts and dried apricots and wild rice mixed with freshly chopped home-grown herbs.

Hattie loves it that you can get around by bike, so they right away buy her a bicycle. Because Caroline's is, of course, hope-lessly too big. So it stays exactly where she left it; a tall old Dutch bike with a large wicker basket, leaning up against the garden wall. Zoe finds herself staring at it when she should be doing her homework, because every time she looks up from her desk the bicycle is right there; right in her line of vision.

Things are trickier for the girls, though, on the face of it, easier for Cat. Not only is she older, but she's highly intelligent, talented, strident, demanding and manipulative; born into a large pater-nal family of doting, warm-hearted and affluent persons with easy top-dog assumptions. So Cat is on an upward trajectory, much bolstered by the energy and skill of her father and her new step-mother. Once the tenant has voluntarily moved on and Caroline is ensconced in the studio, Cat is all too ready to enter it. It's always fun to watch Caroline at work – I mean, she's doing fashion, isn't she? How cool is that? Cat is quick to understand that she was never going to capture the heart of the beautiful Giacomo, but she doesn't care that much; not once she's thought about it. Because wasn't he a little bit weird when you got to think about it? Not to mention that he turned out to be that horrible James's son. In short, the tenant has swiftly and easily disappeared from her life.

That's until one day, five years on – five years on from the 'now' time, making it the year 2000 – when, as a one-year exchange student in Milan, the brightest of her year – Cat looks up and sees the tenant as she sits at a café table in the Piazza della Scala. A tall, handsome, size ten blonde with slightly peculiar eating habits, she

293

is in the company of her adoring current boyfriend. Cat has lots of adoring boyfriends, sometimes more than one at a time. Easy come, easy go. And it could be that the deceptive ease with which she let go of her mother has something to do with the shallowness that marks her emotional life.

The tenant is walking through the square, still dressed top-to-toe in black. He doesn't look in her direction and she's sure he hasn't seen her. She feels no urge to intervene. He is merely the person whose fabulous book once helped to kick-start a school art project that won her a national award; an award that made her the envy of her classmates and caused that creepy Alan to come sliming up to her, just as though he'd never chucked her over in favour of her one-time best friend Michelle. But all that is very so-what and seriously in the past. Since then, she hasn't looked back. She's sailed into the architectural school and now she's using her time in Italy to study rationalist-modernist trends in early Fascist architecture; those beautiful, austere, industrial-looking structures that are so much in evidence around Milan. Cat finds herself quite drawn to the romance of the Fascist aesthetic.

She gets on OK-ish with her mother these days. Or they manage, at least, to coexist. She has always set the terms of their meetings – either in her father's London flat or, together with her older siblings, once a year at the Cape in summer. Never at home. Most recently she has arranged for her mother to pay a brief visit to Milan. The emphasis is on 'brief'. She's booked a small hotel room for Hattie and she's even used some of the extra cash she's got from her dad to book two tickets for Stravinsky's *Pulcinella*. It's not her cup of tea, to be sure, but she likes to keep the visits well structured. Keep them busy; keep them brief. That way they don't end up quarrelling. She takes note that her mother, for her sins, is on to Lola book eight.

Things prove rather more difficult for Zoe, who is younger and a lot less pushy about making her own needs known. Thanks to her mother, she's been rigorously trained in self-denial. And, unlike Cat, she has no extended family of merry, extrovert aunts and cousins, and there isn't an uncle in sight, though admittedly there is, on one bleak winter's day, an unannounced, one-off, one-hour visit from a person who turns out to be her mother's sister Janet, the once-upon-a-time Less Fortunate. She turns up on a day when Zoe is home alone and she's babbling about how she's 'dropped in' to collect her late mother's Hummel figurines that she says were promised to her by Caroline.

'I've only got one china figure from Gran,' Zoe says, and, in the earnest hope of getting rid of the woman, she offers up the little china lady reclining on a china bed, her little china husband holding her china hand.

'Really and truly,' Janet says with a sigh, and she rolls her eyes to heaven. 'You won't have heard the last of this.'

She accepts the offering somewhat grudgingly and is never seen again.

The Gérard affair proves a far more lowering experience, for all Josh's conscientious efforts. Her dad is certainly as good as his word in making contact with the French headmistress and discovering her dear friend's current whereabouts. The boy has departed from the school, she says. It was all for the best. He has been sent to live with his grandmother in a village near Narbonne, which means that he is no longer a part of Zoe's school's French exchange programme. The conifer house has been repossessed. Véronique has left school and has got herself a job. There is no news of Gérard's *très triste* dad, who has doubtless by now been dispossessed of the little forest hat.

Hattie, Josh and Zoe board the Eurostar for Paris, from whence they take the sleeper train for the south.

'We'll make a holiday of it,' Josh says, and he books them into a B & B, though for himself, he'd much rather stay in Paris and take them all to the Comédie Française and linger around the Gard du

Nord so that he could show dear Hattie where he once had his little student garret, in those days before he'd returned to the news of Caroline's father's death.

For Zoe the train journey south ought to have been the best fun, just like being in that going-to-the-seaside ballet that she's always wanted to see. *Le Train Bleu*, with the enormous Picasso backdrop. The two huge ladies, their hands clasped high, running, in their bathers, towards the sea. Oh! Oh! The sea! The sea! But anxiety is keeping Zoe from enjoyment. And the fact that every dog in Paris appears to be travelling south by train for the summer vacation is causing her to brood upon the possible fate of Mimi the chocolate Labrador.

In the village, where they approach the house, Zoe is appalled to find that Mimi is, by her lights, worse than dead. She's kept fixed to a chain at the gatepost, where she has no shelter from the blazing sun and nothing to do but bark. In her pathetic, body-wiggling welcome, she treads in her own stale water bowl, inverting the last of her liquid refreshment on to the greedy earth.

Gérard is not at home, for all that he has been forewarned of her arrival by Josh's telephone call. They find him, taller and more filled out, playing football in the square and he is patently not best pleased to be interrupted by his erstwhile woodland ballet partner; a ghost from his former life, in the figure of a small, red-headed girl who does nothing to enhance his local street-cred.

He shakes hands politely but stiffly with Zoe's father and with her stepmother, then with Zoe herself. He declines the offer of dinner that night in a local restaurant. He shifts unwittingly from foot to foot in his eagerness to be gone. Then his teammates summon him back to the game by means of those bullish male noises that Zoe has always found so strangely other whenever she's heard them emanating from sports fields and recreation grounds back home. It occurs to her to be thankful that she's not wearing the 'Zizou' T-shirt.

'Gérard,' she says. 'About Mimi . . .' She wants to blurt out to him that the dog should not be kept chained up, but she loses heart and gives up.

He makes a little almost-bow and then he's gone.

The three outsiders hover to watch the game for something like half a minute.

'Please, Dad,' Zoe says. 'Please. I'd like to go now, if that's all right.'

School is never quite the same, since Mattie and Maggs are more bonded than ever and when the French exchange comes round again, Zoe, as in a game of musical chairs, is the one who is left standing. She's of an age when she is just about to change, and adolescent introspectiveness comes with a heavy dose of introversion. It begins to dawn on Zoe that her previous, ebullient interactions with her dad – those lovely 'silly' times she always had with him – were quite a lot to do with the two of them reacting to Caroline's grown-upness. The mood between them has changed with Hattie's coming, so that things like their collections of prize news billboards have gradually dwindled until they are no more. Gone are all the 'Brad Pitt Haircut Boys' and 'Cold Flat OAPs'.

All the silly stuff has quietly fallen into disuse.

'I saw a butcher's shop that was called a Meat Boutique.'

'I passed a restaurant that was called The Rumblin' Tums.'

'I was on a bus that said "13 seated plus 2 standees". Then it said, "OR, 11 seated plus 2 standees plus 1 wheelchair".'

'So it could have said, "9 seated plus 2 standees plus 2 wheelchairs"?'

'Or "5 seated plus 2 standees plus 4 wheelchairs"?'

'It could have not had any seated at all. And no standees either. That would have made enough room for 7½ wheelchairs.'

It all simply stopped, because it had somehow stopped being funny.

Zoe finds that she feels self-conscious, once she's joined the ballet class, where everyone else is quite a lot younger, and she's already missed out on acquiring a place at a school for the performing arts. Truth to tell, she's been yearning to do ballet for so many years before her wish is granted, that she is on the edge of having exorcised the need before it gets to be realised.

She misses her mother quite a lot and, when the family move to Bristol, Zoe stays there only to finish her GCSEs, after which she returns to take up residence in the old red bus. She practises theories of self-sufficiency by resurrecting Caroline's vegetable patch and she gets herself a chocolate Labrador pup – a bitch called Mimi – who always sleeps alongside her, like a chunky hot-water bottle.

She does voluntary work with asylum seekers and goes in for a form of minimum-impact living that on the whole works well, though she does once find her equilibrium disturbed when she uncovers the floral Birkenstocks and the T-shirt that says 'Zizou'. Most of her friends are from the Allotment Association, and she enjoys their company. Maybe one day she'll sign up for some form of adult education? Maybe she'll do a course in forestry? Because, thanks to her French exchange, Zoe is still fond of trees and some proper woodland know-how would be a nice thing to have. Zoe isn't hugely motivated. Caroline, even in her absence, remains such a difficult act to follow, that her daughter finds it easier not to try.

And then, of course, there's Jack. Once Jack has got his DNA result he knows exactly what to do. He acquires the necessary papers as the descendant of that line of Marchmont-Thomases, one-time settler upper-crust and basket-weavers of Norfolk. Then he claims his British passport and becomes eligible for residence in the EU. He needs to serve out his two-year junior fellowship and then he can move on. From his point of view such relocation can't come soon enough, because – who knows? – being where he is, there's always a chance that one or other of his deadbeat parents might loom up out of the dark; a phlegmy, alcoholic street person and a dumbo domestic servant, both wanting something from him. The prospect offends his aesthetic sense. Needy, repellent persons, like those Dakar beggars he was once so deft at stepping over, on the Avenue Pompidou.

In this respect, luck is once again with him, since his recently found male parent has a mere eight weeks to live, and Gertrude, poor old Gertrude, stolid Gertrude – does anyone really care about her? – Gertrude is no more. Gertrude, respecter of racial hierarchies, schooled in subservience by previous white households, was always baffled by the Silvers' atypical way of life; was never comfortable around them. Their constant sloppiness towards the time-honoured barriers of race; the shocking way in which they would invite black people into their home – persons, as she judged them, no better than herself, who sat all over the living-room chairs and to whom she was required to serve tea. Tea out of the same china cups that the family used for white friends. Zulu men wearing suits and ties, Zulu women with handbags and high heels, who didn't cover their hair. Right from the start she'd had a problem with the Silvers' repeated urgings for her to use inappropriate modes of address.

'Yes, master,' Gertrude said. 'No, master.'

'I'm not your master,' Bernie said. 'I am your employer, that is all. My name is Bernie Silver. How about you call me Bernie and I will call you Gertrude?'

'Yes, master,' Gertrude said. 'All right, my master.'

In addition, the Silvers were extremely sloppy with regard to their wallets. At first Gertrude assumed that they left money around on purpose, as a way of catching her out. Trousers on the bathroom coat-hook, pockets jingling with coins, a handbag left on the kitchen table. No lock on the telephone. A drinks cupboard with no key. Then it began to dawn on her that the Silvers were just plain stupid. If they couldn't take care of their own money, then they didn't deserve to have it. They didn't behave like normal white people, so what was there to respect? The pay was good and she did her work as thoroughly as she had been taught.

But truth to tell she missed her old billet at the Marchmont-Thomas's house, especially as the length of garden there had made for greater privacy; greater privacy for her and the gardener. Joseph, the ancient Mozambican so approved of by Hattie's dad. He had begun to cut her in on the money he was getting for storing stolen goods; knock-off from an electrical-appliance factory where his son Amos had a job. Amos, together with a bunch of young men, could sell the stuff on for a very good price and the old man always got his share. For Joseph, Gertrude was like a sort of daughter and he could always count on her loyalty. Then came the time when the wretched James was sent down from his boarding school and from then on he was omnipresent.

He had taken to drugging in one of the sheds alongside the servants' quarters, which had confronted Gertrude with a problem – especially since he'd come upon her one day, concealing a stack of transistor radios under a pile of old sacks. Gertrude was not going to sacrifice old Joseph and, instead, allowed James to have her portion as a way of buying his silence. Then he demanded her savings from her and, when she had no more money to give, he'd forced himself upon her.

'You can pay me in pussy,' he said.

Once the pregnancy was too marked to hide, he'd stolen his father's fountain pen and had contrived to get her sacked.

At the point where Gertrude took up her job at the Silvers', she had not a penny left to her name and lots of catching up to do, which was not difficult around the Silvers' house, since they never missed the odd twenty-rand note. Meanwhile the friendship with Joseph was able to continue. Joseph who, thanks to his employer's son, had had to rethink the storage system, soon learnt to keep a sharp lookout for James Alexander Marchmont-Thomas. And so it was that the old man had happened to observe Hattie's brother one night, removing a loose brick from the wall alongside the servants' cistern outlet and then mortaring it crudely back into place.

It cost him some effort, that very same night, to climb on a chair and check things out, but he'd made a better fist of it than James had, eighteen years on. So Joseph found the envelope that Josh had been carrying in his pocket the night he'd gone to say his final goodbyes to Hattie Thomas. The envelope said 'Gertrude', so Joseph promptly handed it over to the person for whom it was intended. That was Gertrude's windfall time because Josh, alone in his parents' house next morning, had meanwhile been to the bank. He had handed her another envelope, also labelled 'Gertrude', and containing, in crisp new notes, the identical sum of money. Then, that evening, he'd headed out for the airport.

Gertrude, too, was meant to leave that night. It had been the Silvers' plan. For her own sake they had wanted her out, just in case the Special Branch came by and made trouble for anyone left behind. Yet Gertrude's plan was to linger there, for just one more night, so that she and Joseph, on the quiet, could gather up the Silvers' remaining smaller items with the object of selling them on. But news unfortunately travels fast and soon Amos and his friends were there – a group of young men who were high on booze and probably drugs as well. They came prepared to cart off more ambitious volumes of stuff, for which purpose they were adequately equipped with a stolen dry-cleaner's van. And they were making quite a lot of noise.

The commotion soon drew the next-door neighbour, who came out to investigate; the very same next-door neighbour, by now advanced in years, who had once apprehended Pru at the Silvers' gate with the infant Josh tied to her back. Being a man who kept a gun under his pillow, he was unwise enough to bring it with him, and to brandish it as he approached the group, demanding to know their business. As soon as the old man made as if to aim, it was all too predictable that one of the hotheads would shoot him first. Then, in their need to make a hasty getaway, the gang were obliged to leave the balance of their pickings in the Silvers' driveway, along with the bleeding old man. They all piled back into the dry-cleaner's van, grabbing Gertrude as they did so, just in case she could have it in mind to squeal.

They drove at speed down Umbilo Road and some way beyond the Dalton Road market where, alone in the anonymous dark, they threw Gertrude out of the van. Then they reversed over her body to make sure she was dead. They took a moment to check her over for anything of value and found two identical envelopes containing identical sums of money. They also found her ID. As soon as they could, they abandoned the van and took the precaution of setting it alight. So Gertrude never appeared at the house of Bernie and Ida's friends, the people who subsequently made such efforts to find the Silvers' old housemaid and, failing to do so, grieved long and hard for that poor little schoolboy Jack, so alone and so far from home.

In the studio, on the morning after the weird girl, and the screaming, and the stinking tramp, Jack is relishing a second cup of espresso along with a slice of panettone. He is turning his thoughts, with a certain effort of will, to the conference on mime which is due to start that day. His studio now has a definite aura of having been violated by events of the previous night, happy as the outcome of those events has proved to be. Jack's plan is to move out as soon as seems judicious, and find himself a different billet somewhere in the area. It won't of course be halfway near as nice, but he is confident that in a couple of years there will be another studio. In Paris, maybe. Or Brussels. Or Ghent. In Bergamo. Or Budapest. Or, best of all, in Milan. And next time his studio will come without any of these messy and unseemly attachments. No Josh, or Hattie; no ghastly girl to leave her scent on his clothes. No repellent, stinking drunkard, or sullen barefoot housemaid. Only himself and the Vespa and the three equestrian etchings. The Giacometti poster and the Moka espresso pot. And the beautiful silver desk.

ACKNOWLEDGEMENTS

Several people were more than commonly supportive to me during the writing of this book. As always, my editor Alexandra Pringle displayed exceptional thoughtfulness, flair and sensitivity along with huge dollops of personal warmth and generosity. My agent Victoria Hobbs was always there for me. Margaret Alice Stewart-Liberty allowed herself to be my hour-by-hour, read-aloud audience at final typescript stage, always did so with a marvellous good grace and always knew which words had double consonants. Anna and Joe Trapido's ongoing involvement with African culture kept alive for me the allure of that continent, while Cat Marais (see Chapter 10) will have caught her interest in the Futurist–Rationalist architecture of Milan from Joc. I also wish to acknowledge that Caroline Silver's objection to Hellmann's Mayonnaise (see Chapter 2) is a thing of the past, since that company has subsequently taken to using free-range eggs. Finally, I am most grateful both to Ledig House International Writers' Retreat and to the Santa Maddalena Foundation, for two fruitful spells as writing fellow.

A NOTE ON THE TYPE

The text of this book is set in Baskerville, and is named after John Baskerville of Birmingham (1706–1775). The original punches cut by him still survive. His widow sold them to Beaumarchais, from where they passed through several French foundries to Deberney & Peignot in Paris, before finding their way to Cambridge University Press.

Baskerville was the first of the 'transitional romans' between the softer and rounder calligraphic Old Face and the 'Modern' sharp tooled Bodoni. It does not look very different to the Old Faces, but the thick and thin strokes are more crisply defined, and the serifs on lower case letters are closer to the horizontal with the stress nearer the vertical. The R in some sizes has the eighteenth-century curled tail, the lower case w has no middle serif, and the lower case g has an open tail and a curled ear.